AWAKE IN THE MAD WORLD

DAMON FERRELL MARBUT

ISBN: 0985545208
ISBN-13: 9780985545208

Library of Congress Control Number: 2012907518
CreateSpace, North Charleston, SC

For Michael F. Shugrue

AWAKE IN THE MAD WORLD

Damon Ferrell Marbut

CHAPTER 1

Amber Knox invited me to dinner one hundred and twenty hours before Brody would fly to New York, and he and I would meet for the first time that mid-evening in December. I'd been walking the downtown streets the night before, slipping into smaller, less noisy bars and sitting quietly among the paired-up talkers along the counters, giving in around 5 a.m. when the last dives closed and crawling home with no foreign body to show for it, just the night alone and the walking, and I'd slept hard until lunchtime. Later in the early Saturday evening Amber called, and after hanging up in came a slight guilt, as I'd missed her graduate school commencement that afternoon, so I withdrew my commitment to the couch in my small living room and readied to leave the house without a shower, in destroyed jeans and a radio t-shirt from Boston, given me by a girl I no longer knew and hardly remembered. Just the shirt, and the recollection of picking her up from an airport with the too-small white-and-red garment draped over her forearm outside the terminal gate. Only when wearing it could I see her face, beaming, as we locked arms down the escalator, heading off to who-recalls. But when smiles begin to fade in the present, as had happened between us, the entire person seems to disappear, too. Amber, however, was a different animal.

I scanned a small bookshelf near the door on the way out and found a book I'd borrowed from Amber, a year prior, and decided to re-gift it to her as a peace offering for my absence, hoping the joke would also earn her reprieve. The verdict would come soon, in back of a small Italian eatery on east Airport Boulevard, the part of the boulevard where it becomes a two lane shortly before it dies its brave death as it melts into Government, a boulevard also, where an old war cannon heavily rests at the junction. The restaurant was a quick few miles from my house off Azalea Street in Midtown, and though I was late, likely taking my time in rebellion to going at all, the large group she'd assembled in celebration, consisting of family and friends who were all unknown to me, was a warm collection of people well-versed in laughter. They consumed a fair third of the place, and it was easy to find them. Amber leaned over the table for a hug as I passed her the book, a childlike look of regret on my face in addition to a half-smile, and she laughed, I sighed, she explained it to her mother, the gift that kept on giving, and her mother extended a hand, smiling, saying *Pete, we've heard so much about you.*

Just as I seated myself at the end of one long table, my view a clean shot of the broad window overlooking the boulevard, and before I could choose a wine, I was interrupted on my work phone by a call from a friend who bartended downtown, informing that a mutual acquaintance had been stabbed in the neck the night before. It sounded drastic and incomprehensible, and I stood to step outside for the details until he said our friend was at work that very night. A flesh wound, he said, and then went on to mention the junkie who'd stabbed him was in jail for attempted murder. I sat back down and was coerced into relaying the story across the table, with chagrin, indicating to strangers that yes, this is my life, yes, I carouse with stabbing victims. Brody, sitting two seats down, and before I knew him as Brody, leaned across the young woman between us and said, *Everything's insane.*

Brody and I would quite soon end up sitting beside one another, as the girl dividing us, a librarian-looking sort, and rightly named, Penny Frick, took to glowing over photographs of her young daughter with a pair of Amber's friends at the other end, newlyweds who were expecting, a couple emitting a series of oohs and ahhs at the pictures that disrupted my focus on feeling out of place. He and I sat close for a good while, with him doing most of the talking at me, around me, with others, his leg bouncing up and down steadily next to mine below the low-hanging table linen. Amber, highly distracted by the attention, indulging in it, too, played kind host and threw a bright smile or raised her eyebrows at me across from the other side of the room.

"You two need to get together," she said loudly, pointing back and forth at Brody and me, completing the declaration with such an apathetic wave of her hand I wanted to pick her brain about it, as I wasn't there to meet anyone. Envisioning an eventual return to my couch, being there was all I'd the energy for.

There was some odd chatter about fish sauce coming from an un-introduced family member of Amber's, someone swore by it, someone said *you just don't know what you're missing*, and Brody and I parked elbows on the flat of the table to listen closer as the man, an Asian-looking fellow, told how it was made in so-and-so's garage.

"Homemade fish sauce, huh."

"Sounds wild," Brody said.

"You guys," Amber called across the room. "I'm telling you." She shook her head at us.

"What's she...do you have any idea what she's talking about?" I asked him.

"One sec, babe. He's talking about homemade beer."

We studied ourselves being studied by the women at the table, which ignited a mutual recognition of our presence together.

"Have you ever kissed a *Frick*?" He asked.

"A Yes would be a lie, man."

Brody flirted a bit with her as I thought about kissing a Frick and was glad to be momentarily overlooked, my knee jutting from the gape in the jeans, my shirt likely unwashed, two-day shadow across my chin.

Our server was extremely kind and she told us, almost individually, that we were all pleasant when the bill was paid by Amber's gracious parents. But she likely ate her words as everyone seemed to then take up the small walk-through space inside the building to take various group photos. An elderly couple nervously excused themselves in a hurried shuffle as they passed through the Red Sea of family, friends, and me and Brody tucking in our shoulders and nodding out of the film's way. In the fray I was somehow assigned the holding of Amber's aunt's purse. It was the right choice to have come, even if to purse-carry. My stomach was at more ease than earlier, sitting around at home self-debating and deliberating with cashews

3

and worrying I'd get nothing accomplished in the pending hours beyond sitting alone in lamentation of bruising myself so thoroughly the night before.

We all exchanged goodbyes in a casual exodus toward the door, warm hands shaking before becoming cold, jackets being slipped into, a few hugs. As we lined up down the ramp of the patio, Amber cupped her hands and announced a get-together later in the evening, to which I falsely agreed attending, knowing it would be late getting started and I already had neglected work deadlines back home in need of attention, deadlines I'd surely neglect, but at least I'd be nearby when responsibility began to rear its head. It was Brody who brought me out of that particular thinking.

"Hey Pete."

"What's up?"

Brody crossed to my side of the car and leaned against the trunk, running his right hand down the back windshield as if appeasing a hissing cat.

"So I've got a girl in crisis. At that huge bookstore next to the Irish pub. Down that way." He thumbed over his shoulder. "About a mile west, three tops."

"What about her?"

"Not sure. Come get some coffee. We'll scope her out, see if danger lurks. On me man."

My suspicion was that Brody was a person one could ignore and it would still carry little weight, a self-talker, elated to have bystanders hear and join in. I was curious about the danger and figured I'd be better off staying awake through the stomach rumblings that night and possibly adhere to new experience instead of moping on home and ignoring the phone. I agreed with a doubtful nod, which he ignored. *Nice*, he said, patted my car and then trotted two parking spaces over to a beat up version of mine, and he disappeared before my car could get remotely warmed in the slim frost. Down Airport I wondered what I was doing and what to expect and thought a bit about whether the strength would reverse roles and find me to make an appearance at the party later. I considered the imminent struggle for conversation amongst the unfamiliar drunks, which seemed unappealing enough to where I'd determined a very resounding No before cutting the engine in front of the bookstore. I could see Brody through the glass as I walked toward the building, being handed a coffee by a male employee with shoulder length blond hair and a thin goatee. Brody waved a pair of fingers overhead as I entered to join him.

"I knew Knox from workshops on campus," Brody continued once I'd returned from the counter with a coffee. "We get together a good bit now that I'm done. She's talked you up before. I think that's what she meant at dinner. That we should get together."

"Why was that again?"

He was looking over my shoulder periodically at his female friend. We'd not discussed her yet and I was nicely surprised at the mission I'd become a part of. Whatever crisis it was I guess Brody had on his watchdog eyes, had it under control. "You guys ever see each other?"

"Knox and I? Not quite," I said, laughing. "You?"

"We never committed to any authentic interest in it. So you're a serious writer? She called you a writer. She said you're serious."

"Oh, right…that's what she was doing."

"So you do? You write?"

I sighed.

"Yeah, I guess…"

"That's good. *Good.*" He breathed into his coffee. "I'm going to New York Thursday, go catch up with an old friend who's got a textbook coming out."

"You write?" I asked.

"Yeah, Pete." He exhaled, set down his coffee, stretched his arms to the ceiling and reclaimed it in his cold hands. "As much as I can. As *often*, that is. This sounds secretive, right?"

"How so?"

"These short answers. Like speaking in code. You published?"

"In a couple locals. I think…I *hope* I've got a novel working. Some other projects going. Little things. Not really yet."

"Right on. I'm bringing a novel up with me. See if it's got legs. I guess it's done. For now, at least. But that's still great. Hey, *motion.*" Brody kept nodding and I was wondering and not nodding. I was wondering about the girl.

"You know anything about what's going on with her and that guy?"

"Nah. It seems unnerving though. She seems unnerved. But then she always does. She's a sweet, sad situation. That's why I thought we should be here." The top of Brody's left knee bounced around the edge of our table. It was dark outside and not necessarily cold, not a Midwestern cold, not ever in Mobile, where natives dared to call 55 degrees freezing. I'd seen a Canadian winter once, a real winter, a year earlier while visiting my brother-in-law's ex in Toronto.

"We?"

He looked at me curiously.

"Yep," he said, nodding.

"What's wrong with just you?"

"Hmm? Nada."

His leg still bounced, palms still glued to the outer edge of the plastic cup.

"You gonna talk to her?"

"Hell no. She's good."

"Did you even say hi to her?"

"Nah." He shook his head and looked over my shoulder. I almost laughed. I was tired but had it in me to laugh. "You have an agent, or editor?"

"Not hardly." I smiled at my coffee in mild disbelief.

A woman squeezed by our table and bumped into his leg. He didn't notice. "Then I'll read some of your stuff this week, right? Maybe bring something of yours up and show my friend Mitch."

"I don't know."

"It could be a good thing, man."

"Are you published?"

"Getting there. A short novel with a small press in Massachusetts. Nothing full-length like this one. I'm looking for good things in the year."

"What's your last name?"

"You haven't heard of it. Like a hundred copies of it, just in the northeast."

"No, man," I said, finally laughing. "I don't know your last name."

"LaCoste."

"LaCoste," I repeated.

"Pete what?"

"Rattigan."

"I could just call you Rattigan. You know, we should start something," Brody said, pointing at me and exhaling.

"Like what?"

"I dunno. We'll see."

"I'm not too confident about the politics of publishing these days. Almost feel like hanging it up."

"No way, babe. Not at all. If Knox says you're serious, no doubt you're strong. Give me a peek at it and I'll take it with me. Yeah?"

"How many options do I have?"

He winked at me and looked again over my shoulder. I felt a four year-old's timidity when sitting across from me was a guy who didn't seem to care if his work to date were received as genius or toilet paper. Bright white teeth, dimpled cheeks, around six-two with blondish-brown mid-length hair strapped back by a navy-colored hair band, blue eyes, tan complexion, seemingly indifferent but friendly, I thought his looks could easily preclude a lack of confidence. He thought a moment and then shrugged.

"None, man. Just think, life can be almost miserable unless you teach yourself to maintain the highs the universe deals out. I mean, yeah, you learn from the lows. You *have* to. But it's empowering to understand it's possible to rocket back up from a really low low, man."

"I guess so."

"No, you *know* so."

"But what are you talking about?"

"That whole 'how many options do I have' thing. I'm talking about *trying*. Why not take a jump, right? It's not gonna do you any harm to experience the gloomy side of effort, right? There's a kind of success in failing, too. They cancel each other out that way. " He suddenly sat up straight. "Here she comes."

I was still stuck on what Brody was saying as stranger danger approached, while the fellow she'd been sitting with had his eyes down and peeled little papers at their table by the entrance's large window. I knew where the talk could be going, and I knew why Amber had grinned at us, at me, why it was a sly grin. I thought I'd already begun doubting myself less, a thought I'd had when alone and still nearing the cusp of doubt. I was ready to dissect things further, but we both yielded to start playing concerned friend to a woman in some untold need. *Take a jump*, I thought, and stood to shake the girl's hand before sitting down after Brody's introduction.

They knew each other through Amber as well, and I realized that after graduating two years back, I didn't know anyone anymore, just fragments of them when I saw something, like the shirt I wore, that reminded me of what was but no longer is. The girl was a beginning poet also trying to figure why her fiction kept falling apart. She was considering switching to Islam but, the crisis finally unfolding, she decided against it because her Saudi Arabian boyfriend confessed at the last minute to being married and that he was returning home to get his wife and children before settling into a job in London now that his schooling was over in the States. Her name was Margaret MacDonald and she was not pleased, not at all, to be sitting with her boyfriend's best friend who'd come to give her the information about the incisive breakup. I sipped my coffee and made a pledge with myself to say not a damned thing. Instead I studied the young man against the glass up front, still digging through the scrap paper and mumbling to himself perhaps about what next to say when Margaret returned. I felt silly and confused on his behalf. It's always the messenger. And we *were* talking about it, the situation, and *him*, just a handful of feet away.

Margaret didn't initially seem too overwhelmed by the burden of a personality, as she spoke with relative slowness and mentioned something about having lived in east or west Memphis, which I regrettably yet immediately held against her as the Grand Explanation for her seemingly lack of a legitimate take on the world. She'd an orange-red hair color, more toward orange, and her voice was thick with a self-challenging defiance against the truth behind her emotions. I sat back into my chair and coffee and hoped not a single person would walk by and nudge me like Brody, because the moment had become suddenly new and interesting, and I'd surely flinch, maybe miss one of them exercising their strange reasons. My knuckles got parched-throat dry as she sat and my voice went bare and white.

"It isn't that I feel it's that big of a cultural difference between us. I mean, don't you think if he really cares about me, something as unimportant as religion wouldn't be getting in the way?" She asked, standing close to our table, hunched forward, expressionless face.

Brody was index-finger-massaging his chin. My lips puckered over my thin straw I'd fidgeted into my cooling drink and I imagine I looked a lot like a curious child, bored stiff from adult conversation.

"Sweet baby," he said, like a weathered trumpeter, tested by years of dark stages, might say before telling glossy-eyed drunks in the front row to clear a path as he shuffled through to the bar. "It does matter, see? We've got power and the will and the right and literal freedom to step back from uniformity and be, well, *happy*. And happy's hard work to some, right? But we can make more choices. That's our birthright. Not just here in this building, but on this very soil, man, I mean, *Nabokov* knew..."

I kid-sipped my tepid coffee and savored each minute of guessing Margaret's musical choices, IQ, favorite soda.

"But religion matters to some people more than most other things. No doubt," he said, nodding. "You said you two had a breakthrough because he stroked your hair while driving to dinner the other night, and he held your hand? But if nothing had happened between you two up until that point, and now he's saying he's *married* or Mohammed's saying it *for him*—which is indisputably shitty, but still, justly informative—you think maybe it, well, and I mean this kindly, *you* were his one final experiment with American tactility?"

"Whoa. Yeah. I guess so."

"But see, it can't *all* be religion. Generally...and I know it's unsafe to generalize, *usually*... but nothing should be all about one thing. And I'm not defending either...you get what I'm saying, right? But also, who's to say he loves you the way you want him to, or if it's the same way you're trying to love him? It's all at least *some* form of love, right? Rattigan here's *all* love."

He smacked me lightly on the arm and I turned my curious eyes upward to hers, with my lips still tight around the straw as I responded.

"I have no idea what's happening right now."

"*See?*" Brody said.

"But *Mohammed*..." Margaret whispered as she glanced past her shoulder at him. Poor man, still shredding paper, still looking down. "Now *he's* offering marriage."

"To *whom*?" Brody asked.

Me, I thought. Mohammed wants me.

9

"To *me*."

Are we really doing this right now, literally *next* to him? I thought.

"I agreed to go get something to eat with him after this. I just...I don't know what to do about any of this. I don't want to paint Sam as a jerk..."

"He kinda is," Brody said.

"...or Mohammed, because when they're both out of this situation they're both wonderful guys. I was so ready to say Yes to Sam when *this* came along," she said, thrusting her thumb toward Mohammed. "And I know it's obviously had to have been here all along, but I can't say Yes to Mohammed and guarantee him the same trust as I did Sam. You know?"

Brody leaned back in his chair and smiled at me because, I suspected, he was rewarding himself for keeping what was then happening a secret from me. He ran his hands through his hair, reset the band across the top of his forehead, giggled, and then took my straw from my cup sitting near his long right forearm and stuck it in his mouth and began chewing. Through the chewing he looked at me again.

"What do you make of all this, Rattigan?"

"Make sure it's an expensive restaurant," I said softly.

Margaret eyed me like I'd vomited myself. Brody laughed aloud, a quick blurt which seemed to even surprise him, and clapped his hands once. Margaret looked at us both, one at a time, as if we had never even had minds. And then Brody, fortunately, rang in with a salesman's closure.

"Come on, sweet baby. He's just saying this is *your* jam. If you don't, if we don't, *anybody* doesn't, assess troubling situations with clarity and courage it'll be a hard road forward. Things don't get easier if someone sits around expecting them to. Rattigan's just saying to be assertive is all. Make way in your life for more serious aggressions that might arise. Don't let your personal identity come to question in your mind just because someone in your life is flagrant with their *own*."

Margaret looked at me, cocked her head and sighed, got this curious look on her face, looked at me again and I got nervous. I tried to take back the straw but Brody leaned away in his chair and patted his chest and kept smiling.

"Why does he call you by your last name?"

"Yeah, LaCoste," I said. "Why so informal?"

10

Brody sat forward, amused.

"Pete rhymes with too many things, but *Rattigan*. That's a tough one. As in, Hey Rattigan, don't forget to take off your *Hat-again*. Takes me right back to the schoolyard."

"Absolute poetry," I added.

"You guys don't need coffee," Margaret said, reclaiming from the table a pen she'd carried over.

"But look, do get in touch with me when the bad weather subsides," Brody told her, wholly returned to seriousness.

"I will. I needed more perspective, from someone my age instead of the baby boomers at my office that seem to think I have all this shit coming to me because of my differing sense of initiative. I can't take this all over again, guys. I mean, do I have it emblazoned on my forehead? *If you're married come offer me a fake view of the world, I'm gullible.*"

"I can't say that you do. But in fairness, apparently it's not a fake view to him."

"I don't see anything," I added.

"You probably would if we were dating."

"Look baby," Brody began again. I grew inquisitive as to how long Mohammed would sit there, alone and unattended, just ripping those sad little papers. Brody didn't seem to remember him, and I fell big into thinking about his writing, if he focused solely on the small micro-moments of a story, while I seemed to unsuccessfully thrive on the madness of the big picture. And then Brody piped up and disproved my supposing, eventually forcing me later in the lonely beautiful night to slip abysmally into the thought that I wasn't seeing quite enough of anything. "The universe is in control of what happens and what we do. The one bit of power it gives us individually is the power to give or refuse to give compassion and love. We do what we can each day, spread joy, and learn more about how we can effectively and lavishly give ourselves to others as generously we can. Not with money or tangibles, but with our spirits...that better not sound dumb... how we can best offer our hearts and attention and concern to others in service to that power. Our *reward* then is when we've done enough right, the universe starts inserting into our personal existences more and more cosmological love that we can celebrate and share with others. It *grows*, baby. *That's* how it grows."

"But what about when people complain that God lets bad things happen to them? Isn't that sort of against what you're saying? I don't feel I've done anything wrong," she said, tapping her pen on the table. I had disappeared off into the examination of my own worldly grievances, a dull set of constructs surmounted just by believing something as simple as that, that giving compassion could better govern how we journey and triumph. It had all been just a feeling before, never heard in words and sentences and smacking of straws and the climb of weakening steam.

"The question there is this, man...the question is, what have you actively done to make your life better? The lives of others, *see*? Worse stuff happens to better people than you and me. All we can do is keep trying. I just told Rattigan. You gotta keep considering that and telling yourself that when you make your choices. This whole situation..." and Brody made a sort of globe with his arms like he was balancing the world for one minute to show Margaret the scheme of things. "...can be overcome simply by *you* giving *you* a more keen awareness so you can get yourself equipped to start positively changing both your world and everyone else's. That's as plain as it can be. But accountability's got to start there." He pointed at her chest. "And here." He pointed at his own forehead.

"Damn. Yeah," she whispered, in the same voice she'd brought to the table. I thought of Memphis again and snapped out of wherever it was I'd gone. "You're pretty involved for nine o'clock at night. I don't come alive until at least 3 a.m."

Brody quieted and sat back into his straw, my straw, as though compliments were his collective source of fragility, his underbelly. We had that in common, though his, I was sure, outnumbered mine. Margaret paused another half-minute before announcing she needed to get back. I felt better on Mohammed's behalf, out there in the love-seeking air, running out of paper, and then I remembered he was after her hand in marriage, he and Sam vying for the same woman, a nasty tangle amongst friends. I dismissed it and rose to give Margaret a hug, which I'm fairly certain shocked us both but then, I was embracing, too, what advice of Brody's still lingered in the air around her shoulders.

When Margaret was on her way back to Mohammed, Brody and I sat in a bit of quiet for the next few moments, staring at surrounding biographies and on-sale books and sundries in our vicinity. There was a huge posterbook of Alabama cities I grabbed, which we thumbed through a bit, commenting on the large, colorful, friendly snaps of Birmingham citizens painting a mural, Jimmy Carter visiting a small town Habitat for Humanity project in the center of the state, flowers and dew-covered farmland both smattered in sunlight buckets. It was nice to be silent, as if we both needed to take something in other than our own thoughts. The pictures, like free mental images, fed into my brain like the dinner hadn't earlier, not completely, and I still found myself stepping over chasms in my memory, thinking perhaps things were going to be really really good now that I could breathe with the knowledge of there being someone out there worth listening to. Brody sat beside me and tapped his thumb upside the table's edge, and when I noticed Margaret had left we both watched her walk beside Mohammed and we laughingly guessed where they'd go for dinner.

"Crazy you said that to her, Rattigan."

"What?"

"I was thinking the same thing man. Same damn thing. Let's get outta here."

He patted me on the back as we stood, and up went the posterbook and on our way we went, deep into the shadows of the parking lot past their table of tested nerves, bad news and hope, manifesting itself in the destruction of trees.

Out in the whirling sound of boulevard traffic, no more than sixty yards from where we'd both parked, we stood as new friends together beneath a broken lot lamp almost twenty feet tall and we stuffed our hands in our pockets. I then picked up a few rocks and one by one kicked them off toward the busy street. I'm sure it seemed I was young and stupid with such a trivial occupation, but that was until he bent and selected a few from the ground. We started aiming for bushes, assigning paper cups to one another as targets across the dark of the concrete. We'd come to an even tie as Brody sent out the last rock just narrowly at a plastic bottle then on its side beside a public trashcan. It reminded me of the things I could still do, like be simple and laugh at myself and feel coherent and necessary.

"I'm serious about seeing your work, man. I'll get in touch with you about it, Girl Scout's honor."

"How many fingers does that mean you have to hold up?"

"I actually thought they just pinky-swore."

"Where are you headed from here?"

"I dunno man. Lots of good energy out tonight. I think I'm down for Mobile's finest chocolate."

"Are you joking?"

"Not at all, babe. It's an infrequent craving that must be heeded. There's a good place downtown."

I shook my head and smiled.

"Hey, man. Something you said made me think in there."

"Yeah?" Brody grinned and leaned against the side of his car as the wind picked up. I walked closer while he patted the space next to him and we leaned together. "What's that?"

"I was wondering what you think about this. About emotions. You think we come across brand new emotions every day? Like everything's conditional, like maybe a series of events happens in some unique way that generates, I don't know, a new feeling? Or maybe a new approach to an old feeling? I don't know."

"Yeah." He nodded, staring at the ground. "I'd say so, yeah."

"So then it's not like sadness or frustration are the same each time we feel them. I mean, if I can see that you're completely elated, would it make sense if I asked what kind of elation you were feeling? Like…"

"Yeah. *Yeah*, man. I see."

He turned to face me. It was my turn chewing the straw.

"As in, what combination of elements, emotions, *things* fell in place to make you feel that particular kind of elation, you know?"

"I see it, Rattigan." The wind kept going and Brody kept nodding and all was nicely clear and intact for an unexpected moment, with the two of us leaning against the car as Margaret and Mohammed went somewhere across town in search of contract, food, fortitude.

"I sometimes get tired of thinking we all just feel the same basic feelings," I said. "No derivation."

"Right on. It's as if all that exists vertically on the food chain are, say, ten different foods and that's it, no variations, no subgroups, no, well, definitely, no *derivations*."

"Like we forget there's a difference in everything."

"Yeah," he said, spitting on the ground in front of his feet. "As well as similarities. We have options to explore, man. We're all part of one vast thing in the world. Sounds silly out loud, but it doesn't make it less true. Most of the time truth sounds ridiculous. What's one way to you isn't necessarily so to me, but they can still be similar, right? So no general right or wrong."

"All one thing," I said, and then we were quiet. A satisfied, rich, mindlessly noisy silence.

"Well, I should get going," I said, shoving off the side of the car.

"Yeah, babe. I'm off to see the wizard."

He nodded skyward, and an awkward handshake preceded a generous and ample hug, loud claps on his back and mine. My wizard was perhaps a book, some writing, something worth going to see, but at home, in fresh, good solitude.

"We'll catch up soon," Brody said.

"Later, man."

I rode Airport down to Houston and cut to Dauphin, the narrower roads more intimate as the wheels hugged the snug lanes. It had been raining heavily that afternoon, so I took the middle lane, as the outside lanes tended to collect thick puddles, and I remembered my friend getting stabbed downtown and I thought there was no way in hell I'd be back at work the day after a brush with death.

––––––

That night of sleep consisted of random ups from bed, water glasses, writing blindly in the dark. New, distraught ideas coming happy at the center of my forehead, coming clear. I was so worn to a good exhaustion from the weight of the night's suggestion that I couldn't sleep properly, whatever that had meant to me in the past, still couldn't bring myself to tug the lamp chord and even minimally participate in full rest. So in the morning, after waking and sleeping and sitting up and thinking and dreaming and dozing and exhaling into the firmament kept docile by the cloak of my ceiling, I woke to read a surprisingly legible series of notes on a new fiction project I was working out, but hadn't worked in over a month, *serious attention* kind of work, because I'd been out either drinking on the Causeway or downtown or in Midtown or more west near campus. Anywhere but where I should have been, off in some vehicular procrastination, same as with work, with the deadlines that were still crying out to be noticed. The day, though, a Sunday, was rich and rife with possibility. It was early and that was my strong time, staring at the clock and wall almost simultaneously, blurring out one vision for the other. I assumed I'd eventually get mobile, look into laundry. The coffee, all of it, was gone leaving an open half-a-soda and a Sapporo in the refrigerator, so I had a glass of tap and felt happily mock-poverty-stricken for about three minutes before tossing a set of underwear and jeans and a few t-shirts and a couple loose pairs of socks in the wash and scratching my head once back at the typewriter.

I'd written tired, long chunks at the end before I'd wrapped for bed, the telephone marvelously silent across the room. The incoherence of the last paragraph especially was completely erased and restarted by the time Margaret called and I'd finished a conversation with Mel over the phone just before it, Mel being this young, deranged and beautiful creature who lived across the city near this tiny, ignored but fine locally-owned coffee shop. We'd get together and get together, as often as possible, but times were getting ridiculously busy the nearer Christmas got, and I'm not sure why. I wasn't doing much of anything. Work wasn't taxing. It wasn't fulfilling, in any imaginable regard, but it wasn't difficult. I'd been see-sawing on the idea of graduate school, and the thought of committing to it was testing my self-control and stamina and I felt maniacal, ready to explode, like Mel, but for work-related reasons. Because work was there and requiring me to perform. I didn't know her reasons, even when, or *namely* when, she slid from my bed some mornings and wouldn't explain why she had to go. She'd simply run her fingertips across my upper back as I lay facedown, not watching her mercurial body—set against the backdrop of my painted-white bookshelves, ceiling-high—recollect and become itself again once gone from beside me, her mouth saying, with vagueness, *I really have to go.*

But Margaret. She'd called my home, a building most often estranged from its renter, her voice that same drab sort of destitute that had me thinking of Memphis. She danced a conversational dance, asking how I was doing, and before I could answer she interrupted with the revelation of her agenda. Suddenly I felt I was preoccupied. And I was, cleaning up the literary oil spill that was my last from the night before, but she didn't deserve that information, not when I was still deciding on how to enter the day. I hung up and let her call back. She launched into herself again and

I wondered, briefly, how she got my number and why she called. It came clear the more she talked. She was looking for even more perspective and had called LaCoste, already, had already acquired my number from him, who'd inarguably retrieved it from Knox earlier. It only could have been them, conspiring, pawning off, I thought. Her grinning slyly, him with his sweet-baby hair band. *Assholes.*

"Brody was out late last night," she commented.

"He found the wizard," I whispered too loudly.

"What?"

"Nada."

The case was that Margaret needed, or *wanted*, most likely, but *thought* she needed, an outside view on the ever-growing catastrophe that was getting too off the charts for her to act with boldness on her own. I didn't know the girl from Elvis but I said, like a half-wit, *Sure, come over. Door's always unlocked when I'm here.* She said, *Give me an hour*, and then we hung up. I internally pulled my hair, guessing my day would be circumcised due to this new trip toward philanthropy, thanks to Brody—he deserved blame—being a spiritual ear or shoulder. But then I considered, like something Brody had said the night before, what good am I doing by not helping, so I checked the laundry and took a quick shower and assumed the coming moments could be much, much worse.

Some other me, then, due to the circumcision, might have sat around and brooded until she arrived, a child grounded from its toys, thinking I'd had something taken away forever. But I grew up honestly and fast when the screen door announced her arrival and then there she stood, looking ready to cry and studying my face to see if I'd allow it once she made it inside and I offered her a place to sit and wallow.

The bizarre, out-of-this-world business that followed was boggling. She waxed melancholy and gloom about going to Sam's house, and Mohammed pretending Sam wasn't there, although Margaret and her friend had spied earlier on Sam's car circling the block—this soap opera mess, what with knocking on doors and leaving letters on the door and watching the door from a distant parking lot in the complex, to see if a hand would sneak out and snatch away the taped letter, which it *did* by Allah, it did. What to do, when a stranger requests stranger advice of an even stranger situation, over a convoluted break-up, breaking apart something that was never quite whole to begin with? I tried to play it smart by not playing at all, nodding and listening and grunting when the appropriate grunts were called for. But then she mentioned Brody, misinterpreting a wild majority of the truth he'd advised and offered, *his* truth, so in getting the gist of a fraction of her own truth, her interpretation, and tearing down the highway of good intentions, I accessed and delivered my own take. After a half hour of pleading with her through repetition she said, *Yeah I guess you're right. You and Brody were right.*

"Are. We still are," I said through fingers covering my face.

I wanted to tell Margaret, someone I didn't know and almost feared from her brazen silliness, that no one controls who it is who loves us, or who we love, right? so the best thing is, right? to wade through living best we can, and *do*, and the goodness we give out revisits us as it arguably should, and in good time. This is fun, I kept thinking, this *has* to be fun, cursing Brody and Knox, just *because*, knowing my day had surrendered its foreskin all over again. I mentioned to Margaret with an almost-look of consternation that some might worry about her scoping their apartment. She agreed with no fight, maybe tired of hearing what she knew, already, facts instead of generic truth being handed back to her. She asked to take me downtown for a sunny lunch.

"Absolutely," I said. "If you can guarantee the sun'll stay. Tough assignment."

She looked outside the window behind the couch where we were sitting and smiled up through the blinds, out at the beckoning blue slivers of sky, for the first real time that late morning/early afternoon.

"I think I've got you covered."

I smiled, too, trying my best to at least give her that.

The dryer buzzed itself off as we clomped across the hardwood and headed out the front, her more-orange-than-red hair bouncing with happier life to it, much more than it had so odiously done while traipsing in from a day I thought had almost drowned her and barely allowed her resurrection. She didn't ask if I'd hung up on her. I didn't ask why she had entered nearly in tears.

We made it downtown in her car in minutes, brief minutes, the roads having mostly dried, but few puddles on them then to continue drying with her tires.

"You ever eaten here?"

She pointed at a tiny corner sports bar with a long, light tan-colored deck built halfway out into the road.

"What kind of stuff do you eat?"

Both of us crushed together beneath a shadowy overhang in front of an old dead theatre that used to play matinee pictures from years before we'd both been born, films no one went to see except the older generations and people like myself and Knox, maybe some lost counter-culture kids dressed as what they thought was an updated nod to past hipsters, before the owners realized it was only going to capture old dreamy nostalgia and, deeming that an inadequate return on investment, shut it down. There we stood, thinking about food.

"Anything, I guess."

"No pork, though."

"That's funny."

I surveyed the block.

"There's a brew pub down there."

"Any good?" she asked, craning her neck past my shoulder, in the slight wind between us, to catch a look. Two older men passed in identical suits, and one coughed a ferocious cough that took Margaret by surprise while I was busy wondering, *why the same suits*, as if maybe it generated some kind of brotherhood or likelihood between them, unspoken but agreed upon, needed, definite like the light chill in the air around us.

"Not sure, honestly. Last time I went there I drank a lot. Don't remember much from the times before. Sports bar sounds good."

"Let's try the pub."

"All right."

A stream of Margaret's promised sun fanned into the front corner of the pub on Conti, a corner to which we were assigned only after the evidence of our unfamiliarity played its part. I wasn't sure if she smoked until then, and we'd paused, or she'd paused, before telling me she wasn't a smoker and so, for the meal, neither was I. The patient server stood aside, watching us, as we discussed the possibility of Margaret's smoking, and I caught her uneasiness, the server's, a short and stocky girl, college-aged, hemp necklace, braids—I felt inattentive and almost cruel and said, *Sorry, anyplace is good for us*. So to the corner we went, my face in the sun, Margaret's back to it.

One girl took our drinks, our server brought them and another staff member, a thin fellow, psychology major—second year, he told us—took our order. I enjoyed the team effort, but I could feel Margaret bubbling with inquisition, could see her eyes wander, as if to question it or complain. To avoid it, I asked about her writing, what she wrote and how often. Her slow Memphis-ness began to eke its way out and I thought there was no way any of it, us, was going to work. *Where's Brody.* She hadn't written much at all. She couldn't have, not with such hesitation. Then again I was an asshole to critique a process of hers I made little effort to learn, a slight hypocrite, too, with so many unfinished projects and littered poems suffocating my room at home, pages everywhere, little flat white clouds on the floor and desk. Margaret talked of being in the dumps and how she had to be there, in the dumps, for quite a while in order to summon the goods of her creativity. I told her I'd read several writers who did that. But we weren't discussing what I thought we were there to discuss. I wanted intrigue and stalking, maybe an affair gone awry, with knives involved. My byline in the Metro section would be stunning: *Memphisian Knockjob Commits Anti-Muslim Love-Hate Crime.*

The manager approached. It turned out he was the same tall, talkative, slightly bizarre fellow from my job at the newspaper, contributed occasional bits in cuisine, a man I saw every so often.

"Got to have two jobs, now that my wife's pregnant, yeah, I'm hoping for a boy," he said, a bit jittery. Definitely him, the same guy I knew from before, or didn't know. But same mannerisms, same nearness to implosion but same good, big heart.

He said he'd been upstairs supervising the cooking because they were down a guy, but he saw me from the top of the stairs and wanted to come by. "Reason to talk about the new brat," he'd said. I congratulated him on the upcoming birth and told him to pass a Hello to his wife for me. He had a lovely, plain-faced, passive-aggressive-but-almost-kind wife named Kris who some considered mentally unstable, though I'd only seen the calm side of her in our few encounters. I remembered she was terrified of hugs. He shook my hand and Margaret's after I introduced them, shook our hands with insane seriousness, as if he'd accomplished something by not falling apart with us, not sweating too profusely on our table, not dying. Once he walked away, even she thought he had something wrong with him. The irony, I wanted to say. Right? Where was Knox? Where was Brody?

"Pressures of the world, I guess," I said.

"Maybe I don't have it so bad."

"That's callous."

"Ok, I hear you."

"Because it seems like you certainly..."

"Loud and clear."

I smiled at her, playfully raised my eyebrows and she relaxed into her chair. The food was brought out fairly soon thereafter, by the hostess. The sandwiches were dry, as in chewing the stuffed inside of a vacuum bag dry.

"How do you mess up a basic grilled chicken sandwich?" I asked.

"Mine's pretty tough, too. I have no idea."

"Is that a silly question?"

"No."

"I didn't think it was either."

"I just can't answer it," she said, tearing off a piece of the bun.

The manager swung by again.

"So how good is it? Is it good? Good stuff, right? I love that jerk sauce."

"It's fantastic," I answered, trying not to choke on either the meat or my feigned enjoyment.

"Mmmm," Margaret added, nodding and chewing bread.

"That's what we like to hear."

He grinned, patted the table and jetted away, with the words *good, good* trailing behind him.

Our server returned, apparently working a large corporate luncheon up on the balcony, hence her invisibility and the fear in her eyes. Margaret paid the check and thanked me for listening to her, although I was still in the dark as to what I'd been told. I grabbed a pair of thin plastic boxes from the host station and we packed up our dry sandwiches to take with us. The early afternoon was bright, so much that the yellow rays looked almost white against the tops of the taller buildings we passed as we swept through the downtown streets, the old furniture stores and music halls, a bookstore, a muffin joint, a chocolatier.

She drove us against the sun back to my house, stopping at my request at a convenience store off Government Boulevard for beer and a few lifted single packets of joe. I was glad the trip had run short and clean of any conversational mess comparable to that from the bookstore. I stepped to the driver's side to thank her through her rolled-down window for lunch, but her face had returned to sullen, less preoccupied than when I'd gotten her to finally laugh with me over the sad meal. Or maybe she was preoccupied differently, that the afternoon ahead would be a recession into angst, self-doubt, but hopefully, at very least, no private-eye missions of stealth that could lead to an apartment complex shootout over the matter of her heart rendered asunder by two strangers, one of whom she wanted desperately to call "husband."

After she drove off down my street and turned right on Ann, heading toward Government, I exhaled a large, long exhalation and slowly jogged up the steps to my porch and keyed in the door, ready then to get back to what work I had before me, with no sullenness attached. An actual interest in it had suddenly unearthed itself, borne of her dejection and the quiet space I'd volunteered to fill beside her.

A light blinked on the answering machine that sat on an end table near the door to the laundry room and kitchen, my small rental home a shotgun, rooms aligned on either side to go straight back until hitting the thin weeds growing in the concrete cracks just outside my back door. I tossed my keys on the couch and pressed the play button as I passed through the refrigerator to put up my pub fare—*of course*, I thought, *the food was awful because I was sober*— and grab a beer, after the fact. Brody's voice jarred the quiet of the house. He was nearly shouting and talking some excited gibberish I could barely make out from the kitchen. I caught an apology of sorts when I walked back into the room.

"…and it was completely sick of me to pass on your number to her, but I guess I'd convinced myself it was a good thing to expose you to more of the world's varied lunacies, I don't know. Or maybe, yeah, come to think of it, I was avoiding her, definitely babe, like the Plague. The *Plague*, Rattigan. But I'm serious about catching up with you later to look at your work, no doubt I'm looking forward to it, so give me a call back, I dunno where I'll be, maybe around, and we'll set something up. Later, man. Be well."

The second and final message was also Brody's voice, apologizing again, laughing, leaving his number and then he hung up.

I called him back and got his machine, that had no greeting, just a few seconds of silence and then the sound of something breaking before it beeped.

"Hey, LaCoste. You owe me huge, man. You can't know. But no worries, and yeah, call when you can. I'm on lock-down here all night."

After shaking my head at the phone and replacing it on its cradle, I recognized a disinterest in an attempt to write, immediately. My energies were conflicted, stretched between the possibility of catching up with Brody versus the awkward finger-fidgeting in the car to and from lunch. I sat on the couch with my beer, unzipped my hooded sweatshirt and propped my feet on my makeshift coffee table, an old WWII army trunk I'd found at Goodwill, and I let the light from the window behind my head crawl in on its own and sniff around. I could hear neighbors in their yard arguing about necessity and logic, something to do with taking out the trash, two impassionedly wailed arguments from the married couple I only knew in terms of waving across our lawns some mornings. It was hard to avoid a smile at the image in my mind, her hitting him with the lid, him kicking the wheels of the bin, and it would have been too disappointing to cross the room and flick the front blinds and have it disproven. I sat, instead, and finished my beer and then fell asleep.

Just short of an hour later, I blinked awake and rose to throw on half a pot of coffee. As it brewed, I stood in the kitchen by the sink and jowl-muscled my way through the remainder of the sandwich, satisfied more by the ketchup-soaked fries I stuffed in between the meat and bun to simply endure the process. Once the coffee finished, I fixed a cup and had a smoke out on the porch swing, observing the human nothingness occurring on the street. No bodies, no voices, just the tiny scratch sounds of leaves brushing leaves in the mild wind. I had compiled interview bits for a piece due in, and I needed it finished soon, needed to at least assess the chaos of the scattered information scrawled in an unfortunate-looking, abused leather flip pad that I carried in my back pocket while on assignment. But when I entered my room, raised the shade slip in front of my one window unblocked by tall bookshelves, lit a candle on a shelf and sat at my desk, I decided to look over the notes from the previous night instead, a series of images that somehow throughout the course of the day had proven to have its own clarity and needed, without question, to go into something. But

the question was...what? Nothing new, certainly not, as none of my exist-
ing projects were finished. Nowhere near completion. I sat until the entire
cup's emptiness and ruminated, occasionally flitting an eye at the interview
notes, wanting to tell them to hang on, I was getting there. My attention
then turned to the candle, its grayish smoke almost black in its linear climb
to the ceiling. I was caught by, or had willingly surrendered to, a post-nap
delusion of productivity. But I would get nothing done.

The phone on my desk rang less than a minute later, just as I'd begun
to call myself a mentally lazy, scared shitless kid.

"I tell you I'm going to New York?"

"Brody. You bastard, hey. Yeah, you did."

"Bastard?"

"Huh?"

"Margaret call you?"

"Yeah, she did. *Yeah*, she did. I thought you knew that."

"I don't think I did."

"You're message made it seem you..."

"She was really in a pinch with herself, babe. Thought you could help
out."

"Why me?"

"What did I...I left you a message?"

I sighed a laugh and shook my head, smiling.

"You did, Brody. Two, actually. One was almost penitent."

"Nice."

"But anyway, yeah. She called, came by, took me to lunch. The whole
she-ba..."

"Why are you laughing?"

"I have no idea."

"Let's go shove off somewhere."

"Where?" I asked.

"Come on, *Rattigan*. Does it *matter*?"

"No."

"Why, you busy?'

"No. What are *you* up for?"

"Dunno, man."

"She said you were out late last night," I told him.

"It was wild, man. Very, very good. All kinds of cage-free animals out."

"You hung over?"

"Hey, give me directions to your place. I'll come over."

"Now?"

"Yeah, now."

"Ok."

"Why, you busy?" he asked again.

"I should be, but I'm not," I said, up and pacing the room as far as the cord permitted.

"So let's hear them."

"Hear what?"

"You're *killing* me, man."

"Oh, directions?"

"I mean, it would be surreal if I could just *know*, you know? Maybe click my heels three times and say…"

"Ok, ok," I said, laughing. "Pay attention. It's pretty simple."

I gave Brody directions and we hung up. Half-expecting him to show, I surveyed the room and the assorted piles of work and faux-work and waved an apathetic hand at it. I thought of the house, too, in general disarray, dusty. Rather than tidy anything into a liar's form of order, I took a quick shower to steam out the weariness from my diversions.

A few minutes after throwing on slightly fresher clothes and then blanketing them with the same old gray sweatshirt, I heard Brody letting himself in, calling out my name, distrustful of his selection of houses, although I was the only red brick on the street. He'd stopped first at a friend's place west from mine, Reagan, an old classmate, rather, a girl I didn't know he knew. She lived in one half of a two-story duplex, the only red brick on Rickarby, coincidentally, and as I came out of the kitchen with a beer he'd already shuffled into the middle of the living room, studying the walls and books and sparse furniture as he told me how he'd sat in this old metal porch swing hanging from the thick of a long ancient oak tree limb in Reagan's front yard, crammed tightly beside Reagan, whose girlfriend was in town from New Orleans, then the girlfriend, Lisa, and Ethan, Reagan's roommate. Brody was wearing a long-sleeved t-shirt, jeans, and a bright purple bandana had replaced the hair band from the previous night.

"Little chilly to be outside too long, isn't it? You want a beer?"

"Sure, man. But no, it wasn't bad. We were talking about guitar lessons and harmonica players and the elderly who still run marathons. Those are good people, Rattigan."

"The elderly?" I called from the kitchen.

"Reagan and Ethan. That Lisa's a *fox*, man. Good visit all around. I would have been here sooner, but..."

"I didn't know you knew Reagan. She's a good girl."

"Thanks," he said, and took the beer. "Yeah, I don't know how I know her."

Brody was exuberant and stretched his arms wide for a generous hug and then a grasp of my hand and forearm with both his hands, his eyes studying my face. I clapped his back and smiled and then pushed him off. He spun and walked in the direction I sent him and stood in front of the bookshelf by the door, tapping his foot and nodding, saying *uh-huh* at each book he recognized, had read or hadn't. He was teaching himself about me. I walked past him and raised the front windows just enough for a cool sliver of December air to stretch out into the living room, and then made for the couch as he continued his scan of my house. It was like setting down a puppy in a new place, in need of time to roam and sets its own parameters.

"Well anyway, that's what I told Margaret, man. The exact same thing," he said once seated in an old barrel chair beside the couch, once adjusting the thick green cushion beneath him. "Exact same. I mean, come on Rattigan. Who we want to be is who we are already. Past that it's just about acquiring things, which really has nothing to do with who we are, right?"

"Of course," I said.

"I tried telling her. I mean, it's not like love's any kind of obligation. And the kind of love she's after won't just jump in her lap."

"Especially if she's trying to force it."

"*Exactly*. It's all love, everything is love *first*. She's improperly identifying what she wants, is all."

He shook his head while he tapped his foot on the wood floor at the outer edge of the mid-sized rug beneath the war trunk.

"I think she doesn't have much confidence."

"This is a great sound, by the way." He nodded at his foot. "But yeah, she asks me sometimes what I think of her confidence. Know what I tell her?" Brody scratched his left wrist on the corner of the trunk.

"Nope."

"Great coffee table, man."

"I thought it was cool. Surprisingly cheap for what it…"

"I tell her she's gotta understand her obligations in life as a whole, and embrace them, you know?"

"What are your obligations?"

"Dunno, babe. Still finding mine." He slapped my knee and sipped his beer, studied the side of the bottle and set it down. "Really. Killer table."

"Goodwill."

"And she's still finding hers, you yours, me mine. We pick up what we need to know along the way. We're continual students, right?"

"How does that affect her confidence?"

"How does what?"

"Still finding obligations. I'm…I don't know what you're…"

"It's like this." Brody put his hands together. I remembered the globe he held in his arms the night before. "Sometimes we just get in the car and drive, and sometimes it's nice and empowering to not know where we're going, you know? Just get in and drive. But nowhere *always* eventually becomes somewhere. It has to, by definition. You get lost, you say you're out in the middle of nowhere. So you go ask for directions, help, maybe advice, and you find out from a gas station clerk, or nice person in a food market, and so on, and you find out you're actually somewhere specific, so your confidence level heightens. So now if you simply tack a destination on your journey it makes the in-between all the more surreal and pure and enjoyable because you know for sure that the in-between's gonna end, way before the destination arrives and ultimately ends as well."

"And becomes something else."

"Definitely. It makes it beautiful, man. The whole ride."

"So you're saying that if she'd just relax into knowing that the means will take her to some kind of guaranteed end, she's better off setting a broad goal for herself and just working in the meantime to make the getting there all the better."

"That's it. Like what we talked about last night. Let the stronger power take over and, who knows, you just do what you can to make good in your life and others'. The kind of love she wants comes way after the big love takes shape. But there's a larger—what's the best way to say it—*spiritual demographic* than just her and that business she's entangled in."

"Does that mean we can stop talking about her?"

He'd been looking past me as he talked, but averted his gaze and looked at me and laughed.

"That's great, Rattigan. Yeah. It's exhausting. Good, no doubt. Important, but I get you. She's probably kind of become all-encompassing for you these two days."

"Thanks for the handoff."

Brody leaned forward and slapped me on the back and grinned.

"You still owe me, man."

I got off the couch and went for another couple of beers. The screen outside the back door was flapping lightly back and forth in the wind, and I stepped out to reset the ineffective latch. A neighbor, several houses east, had a few teenage sons, one or two of whom I'd seen nosing around in my back yard, likely curious, but I always kept the door itself locked. I wasn't concerned they'd steal anything, even though I was sure they'd popped open the screen several times and had at least tried the lock. It was more a concern of being asleep and waking to the sound of fourteen year-old feet scurrying across the hardwood, it was a concern for the awkward conversation that would ensue when our eyes met, just before he or they took to a sprint out back, a beer in their hand from the fridge maybe, a toaster, who knows. I didn't have much to take.

"What you get into last night?" I yelled from the kitchen. When I made it back into the living room, Brody was standing again, across from the couch, looking at a picture of my sister and brother-in-law in front of their new house in Atlanta. I set his beer beside his old one and regained my seat.

"Went downtown a bit. That's where I first ran into Reagan and Ethan. He was pretty unraveled. That's why I went by today. To see if he was still in this galaxy."

"Unraveled?"

He motioned a drinking sign with his free hand and set down the picture on a small stand beside the television.

"I thought maybe you hit the bars hard, too."

"Nah, I just kind of floated around."

Brody crossed the room and sat and exhaled as I propped my feet on the trunk.

"I had some wild dreams last night man. Kept coming. One after the other."

"Like what?" He asked, turning on his cushion.

"They haven't come back to me yet."

"That drives me nuts, man. I usually try to write down what I can if they wake me up."

"Happens all the time," I said. "So what are we into tonight?"

"Where's your room? Point me."

"To the left of the bathroom in the hallway."

I watched him walk off into the non-hallway that bore entrance to the bathroom, my bedroom, and the other bedroom which, in theory upon moving in was to become an office to do work writing and then my own, but instead it became a sort of death cave, housing boxes of old trophies and medals from when I played sports up through high school. There was a long, old carpet handed down to me from my mother when she redecorated her house across town, but it was still rolled up and neglected and actually unneeded. A few wastebaskets were in a corner, a sign I'd meant to construct an office there, and had meant to throw away a lot of drafts, as maybe the intention to fail, or expectation to fail, was pre-set. Perhaps that's why it never became an office, in that I was handicapping myself and maybe I knew it. I got off the couch and followed behind him, glancing at the shut office door.

"*Ok*, Rattigan. *Definitely*."

He was sitting on the bed and looking around the room, from the chest-of-drawers to the tall slender book shelves to the brown desk across the room from his vantage point. He eyed the high ceiling and the natural light seeping through the window from beneath the drawn shades.

"This is a great room for work."

I followed his stare to my desk, cluttered and confused and tormented.

"Here you go."

I handed him his beer. He ran the glass bottom along the lower edge of the bandana and then pulled it to his chest.

"Cheers, babe."

"It's a flat out mess, I know."

"Look at all *this*."

He rose from the bed and peered down over the paper mountains on my desk and on the floor beside it. His eyes were uncomfortably luminous, curious, looking for answers, a child ready to grab everything from the counter if allowed, if told he could have just *one*.

"Where can I start, Rattigan?"

I had copies of three unfinished manuscripts—100 pages, 115, 85—somewhat neatly stacked on the desk corner directly behind the typewriter, and other than that there were lumps of folded sheets, piles of poems labeled "unedited," obvious, "edited on file," which meant they were fixed and complete and a clean copy of them was in a separate folder on shelf, or "collection pieces," meaning they weren't atrocious, good enough maybe to sneak in a collection, hidden and hopefully suffocated by my strongest. Several short stories were in mild disorder on a shelf near his left elbow, but his attention and fingers were on the diagonally stacked incomplete non-novels with no tag, no sign of life, nothing.

"What are these?"

"Novels I started. I dunno. Could be novellas. Could go all the way. Not really sure."

"There are two. No, *three*?"

"I don't know what to tell you, man."

"Try," he said, running his thumbs along the sides of the piled pages.

"I guess..." I began, nervous at what he would or wouldn't say, not wanting him to touch them, either. They were mine and would go nowhere, and I wanted sole access to that lack of confidence in the process that gave birth to them, a process that promised their lives would be stolen back once given. "I guess...I get this enormous amount of ideas but can't seem to stick with just one. Like I want to do too much at once. It gets overwhelming."

"Yeah, Rattigan, but these are over 80 pages each. How long have you been on these?"

"Total?"

"For all of them."

"About ten months, maybe a little more. Under a year."

Brody quieted a moment and then retracted his hand from the papers. We both sipped, audibly, two sippers in natural light standing over the incompletion of at least one of our young lives.

30

"That's why Knox talks about you so much man."

He threw his arm over my shoulders.

"You're prolific man. That's a serious situation. You're no joke."

"I dunno about that, Brody."

He stepped back.

"Well, you don't have to know. Not right now, as long as you just stay..."

"I can't seem to get to them in a way that, it may sound stupid, in a way that satisfies me."

"How so?"

"I get going, and I'm insanely serious about it, and then like a train something else comes in. Drives me nuts, man. Something I feel I can suddenly say better, something more relevant to my life and my ideas at the moment. Like I'm not ready, like I'm still in practice, or they're not the right thing to go forward with yet. Like I'm not the same person every time I sit down to work. I'm not sure how to explain it."

"I was there, babe. A *long* time. Still probably am, but it just doesn't feel like it. What do you do?"

"How's that?"

"What do you do to deal with it? Because confusion over process is a crazy..."

"I go out for drinks, mostly. Kind of numb out from the pace of it. Somehow that kind of helps me rescue myself from how painful it sometimes seems to..."

"Bullshit," he said.

"Say again?"

He put his hand on my shoulder and looked directly at me. "Calling it pain is counterproductive. It's inaccurate. Whatever it is, it isn't pain. But regardless, what it *really* is is what saves your ass. It's what teaches you, us, everyone, about the struggle to become whole. You can't let hesitation about yourself be cause to ignore how important that is. Time's too limiting, and it's too pretty. Rattigan, honestly, of all the beauty in this world, you've gotta understand that the little bits you get, you hold on to. We're offered more of it than we can manage. We spend our whole lives trying to find every related piece of it. So don't dart away. And don't goof around and call it, don't call *this*, pain. There really is pain and hurt, out there, right? And in here." He poked his chest and then his forehead. "But I think the *pain*, regardless of its actual name, that results from mislabeling it, is worse."

Brody took a deep breath and let out, patted the side of my face and cheek. I thought he was going to kiss me. But he just relaxed into himself again and smiled his regular smile.

"Got me, babe?"

He bent down to catch my eyes as they drifted toward the ground.

"I do, man. You're right. And I mean that I do."

I patted his hand on my shoulder. He grabbed the top of the three manuscripts and tucked it under his left arm.

"Come on."

We left the bedroom, and as we reached the doorway he turned. I copied.

"Comfortable bed, man. I doubt it's just you all the time."

"A girl's been around."

"Yeah?"

"It's not like that."

He laughed, and we went back into the living room, thankfully switching topics. I didn't wish to revisit Mel being there, not being there, not saying why or why not, nor was the introspection that brought her back, ghostly, a welcome thought. In my room there was infrequent touch, touch I wished to continue, touch I *wanted*, but it felt impossible at that point to explain it to Brody, and difficult to explain to her, why I needed the silence of my house, when I was getting so little done. My bed should have, *could* have, been a carnival of her flesh suffocating mine, sweating together, in mutually heavy breathing, but it wasn't.

"Nah," he began, as we assumed our posts in the living room again. He'd asked about my process, and I still couldn't answer. "Just imagine if everyone had a balance with it, with their lives, too, and not just writing. It's possible, and really, almost inevitable. Or at least it *should* be. But practice is a must. I couldn't allow myself to be consumed by the unimportant junk of life all the time and do my best work. My guess is that it's best to have conviction about what exactly is and isn't important, first, before the balance can be understood. Imagine what we can change for the better if we're active in our design. What we can change for others after we change for ourselves. And it's not necessarily some altruism trip I'm on, because..."

"It sounds like it," I joked.

"Maybe," he said, smiling. "Maybe it does, but the label weakens it. Can't we just understand the nature of something without having to give it a name?"

"Yeah. I think it's good to see it that way."

"To *live* it that way, Rattigan. Would you rather see something or live it? Participate in it? We have choices, babe."

"That's true."

"And *this*." He waved his beer. "Sure, I'm sometimes interested in, I dunno, altering the madness, but not *erasing* it. Right?"

"Definitely."

It came more clearly then, simply, but especially in the form of guilt, as though I'd been chasing down the wrong kind of life, an improper marriage of efforts, between work at the paper, paying-the-bills work, and the fulfilling, yet sometimes prohibitive work at home, the real work, or as Brody called it, the goods. As he chattered on, eyes glazed, talking until his point was reached, his suspicions considered and then examined, I thought of barely being able to get by, the near-squalor of it, smacking of counterproductive perceptions but not romance. To get past the dreariness I'd assigned it, it seemed I would have to put an end to the wallowing.

"I mean, I'm just one small part of you, and you me. It might sound too broad, I get that." Brody still looked into a distance slightly inaccessible to me, somewhere through the wall by the front door. "But everything blends, Rattigan. We're all at least *partially* undiscovered. At least, so *far*. I mean, this big place, this whole *thing*? This insane world is still so new even to itself, changing, *having* to change, looking for its own footing. And we're *in* it, lost, and remarkable for it, I think. For getting our ground, too. For recognizing our small role and playing our hearts out. It may be a lame metaphor, but most are these days anyway. Doesn't make it less true."

I eyed the unfinished manuscript he held tight to his side under his arm. We talked a little while longer, mostly about New York, his Manhattan host Mitch, a writer and editor. Brody offered no story behind how they had met, how they were aware of each other with so many states dividing them and their realities, but if I asked him I was sure it would be the same, a stock answer, that he wasn't sure how they had come together as friends. And then he was off, asking me as he bustled toward the door, shivering some and rubbing his arm to warm it, if I would pick him up on Sunday at the airport at six at night. He'd asked Knox, as his car was in the shop—for what, he didn't say—but Knox was also leaving town.

"I'll try to call you from the city," he said. "Have a killer week, and really enjoy this nice weather. It's beautiful out."

"But you're freezing."

"It's still beautiful."

He stood on the porch, smiling, huddling into himself.

"Ok, ok. I will."

After Brody was gone, I turned to survey the house again, closed the cracked windows and cut the heater on after setting a small pot on the stove for tea. When the water was ready, and as the tea steeped, I carried the cup to my room and sat at my desk, staring blankly at my typewriter, a behind-the-times beauty, old and angry and refusing to die.

———

Over the course of the next several days, before he was set to leave, I didn't hear from Brody, didn't expect to and almost didn't want it, preferring him in his own space in order to re-establish my own, the silence having returned, a resurrection of focus in place, on articles, only, but a solid step toward what was beginning to matter more. Knox called, from Thailand, to tell me she wanted to buy something for me but wasn't sure if I'd wear a dress.

"Wait, you're in *Thailand?*"

"Yeah!" She shouted over unrecognizable noises in the background. "Sublime, Rattigan! Sublime is such an inadequate word for this place!"

"I thought…holy shit…I thought you were in *New Orleans* or something. What the hell are you…how are you in *Thailand?* How did I not…"

"Grad gift from the parents, man!"

"What about your thesis?"

"Details, man! That's a Spring thing!"

"I'm not wearing a fucking dress, Knox."

"It's called a 'sarong' you big baby! Live some!"

"In *Alabama*, though? You're so far gone right now."

"I gotta go! I'm sending all kinds of love, man! Feel it!"

And then she hung up.

I committed to a full Wednesday at my office at the paper, finishing a cover on industrial progress in the shipbuilding area of Mobile's port, all boring and useless shit, but necessary, the pith of someone else's matter. Days before, I'd spent an hour with the Vice Chairman of a major steel company from Germany, a stern man, but pleasant, skilled in concision and eye contact, almost paternal. As soon as the interview had concluded, and due to my slipshod reportage in not writing the important details down, at all, I forgot his name and had to search for it through recent backlogs on local commerce that I didn't write, hiding from my editor that I was sure the man's name was something Helmich. No, I was sure it was something Tonn.

I took a long walk around downtown for lunch that early afternoon, musing at Brody's commentary, as well as how I'd been living over the two years since graduating college, a bit aimless, which up to then, because of its familiarity, the not knowing, seemed agreeable, which had suddenly revealed itself as the unnecessary conservation of mental energy. What he'd said had taken on its own fast gravity, that it wasn't contributing to anyone's betterment by sulking, not even my betterment. I thought of Knox, too. *Live some.* I get it. I *get* it, I thought.

Past Government Plaza I entered a lunch-only concept one block down from the police precinct. It was a small restaurant that had opened a few nights in the past to have poetry readings. A nice idea, but the only one, and the last ever, I would attend was run by this strange, big-eyed bird who said "Peace" after finishing each of her poems, which I allowed to bother me—as in, *Nice move. Say "Peace" after each poem and subliminally guilt people into thinking you've got the goods.*—and then the other attendees, nay *performers*, were instructed to rotate back and forth, volunteering in an odd dance of failed organization, bringing crumpled papers up to the front window, nay *stage*, to read. One girl sobbed out a slop-box about her dog. An older man could barely read his own handwriting, stuttering through the hardest hitting lines about, no lie, his heart and soul and flowers. And that was just the cake. The icing, it turned out, was that it was a competition, so whomever received the loudest applause after each round won a portion of the pot they'd all thrown in on prior to beginning. I remember leaving the joint incredibly drunk and disgruntled. But during the day, the soft-spoken owner and his wife bounded through the busy dining area, the quiche was good, the fruit fresh, service fast, and I ate and smiled like a madman, alone at the table, recalling something I was confident none of the businessmen in the place had likely ever witnessed. Maybe it had just seemed hyper-silly to me because it was personally relevant, and also, that I hadn't read in public, not since school, and I quietly envied them, goods or no.

Back home around six, an uncommonly late work day, I put on tea and, not yet hungry, aligned my body with the typewriter at my desk, after thumbing through the last five or so pages of an ignored manuscript, a psychological story I'd told Knox about a year earlier, about which she offered encouragement, a green light that yielded the 115 pages of dark, sad language from a woman who'd endured a still-born child and, rather than acquiesce to the devastation, she had split into an altogether different someone, distancing herself from him in her imagination, observing him, lovingly, but with almost insufferable mania of epic mental disturbance. A celebration of words, essentially, with no real direction yet, no identifiable story, but I was enamored of the vowel beats and sharp, tough consonants housing the message of the word itself, which melted into more words, then sentences and then pages, and it had become this depressing, thick swamp of a fictitious woman's bare emotion. But I recognized the ease with which I had written it, how surly and unsociable I had been during the few months of its steady oncoming, and *that*, as I sat that night and looked it over, was its own suggestion that I'd put those feelings in contexts and worlds far from my own to feel less glum about, no doubt, me.

I worked on it anyway, into the late night, to see if perhaps the quasi-epiphany would change the language, and at very least, get my fingers on the keys again, give me something to do besides think of things I didn't wish to do. And I was grateful Brody would be flying off the next morning, although I had no idea how he'd planned to make it to the airport, not knowing his other acquaintances across the Midtown streets where I lived, and would later find out he did as well, three short miles west. And since he had so many ideas about the fluidity of the world, I knew it would be best I get on with him when he returned, but have something of substance to show for myself when he descended from the clouds. With Knox buying me man-skirts, and Brody to soon collide with New York City, I had no one to blame but myself if I didn't write, if I didn't have an energy to match theirs in our future reunion.

The old wood of my desk chair was comforting and creaking slightly, and I wrote and wrote pages of the continued pretense involving a good idea that had gone haywire, got high on each minute of it and much, much later fell asleep in a blissful slump on my bed.

Brody would call in the middle of the next day, from the Charlotte airport, excitedly yelling into the receiver that he'd finished reading my work he'd lifted, that he was then threatening with real joy to run with it.

"You've got surreal talent, Rattigan! Right!?"

I laughed, having slid back into my desk chair, as the phone had wakened me. I wondered if I'd ever yelled through a phone when calling home from elsewhere. I wondered if Mobile was actually that stagnant, or if it was just the feel of motion that shoved the voice into a roar.

"I'm glad, man. That's really great."

"I mean, if you don't think this is *good*? Go jump off a cliff *now*, man!"

"It's not done, Brody."

"Then finish it! It's that simple! Hey, I'm about to be cut off!"

"What?"

"I don't have anymore change for this thing! Be well!"

It was inarguably a happy exchange, and I was glad to hear his reaction. The nervousness of the manuscript's departure, and not knowing he'd kidnapped it for the travel, had come to a close at the base of my stomach from having been forced into his feedback on something that very well could have been on its way to the fire. I was half-asleep but more awake than before, speechless and still laughing at his exuberance. As he hung up I slouched in the chair, exhausted by him and that nudge, that push of his toward continuity, and then I sighed, wanting to reclaim some old audacity of my own to get up and just go.

So with him off, and silence resettled, I decided to stretch out into a self-imposed agenda and to adhere to it with strictness, to attempt things I'd let fall to the wayside. I rose early most mornings to cook solid breakfasts, of English muffins and eggs and hot tea, rather than tearing at a piece of bread on the way out the door. I turned on the player in the living room and left it on all hours, public radio mostly, for when they broadcast jazz or classical spots and interviewed composers. The language of the house needed adjustment. And most importantly, two days after Brody had gone, a Saturday, I remembered an obligation I had turned my back from, a guarantee on which I'd not delivered. So after breakfast that weekend, I showered and dressed in slightly more formal clothes, pulling a suit coat off a rack in the old, dead non-office in back, rather than the sweatshirt I could hardly force myself to stay out of, and made the forty-five minute drive across the bay to Magnolia Springs to visit my grandfather.

His cancer was slow and antagonistic, not swift and as final as my father's had been. My father's was of the lung, but I wasn't sure about grandfather's. Maybe bone. Maybe more than one kind. Mother's reports on his situation were always so unnecessarily dire, as if the moment itself was not, so in my loathing of her brand of informing, I'd lost many details. Papa was losing weight, though, too quickly, and it seemed a prelude to his sure passing after a long, grotesque bout. My mother would leave updates on my machine, and as the cancer progressed, my visits had diminished in number. I hadn't gone to see him since the latest news of his weight loss, trying to keep his physical weakness and close proximity to death just in my imagination, in a small cabinet of it, leaving more room for how I remembered him while growing up, strong and reliant and somehow lackadaisically powerful, as if he were accidentally supreme, but softly apologetic for it. But then, that Saturday morning, it was my first thought coming from bed, and it grew into a wild, stinging revelation that came in a rush how I was being a coward. The thought of it, the damage of its truth was such a piercing pain that I had no other presumed recourse but to go see in person what I'd been pushing away in my mind.

Papa was sitting in a wheelchair on the porch with my Uncle Jimmy, who was as skinny as my grandfather. Jimmy had a thin, reddish frame, a tightly-pulled jawline, yellowish eyes, and as I pulled in to the dirt drive leading up to the front steps, got out and waved and walked up, I couldn't figure out between the two who actually looked sickest.

"There he is," Jimmy called out, standing from beside Papa after, yes, putting out a cigarette in an ashtray on the floor at the foot of his chair. I shook Jimmy's hand as he smiled a wide smile, and then I bent to kiss Papa on his forehead. He reached a hand up slowly to touch my arm.

"It's Skeeter," he said softly.

He was wrapped in a thick blanket, not wearing shoes, but Jimmy would later tell me he'd double-layered Papa's socks, a man who never wore shoes in the house and spent most of his retirement days on the porch, waving at neighbors walking their dogs along the country highway.

"Pull yourself up a chair," Jimmy said. As I did so, knee to knee with Papa, Jimmy went inside and came back out with a glass of tea and handed it to me. "I'd offer you a beer, but your grandfather here says if he can't really have any, I'm shit outta luck."

"Did you make this tea, Papa?" I asked.

"Well," he began, exhaling, looking perturbed. "Jimmy had to. I can't get up too good."

"That doesn't matter at all."

"It just won't be as good. Not as good as mine."

"*Papa*," I said. "I know how bad Uncle Jimmy is in the kitchen. I hope he's not in charge of your meals, too."

"You little shit," Jimmy laughed, looking past me over the porch railing at my car and then furrowing his brow. Here it comes, I thought. He owned an auto body shop in Mississippi, was in town in rotation to take care of Papa, since my grandmother was already deceased and my mother and her sisters were too lazy, well, as lazy as I had been, to drive over from Mobile and stand post for his day-to-day needs, which Jimmy later said were changing fast. He walked down the steps and into the front yard, leaving Papa and me to ourselves.

He gave me brief tutorials on how his medicine regiment worked, as well as the multiple hospital visits for chemotherapy and follow-up. Papa seemed understandably frustrated at the language that had changed in his own house, sounding nothing like public radio or string quartets, but that of onomatopoeic declarations of pain, when the pain came, then the talks thereafter, concern for when the next wave might come and where, giving Jimmy constant updates on the time and location, as well as the length of the pain's tenure. He struggled to lift his shirt to show me his emaciated torso, the skeletal frame beneath all the layers, his ribs easy to count individually, and that, *that* was the moment of realization that this powerful human contribution to my younger life was now the one in need of nurturing and I hadn't any idea how to give him much beyond simply sitting there and sharing space. I wanted to do more, of course, but I still felt inadequate because there was no real answer as to what *more* was. I couldn't determine how to tell him about the world beginning to open up in front of me, and he had too little energy to talk to me about football. Just pain, since there was so much of it. After we'd gone inside, I watched him doze off during a game on television, and I imagined him just sliding off into oblivion, then and there, in that same recliner in which Nana had, three years earlier. But every now and then he raised his life-exhausted eyelids and would look at me.

"I wish I was better company."

Later, once Papa had fallen into a deeper sleep, Jimmy followed me out to the car to bemoan the reality of my grandfather's worsening condition, and he struggled to maintain eye contact with me as though I wouldn't believe him without some type of stern acknowledgment, or as if he doubted I'd comprehend the severity of his tone, the meaning of his words. His wife, my Aunt Barbara, was a traveling nurse, stationed at the time for a six-month contract in Northern California, so it made sense he would offer a mountain of diagnoses and prognoses as we stood around my vehicle. I listened patiently, but I was ready to leave. I'd seen it and didn't wish to keep discussing it, not in front of those ferocious Uncle eyes.

And then what he'd really been sitting on, and without changing his tone or stare, was a condemnatory lecture regarding the poor upkeep on my car, how I needed new tires, rotor work done, a better sense of knowledge in terms of preemptive care before something major happens. All this, before launching again into even more frightening intonations about Papa.

"I understand. I get it."

"Do you, Peter? 'Cos I hope I'm making myself..."

"Loud and clear. Come on, Jimmy."

"I..." He took a deep breath, continued to study me and then dragged me toward him for a hug. "You're a little shit. Am I right about that? Huh?" He took a step back, laughed and lit a cigarette. I stared at it.

"Don't worry, Peter. It isn't in his *lungs*."

He stood behind my car and waved as I got in and idled to the other end of the drive before pulling back on to the highway. I didn't know that afternoon what would eventually happen, but I was there, at that moment, to hopefully somehow shoulder *something* on behalf of my grandfather's suffering. I thought what Brody might have suggested, imagined him even coming with me to visit my grandfather, how pure and good it would be. I was the more isolated of the grandchildren, never bringing anyone with me to family gatherings or holidays, rarely showing even on my own, and never, never obtuse enough to bring around a girl I was really into. But Papa would have liked Brody LaCoste and things, for me, could have been a whole world better with someone around to distract Jimmy, in the middle of Papa's sleep, from jawing on about tread and worn down rotors.

Papa's repetition, how he weakly and ceaselessly had apologized throughout the visit for being a lacking host, made my heart and throat drop. Sitting near him, with the television on low and with Jimmy out puttering in the yard, I had closed my eyes and tried, with any and all strength, to somehow vacuum the disease from his body, to pull at least some of the pain out of him and root it deep within myself. I wished, with a mad rush of intensity, for a connection with any power I possessed, to give him, if anything, just a half hour of honest and true rest. I opened my eyes once noticing his snoring and heavy breathing had stopped, and I'd left him sound asleep.

A week later, however, I would receive a message from Jimmy that they'd visited the doctors the following Friday and a conclusion was drawn that a miracle had occurred—Papa's words, his translation of the doctors' language—that there was no trace of his cancer at all. I was stunned and, before I could feel naïve or maybe just *wishful*, I wondered if I had opened something within myself that had been locked and unnoticed, some sense of spiritual muscle. I'd eventually have to sit down with Brody and talk it out, a curiosity at what we'd been mulling in regards to the process and power of being alive. At home that night once hearing the news, I would sit in front of my typewriter and hold my face in my hands and think to myself, *Now it all begins.*

But in the meantime, work consumed my Sunday after Magnolia Springs. The mayor's son was once again in rehab, and the insatiable local masses needed dirt. So I went about gathering the proper information and phoning the right higher ups in order to gain access to Mayor Dole who was at his home in West Mobile, but after first agreeing he declined at the last minute and I was still stuck with a deadline which produced a terrific fiction piece on how "the Dole family was admirably unified." It was absolute swill, my editor loved it, not knowing I'd had my interview cancelled, and

Mobilians got their fix. I'd written it after a brainless drive to the airport, where I waited two full hours before realizing Brody was out of town until the *next* Sunday, staying out of town much longer than I'd remembered, having his dates completely wrong in my head. I'd written them down on a blank sheet of typing paper and taped it to the side of my desk that faced the bedroom's door so as not to forget, which proved to have exactly zero effect. So, shaking my head and the hand of the airport bartender, as I was her only customer, I went home and carved the Metro piece into the ingenious stick of shit it would become.

CHAPTER 2

The rest of the week, in wait of Brody's return, was of unconventionally low pressure. I took several walks through my neighborhood and made real work of getting out of my own way. I slept often, in cycles of long naps and then waking to play around with older poems, slowly thickening the "edited on file" folder that for too long had been sick and thin and almost in need of an Uncle Jimmy. My grandfather's recovery was my victory, too, and I wasted none of the week in its over-analysis, ensnared by no real sense of structured thinking or responsibility. In fact, the morning of the Sunday Brody was to return, I found a handwritten note, written on the back of a receipt for an oil change, and it was stuffed in the circular metal knocker on my door, a note which read: *Please follow the new civic timelines for receptacles being left in the yard. No one is exempt.* It wasn't signed, but it was evident that my newly developed insouciance for the week wasn't cute and was actually looked down upon by neighbors, frowning at my failed sense of duty. I heard my phone ring through my open door as I wheeled the empty trashcan to the side of the house, and I jogged inside just to barely miss it. I wondered if Knox was back, or if my mother had heard about Papa. I couldn't talk to her about my realized strength, but his health would be a good talking point at minimum, not as typically glum as most of our conversations, not so end-of-the-world. It was cold out, getting later in December, but the sun was still everywhere, even on the lawn and rooftop of the cowardly person who refused to sign off on their contempt for my recent lapse in routine.

Groaning at the sound of Margaret's voice, I wondered what kind of genocide she'd committed, or how many children she'd run over in a tear-soaked rage. She needed to see me, the message said. So after a callback and around eleven thirty we met at Bakery House two blocks from home for a brunch and, I was sure, stimulating conversation with a girl I didn't know the first thing about.

I laughed during the walk over, thinking Brody may have been sharing Margaret with me like a secret. *Here*, he might have said. *Here's this great cartoon you'll enjoy*. And sitting across from her once we were settled and had said our hellos, I thought if an ACME anvil fell from the sky it would land smartly on her as she continued to talk, with little injured birds spiraling up and out of her head.

"That's terrible," I said, sipping from a slender vase-looking glass as we sat outside on the dining porch.

"I know. She'd signed the check, and there was almost six hundred fifty dollars in cash in there."

"And she just dropped it?"

"First off she just thought she lost it. That was what she first told me. I'm glad they gave her a few extra shifts later in the week, to try to make up some of the cash. Her rent was already late."

"But what actually happened?" I asked.

Our server darted in and out of the scattered concrete tables, with a bewildered look on his face. He looked familiar. I thought he might have been the fellow Knox spilled on about, a young man she slept with a year or so earlier that had that noteworthy equipment, a guy who went everywhere alone and smoked a lot of dope. I'd met him once in a bar when out with her, but because he wasn't talkative I quickly forgot him. But he was quiet and friendly, smiled half-smiles, had good energy. Maybe it was Knox's erstwhile crush, or maybe it was just a cat named Fred. Margaret's story had no drive, no necessity, and I was curious as to why she'd needed me on the message, with urgency in her voice, just to talk once in person about a friend of hers who worked with Brody that lost some cash. But a story, I was learning, as with the brief moments with Papa, was still a story and needed to be heard, to be listened to even if discriminately. That, and I had nothing else to do until leaving to scoop up LaCoste—stare at the clock at home, read maybe, or get off on the continuing saga of Margaret.

"Apparently she dropped the wallet next door to the bank when she was cleaning out her car at that little vacuum station. You know which one I'm talking about? Across from Springhill's campus? Or maybe...shit...I don't know. It's in there somewhere, where that Asian family owns that big liquor store."

I shrugged as she fidgeted with her thin pasta and continued, with fading confidence, the story until she managed to, at long last, climb into the heart of it. A thin man in wiry glasses slammed on brakes in his white sports car in the parking lot, and he yelled helplessly out the cracked driver's window at an older woman talking on her cell phone and blindly strutting across the parking lot and through passing traffic. Margaret followed my smiling stare and she rolled her eyes and grinned.

"People are so *angry*, man."

"Seriously."

"I'm sorry. What about the vacuum station?"

"Oh, yeah. The thing is, she *had* to have dropped it somewhere around there, because she went inside to get some paper towels and realized her wallet was gone. And there's this house on the other side of the station's property line, right? So Aimee starts crying and asking people inside about it, but no one had turned up anything. On the way back out to her car some fat black woman was sitting on the steps of the little house next door and said, *You lose something?*"

"Fat black woman, huh?"

"I'm just describing her, Pete."

"Right."

She stopped her fork in mid-air and squinted at me. I shrugged again.

"So anyway, Aimee's crying harder at this point, and the lady held up her wallet and said she found it but there wasn't any cash in it."

"You think maybe she'd gone through it?"

"Not sure, but it seemed like it, says Aimee, who's now in hysterics and begging the lady for her money and the lady said, *Go on, honky, get outta my yard.*"

"Ouch."

"I felt so sorry for her."

"That's a big chunk of money to just say goodbye to."

"I know. But Aimee's dumb ass just *left*. I mean, I'm not trying to be racist, but…"

Here it comes, I thought.

"But I know how black people are into voodoo, so I was thinking about going to this meat market down on the Parkway and buying a hog's head and putting it in her yard with a sign that says, *Thou shall not steal.*"

"Is this what you needed me for? *Really?*" I asked, finishing off the vegetables on my plate and pushing my lemon to the bottom of the glass with my straw.

"Oh. Not exactly."

"Because your 'black people' rip makes me want to cut myself."

"I didn't mean all black people."

"I don't care."

We sat in no other kind of silence but an awkward one. The sun was ugly on her face.

"I got married."

That's when I understood. The only thing she could do to prevent herself from revealing it too early was to talk about Aimee, thereby passing along a precursory story that suddenly didn't seem too large a concern of hers anyway, her friend's loss of money or even her frightfully serious, but likely noncommittal, desire to engage in the distribution of decapitated swine. The core of the midday meal was this news, at this very minute, in the lightning-fast seconds it took for her to process when the interjection of it, the admission of it, was appropriate. A definite cartoon, I thought, anxious to get to Brody and harangue him for the mess he'd divided up between me, his advice for my own new direction, and a sort of subterfuge girl, plump and unsmiling, with fading-out orange hair.

"Ok, I get it now. I guess…congrats?"

She shrugged her shoulders, her eyes obliquely focused, searching the table and not me for validation, council, something.

"So everything worked out for you and Sam after all."

"That's the thing."

"What thing?"

"Mohammed and I got married."

I sat forward. The afternoon flashed like disturbed kindling. Everything got good, fast. Her last four words made the walk to the restaurant worthwhile.

"Sam's best friend?"

"Yeah."

"That sad cat from the *bookstore?*"

"Yeah."

"Who you don't even really know?"

"But it's not like that."

She paused and looked unsure of herself, before mentioning it was a quick ceremony with no one else present. They were moving to Silicon Valley when he finished his degree. All this, just days after her distraught concerns over the outcome of, the end of days between, Sam and herself.

"Well, good luck with what's ahead."

And with that, there was little left to add. I stayed at the mock work of straw-pummeling my lemon wedge beneath the ice in my glass. Margaret looked uncomfortable in her chair as she spread the last of her pasta across the plate like a child convincing its parent it had eaten equal amounts of everything. It was almost pitiable to see her squirming in the nervousness following such admission, as if saying it aloud hadn't freed her like she'd hoped, but instead, it had put out into the air between us a cloud of mis-calculated permanence, one of a reality that she and her inner Memphis nature, by way of Mobile, was going to feel ignored and alone while living with a stranger in California. My support, though, surprised her when she divulged a burgeoning interest in Islam.

"No one yet has given me that response."

"I'm all for learning new things, man. Honestly. But at the risk of sounding professorial…"

"It's fine."

"Just think of what motivating forces are behind the interest, is all. Right?"

She nodded without looking at me. Of course it was far from my respon-sibility to tell her what a colossal mistake she was making, as it wasn't my statement to offer, nor was it my mistake. If hurt and languor were her bag, her deal, then so be it, which wasn't to say emotional chaos would occur, that her identity would be surrendered if not stolen. But from my seat at the table, it seemed her decision was too fast and borne, possibly, of going a long time without feeling wanted.

I thought of a mechanic who'd filled my ear one afternoon a few months earlier, a shaved-headed fellow a little younger than myself. He'd just been through a divorce, he'd said, and as he called me out to the pit to do as Uncle Jimmy had done, condemning me for the substandard upkeep of my car, he pulled me into a specific discourse that, until this particular moment with Margaret, hadn't seemed would ever resurface in my mind. I wasn't sure whom he was referencing, and from what point of expertise, but his adamancy was impressive. *It's always the fat ones*, he'd said. *Always the fat and lonely ones who get sucked in by some dumbshit of a guy who wants somebody to control and is tired of chasing down the good-looking women he can't have in the first place. So it ends up being a man who hates his wife because she ain't who he wants, and a wife who's too scared of being fat and alone forever who'll do damn near whatever she's told. So me? I'm dreading gettin' back out there.*

And it wasn't that I had an insider's information about their relationship, as there didn't seem to be any. I didn't deserve it or want it, which she could tell. That she knew, hence, her quest for outside advice, to ask someone it was easy to ignore. But she never once asked if she were being unwise which, to me, meant her Achilles Heel was that she wasn't yet bold enough to doubt herself.

We instantly began our goodbyes after our server, under less strain by then, had picked up cash I'd folded into his book. I watched Margaret slowly cross the parking lot, keen on avoiding angry little men in angry little cars, and she climbed in her purple compact and disappeared down Dauphin Street. I sat a short while longer in the lingering afternoon of late December and sighed, long and deep, out into weather that had yet to decide on fierce frigidity or a steady, pleasant cool until March brought in sporadic rains and the hint of the inevitable, aestival heat. I never saw Margaret again.

———

It wasn't until long into Brody's rehashing of New York that he'd mention he found a girl. He didn't meet, he said. He *found.* It was an epic *happening.* But after diving into the description of her, he hadn't changed cadence or tempo of passion from the rest of the story, seeming as though he'd also made love to the city itself.

I arrived at the airport earlier in consideration of the new, elevated security checks. Too early, in fact, as his flight was delayed, and so I sat in deep study of the back of my hands. The arrivals lobby area was gray and boring, the lighting dull and inappropriate to the point I felt I was a child again, in church beside my parents, trying desperately not to fall asleep, to begin snoring, to incur my mother's disconcerting pinch on my forearm. I heard loud laughter before I saw Brody, and as he rounded the corner from the gates I saw he'd made friends on the plane, an elderly couple and a grandchild. I stood as he pointed at me and grinned, and then he stopped to set down his carrying bag and squat to tousle the little boy's hair and slap hands before standing again to shake the couple's. It was good to have Brody home in Mobile. I was ready for the pace to pick back up, suddenly and momentarily guilty, inexplicably, for having allowed the slowness that had permeated my time alone. As I rummaged through my head to determine what I could tell him apart from Knox in Thailand, Margaret and the Valley, trash receptacles and a few poems, he began to pick up speed and nearly knocked me over.

"You're *here*," he said, squeezing my face and planting an audible kiss on my forehead.

"Of course I'm here, man." I laughed. "So are you."

"I know, man. I *know*."

He adjusted the strap on his shoulder and palmed the back of my head, his elbow in the center of my spine, as if I were a baseball he was readying to hurl down the escalators. Too spirited to get home and unpack, Brody insisted he take us to a small lounge near the restaurant where he occasionally worked, to have a drink and talk it all out. He wore a button-down white shirt beneath a light sweater, faded jeans, and he looked extremely thin. I imagined he hadn't slept throughout his entire stay in New York, opting for exploration as sustenance over the patience necessary for food and rest. I also imagined that if he'd dressed like that the whole week, he'd frozen. But since he was back, I felt heat from his elation as we trotted through the sleepy ground floor, waited a few minutes to grab his suitcase and then pushed through the heavy glass doors that led out to short-term parking. I drove east down Airport Boulevard with the music low, as he cracked his window and sighed, occasionally smiling over at me while shaking his head. *You just don't know*, he kept saying. *You can't know.* We turned into the small parking lot of a smoky, quiet place called The Blackbird, named after a Miles Davis track. Once seated inside, and after fanning away cash I offered him toward our drinks, he moved us to a comfortable couch in the back of the dark bar. Brody's story surged.

"Ok, get *this*. I caught a cab to the airport but realized I was hungry en route, so I bribed Dan to stop off for breakfast at the Waffle House out there on Schillinger, and right as we sat, man, our server gave me a dollar bill and asked me to select from the jukebox. You're right, it *was* weird, but she said she liked my selections, mostly Sinatra, so it worked out. Dan was a nice guy who didn't have much to say until we stopped to eat, the stop by the way costing me about thirty just to get him to agree. I know, I *know*, Rattigan, but everybody's got bills. He seemed relieved to get some conversation and hot coffee going before the sun came up and he had to get home, oh man, to his granddaughter he was watching while his daughter picked up her husband from the airport in New Orleans. Apparently he'd been surfing in Ecuador? San Salvador? I can't remember. And he needed to be immediately rushed to the hospital after landing because he'd been suspected of catching malaria? Maybe he said malaria. It was rough on the old boy, you could tell, by how he talked about it with this kind of quiver to his lip, his tongue darting, like maybe he had dry lips from even the recounting of it but was too afraid to stop and do the story a disservice, or continue and experience it too connectedly in front of a stranger. Which reminds me, babe. You gotta help me remember to call him. I promised. What? *Yeah*, I got a cabbie's number. What planet did *you* move to? But it was nice that I could tell in his face that he knew I'd call. People these days think any kind of goodwill or, I don't know, move toward generosity is just a move that never comes into fruition, an offer that never learns how to quite embody itself. It's a shame about that, Rattigan. A real shame.

So then we ate, which was another twenty-five, and he dropped me at arrivals, and I tipped him and clasped both his hands with both of mine through his rolled-down window, and I touched his shoulder and, sincerely, he seemed like it was something he realized he needed but hadn't had in a while, you know, at that very moment. Human contact? Compassion? Whatever it was he was getting from me, I promise you I was trying to give it with all I had. Exactly man, it was exactly like you pulling that pain out of your grandfather. I believe in that. Hey, remind me about that, too. We'll go see him when we get the chance, wish him well, wish him peace.

I got turned around and confused at the new process of flying these days, security clearances and all, like there's war happening right here at home. Who knows? Maybe there is. But I can't tell you how much anger and apathy and distrust and leering all went into the jobs of these poor TSA folks. They've gotta do their job, I realize that, but everything's a conspiracy, everything's assumed dangerous. It was so strange how guilty I felt just going through their motions, you know? Thinking, man, I've got tweezers in my suitcase, am I screwed now? Will I be able to fly?

So to counter the paranoia I walked through the lobby and up to the desk and the whole time I wore this beaming proud smile with all the good I could emit, so people could maybe think, for just a little while over the holidays, that there was nothing to worry about with at least *one* someone. It's a hard, hard bucket of responsibility to carry sometimes, being *that* aware of how important your every move is, I mean, if it's to be accommodating to your fellow person that you're after. It's a joy, too, don't get me wrong. But then there's a pain that comes with knowing there are so many other people just floating along through the process of living, unaware of how their indifference to or ignorance of the general suffering of us all under the same damn blanket and code of existence is a hindrance, a true damage to the soul. What I'm saying is that America's turning into the kind of country that'll use any excuse, even something like a war, to be mean to one another *here*, and laugh at those who say we have to show some kind of solidarity *because* of the conflict itself. But no matter how much hate and death there is, no matter who's causing it, unity's got to be some kind of goal, right? What I'm saying is...I don't know...ok...I'm *saying* that when I walked through that lobby, lost and unsure of where I needed to be, I just smiled and thought to myself that maybe there's no solidarity with the self in this country, that it's sadly likely that people that look like you and me who we walk by every day just seem to be adrift in a sea of unawareness that's eating us all up on the whole. So at the desk I just said, *Hey there, good morning*, and the nice brown-haired woman flashed an alert smile, her cheeks dimpled and she helped send me on my way. I went up the escalator and stared at my feet, thinking about all those times as a kid Mom would tell me to be careful or I'd be sucked into it and never seen again.

The line snaked around in front of those X-ray machines, and I noticed people all around were slipping out of their shoes, so I reached down and untied mine and talked to a good-looking kid about our age who was rail thin, skeletal almost, and we even had the same travel bag, though his had a laptop in it and mine had notebooks and old disks and your manuscript and just a few minor things. A book I bought for Mitch in New York, some tissues for the cold. I went through the screening area and studied how they scan you and pat you down, how they profile you, too. That business *happens*, Rattigan. Not just at the airport. I had a friend who got arrested for accidentally leaving a half bag of jelly beans in his pocket he was eating while at the store. He walked out with the rest of his groceries and forgot to pay for them. No lie. He was from India. It was so unbelievable. Sweetest guy you'd ever imagine. I mean, yeah, it was technically a theft, but who hasn't done that before, right? Karma worked me over a good bit for stealing on purpose when I was in sixth grade. I learned early. Me and this kid named David O'Connell stole beer just down the street from our neighborhood, several times. We'd just climb on his Moped and come back home, drink the beer beside these big wisteria bushes on the other side of his backyard fence. And that had all been on purpose. But an *accident*, man? And jelly beans, no less. It cost Varun's family something like 1400 dollars to get him out of that one. I bet you my right fingers that if it had been me, they'd have *given* me the damn candy if I'd have been the least bit apologetic. Sad, sad world, Rattigan.

Oh, and this won't surprise you. While I was downstairs philosophizing to myself about the melancholic intricacies of American society, and of course, still flashing my best grins at the busy woman at the desk, I forgot to check my biggest luggage piece. Mindless, right? But the lady at the gate said, *Darling, you've only got fifteen minutes to go check it in and it surely won't fit in the overhead*, so I was lightning minutes away from getting despaired when her face studied mine and recognized, I guess, inexperience and apology all wrapped together in my face, and then various compassions broke out on hers, and then on mine as I was trying to thank her kindness. It was this amazing little moment where we understood the situation and each other so immediately that after she offered to get my bags taken care of without me having to rush back through the screening and shoe-removing and getting sucked into the escalator's abyss, all I could think to say to her, with my most genuine look of respect, was *Thanks so much, Ingrid, you have a wonderful holiday season.* And she melted and said, *You too, darling.* Because of her, Rattigan, come to think of it, right now I'd say I already have. See? Those are the kinds of faces and memories you want to keep with you and share with others. That's that big great universal love.

But once I got on the plane, everything seemed to finally be setting itself into motion. At first I planned on a quick nap because I'd only gotten a couple hours of rough sleep, fighting dreams and ideas, and even once getting up to list them out on paper before waking up later and forgetting them. *You* know how that goes. Anyway, I thought I'd actually gotten assigned to a row with no one else beside me, since body after body kept shuffling past without stopping to do more than glance at the letter before moving on. Wishful thinking, definitely, because stretching it best I could would have been nice for sleep, but then this middle aged woman and her daughter, a couple years younger than you and me, plopped down next to me and offered me gum. So instead of closing my lids, man, I sat with them and we smacked away, and I'd find out shortly after the seatbelt light flickered on and the female robot voice sounded out through the plane about regulations and what we could expect of the flight, that whole bit, that the woman next to me had another daughter across the aisle, so the crossover conversation between them began and was giddy and pervaded by laughter and hopefulness, and I caught this great high off their high and decided I wasn't tired any longer and, who cares, if I had to have sleep I could force a few winks during the connecting flight from Charlotte. So I nestled in my seat and dug through my travel bag and sank deep into your story, which I'd started a little before lights out the night before. That's likely a big player in why I couldn't rest all too well. It's really something, Rattigan. Got me thinking about it all. You're really there, man. I don't...I don't know where to start. I wrote on the draft, so I hope you...oh, you don't? You sure? *Nice.* I mean, it's good stuff I scribbled in, you'll see, all good stuff. I just couldn't remember everything I wanted to read back to you, man, to let you hear some of those harder-hitting lines from a different voice that doesn't sound like your mind shouting back at just you.

But I did take a quick break before take-off to look out my window across the tarmac and out into the day just waking up, and the sky was that kind of fresh early morning pink, man, and I couldn't wait to actually be in it, you know? To have that transcendent shift into weightlessness all around me, dangling in the sky in the guts of a bird with big metal wings. I dunno, it sounds crazy but it was good. So, so good. And while leaving the ground there were those half-scared howls of first-time flyers, so I closed my eyes and smiled wide, feeling those plane wheels hit small bump after bump until meeting that independent smooth cold December wind, and then we were sailing. I looked all around to my left, up ahead, behind me, man, like an excited young boy, everyone eye to eye with that pink orange foggy horizon, and I glimpsed and understood the wonder of my fellow fliers. It was so surreal and innocent altogether like a poem so intense you scream it out. And by the time we neared Charlotte, the sky had transmuted into a white layer beneath this almost completely indecipherable light green-blue and then blue, babe, so much blue, crazy-ass blue oceans of blue.

At the airport I had about twenty minutes to find the right concourse and—yeah, I know they have *signs*, Rattigan—I had to ask directions since I was trying to make it to my gate but still get time to call you because I'd finished the pages—see, I had you on the brain—and then hit the bathrooms and grab a soda. It's all funny, now, because I think about how I felt panicked I'd miss the plane, so I was walking this near-frenzy of a walk and trying to send peaceful vibes throughout the crowds but still managing to get a little frustrated at the stoppers and left-turners and right-turners who upset the flow of the rest of us in a hurry. It was like I was more trying to balance my imbalance internally and still be punctual in the corporeal sense, so yeah, you said it. No doubt I looked insane. But whenever I got back from New York, after walking those hectic streets again and jumping inline with the pace of that urban roar, Rattigan, I tell you, when I was back through Carolina this afternoon I hummed through the crowds like a silent missile. It was like I could communicate with my legs just operating independently from me, like I could look down and congratulate them on jobs well done, like they'd needed New York again, like it had been too long.

I eventually dozed though, on the way up, crammed next to two unfriendly cats, this one in particular who grunted beneath his low hat, and then one who sat there making these impolite, inaudible declarations of anger all balled up in his face. But get this, babe, this'll kill you. I *swear* it happened. I overheard them talking about the younger of the two's grandmother who'd just had open heart surgery, and when she came to and was still all disillusioned from pain and drugs, she patted her daughter on the arm and whispered in the direction of the doctor, *"Tell that man down there he better stop looking at my pussy."* I mean, can you imagine some ancient gal coming off with something like that, Rattigan? She's at least *earned* it, right? That's how I'm gonna be, man, I'll be a hundred and fifty and still making waves. It's gotta be in motion already. It *has* to be.

But at the airport in Newark I got lost again, completely turned around after this lady at the counter where you get public transportation passes into the city gave me these labyrinthine details about navigating through the place, and then some guy smoking a cigarette in the doorway to the outside told me I was confused and in the wrong place. This nice couple from Shreveport, who said they go to New York five or six times a year for the shopping, they took pity on me and gave me good conversation the whole way toward this place where you stand to wait for your respective buses, and they were even getting on the same bus to Penn Station, man. I'm talking *serendipity*. So we skimmed by signs of Secaucus, Hoboken, eyeing the sprawl of New York, the Statue of Liberty staunch and out in the middle of the glossy sunlit water, Lincoln Tunnel, I think maybe the New Yorker building, on this rocky, wild bus ride with a sweet driver with big, muscular hair who seemed embarrassed that her music was too loud when the radio clicked on by accident. Somebody facetiously yelled from the back to turn it up and we all laughed, because no one really wanted to hear anything but the roar of the wheels and the engine as we collectively stared at this poor woman who'd stopped off the turnpike to vomit.

It was cold out and windy, and I was trying to take down some ideas in a notepad before I forgot them, but then we were being tossed about so violently that at each and every turn we glided around, I just shrugged it away, forgetting whatever it was trying to eke its way into my forebrain, and so I just enjoyed the bustling, ravenous rush toward the city. What? Hell *yeah*, I'm being serious. She just pulled right over on the shoulder, opened her door and puked all around her feet while holding back her own hair. *What?* What kind of *car* was she driving? You're killing me, Rattigan. *Killing* me.

Anyway, at Penn Station I knew I was more lost and I was loving it, having misplaced the exact address for Mitch's apartment downtown, somewhere in my bag, with no time to stand out on the sidewalk and squat down and dig through. The Louisiana couple tried to give me advice based on what little I recalled, even when all I gave them to go on was an Au Bon Pain, and a Strands? I know, man. What was I thinking? And come to think of it, maybe I made up the Strands. But I thanked them and said I'd be fine, figuring the worst that could happen was that I'd end up somewhere in Chelsea just a handful of blocks up from Mitch's area, check out a jazz joint and ask some old scene hero if he could point me in the right direction, or maybe dart into a gay bar and grab a beer and see if I could get anyone's attention for some friendly advice, you know. But somebody told me later on that Chelsea's a market for the young and pretty, and I decided I'd be, I dunno, messing with their territory by coming in all high and sleepless and curious about how to get from A to B, instead of sitting to wax on heart matters. What's that, man? No, *you're* young and pretty.

But after some aimless strolling around and just staring up into the expansive sky and studying the faces of people blistering by on the sidewalks, with these fiercely determined looks in their eyes, I figured it best by then to just hop a cab and give him what bits and pieces I did have, get on down to Mercer Street one way or the other. So I flagged a car and he nodded toward his popped trunk and I loaded up and climbed in. And again, this won't surprise you, Rattigan, but this tiny old lady dressed in an eternity of purple blinked at me from inside the car, recoiling a bit before asking, *Uh, hello? Can I get out first?* And I started laughing and looked around, as if maybe there was a camera on me or something, like maybe it was staged. Like it was a new game show, *Stun the Kid from 'Bama*. It was beautiful. And so I moved to let her out, still laughing, but she didn't laugh and neither did the cabby. You're right, man. I thought it was funny, too. So he drove me through Chelsea—I keep referencing Chelsea, I know, as it seemed we drove around there for days, like maybe he was milking the fare, who knows?—and as it turned out later I was supposed to have told him 8th and Broadway, but he managed nicely with what I managed to unearth from my carry-on and he plopped me down right in front of

Mitch's huge apartment building. I tipped the reticent cat and emptied out into the street, ran up the steps with my increasingly heavy suitcase and jetted through the revolving door, showed identification at the front desk and took my spare key Mitch had left for me, my name on the envelope and everything, hopped an elevator with a model who'd been out walking her dog. What? I'm assuming she was, man. Mitch said a lot of them lived in the building.

So I hit the 28th floor, and Mitch was standing in the doorway of his apartment right across from the elevators. I guess they rang him from downstairs and said I was there. Anyway, we got caught in a big, redemptive, it's-been-way-too-long hug and then stepped in, where from the door I saw the bed he'd made up for me in the living room, this small thin perfect bed right there in the middle, and just past it his view of the West Village, the Hudson beyond it, Jersey beyond that. To the left looking south you could see the sky above the area where the Trade Center was going to be rebuilt, and to the north you could see this staggering view of the Empire State Building which, I have to tell you, looks like a giant big symbol of fortitude when the sun's going down over Staten Island and the pinkish red orange hues blast the side of it with this kind of quiet strength that seems to electrify it, shock it into being bigger than itself, the same way you get or I get or anyone gets who sees the winking eye of the universe and *understands* for a moment. And then not two minutes and the wine was poured and it was great, man, just sitting there and laughing without saying a word. He's been retired for several years, so I'm sure the energy I was bringing would be a reminder of sorts for him and his past selves, and I was definitely sure that his energy, staid and direct, would be a reminder for me, too, that I may not live a full thousand years but I can always maintain a spark and keep living life to celebrate it, and not forget the purpose of the search.

We jumped into suits after I showered off the airplane scent and the feel of being cramped, and we laughed our way into ties—I know, man, I had to borrow one from Mason at work—to go walk the city before dinner. Mitch said I need to learn to tie a bowtie, since that's what he was wearing, and I considered it and this is what I came up with: that it would be a great trick at dinner parties, but it doesn't seem to match, I dunno, *me*. He said it would be a terrific skill, and I agreed, but a *suit? Me?* Can you see me in a suit, Rattigan? A *suit*? It was upscale, man, wild and way up there. We walked this alternate route out the other side of his building—I'm starving mad at this point, wanting to eat up everything—so after a short ride we walked to and through the giant echoing stirred-up Grand Central Station and past Trump Tower and Cartier, we joked about trying on tiaras. *What?* Didn't you say Knox wanted to buy you a *dress*? It's all love, man. Anyway, my coat was allowing the city wind in on through to my button-down, but it was a nice crisp sort of breeze, and in fact, the whole time I was there it was just that, nice and crispy, sunny and in the thirties, so oddly against what I expected for late December that I even got a rise out of Mitch when I said it wasn't cold enough.

Suddenly, though, there we are zooming tourist-like past Radio City Music Hall, NBC Studios, the Rockefeller tree and the crowds with their cameras, as though he was giving me the basic sweep again before dinner. Between these main nights I'm telling you about, these *pivotal* ones—and I know they sound stacked on top of each other, so please, babe, bear with me. There's an abundance in my head I'm trying to hang on to—I gave myself a refresher tour as well, self-guided, just kind of ambling along and staring up at the tall buildings, dipping in and out of random shops, drinking maybe too much post-nap afternoon coffee. I slept a good bit during the days separating our nights out, if you'll believe me. Made a few friends at this killer deli in Soho. Listened to a lot of classical at Mitch's, talked books, and I let him take a look at the notes I wrote out on your stuff. Oh, come *on*, Rattigan. You *knew* I would. He said he's interested in the final product before we get him a copy. That's right, I said *we*. You win, we win. You're mine now, man, so that's how it goes, and I'm yours. We need to talk one day about victory. I've redefined it, you'll see. But anyway, I told him, *Yeah, Mitch, I'm interested, too.* So that means you've got some work to do. Haha, don't *slug* me. I'm doing us both a favor.

So where was I? Yeah, thanks, *Rockefeller*, with no one yet on the ice rink down below to photo, so we saw mostly people just clutching one another in the chilled early evening and smiling at the bright glow from the tree, taking advantage of every moment away from their respective frays to just stand around and love. I even bummed Mitch's camera and snagged a tree shot from the distance just before we turned the corner to head on to Four Seasons somewhere around Park Avenue, I can't remember. No lie, Rattigan.

He had reservations already set. And when we got there, I was tired and high and craving something thick to go on top of the wine and an empty stomach, but our table wasn't yet ready, and we hadn't talked any business about writing or publishing because there'd been so much grandeur that there was no real use or place for it just then. We sat and waited in this long marble hallway, this glorious and massive Picasso original hanging down this high wall just across from us. I think it was from 1919, man, so close I could have touched it if I were out of my right and left minds and chose to make a decision like that with absence for a brain, so we just studied it and laughed some more and eventually made it on down to our table in this huge brown room lined with dancing, swimming copper and decorated trees in the middle, trees just barely the size of giants. We had martinis and discussed Mitch's lovers' concern for him that there is a true, potential risk in this world today of being hurt for a human's abundant kindness, and you know what I told him? You know what I think of that? I think we keep going on freely in the universe, and what goodness we release doesn't just vaporize into the air, man, it lingers. It *remains*, Rattigan. I told him if Chris wants to be free of that kind of worry, he should just sit back and celebrate all the joys and downfalls and heartaches and beauties that occur every single day in our lives, and leave the full-scale kindness to those who don't fear the occasional fellow who doesn't understand or respond. It was pretty bold, now that I think of it. Maybe I was feeling the liquor. But it was rich and intense, and I couldn't seem to get off on the dinner unless Mitch showed some sense of recognition of the fact that you gotta keep perpetuating love, keep finding it, *creating* it. It's where hope has its source.

For example, man, I haven't told you about just a few weeks ago. I was driving down Airport Boulevard, just past Florida Street where the lanes narrow and those killer older homes lean right over the street it seems, with their dramatic long facades and eyeless windows. Those old doctor's houses. *Exactly*. There was this car broken down in the street, so I pulled over, maybe a block past the couple who was pushing the car into the right lane alongside the curb, and I jogged down to help them push and they let me and didn't thank me, didn't need to either as far as I'm concerned, as I'm sure they were frustrated or distraught or embarrassed or all of the above. But they both got in the car and let me push them alone about three or four blocks until we hit this downward slope just before that station up there on the left. So I kept running behind the car until they pulled over, and I wanted to see if there was anything else I could do to help, even after they'd sat in the car and let me do all the work. But the man steering the car asked me for money. For *money*, man. I wished him well and took off back to my car, but *man* was I a little boiling about the whole process. You get this worldly sense sometimes that there's this nefarious hodgepodge of apathy and opportunism in this country, where no real generosity exists any more, since it's all so laden with greed and stipulation. All that's going through my mind, right? During the trot back to my car. But then I checked myself and looked at the sun beaming down over the trimmed bushes and the semi-circle driveway I was parked in front of, and it was then I realized the universe was giving me a needed reminder, that everyone deserves help, no matter the situation, that there's always someone *next* time that will perceive the benefit of someone's efforts, and *that's* the reward, man. To keep looking forward to how you can change at least *somebody*. To know your good's going to at some point translate over into others' actions. That's how you change yourself, to not give up on that truth. And so I told Mitch all this and we clinked glasses as our server from Romania, this guy with a swollen third-trimester sort of belly, joked a bit with us before bringing the check. We walked past the Picasso and got our coats, and once we entered the street again toward St. Thomas Church, you could tell by the way the streets had lit up along each avenue and pavement we crossed over, that something pure had been revealed, rehashed, I don't know, something had been brought closer to life.

And then we get inside the church to see Handel's *Messiah,* and it was then I'd say I felt most out of place in a suit. I mean, there were women in gowns and older businessmen in suits who looked like they *meant* it. It was all this hilarious swirl going on inside me, and I just sat beside Mitch and listened not too closely to him joyfully exchange passions with some woman in front of us who claimed there was nothing more clear about the existence of God than the sound at the end of the second wave, movement, I don't know what to call it, where everyone stands, and the choir of mostly younger men belt out the most famous part of the entire piece, this jolting harmonic shout of Hallelujah, over and over. You've heard it before, Rattigan, and *damn*, it was something to experience in person. Mitch had tears in his eyes and studied me studying the sloped looming walls of the church and I tell you, it does make you feel like you don't know about anything at all when you're feeling all this joy, and then seeing it, how it's twisted all up in your entire sensory threshold, and you catch someone who's felt it and lived it before, remembering his first time with it, all over again, just by watching someone else get all tangled in a new, inexplicable, who knows, *rapture*, maybe. It turned into this whole new responsibility, what I was giving my old pal Mitch by standing there and getting wholly absorbed.

On the way back to Mercer, we stood in the center of the subway and giggled about destiny as Mitch said something about "subways these days," something with a bit of sarcasm, and I just nodded and he laughed this great high squeal. Once we got home, I threw on a sweater and some beat up shoes I still haven't been able to destroy and I made my way alone out into the street, because I knew I had a date with a poem before it then hit me I needed to go find it somewhere, needed to go seek it out, out *there,* and not wait for it, somewhere both lucid and deceptive around Chelsea or Hell's Kitchen or Union Square, somewhere where streets you've long forgotten hover around just eyeing you, like they haven't forgotten you or that you no longer recognize their faces.

An old friend from high school in Birmingham—you didn't know I was from B'ham? That's good stuff—well he was originally from Chicago, wait, *is* from Chicago, a kid I knew in Birmingham after his parents moved him there who now goes to NYU, he was on his way home and—yeah, this is how crazy the world is—was standing around in Astor Place as I shuffled down the sidewalk toward some steps into the subway. I'm cold and elated by now, and I hear this *Brody, Brody* series of shouts as I walked. Why would I lie, babe? This stuff *happens*. We grabbed each other up off the concrete, man, an unreal reunion, and he said something about standing on a trolley, whatever that meant. Then we rocketed uptown toward Union Square, walked a few laps around the park. This cat Brian, a writer of his own bizarre forms that mainly just demonstrate his vocabulary, which is impressive, but his stuff chokes on itself for the most part because it's these mind-scramble ideas with such overt attempts at cuteness he sometimes gets you sick rather than gets you off, but he's a nice guy all the same, and has this dreamy look in his face these days that almost makes you think he's near to being deep into himself, but won't surrender to it, that he's just now figuring if the world fails him or he fails himself, again, babe, whatever *that* means, he'll end up teaching high school honors English back in the Chi-town suburbs and pulling out his hair when he can't determine on his own why it is he's unfulfilled.

So after we exchanged contact info and he poised to take off further uptown, I took his pointed-finger directions down into the East Village, to this small smoky and blue bar that lined up alongside the left once you walked in, with these great big thick-cushioned black seats lining the wall to the right. This thin guy in dark sunglasses and an eerie smile was in back playing some boggling records that had this heavy dripping sort of rip on traditional jazz, but it was nice and everyone around me seemed pleased by it, so I slipped out of my jacket at the bar and had a beer, sitting there a minute thinking maybe someone would come along and find me interest-ing so we could strike up some magic, some young lovers with great sto-ries to tell, maybe a good-looking neuroscientist whose brain I could pick about the study of emotional pain center flashes through EKGs, someone enthralling I guess, I have no idea, now, but just someone unpredictable.

Another beer and I got what I was looking for, these excited Columbia U. law students who lived in Queens had come down for some of the Village scene, and *man* they talked so loudly and with this mighty vigor that I, at some point, struck up some chatter with them about nothing in particular, and then there we were bouncing down Avenue A to some gay bar with a neon rooster in the window, because Becca said her friend John was after the lead singer of some band who hung out there often, some band just getting big around the country. They had asked if I were down and I told them sure, and that time was wasting. About ten minutes later, after they both grabbed a cigarette in the light chill outside, we were there under these deep alluring red lights and black lights and people groping in this wild, visceral pond of drugs and longing stares, and John buying us round after round with a preoccupied look on his face until sure enough, here comes this wiry distracted-looking fellow without a shirt and these thin overall straps covering his sweating upper body. Honestly, Rattigan, you get into the right kind of music in the right part of anywhere in existence, no lie, you begin seeing little fleeting moments like that, and you can really dig down into how innocent and awkward everyone is in the world, even you and me, even when we set ourselves up to meet with *maybes* in terms of love when we're already surrounded by so many *yeses*. So then Becca just kind of beamed at them, leaning their shoulders against this tall wooden post just across from the service well of the bar, and then she went and stuck a five dollar bill in the elastic of this thick-muscled male stripper. We were laughing and studying the variety of people going in and coming out of the unisex restroom that had no door, until John came over and we met the singer, Tighe, and a friend of his who'd been in a movie we'd all seen, a confused-eyed young man who almost tipped over when I clapped him lightly on the back. And John and Tighe were looking fairly familiar together by then, so Becca and I had one more drink and I was pretty heavily on my way, so with a great buzz and all these competitive, superior loves churning inside me, I hugged them all goodbye after getting their numbers, and I walked in jagged lines back through the village toward Mitch's apartment, where I fumbled around with the key but couldn't get in through the door. Yeah, I know, babe. I *was* that tight. I had to go downstairs to use the lobby phone, but instead of acquiescing to my right mind and phoning up to the 28th, I dug Brian's number from my pocket and got his directions for that much-needed sleep. What? Of *course* I slept, Rattigan. I already *told* you. But anyway, after stopping off at this late-night joint with greasy, fantastic pizza burgers and brutally insulting employees, I ate my messy sandwich over a trashcan on the corner of Nowhere and Somewhere, finally at home in the city, turned around and out of sorts, just standing there weighing in on how ridiculous I'd look anywhere else in the world and, then, laughing aloud to myself, at myself, *with*, I hopped a train to 26th and 1st. Brian was still up working on a paper for school, so I thanked him with all the exhausted esteem I could muster and rolled up a bath towel of his for a pillow, just to sink into a deep, perfect sleep until he woke me a few hours later and said, with heavy baggy eyes, that he'd pulled an all-nighter and he'd walk me to the train.

Back at Mitch's we laughed at the story of my burgeoning confusion about everything in existence, even a situation as seemingly approachable as the use of a key, and when I got a little playfully self-deprecating he said, Don't say *fault*, and then he poured us a glass of white wine. I'd say I made, ball-parking it, thirty trips back to Mercer over the week. Seriously, it seemed I was roaming and either fitting into an agenda or escaping one, but always, always, around every corner there was Mercer,

63

I was always somehow headed back to Mercer. It was like a beacon, man. Of *course* of light. But anyway, there we were having salmon for breakfast, and I was wide awake in a stir of our collective happiness. The whole conversation of the morning dealt with these guarantees we'd given ourselves at various points of our lives, where it would always be that exact feeling at that very moment we'd chase down, with a fury only as passionate as we could use to compliment the search. We stared out over the Hudson as we stood beside his two large cactus plants to the right of the window, and we said everything was *wonderful*, over and again, everything was sometimes *striking*, but most always wonderful, like when he used to live on Bleeker Street back in its "best days," but he didn't expound. We took turns napping between talks of NYU property ownership, Times Square, Long and Staten and Fire Islands, enormous ocean liners distinctly visible in the river between where Manhattan and Jersey never slept, the sun coming in on the cacti, friends who'd died in late mornings while directing movies in their sleep.

We slipped into a mutually agreed upon set of outfits. I think I was just wearing a different but similar looking black sweater as the one I'd slept in at Brian's the night before, threw on an old, folded black leather jacket from my suitcase, and Mitch poured us more wine before we headed downstairs to leave through the Mercer Street exit of the lobby. We stopped over at this tiny office in the corner and I met Liz, this woman who looked to be somewhere in her fifties but who was happily, and proud to inform, well into her seventies. She was this delightfully energetic, long kiss of a person, buried beneath crumbs from snacks on her desk as she spoke about shopping in the financial district and not to go "fancy-shmancy" shopping with Mitch because she knew of better places with the same quality and half the price, and Mitch would later tell me she was devoted to her mentally-retarded daughter and had even been given an award from Governor Pataki for her work with people with like conditions in the city. How beautiful is that? And apparently it was her job at the apartment building to interview potential residents, Mitch told me, and she'd given him a hard time about the price of his bowties when they first met and instantly adored each other. She was a sight, man, exhausting and filled with this wild kind of love so furiously strong in her eyes and forehead it seemed to make the rest of her body sag in her chair. You imagine being that far into life still stuck out in all that goodness? That's going to be me one day, for sure. You too, Rattigan. It's in your face.

Mitch was being, yeah, I'm saying it, *obfuscatory* about his plans until we'd stopped off at The Algonquin and tipped the matre di for the following night, and then I realized he was getting us the sweet seats and just enjoying hanging on to his secret, so we went down to Sardi's. I bought us twenty dollar cocktails beneath all the animated caricatures on the walls, signed by the stars they'd been drawn for, as some unexplained urban pounding came from this upstairs area, and it was too surreal a sound to be escaping to the downstairs' more hip feel, so we moved on to dinner at Triomphe, one of my favorite microscopic restaurants where everyone basically sits elbow to elbow, it's so small and boxed and intimate, and we ate foie gras-stuffed prunes and I had a martini, and our server was this beautiful blonde with an almost apologetic smile that I kept trying to connect with each time she traversed the passway between the back of my chair and that of the man's behind me at his table filled with, what I took to be, his roaring, handsome family, but she was way too busy to flirt. And I wasn't sure, either, with all that booze swimming around in my head, if I had any intentions on it myself, so Mitch and I ordered coffee and chestnut crème brulee and talked about how much we liked the words "prelapsarian" and "crepuscular," how *wonderful* they are. Later in the night we'd add "interpolation," "swell," and "gams," the latter after passing a huge billboard in the colorful, alert Times Square, with some unknown beauty with her skirt all tossed like Marilyn Monroe's. Rattigan, the grandeur of Times *Square*, and all the people swimming in *between* one another? I heard a guy call out to a passing cab, one that was nosing too closely into the street-crossing crowd behind me, to go fuck itself, and I laughed with this unutterable joy, and when Mitch heard he turned against the cold wind and realized that if he asked why I was cheering into the sky, or about the object of it, the real truth of my exuberance would fade into this romantic but inadequate attempt at explanation. But I knew he could see it, so he smiled a wider smile and all I could do was sigh a sigh of relief and stay within feet of him as we turned and navigated and dove back into the streets.

No, man. A cabbie getting told to fuck off isn't *grandeur*. It was the pulse, right? The whole that night was the sum of its parts. You're too much, babe. I missed you.

But anyway, we got seated at *42ⁿᵈ Street*, just in front of a man from Rhode Island with a zeal for life, and accompanying him was his bored daughter. We met them both for a more lengthy bit of time at intermission after I ran off to the restroom downstairs behind the bar where I'd return for a beer that I bought from this polite and overworked Asian woman who said *Thank you so much* when I gave her ten bucks, because *honestly*, man, she looked like she'd been strolling through a series of unflappable tortures back there, all smothered in a sea of impatient fingers snapping for something else it was they thought they absolutely needed. But the *show*, man, just visual aesthetics alone should bring someone there, and the songs were lively and the cast was attractive and working so hard, and the beat of their soles against the stage was this deafening, brilliant thump. I'm not sure, but I think next week and it's over, maybe the first week of January. When it ended all the actors and dancers were standing out madly waving to the audience, bowing. I wanted to cry, babe, so suddenly connected to their sublime, pure efforts. And so we aisle-hopped in the middle of the long standing ovation, and patiently followed the steadily dissipating crowd out onto and over the sidewalks and made our way by train down to 8th and Broadway where we parted and, after a quick chat on a corner with these two attractive girls from Massachusetts, I made it back over to the East Village. And that's where I met her, Rattigan. *That's* when it all happened.

I walked into this small joint around 4ᵗʰ and 2ⁿᵈ, some sort of wartime name, like from WWII times. Not now. Yeah, man, I agree. I wouldn't know what a bar would be called during this one. Damn, these *two*. Doesn't that scare the shit out of you, about living in wartime? I don't know how to process it either. Not yet. It's like it almost needs to pass so some sense can be made. Who knows, right? My reconciliation with that's just out my scope at the moment. But that's bringing it all down right now, I know. Sorry, babe. We'll talk it out at your place some time.

So anyway, I walked in and checked out the place and felt strangely alone because, you know, it only takes that one startling judgment from someone's eyes across the room and you think you may have to start flexing your negotiation muscles in the event it's danger you stumbled upon. But when I made it to the bar everything just kind of shut down, because there she was, this beaten old hat on backwards, and she was a little slouched forward over the bar, giving it to this one guy about minding his manners.

Rattigan, it was love right then. And I know how young and puerile and inexperienced it is to just belt it out, man, I *do*, but don't you agree that if it comes so frequently in various forms out of us into other people, it can certainly leak out of someone else, into *us*, without their knowing? *Nobody* can know every instant of someone thinking you're fantastic across the room.

But then she made this peculiar little face when I asked for a beer, like I'd asked wrongly, but then I realized it was asked unfamiliarly, so I paid her and she went off to being busy a few minutes until two of her friends came in and sat down beside me at the bar. I tell you, once I fell in with both her friends it was like that's what was meant to happen, like maybe she and I would have both been weak enough or content enough to just exist on opposite sides of the bar and never find out what could have happened unless some kind of catalyst came along to help initiate the process. We were introduced, and even after her friends had drunkenly swapped numbers with me and we had our final laugh about some guy accidentally spitting up rum on my back—*yeah* he did, but he bought me a round, a good kid—I still sat mesmerized by the ethereal quickness of it all until she and her co-worker, some tall guy named Steve who kept bringing shots over for him and myself to celebrate the craziness of the night and her apparently shared enthusiasm, had closed down the place, and she and I were whipping off in a cab toward the Upper East Side where she lived in a tiny walkup with candles in her window and a flower she'd named Rose that I think was an iris. Oh, *she* knew it, Rattigan. Don't make that face.

We spent the whole long morning in bed and couldn't bring ourselves to attempt making love at first, and I think it was a sense of ruining the innocence of the night's pure, again, man, *serendipity*. So when I untangled from her and dressed and headed down across the street to catch a cab back downtown, I remember looking up into her window and hoping her face would be there, this longing and yearning that bore down from her eyes to match the inside of my chest, a yearning that would stretch over the hood and the slowed taxi, but she never did, Rattigan. I remember thinking right then, as I waved up toward the window anyway, that it was terrifying and marvelous and ridiculous and correct that I was in love with a girl named Kera, as sure as I was in New York City.

Back at Mitch's he greeted me with a kiss and a glass of wine as we had more salmon. I told him about Kera, and then we looked at a photograph series taken by his lover in Germany, before very briefly entertaining his old friend Gary from upstairs, a veteran and hugely successful city caterer who seemed nervous and fidgety as he talked about his favorite sherry, a look that to me meant he'd spent a good part of his life not trusting anyone to share his same loves, even if they were unfamiliar at first. He looked worn by the quietness of the afternoons since his wife died, information I'd later learn, but it didn't require me knowing anything about the specifics of his tired jaw line and tapping foot beside the coffee table. I did like you must have done with your grandfather, man. I just gave in as much compassion and warmth as I could, and took out as much grief as possible, and even though I felt heavy from it and the wine and the salmon, I'd be cheating you if I didn't tell you he hugged me on the way out, yeah, Gary did, like he'd needed some help and didn't want anyone to offer it, but really just to give it and let that be that. After Gary left, Mitch put on a new suit and I put on my same form of one, for our last night before I flew back today. What? *Yeah*, I've been gone this whole time. I thought you knew...oh, you *did*? The airport *last* Sunday? I'm sorry, man.

But Mitch, he was preparing to go to mass at St. Joseph's in the village since he'd been ushering there for years, and I could see it meant a lot to him as he somewhat nervously suggested I stay home and rest until he returned and we headed together to the Algonquin. And man, I was as tired as I've been in months, but there isn't a thing on this planet that could have physically kept me from going to his church and sitting there in back with some NYU students and sweet noisy congregants and feeling out of place as ever but feeling on top of the world, too. Mitch was sharing his joy. It was all I could do.

And his preemptive tip to the maitre di the night before had worked at the Algonquin, because we ate five feet from the stage, and when Andrea came on she even held Mitch's hand a moment and sang a Cole Porter tune right into his eyes, and it felt like the entire night had exhaled in the room and we were all sitting beneath a cloak of solidarity, with everyone just kind of looking knowingly around at one another and remembering older, sweeter feelings each time Andrea smiled her bright smile and whispered about nostalgia, about whether or not it really exists beyond what we can only know alone in our hearts. And glancing around at two men from Baltimore who were holding hands, this older married couple to Mitch's left toasting champagne, and a middle-aged woman singing drunkenly along into her husband's shoulder as they sat facing the back of the piano player, I suddenly had this wild rush of relaxation that was followed by an eager need to see Kera, even if it meant foregoing the brandy out in the lobby with Mitch after the show. And when Andrea finished her last and everyone romantically, tiredly began to shuffle toward the door, I walked with Mitch a block west where we stood on a corner and embraced beneath the silent glow of the street lights. I watched him south down the sidewalk until I couldn't see the top of his hat, before he was completely enveloped by the human roar, and then I took off into a long pace somewhere into the 70s in search for that beautiful, small creature I'd met in a hat just a handful of hours before. When I got close to her I kept her in my imagination until I could barely make her out, standing opposite me on a slowly depopulating street corner, and my feet were sore from the fervent slapping down on the concrete in my rush to see her, and then when she saw me she waved and we hopped a cab to her apartment again, just after eating at this brightly-lit diner where they put too much spinach in the omelets, but were generous with lemons in their hot tea, and where Kera said, *You look handsome tonight, Brody*.

And Rattigan, we made love all last night and both nearly cried in her hallway on the fourth floor, and asked one another if we'd be all right, and when I went down to the street to grab a final cab out I looked up before climbing in the car and there she was, her bedroom window open, dropping select pieces of Rose down into the windy street below. This stuff *happens*. I blew her a kiss off my fingertips, and she held up an index finger and wrinkled it a few times as I hauled off again to Mercer. On the way through the lobby I stopped by Liz's office but she was gone, locked up for the day, but a photograph Mitch's lover had taken was taped to her bulletin board, a picture of a rose. Maybe its name was *Iris*.

Mitch and I had a fresh breakfast including talks about how he'd once known Anthony Burgess and Joseph Heller and Kurt Vonnegut, and he gave me a coffee mug that had once been on Toni Morrison's desk at Random House. I *know*. We even extended the conversation of Gary's the day before with talks of chalices and Genoa, sort of like a toast to him. And then down in the street once the car arrived, we laughed a bit and started planning the next trip up and he said he'd like to meet Kera. I'm sure he thought I was foolish, and I probably am, but when you find love, brother, you take it and run. We exchanged a huge hug right there in traffic and I slept during the short ride to the airport, just as the forecasted freezing rain was getting ready to fall over the city.

In the airport I met this spirited woman named Prendergrast who had an Irish dancer for a daughter, a musician son in his late teens, and this joyful penchant for reading and travel. She asked my name to find my work if she could one day, and I told her, *Not yet, not likely, but you'll eventually find it*, and we shared a big smile together. I was going to sleep a bit longer in my hard bucket seat by the gate, but I started scribbling down a poem about sitting in Newark and writing poems, and this cute little girl, maybe six, came by and looked over my shoulder before being called away by her apologetic parents, this little girl I had blushing and hiding behind her iron grip on her mother's leg each time I made a face at her. And man, I'd tell you I slept on the way home, but once we took off and I got out into the sky again, I felt so charged by the coming down of everything, I had no other choice but to look out the window and try to make sense of the pace of existence. Seriously, we can think about how maniacal and out of control the world can be, but from an airplane, somehow it seems so vastly simple, so connected, so worth continuing. So you bet, Rattigan, by the time I touched down here, I'd already discovered another wealth of spiritual responsibilities we've got to acknowledge and get working on, but we'll get into that all in good time. I missed you man. Let's get one more drink. I want to hear about you."

CHAPTER 3

Christmas Eve fell on the following Thursday. I was late to my Aunt's house just outside of the city due to my editor, Richard Fuller, keeping me and two others late in the afternoon in superfluous conference, Fuller being a long-winded martini drunk who was slightly balding, notorious for long nights of walking around random bars at random hours downtown and seeking love in the most arbitrary of hearts, men or women. An hour past schedule in getting to Beatrice and Ralph's around four-thirty, I stopped to grab Knox from her small guesthouse in Springhill, a broken rule for me, a first, to bring a guest. She was foregoing the drive up to Huntsville that season and wouldn't be allowed to sit around her small home alone. I was relieved by her availability, because I hadn't written as much during the week as I had intended and was in need of distraction, also seeking an ally against the clash of lunacy that usually occurred during the holidays with my disjointed family. My sister Leah and her fiancé Matt were in from Atlanta and already wine-drunk by the time I'd poured my first glass, I heard my mother swearing to God from across the main room as she dropped and broke a crockpot of cheese dip, followed by a round of invective from Leah calling her, among other things, a jackass, while scooping some of it off the carpet with a chip as Knox attempted to hold down her second sip of red. My grandfather was standing, walking around the living room and eating a respectable amount of food. Beatrice glowed with a sad happiness, regarding his movement and regained strength, still looking as wearily content as he could, even through the diminishing pain. He had two gift bows pinned to his chest like sparkling, thorny breasts, which my cousin Hannah had elatedly attached to him once they'd hugged over her newest painting she'd given him for the season, a follow-up to one she'd done two years earlier, a puffin lounging in a loveseat, a tobacco pipe dangling from its beak.

The yap of Leah's young American bulldog sounded down the hall, so after an official introduction of Knox to my family, we walked to the back of the house with awkward, giggling grins between us to go see how big Jelly had gotten in fourteen weeks. Jelly, a biter in her youthful excitement, pawed frantically for a moment at the upper edge of the animal fence that divided her from the hallway and living room, before giving up and nosing our hands with frustrated realization that we were there not to free her, but to give her sympathy disguised as adoration. She sat and sighed loudly as we returned down the hall to a large, curious meeting over the buffet-styled layout, a series of questioning eyes all surveying the food, determining the content of a specific spread here, the inner wrappings of pinwheels there.

Aunt Josephine was in the kitchen, whispering low to Ralph about grandfather's condition, and she'd later go on to getting a hyper kind of drunk and spill cheap blush around the same area as the then defunct cheese dip my mother had been so deftly chastised for losing. My mother grasped both of my hands and looked at Knox with a full, uncharacteristically joyous expression, as if everything was ending in the morning, the night at hand was the only night she would ever remember. Hannah and her sister, Celie, called from the living room. Celie was a type-A, energetic administrative fundraiser for a Jesuit college in town, her first big career move after graduating from Converse in South Carolina, and she was waiting for the corporation she founded with two gay men who lived near me in Midtown to take flight. I followed Knox toward them, through the food room, and we sat in a small circle on the grayish, thin carpet and, much like we'd done years before as small and unassuming children, minus the alcohol, we huddled in our laughing mass and began telling stories from those years while purposefully excluding the boyfriends and fiancés, Knox being allowed because she was unexplained, not easily placed in a category by my family as I pressed them on to her. No one understood how to label her, so she was in. That, and she cursed like a sailor, like my generation of the family when together. She was also into acquiring a fast drunk. Eventually the talks would break off into their segmented interest groups. Hannah, about her new gallery showing and Darryl, her first boyfriend now rehashed from the past to be her current—Celie, about her own boyfriend, still en route from his family's high-tension soirees in Baldwin County over the bay—Mother's babbling to grandfather as he sat in a reclining chair nearest the door, as he fanned her off by saying, *Oh yeah, I'm fine, this is my second plate. Where's Skeeter?*—Ralph sitting beside Beatrice and scratching his back with a fork, yelling forgivable perversions across the room to Leah in an effort to not embarrass but test Matt, to which my sister would reply in her typically raucous manner when drinking, *Fuck you, Ralphie*, laughing behind her hand with an equally drunk and roaring Celie as they fell back onto the small sofa across from Knox and me, throwing their legs over one another in celebration of being able to demonstrate their developed vulgarity, for one night, for one ribald and enlightening collective a year. And then Knox and I, increasingly more unaware of the rest of them as we chattered over a pair of jazz albums I had Hannah put on in the new player she'd purchased her mother, Beatrice, a woman still new to technology, a woman who chalked up her ineptitude regarding it, like me, to apathy.

"So, you're moving out *when*, exactly?" Knox asked me, as we sat on a small sofa by the foyer.

"Next week sometime. I think Wednesday."

"For *how* long?"

"I'm told a week."

"That's so inconvenient."

"It should be worth it though. I had to sue to get anything done."

"Who was it, again, that paid for the lawyer?" Ma asked in passing.

I sighed. Knox looked at her and then back at me before rolling her eyes.

"How much is getting re-floored?"

"All but the kitchen and bathroom."

"Fuck that."

"I know."

"So why don't you take me up on my place, asshole? Why are you being difficult?"

She slapped my arm.

"Hey bro. *Bro!* Remember this?" My sister called from beside Celie on the sofa.

I turned just as she made a twitchy face she and I used to make as kids, sitting in front of cartoons in our parent's house a few years before the divorce, then high school and then our father's death. Celie howled again, the type-A howl I thought bordered on clinical mania, as Leah's cheeks were at a silly state of redness which really brought out her freckles. I looked at Knox, and her face was a strange sort of reserved, studious of them, almost scholastically, as though they were nearly incomprehensible. They were. I gave my sister a thumb's up.

"I might, I might. We'd just be living on top of each other is all. Such a small place for two people like us."

"Come on, man. I can clear out some cabinets. It'll be like old times."

"But I need time to write."

"So do I."

"More wine and we'll talk about it?"

She nodded at me, while staring across the room at Ralph, scratching the side of his neck, then, with his fork, before returning it deep into his casserole.

After everyone had initially eaten, Beatrice raised her glass with a solemn face, turning down the volume. She sat on an old-fashioned chair that had been placed almost in traffic's way to the food, and we all sat still and at attention, as Beatrice was known for incredibly serious banter while in the bottle. But we knew it was due to the pressure of grandfather being so wildly sick, and then, how indescribable it had been to see him recover so vastly and in such fast form. She offered a toast after a generous welcome to the guests, present and not, and then we all sipped.

I stepped outside to take a call from Brody on my work phone, after briefly being ushered out by Knox, who lit a cigarette behind me as we hurdled over the low bushes and walked into the middle of the front yard. Shuffling through the front door, we passed a highly-concerned looking Todd who'd at last arrived, no longer Celie's boyfriend, as it was revealed— at least to me, ever the last on the family list to know—during the meal that he had become her fiancé, a staunch Republican with loudly-voiced opinions about the public view of what he referred to as "the people's potentially best administrative entity in decades, if only they'd..." He nodded determinedly as I clapped his back and Knox shut the front door behind me.

"Where *are* you, man?" Brody asked.

"Family in Semmes. I thought I told you."

"Did you?"

"Maybe," I said, reaching for Knox's smoke and taking a drag after looking over my shoulder at the house.

"Well, what are you *doing*?"

"It's Christmas Eve, Brody."

"Yeah, same here."

"What?"

I shook my head at Knox and mouthed, *Brody*.

"So that's where you are? Just at the family's?"

"What do you mean?" I asked.

"I don't know, man. I just think we've gotta be into something more than just this holiday. My family's all over the place. It's nuts watching it all unfold, all this disorganization. I feel like I'm more than just here. You know? I'm not sure what I mean. It's wild and fantastic. My father's getting shitfaced and talking about money and taking initiative. I think his brothers are measuring their penises out in the street over their new cars. I *had* to step away. You talk to Knox?"

"Yeah, I kidnapped her. She's been helping me hack through the jungle in there."

"In where?"

"Inside. We're out front for a breather."

"*Nice.* You guys getting into anything later?"

"Don't know yet. Probably. Ma's after this I think, to see what my sister wants to do. Might go for a drink with her and Matt if they're not too tired from the drive today."

"Where do they live?"

"Atlanta. Alpharetta, actually, just north of..."

"You ever read Aristotle's *Ethics*? I mean, *really* read it, critically?"

"Some of it, why?"

"It's been saving my ass up here. Haven't read it since seventh grade. So good to finally revisit the..."

"How is...wait, you were reading Aristotle at thirteen?"

"Better than stealing beer, right? I was a reformed man by then."

"I can see that. How's Birmingham?"

"Hey, I'm found out. Gotta go, but we'll talk. I'll call you!"

I heard an older man's bellowing voice in the background, *What the hell are you doing in the pantry?*

Knox put out her cigarette in the dirt and kicked big, crisp leaves over it. Shuffling noises came through the phone. I followed her through the bushes, over the thin sidewalk and back inside, hanging up after a failed attempt at a goodbye with LaCoste.

Todd was standing with his arm around Celie in the foyer, and he had a furrowed crease across his forehead and between his eyes, Ralph apparently having just lit into him about the responsibilities of war. Uncle Ralph was a veteran of Vietnam who had forgotten if not blocked out most of his experiences overseas but, if slipping accidentally into a drink, he would recall and talk about his past injuries, his visions of those he'd watched die, men he remembered with a melancholic, somber pity. Knox was rolling her eyes in defiance against the holiday turned debate, an argument she called "fists hitting fists." It was humorous to watch her search the room for support, a plethora of curse words mounting her lips like a jockey. Todd had what seemed to be a permanent, stern confusion about his face, as though he were trying to make sense of Ralph's being a decorated military man and Democrat, unable though to come up with any self-satisfying reasons that could preclude a heated conversation about his ideas on "necessary aggression." I thumbed Knox into the kitchen for one last glass, but their talks had consumed her patience and she was ready to leave, so we snuck through the line of pacified observers, Josephine and my mother, where we began our thankful goodbyes and, fast as we could, got back on the road into Mobile. I laughed the bulk of the way as she wore out her diatribe against the fogging windshield, voracious screams against murder and lies and corporate bottom lines and corruption and sundry epithets about war, economy and chances in hell.

"Yeah, Brody seems adamant about it," I said as she climbed out of my car at her house. "He thinks I should move in with you."

"You should, Rattigan. I could definitely use the company, even if it's you."

"He wants you to cook for everybody when his New York girl comes down."

"Fuck that," she said, shaking her head as she stood outside my window. "I mean, I'll do it, sure, if you help. If *he* helps. I dunno. I need to put up some kind of resistance first."

"It could be fun," I said, dropping my car into reverse.

"Yeah, for whom?" She yelled as I backed out.

I honked my horn as she flipped me off beneath the clear sky, just after ten at night, and instead of driving directly to my mother's house in West Mobile, I took a left out of Knox's neighborhood and drove the mile down to the interstate connection on Dauphin Street and headed south for I-10 toward Florida. I needed a quick burst of solitary motion, some thought-airing, to hit the Bayway at one-hundred miles an hour, just me and the growl of the engine around my feet, restless already, apprehensive about the days ahead, the work at home that needed doing, since Brody had darted back overnight and would soon be dealing out commands. Moving all my belongings from my house for the construction, too, even if the expenses were being covered by my landlord, was its own chore, an unwelcome distraction for which I had to, for some reason, in order to prepare, drive incredibly fast in the long, cold dark, with the windows cracked. Once I'd made it back to town an hour later, to find my sister and Matt already asleep, I wished my mother good luck as she whisperingly cursed the angel on top of her Christmas tree, an angel that kept tilting to its side, threatening to fall, swearing in silence it would do it, it would jump.

Christmas Day consisted of a few phone calls from friends visiting town, ranging from a graphics artist in San Diego, a freelance writer in Houston (a former staff writer I'd sometimes see before she moved off to Boston for a degree in Publishing) and Brody, on the run from his family and back in Mobile, with some jolting shout about having "snatched Knox from the depths of singularity and shoving her madly into the big collective void," her wild cackle in the background sailing through the line before they hung up. A writer friend who'd moved to Los Angeles and had achieved fairly quick success in screenwriting, Jerry Thales, a professor-turned-friend that

Knox and I had studied under for a year in college prior to his early retirement, was in town over the bay in Fairhope and had called to plan a meal with me the next day at one. And as I'd turned down the invitation for late lunch at Ma's across town, I settled for a sandwich at home and decided to tell Knox, next time we spoke, that I'd take her up on her offer to move in, temporarily, and then I spent the afternoon figuring what I could take, and what could remain in storage, to avoid the risk of putting her out.

The night of the holiday was spent in front of my tired, old machine. I worked and edited as late as I could, after even a full pot of coffee couldn't make my eyelids stay up while permitting the rest of my body to fall asleep. When I woke in the morning, I stretched my arms toward the back wall, which was a little more out of reach since my bed had rolled away from it during the night. I walked the house with Brody on my mind, the move to Springhill and how I'd manage assignments from Richard Fuller with so much suddenly bouncing around on my schedule, re-learning Knox in close quarters, if it would even work, the unexpected feel of being young again, and most importantly, making time to get more to the root of my process in a new environment, when I was at last beginning to get a better glimpse of it alone at my own home.

After a shower I took off over the Bayway again, this time taking a right ten miles out of the city, past Daphne and eventually into downtown Fairhope to meet Jerry at a restaurant he called to remind me was "really awful." I walked in to the old café after circling the block a few times for parking. It was a country cooking joint, with middle-aged women smacking gum from the sides of their faces, sweet and somehow simultaneously indifferent women who were unfamiliar with the menu whenever we ordered. *It's not awful*, I'd later tell Jerry. *Just idiosyncratic*. Jerry, a handsome athletic man in is early sixties, sat in a booth off to the far left and stood to greet me with a hug once I stepped through the thin brown corridor that led to the dining area.

"That's a peculiar relationship they have," Jerry later said, of Brody and Mitch, as he sipped water. "Is it sexual?"

"Not at all. They just work that way."

"But you said Mitch is gay, right?"

"Right, but you should probably meet Brody. He doesn't see anything that way."

"Neither do you. You never did. You were an asshole in my class, but you weren't judgmental."

I laughed.

"It's a hard line to walk," I said. "But I'm lucky, I guess. In that respect."

"Better to be an asshole sometimes than always a prick."

"I think you're right."

"Remember when I showed you a picture of the one I'm seeing in L.A.?"

"Yeah."

"Peter, since I retired from teaching I've gotten my whole life back. How did I stay in academia so long? It's probably best that you went to the newspaper. Do you ever want to teach?"

"I'm not sure."

"I think you're doing the right thing," he said, studying me, nodding.

"I'm just trying to have enough time to write."

"That's good. You should. Just keep writing. I work four hours a day, every day. No deviation from it."

"But you're retired."

"I'm busier than I've ever been, though. I'm running the foundation, trying to sell scripts." He grinned. "Getting *laid*. I mean it, Peter. My whole life's restarted."

"That's really, really good, man."

"What ever happened with that first story you wrote for me, the one about the debutante and her husband?" He asked with a wave of his hand. I never liked the story and decided years earlier not to do anything with it. "The thing with 'crickets' in the title."

"I never sent it off."

"You've got to. You should. It's fine the way it is. You've got some really beautiful writing. You're just not completely 'there' yet."

"I don't know where 'there' is, otherwise I'd go. You know?"

"It comes from practice. Fuck up a million times, barely get it right, or go way off course. But you have to keep your fingers loose and stay at it."

"I know."

"You over-think the process, you won't learn from it. That's where the academic side actually helps, even though I know you always had a problem with that."

"What do you mean?"

"You aren't selling yourself short, Peter, by carefully observing how it is you do what you do. Even if it pisses you off, when you find something not working. Better to teach yourself why it isn't working than just throwing in the towel because it's not what you'd planned."

"I know. I'm getting *there*, at least. I'm starting to understand that."

"I kept about thirty stories in circulation when I was first starting out. This was in the mid-sixties, of course. I don't know how it all works now, but I just kept sending them off, getting rejected here and there, and then re-sending them elsewhere until they were all accepted. It took a lot of work, but the work was actually just patience. You know?"

"Yeah."

"Once patience no longer feels like a labor, then you're set to really do some great things. But that can spill into your entire life, right? Not just writing."

I ate more from my plate and remembered his seminars, where he'd noticeably hold back from tearing into a student who'd spent the entire semester ignoring everything he'd pounded into our heads for months, suggestions he was reformulating then at the table. Sometimes he would let me run a session, and I suppose those were the asshole moments, when I would say on his behalf what would get him raked over the coals by the administration.

"I just haven't found the right book yet."

"Don't push it. It'll happen."

"I've written so much, Jerry. I'm sleepless most nights."

"You're young. You can handle it."

"But I'm not looking for advice on process anymore. I understand I'm twenty-six, and that maybe I've got a good bit of time. That's the one thing I'm fairly sure of, that it all changes the more everything progresses. We talked about it in your *classes*, man, even with the more naïve students ripping on about their silly certainties, about the growth/recession of learning and how time doesn't guarantee that we'll ever be aware of *anything*. I just don't want to take anything for granted in the *now*, you know? Brody and I've been talking it to death."

"Good. He sounds good for you."

"He's a wild kid, that's for sure. A beautiful person. Fascinating to watch him just, I don't know, do what he does."

Jerry's face lit up.

"That's wonderful Peter. It's interesting how we find such amazing people. I'm still finding them. And really, what do I know?" he asked, shrugging his shoulders and thanking the server for refilling his glass. He signaled for another glass of wine for me, and I smiled at her. She smiled back with a slight grimace, as if the day were getting longer by every request, refill, every kind response. As she walked tiredly away I felt a quiet defensiveness for her, disappointed with the universal lack of behavioral ethic amongst human beings that might have forced into her that glued-on grimace, that strained co-existence in her eyes as she watched the clock. "You know, I told Jane I was gay the week before we married, and so when I was your age I was already married six years. Isn't that wild? We've been married forty-four years and I'm just now regaining my life. I've never lived on my own."

"You seem a lot more relaxed."

"Well, in fairness, are you happy? Do you like living on your own?"

"Of course," I said, feeling the fullness of his elation over his freedom, curious about the solitude of Jane and where she lived around Fairhope, keeping the house and teaching local English courses while Jerry was out in the Californian wild of his new spirit, furious now and loosed from its obsequious dormancy. "I get a lot done with my time." I lied.

"And I've quit reading fiction. Have I told you that?"

"No."

"I read non-fiction." He looked at me for reaction and I nodded. "And books on spirituality."

I lit up and sat forward. The check came.

"That's crazy, Jerry. I was just telling Brody last week I was thinking about reading into Buddhism and Hinduism for a while, or texts on the soul like that Zukav book you had us read. Because all these books I've been reading lately have been a serious drag, this modern effort to do something *new* instead of just telling a seriously truthful story." I was encouraged by the newfound commonality between us, because I'd never doubted him until I finally had gotten out of the entrapment of making too much a run at academically charged writing, and I realized that maybe he just needed to step away from it, too, to gain a fresher perspective on all the nerve-wracking lectures he no longer had to pretend he believed in or enjoyed.

"I'm reading a new one of Zukav's right now, actually. It's really interesting what he does," he said as he swiped the ticket from the table.

"Come on, Jerry. I was late getting here."

"So you should pay for being late?"

"Yeah, it's my penance," I said, but he shook off my offer and set down cash.

"What does your friend think?"

"About what?"

"About avoiding fiction."

"I don't think he feels we should ignore it entirely, because he thinks once you get solidly grounded in your own style you can read garbage and not be too affected by it. I don't know. I'm guessing about him. I'd say he appreciates the essence of what something says more than anything else, as long as the story isn't trying too hard to be clever, or as long as the style is relevant and not contrived."

"And you agree with him?"

"I do. It makes sense," I said as we stood. "But with Brody I suppose it's more about chasing joy. I think that's what I get from him. Too much specifics with him I think kills the fun he gets out of the talk itself. He gets off on just getting *near* the answers, if that makes sense."

"I wouldn't be your age again for the world," he said and smiled a wide, gentle smile. I punched him on the arm as he passed in front of me toward the corridor, and then through to the restaurant's front.

"I wouldn't be my age again, either," I said, grinning, once at his car.

"I hope you plan on enjoying it anyway. It's good to like your life."

Jerry asked where I'd parked, and I pointed across the street to my spot just outside a tiny, closed consignment shop. He smiled again, and I gave him a hug as he thumbed through the keys to his son's old SUV that he was using while in town.

"Peter, it's good to see you. Keep going where you're going."

"Love to you, Jerry. Thanks for lunch."

"Love to you, too."

———

The middle of the next week arrived in a rush, including a call from Brody on Sunday, with wild excitement that because he'd missed his Christmas party at work, his boss had clocked him in two weekends over the holidays, as their dishwasher had been fired and no replacement would be found until closer to New Year's, and it had been decided the extra money, according to the owner, should go to Brody as a means of saying he'd been missed. Brody, feeling he wasn't hurting the company upon their managerial insistence, woke me in the morning with a thrill in his voice, just for me to laughingly congratulate him and tell him in a raspy, just-awake voice, that he was nothing but a beautiful lucky asshole, to which he responded *Yeah, I guess you're right*, and then proceeded to ecstatically tell me about a dream he'd had the night before. He'd been walking down a crowded urban sidewalk, the thickness of the overcoat-ed people ahead of him broke apart, and there was a man standing before him in shorts and a rough, ruddy goatee and a hat pulled down but not too far to conceal his entire forehead. He had a deep bucket of ice on a table with his hand pressed flatly inside the bottom of it, and he nodded wide-eyed at passersby while counting off each second aloud, in a punctuated, almost accusatory tone, as though each tiny click of the clock was his private revelation of some larger greater truth, and people were simply passing on the street without its recognition, without believing him. I asked Brody if he knew what it represented, and he said he wasn't sure, but to give him the day and he'd have something. We said goodbye after a few presumptions, some warm-up conjecture to a future dream-talk, and then I shoved from bed to take on my prep work for the next two busy days at the paper.

We had a system for reporters in the field called "day cover," a term created by Richard when he came on as editor just before I was hired, a term I had never even heard used in journalism slang. It was basically a label for what I and other reporters did already, a label in quasi-definition of our responsibilities, that if we managed all groundwork outside of scheduled interviews that we were in charge of setting up after assignment, and then the concomitant field runs, we weren't required to sit 9-5, which never would have happened in the first place. I was disgruntled by being too often turned away from features, more interested in writing about local art fairs and museum exhibits than governmental goings-on, for which I was mostly designated. Not getting my druthers translated into a rough defi-ance against set hours. But besides that, there was no space for the lot of us to hover around at the office. In fact, my "office" was a desk in the middle of a cluster of cluttered desks, a desk I shared with an overweight ex-fraternity fellow named Andy who I never saw in person, but rather, signs of his hav-ing been there, crumpled chocolate bar wrappings and field notes in his thick-fingered, illegible script.

Regardless of lacking devotion, it had become important for me to make Fuller's "day cover" so I could not only be out early on Tuesday to move must-have items into Knox's guesthouse, during the one day I'd allot-ted for it, but to be out of office as much as physically possible in general to simply live, to write, to peer into Brody's *vast explosive supernova of being*. That afternoon, I aimed to step away around one-thirty after bringing in licks on an economic piece which focused on area restaurant profit margins, staff size and rent as predominant overhead before payroll, blah-blah, in collaboration with Noel Halliday, who got to write the better parts of the story, about the dining experience itself, a man whose daughter had been a year ahead of my sister in high school. He was a kind, burly fellow who was acting cuisine editor until he could return to part-time critic, in order to focus mainly on his freelance work with three or four travel magazines, his "*true* passion," he'd say, with a removed brilliance in his eyes. He and I had sat together for a good solid hour of agreement over the articles, laughing about our joint misunderstanding of the dual roles he played in our prodi-gious new building off Water Street, and then we shook hands at the north end of the long second floor office rows, which seemed dismal and irrelevant on days such as that, when the sun was inches away from everywhere, and more pressing things existed such as a wild, thorough hunt in the long night ahead, with a tremendous lack of conservative prudence as were plan-ning Brody, Knox and me.

Brody met the two of us at a small rotisserie joint in the middle of our second drink. He was dropped off by a girl named Malea, whom he'd met the night before while downtown having beers in a small martini bar run by a heavyset thirty-something named Derek, a man who lived with his mother and was known in the bar circles as having a penchant for dwarf pornography. According to Brody, Malea had exhausted him thoroughly in some middle-of-the-road hotel across from the bars off Joachim. *All night,* he said, and again in the morning, the same morning he'd decided to take up smoking for a reason he wouldn't disclose, but he refused with such constitution that Knox and I laughed it off as he squeezed beside her and shook his head. I'd been discussing animal cruelty with Brody for a few days by then, and decided I'd take a swing at turning vegetarian. It didn't stop either of them from diving into a sliced duck appetizer while I got tight over scotch and a dressing-drenched Caesar salad. Our server was a serious girl named Sarah, if I remember correctly, the name and not the seriousness, cloaked completely in black by uniform code, and she managed a laudable amount of smiles as Brody and Knox pulled off a series of jokes to her liking, perhaps to set the tone for our lightness, our predictability as guests. Jazz played overhead and stretched across the restaurant, with wide, dark columns dividing each section from the other as though something from the ceiling had melted and formed in an awkward vertical pile on the thin, long carpet. We ordered a round as Brody adjusted his bandana and Knox added two more appetizers to our selection, a wide smile across her face.

In wait for the food, Knox received a call from Brian, a friend of hers who worked in a restaurant across the street. So as she stepped outside to take the call, Brody and I put our heads together on the possibility of martinis to surprise her when she returned. But I was more curious in the hows and whys and whats of his night out before.

"What about Kera, man? What about this legendary, New York City love you had…"

"See, that's just it. She started misinterpreting the energy I was sending."

"What does that even mean?"

"In what context?"

He grinned and sipped his drink.

"In *any* context, Brody. You know exactly what I mean."

"Go ahead."

I laughed.

"Well, how so?" I asked, sipping the last bit of my scotch while perhaps-Sarah passed, stopped and then nodded to Brody's request for the martinis.

"How so, what?"

"Her *misinterpretation*. I'm still lost on this big love thing."

"Ok, I think I've got it. You'll see what I mean. I've got a personal silence I need sometimes that's, I don't know, like when I'm trying to get some work done. But it isn't the same as writing time. It's a kind of roam-around-in-the-mind time, Rattigan. *That* kind of silence. See, I knew *you'd* get it. And so you understand how it's hard to explain to someone who has a different value system for silence and time. Does that make sense?"

"Or at least a different definition."

"*Exactly*. So then, she starts telling herself I'm just flailing about in the world, just looking for some carnal fix, which wasn't it at all."

"But you were serious about her, right?"

"Come *on*, man. You ever been serious about someone, and then the language suddenly changed, and you realized maybe the whole time you'd been speaking in different tongues and had convinced yourself a clear translation was there? I don't know why it happens, or how. Maybe it's everything that surrounds the moment leading up to it that's so enthralling. I dunno."

"I guess so."

"The thing is, I thought it was it, *it*, with Kera." He shook his head. "But it only seems to take a few imperfect sentences these days for a person to realize there's a load of connotations involved that weren't there before. Some might call that being shallow, but not me. I think it's a testament to giving dedicated attention to heart matters."

I laughed out loud.

"But *flowers*, man. She was throwing them petal-by-petal down the wall of the building."

"Flair for dramatics."

"But you were digging it."

He grew quiet a moment and then grinned.

"It *was* movie-scene-kind-of-romantic," he said softly.

"*Now* who's killing who?"

He winked and took a sip.

"But seriously," I said. "I've been there. I've wanted to, I don't know, maybe not necessarily live in that movie, but be included in some of those types of scenes. Definitely. I just don't think a person can enjoy the fullness of a moment if they bury themselves in some introspective interpretation of it as it's happening, which I've been *supremely* guilty of in the past."

"That's it, Rattigan. Maybe that's the *it* of romance. Maybe you just said it. Enjoy the now, experience the now, but don't keep telling yourself as it occurs that this *is* the now. That weakens it."

"Is that what I said?"

"That's what I heard. Case closed. We've got it all figured out."

"We can die now."

We laughed into the bottoms of our drinks as our server brought a tray of long stems, and shortly thereafter, Knox bounded back in after apologizing to an older woman at the bar for almost colliding with her as she zipped past the host's stand.

"What did you fuckers do?" Knox asked, slipping in beside Brody and kissing his cheek. She clapped her hands like an excited child before entering a humorous state of reverence. With wondrous eyes, she peered over the rim of her glass and down at the ice shavings on the surface. "I want to stick my tongue in it."

"We're going to attempt a bit of class."

"*Attempt*," Brody added.

She lifted her head and made a face.

"How the hell does a martini make someone classy?"

"I have no idea."

"Let's call it 'feigning poise,'" Brody said.

She rolled her eyes and smiled at him.

"I call it cold and dangerous."

"You seem excited about something."

"Hmm? *Oh*. Brian wants to meet us out tonight. Have you met him, Brody?"

"There's a good chance."

"He's *beautiful*. He works over at that upscale place across Airport. Rattigan, you met him with me once."

"I did? Wait, this place is upscale to me."

"I mean *upscale* upscale. As in, if I ate there I couldn't pay my power bill."

"Hard way to let your light shine," I said.

Brody grinned at Knox.

"That's not such a bad thing."

"What?" She asked. "Not being able to pay my…guys, *focus*. He and his boyfriend want us to hit the drag show at Downtime tonight. His boyfriend? Jonathan? *Also* beautiful. I hate them."

"Let's do it, man," Brody said.

"*Hate?* Strong word. Why's that?" I asked her.

"Because they're gorgeous." Brody said. Knox slapped his ribs.

"And unattainable," I said.

"*Guys.*"

———

A joint pulsation of loud voices and music thumped through the thin door of the bar as we tossed our cigarettes into the street and fumbled for our IDs. A tall, plump man in half-drag guarded the entrance. He had sparkling glitter on his face, as well as silver paint at the edges of his eyes to counterbalance a dark mascara, and when he smiled to expose a row of crooked teeth, the entire picture of him made it seem he'd been a sorceress of some kind from, if not this one, a past life. I was somewhat gone and fully unfamiliar with this particular type of bar, but my company was a pair of drifter sorts who alighted at the prospect of new things and suddenly I felt stodgy and silly, I was my cousin's furrow-browed fiancé. But it washed once I realized the core of the moment, and that my esteem for Brody and Knox was borne of a burgeoning desire to allow in, with keen instinct, the energy of whatever "it all" was beginning to include.

"*Hey babies,*" the doorman said as he checked Brody's ID and then waved us in. "I'm sure you're all fine."

I can't recall whose arms were locked in whose, but we thanked him with likely a foreign, invasive exuberance and spilled onward. Brody later told me, smiling in near-pride, how he could see in the man's eyes that, no matter how casual he may have been toward us, it was a surety we were deemed insane the moment we passed into the bar. It thrilled Brody to be seen as a madman, thrilled him more to have constructed a group of accomplices.

"Fuck that!" Knox screamed as the house beats inside the door punished our ears. "I feel like I'm out of the club, man!"

"What? *Why?*" I asked.

"For having a *vagina*. You see that look he gave me?"

Brody was ahead of us, looking over the tops of people crowding the bar. In the small cracks between bodies I could see the tank-topped bartender's sweat on his shoulders as he danced about behind the counter, fueled by the drug of money from drunks.

"Yeah, man! He totally read you!"

"I think he likes you!"

"*What?*" I asked.

"I said he wants to have your babies!"

"Aw, fuck you!"

"Fuck you *back*, heartbreaker!"

I gave her a light shove into Brody, who turned with a smile as Knox laughed at my extended middle finger. His lips formed the beginning of a question, but the music was too explosive and so he shrugged and waved for us to follow him into the fray. I made for beers after they'd found a quieter spot in the far back. I stood three deep at the bar as Knox took to the search for her beautiful boys. Brody stood at the edge of the smoky main room after draping our jackets across a black leather sofa to mark it as taken, and he steadily stamped his foot to the force of the electronic growl from overhead, studying the dance floor and the reckless, unbound people who filled it.

The bar itself, Downtime, was like many late night bars, with its elements of darkness, withheld secrets, a subterranean buzz going on as men and women grinned and leered and meant the same thing with their stares as did the gears grinding behind their foreheads. The energy was strong, most bars in Mobile having similar vibes even if categorized differently, even if catering to a different demographic. Used to my ordinary articles at work, I'd never been assigned this area of the downtown scene, not a single, rare feature for pride parades or charity auctions held at the neighboring gay bars, nothing, as if not just my editor but my employer left that part of the city's narrative to independent magazines found outside coffee shops and grocery stores. That fact, and my own, older stricture that characterized my wanderlust when walking the downtown streets alone, made the bar newer, foreign and curious, it made it good because of these things. The beautiful thing about Downtime was the mix of lonely, hopeful hearts and writhing bodies and ceiling lights that darted downward into the randomly-mixed flesh, and then the speaker sound so omnipotent it seemed the walls had been beaten into submission years earlier to the point they'd grown strong and impervious to its commandment. All this contributed to a lightness the dark itself could not erase. Joy was there it seemed, and perhaps it was due to the channeling of everyone's energies versus the collective punch of mine with Brody and Knox. We were a part of it and not a part, rising bubbles meeting in the wind, touching momentarily, drifting back asunder, yet still capable of reunion, to implode or explode together.

The actual bar was oblong and finished with a shine that reflected spilled liquors and sparkling light from the spinning ball over the dance floor. Through the smoke, I could make out the DJ in a booth near the bathrooms, bouncing his head with his ears cupped by headphones. The only thing he could likely know of his progress deep into night was how continuously everyone moved with no doubt of his judgment. I finally got a few beers from the bartender who seemed thankful at my patience, and then I made my way back to the couch and sandwiched between Brody and Knox who appeared engaged in conversation, the music having been escaped just enough to hear each other without howling toward the roof.

"*Hey babies*," I said, rationing out the bottles.

"Thanks, man."

"Cheers."

"What are you guys talking about?"

"I was telling Brody how the thoughts in my head are turning up louder to compete with the music. It's like they're being shouted back and forth, man. I dunno. My senses are on *fire*."

"Where are your friends?" I asked.

"Probably getting pampered, I'd guess."

Knox smiled into her first sip and looked at Brody.

"How would you know, Lacoste?" I asked.

"That's what pretty boys do, right? I'm interested to see what kind of disappointment Knox is setting herself up for."

"What the fuck does *that* mean?" She yelled.

"They just don't dig the ladies, is all. I know how you chase up the skirts of men you can't have."

"Oh come *on*," she began, while slapping at his leg as my neck swiveled back and forth between them. "That was one guy, man. *One* guy. You're fishing for something, Brody. You're jealous because I don't invite you to kick off your heels on my bedroom floor."

He grinned.

"May I say something?" I asked before being quickly ignored, a low-paid ball boy on a tennis court of unassuming giants.

"No, sweet baby. I'm afraid that's…"

"Oh, don't *sweet baby* me, LaCoste," Knox said. She was laughing, shaking her head, squinting her eyes and pointing her finger at Brody the same way she did when highlighting important elements of her dreams to me, talking with frenzied hands, on mornings she'd call me to a coffee shop for help in hashing out the obscurities of what kept her tossing some nights in the sheets. She slept a lot like myself, though I imagine for different reasons, hers being a more deep and sated rush than that of my sleep, a churning insecurity that when I would next sit to write, it would fall apart and eventually go up in flames, leading then to Brody pushing me into completing things I'd rather watch die than attempt to sew them back together and see them grow whole again. The concern was based on Brody's correctness about it. Jerry's, too. *Sons of bitches.*

"And what *would* you know about pretty boy pampering?" She continued. "You lucked out in the gene pool and here you are in rags and two-day scruff. At least my guys take care of their appearances, rather than take advantage of them. You'll be an old crusty bastard in just a few months, LaCoste. I know. I *know!*"

Brody seemed to be losing interest, because he was laughing more at the buttons pushed in Knox than actually discerning his own rebuttals. Perhaps that was the point, to entertain himself. And Knox sensed it, laughing harder while she stammered through statements to fire at him, fighting more with herself to say it straight-faced than serve an ace.

"Are you planning on pregnancy through osmosis? Because I don't think a gay guy would…"

"I wish I had a knife on me."

"Guys?" I said.

"*What?*" They yelled simultaneously.

"First of all, shame on me for sitting between you psychotics, and secondly, there are two guys staring over here, so I'm thinking maybe it's Knox's never-can-haves she's raving about."

Knox stood.

"*Asshole*," she blurted directly to me and then slapped at my head. "Don't side with that…piece of…" She let out a sigh and rolled her eyes before looking over to where I'd pointed. "Ok, yeah, that's them." She began to step down the few stairs that led into the main area of the dance floor and bar, turning first and saying, "My *new* favorites." And with a smile, she was off into the lake of people, hoisting her beer above her head as she maneuvered through a tight line of bodies and disappeared.

"She's after *mi corazon*," Brody said.

"You guys need boxing gloves."

He laughed and pulled his knee onto the sofa.

"So what about tonight, man?"

"What about it?" I asked, lighting a cigarette before he took the pack and lit one of his own.

"Don't act so *removed*, Rattigan. What *about* it?"

"You mean being here, or in general?"

"You know what your, well, I don't want to say *problem*. But yeah, you know what your problem is? I mean, presuming this could be called one?"

"Ok, ok. Let's hear it, man. What's my problem?"

"You're fussy."

I gawked into the dance floor. He smiled.

"What does that mean?"

"You spend a damaging amount of time playing this game of avoidance with yourself, when truly there's an obvious roar bubbling at your surface." He patted my chest. "You letting the man get you down?"

I laughed.

"No, Brody. The *man* isn't getting me down." I was clear on his meaning, and I also knew I was lying. So did Brody. "Are you saying I take things too deep into the literal?"

"See, you know what I'm talking about."

He slapped my leg. A young couple of guys walked hand-in-hand past us to another couch and overlapped their legs once seated, exchanging light kisses and laughing about something we couldn't hear.

"Well, for example," he said, pointing at the couple. "If I said that looked like stasis and familiarity, you'd probably come up with some sub-definition of their terms together, rather than settle for the universal acceptance of what could be some kind of underlying and real passion between them. Right?"

"Are you saying I'm homophobic?"

"No sweet baby, I'm…"

"You're a dick."

"I'm just saying…"

"Fuck *you*," I said in sing-song.

"I'm just *saying*, Rattigan…"

"I think I'm deaf. Yep. Just now I became deaf."

"Listen, babe. No harm. Honestly. I'm just saying you're demonstrating that you've got this plush underbelly you're trying to cover up by being this hyper-objective observer. That's *distancing*, man. Not good, especially when the fact is, really, that you're afraid to start putting your life in motion because maybe then you'll discover why you never finish what you start with your work."

"Are we gonna have this talk *now* Brody?"

"I mean, that fear's healthy for a little while, sure, but…"

"*Now*, though?"

"Good a time as any."

I sighed. "This beer isn't big enough." *Get us away from now*, it whispered.

"There it is."

He winked and then rested back on the sofa.

"What?"

"Now you're being honest. Tell yourself why it is you just said that."

It was then that I invariably understood why I hated and loved Brody LaCoste. He interpreted my expressions before I could, or even thought to do so. I loathed my transparency. But the night had just begun, already seeming long and meticulously designed, though I wanted none of what was coming clear to me, in that all Brody was really saying was, *shut up and breathe*. I thought briefly for a moment about my job and then sipped my beer.

"Ok, ok. I get your point, and I agree to some extent, but…"

"To some extent?"

"It's just not as simple for me as it is for…"

"Hey guys, I've paid for sex!"

93

It was Knox, hands locked with two, yes, handsome boys. I figured out suddenly why it was she let her imagination run wild when it came to her attraction to their natures. I was unsure which was Brian and which was Jonathan, but they both glowed with the radiation Knox seemed to press upon Brody's potential looks, whereas I knew, clearly, that Brody would rather be thought hideous in tattered t-shirts and holed-out jeans than be considered beautiful in something as domestic and even somewhat sophisticated as clean, polished clothes. No wonder the tie in New York had confused him.

"Lovers' quarrel?" She asked.

"Ella ya no tiene mi corazon," Brody whispered as he squeezed my leg.

I wanted to punch and thank him simultaneously, wanted to ask, *Oh, so you speak fucking Spanish, too?* But I laughed instead. Knox had a glint in her eyes. She seemed breathless, animated, alive.

"Yes," I answered her, nodding. "Yes, it *was*. But I'm through with this guy. Who are your friends?"

Knox clasped her hands together like a cheerleader. Behind the three of them I could see the floor lights glowing, and my eyes glossed. I was uncollected and suddenly felt good about the world, part of me wishing Brody wouldn't have been so forthright. But then, much of me was warmed that he had taken the time. Things were beginning to nicely burn.

"This is Brian," she said, opening her palms to display him. Brian was the taller, thin and blond, a permanent half-smile on his face. "And this is Jonathan."

I thought Jonathan seemed out of place in his own skin, and then I considered myself. Brody's insinuation was right, again, that I'd busied myself with only looking out and not in.

"Hi," he said softly as Brian bent to hug Brody.

"I don't shake hands, man. Sorry," Brian said.

Brody kissed his cheek during his ascent from the couch.

"Bring it in, babe," Brody said.

It was too simple and fluid for me at the moment. Considering what mountain of curiosity I'd had in the recent past about my own imposed hesitations, the crumbling of the world down to its basic valley of forms was evident only in what I allowed in myself to change and evolve. It had nothing to do with where we were and what we were collectively living, then. Instead, it meant I had a surfeit of worthwhile answers to embrace.

"This is Brody," Knox said. "And Pete."

"Hey guys," I said, tipping my beer as I half-stood.

"Just call him Rattigan," Brody said.

Brian squeezed my shoulders, and I watched Jonathan nervously switch his eyes from me to Brody to Knox to somewhere around his knees or shoes and then back to Brian, some kind of studious and simultaneous loving look at the base of his creased eyebrows. I felt nervous for him, maybe unfamiliar with being thrust into introductions and confident, dark, positive shadows. Knox's face was illuminated.

"Have a seat," Brody said, extending his arms to the space on the cushions around us. The three of them moved around the coffee table, and Jonathan adjusted a small chair at my right to face into some kind of circle for us to use as a conference area, now no longer in a bar it seemed, but rather, a place for ideas and an unrelentingly good, welcome energy. We clinked bottles, and as naturally as Knox sat taut at the edge of her seat, I fell back into the sofa with a comforting willingness to take everything in.

"I'm so glad you're downtown, lady," Brian began with Knox. "Is it crazy being here? Gonna be tough getting laid in this place."

She laughed. "Maybe by a *guy*."

Jonathan smiled as Brian laughed. Brody was smiling and studying their exchanges, I was studying Brody, and Knox looked at me as if my body language was indecipherable, as if I were *distancing* myself, so I sat like her at the cushion's edge and pushed up my sleeves.

"Who knows, man? Night's young," Knox continued, raising her eyebrows at me as she shrugged and sipped her beer. I smiled and made a quick face at her.

"What about you guys?" Brian asked Brody and me. "How long have you been together?"

I was so interested in their casualness it took a moment for his question to sink in. Knox spit up some of her beer and Brody started laughing. I finally caught up.

"Oh no," we said at the same time. Knox howled. Our new, unsuspecting friends were confused.

"I'm not with this asshole," I said, shaking my head. Brian's face went from nervous to apologetic to relaxed.

"He won't give me the time of day," Brody added.

"I'm playing hard-to-get."

"It baffles me."

"No, Brian. I'm sorry," Knox began, wiping at her lip. "These bastards are straight, but I've been thinking they might as well be a couple. They argue like bitches."

"No we don't," we said, again at the same time.

Brian laughed. Jonathan, still, was in a den of wild animals. His disposition seemed that of a listener's, the man in the shadow. I liked him instantly then. I *knew* him.

"*See.* That's what they do. It fucking *kills* me. They're masters at banding together against me. They're as inaccessible as you gay boys."

"We're fun to love," Jonathan said quietly.

Everyone joined in laughter at him, *for* him, the pretty minimalist.

"You know, it just occurred to me, little missy, that you have a potty mouth." I feigned a serious look at Knox.

"She does," Brody said. "Knox, you *do*."

"See what I mean, Brian?" She held her arms out, palms-up, in defeat. "No slack from guys."

Brody sat forward.

"So Jonathan, what do you do? I know it's a pathetically American question. Sorry if that's..."

"Actually, I have an unusual job. I mean, you guys might think so. I work for a sail-making company on the parkway."

"No shit?" I asked.

"No shit," Jonathan answered.

"No shit. *Huh*," Brody said contemplatively. "Please don't tell me what that entails. It's too cool of a job in my mind right now to mess it up with description."

Brian kissed Jonathan's cheek. "It *is* a pretty cool job. He's waiting for me to finish school, and then we're hoping to move back to St. Petersburg."

"That's where I'm from," Jonathan said.

"Let me guess, Brody." Brian smiled. "St. Pete too cool to talk about?"

I squeezed the back of Brody's neck. "Five minutes and they've got you. Impressive, guys."

"You know, Rattigan…" Brody turned toward me, smiling. "…I've got an idea about you, if anyone wants to hear my theory involving…"

"Shut *up. Jesus.*" Knox interrupted. "I want to dance. Who's with me?"

An exchange of looks passed around our circle. I may have even let a groan in defiance, but the straightening of our legs from sitting to standing confirmed the unspoken consensus, and I found myself draining my beer and following the group down to the floor. As we got closer to the music, Knox warned the guys about Brody, that if he called either of them "sweet baby," to smack him.

I approached the floor, ensnared by recollection in the darkness and smoke, thinking of a story I'd written about a trip to New Orleans, one year past and so far removed from the moment that I couldn't think at the time if it had happened at all. I'd gone with two girls and, immediately after pulling on to Canal Road, strutted into the first large, loud bar off Bourbon Street—in the narrative, I think I referred to the dancing bodies we observed from an overhead balcony as an "alphabet soup bowl of flesh and hands." This description came to mind with an unforeseen fastness as my feet hit the bottom of the steps and we landed in the middle of the chaos, the good chaos, where hopefully I could forget the enslavement of work and surrender into a desultory need for touch, rather than bolt myself down as continuously as I had before, to where all I wanted and needed in a moment would surpass my understanding of it, leaving me with a lame and crippled sense of its failed recognition. It was becoming my night, mine alone, though the drumming of our uniformity was staggering and powerful, and I was falling in love with a force which, before that very second, had only existed as a raw, ignored hint.

It was after three in the morning when the five of us left together, sweat from inside stinging coldly on the skin beneath our sweatshirts and jackets, and we two-car caravanned to an all-night breakfast diner off the I-65 beltline. I was worn and drunk and filled with drowsy satisfaction as Brody and Knox and what was left of myself followed Brian and Jonathan down Airport Boulevard, hopped the service road cut-off and parked on the well-lit gravel outside the restaurant. We piled out, garrulous and jawing on together about Knox's recently developed obsession with historical witch hunts and burnings.

I suppose at some specific moment in the early morning, caught in the middle of a dance floor, caught swimming in the soup, I understood that we were all the same person right then, right when I was most likely the last to think it. Nothing defeated entered my mind as I thought this, that I was always the last to crack the self-shell and adhere to it, the elusive—or maybe not so—*it*, a construct in a life beginning to live itself out in a manner which deeply needed acknowledgment and room to run. There was beauty in such a notion, the allowance of its gentle approach, the wax and wane of its intensity no longer overwhelming, but welcome, *necessary*. I slowly trailed the band of dreamers up the concrete ramp and through the door.

———

"I haven't eaten at this grease box in years. Whose idea was this?" Knox asked, studiously looking around the table. "My arteries are doomed."

"Brody's," Brian said, nodding at him across the table. I sat between Knox and Jonathan in the booth, with Brian and Brody sitting in chairs opposite us, their backs to the kitchen.

"Shocker."

Brody played with the salt and pepper shakers as though they were talking dolls.

"I need to be in bed, LaCoste," I said. "This is past daddy's bedtime."

"*You* need..." He said, without looking up. "...you *need* to live a bit. Sleep all day if you want."

"I'm moving the rest of my crap in at Knox's tomorrow. I'm already behind."

"Get off the nipple, Rattigan. It'll be fine," Knox said, reading her menu between glances around the dining room for a server.

"You hearing this?" I said in disbelief, while elbowing Jonathan. "They're really awful people."

He laughed. It was one of few relaxed smiles of his I'd seen during the night. I'd been in a nest of arms and hips with him, for shit's sake. And at the same time, in the thick of the shadowy bar, three *other* whirling bodies, so I grew curious at his pervasive nervousness around me, around us.

"You're pretty reserved, man," I told him, quietly thankful we'd gone to a place that didn't serve booze.

His cheeks turned red, but he smiled.

"It takes me a while to get used to people, I guess."

"LaCoste is a handful, so I know it's hard to get a word in edge..." Knox began.

Brody looked up and, grinning, he leaned forward.

"We gonna play the comparison game? We really gonna make a determination as to who was flapping lips all night?"

"You bastard," she said.

"It's always like this. I'm adapting," I whispered to Jonathan.

A middle-aged woman greeted us, or *saved* us, rather, and I could tell immediately that Brian had worked years in the business, as he craftily managed to give her some sort of strong, confident assurance that we were a good table, good money, a little out of orbit, but not to be perceived with trepidation. He said it with so much more simplicity than that, and it became inarguably clear that Brian and his boyfriend were on the far, unfamiliar other side of normalcy from the three of us. I was exhausted and happy, but still somewhat brooding, Brody had all but named the shakers and was on the second act of a play he'd written for them in his head, and Knox was talking to herself while mulling the menu, occasionally taking pause to kick me under the table each time I picked at my lip. Somehow, likely as a result of Brian's coaxing, as well as our server's conditioned patience with late-night drunks, we placed our order and, realizing the struggle we'd forced upon her, we put the lunacy on hiatus long enough to sincerely thank her. The vacation, however, would end soon after she disappeared into the kitchen.

"Exactly, man," Brody nodded toward Brian as their conversation grew in intensity. "Believe me, I understand. I work in a restaurant right now, too."

"Oh. *Oh.*" Knox said. "Don't let him trick you into thinking he actually works. This woebegone poster boy for the Salvation Army actually just bounces about, works when he needs rent or travel money, essentially eking his way by. I can't fathom how you managed to say that with a straight face, LaCoste."

Brody laughed.

"I'd do it if I could," Brian said.

"Me, too," Jonathan added.

"I probably should," I said.

"Now you're all making sense," Brody said, looking directly at me and lightly tapping the table with his palms.

"It's true, though. No shit, Brody, and I'm not busting your balls. Servers and bartenders would make phenomenal psychologists. The job itself is a mastery of the human social condition. I put in two years when I was finishing my undergrad and, no kidding, the way someone ordered a drink would be enough for me to determine how horribly or how well they'd treat me while they were there. I could even tell how they voted in past presidential races before we got to talking entrees." Knox thanked our server as she set down her plate in front of her.

"Then in that capacity, a job in the service industry can be beneficial to say, a writer, am I wrong?" Brody asked Knox, again looking at me. "In terms of shaping characters? I mean, it isn't the only reason I do it. The money gets me by while I'm waiting for my publications to work out. But yeah, no doubt it would be nice if some kind of additional gratification existed with it."

"Thank you very much," I told the server.

"You're amazing," Brody said to her.

"Thank you," Jonathan added.

"Cheers, thanks again," Brian said, adjusting his plate in front of him, keeping his voice low until she walked away. "See, I hate it. Everything about it. The coke addicts I work with, the pissed off cooks, the self-right-eous customers, the power-hungry managers. But I do it because the hours are consistent with my school hours. Once I graduate, we're out," Brian said.

"Now I think *that's* a legitimate sacrifice," I said, nodding at Brian. "But LaCoste, what kind of gratification are you looking for?"

"Some kind of satisfaction from the effort of it, I guess. Not really grati-fication. Or yeah, maybe that, too. There should always be at least some element of your job you find gratifying, right? But how would I know?"

"That's just it, *sweet baby*." Brody smiled and Knox laughed as I sat up, fueled not by having eaten the needed food, but rather, by its arrival. "Gratification has selfishness at its root. Think about it. If we want to feel gratified, isn't that saying we want to feel some sort of spiritual or emotional reward for something we've done?"

"Sure," Brody said. "But…"

"So if we perform acts toward others, seeking gratification for it even if subconsciously, we're still trying to satisfy a craving to feel better about ourselves. So is it possible to alter our perceptions toward the acceptance of gratification in terms of letting accomplishment be our reward *without* feeling that our new, I don't know, elevated spiritual contentment doesn't feed ego?"

"I'd say so, babe. No doubt."

"Definitely," Knox added, taking another bite. Brian had a peculiar look on his face, divided between Brody and me, one that either expressed growing interest or poorly concealed fear.

"Examining our biases is one, right? Maybe regarding our natural inclination to think mechanically and even stereotypically about usual events and situations in our lives…" I knew I was including my earlier reluctance to unwind at the bar. "…so maybe we should keep working toward comprehending the importance of the *now* of each moment, each moment's own weight, and work to somehow deconstruct the lust for triumph, or at *least* change the meaning of it, since desiring the wrong thing can lead to failure. And that's another thing. I'm not talking that 'failure is just a smaller success' bullshit. But the bias thing, that examination, maybe it could eradicate the fear of failure, too. Maybe these things can chip away at the common way we manipulate or, who knows, at least *overlook* how casually we talk about satisfaction."

All was quiet for a moment. I felt I'd been talking a year, considering how much effort it involved going from observer to active participant. And then we all laughed, I suppose once everyone saw my face finally recognizing their silence.

"No, seriously. I know where you were going, babe. And I agree. *Con todo mi corazon*." Brody grinned at me.

"Is that all the fucking Spanish you…"

101

"But I was leading to the fact that I wish I could have some more like-minded people, like *yourselves*, at work so it would offset the grueling sort of feeling I get from the negative sides of it. Selfish, maybe. It can definitely be called that, guys. *It* can be called *anything*. But the beauty part is, *Rattigan*, that your eggs are probably freezing by now, when I could have told you a while ago that I just wanted an easier ride when I'm on the clock."

"They're full of shit," Knox told Brian.

I shook my head and laughed, picking up my fork and raking through scrambled eggs that covered half my plate. When I looked up, Brody tipped an invisible hat toward me.

"Well done, sir," he said softly.

Knox was smiling, cheeks red, still alive, eyes swirling, dancing. Our server returned to our table to check on us and Brian, the untold leader of our pack, assured her all was well. Knox asked for our tabs as Jonathan finished his pancakes and I put my neglected fork to work.

"My eggs aren't cold," I said. "Asshole."

We left neatly folded cash in a pile at the table's center and again thanked our server, maybe a little too heartily, due to the earlier discussion. It seemed to make her nervous, as though our abundance of gratitude, at such an hour, was possibly insincere. It saddened me for her. A table of younger kids, mostly adorned in black and passing back and forth between them some portable music gadget, paused to suspiciously watch us noisily move to stand and shuffle toward the door. Two cops stood by the front tables of the smoking section and handled Styrofoam cups of coffee, nodding to us as we threw our most sober smiles at them. Outside, we stood beside Brian's car and traded hugs and numbers, after a few minutes of pre-sleep delirium talks of the weary. But the effort's unity was beautiful, each of us taking turns stepping in to embrace new friends, to squeeze out the former stranger in one another as smoke rose from the diner's roof in the background. And before Knox, Brody and I sped off to crash at her place, my soon-to-be new home, I thought for a razor-cut moment that no, we weren't full of shit. Knox, I conceded to myself, had said it to melt the terror that had frozen the guys' eyes once we, during breakfast, launched into the business that had recently, rapidly become our conversational lives together. But no, I thought. Something good was happening.

We made it west down Airport before turning right on to McGregor, yet another boulevard, Mobile being a yarn ball of them, toward the neighborhood entrance and then the driveway of the main house behind which her guesthouse hid. As soon as we were through the vine-infected courtyard and inside and fully or partially disrobed, I fell into bed against the far right wooden frame of the bed, Brody in middle and Knox on the far left, closest to the bathroom. A series of sighs explained that no more talk was necessary, and we fell heavily asleep.

Knox and I mutually stirred around one in the afternoon to find Brody gone. Our brief consensus was that he'd found a girl to swing by and pluck him from a potentially wasted day of sleep. Most of Brody's advice seemed a passive challenge for others to ignore him and push off into one's own direction. Knox groaned as she pushed from bed and walked the squeaky wooden boards to the microscopic kitchen and began grinding coffee beans as I slipped off my side of the bed and hit the bathroom. Of the few things that remained at my Midtown apartment, my answering machine was one, along with a couple of pieces of furniture I hadn't given myself time to take to my storage unit near my mother's house a few miles southwest. Knox's cell phone had a dead battery, and with my work phone still in her car, I felt a needed disconnect from work, from everything. If someone were to call for proof suggestions for their piece or mine, if Andy lost something in the disarray of our "office," if Richard was hung over and had invented another work term for me to ignore and over which the higher ups could call him a visionary, a journalistic *seer*, if Noel Halliday needed clarity from my jumbled, fake-economics-major numbers from our collective, they'd either have to wait or get past their concerns and forge ahead without them. I'd been too, not generous, but too *available* with the help I was doling out. Or maybe that was just part of my job. But the previous night had rendered superfluous that notion.

We finished the coffee and drove together, on her recommendation, to a small café across from the Jesuit college, an institution of impenetrable snobbery and false sophistication, where the education offered was solely based on preserving personal image as part of some mystical other, rather than developing into one's own institution of power, a school that almost condoned an ignorance regarding the necessary path of academia that, if embraced properly, could have freed the majority of its students from what type of person they were becoming at that point. Most of them, that I had met, didn't want or even think to want a way out of the clutch of such a conservative paradigm's influence, all under the purveyance of a supposed liberal arts degree. The dichotomy, to me, was infuriating. I'd been with a few girls in both the business school and the athletics department when I was an undergrad across town, divesting myself of tuition at an assembly line school that released its students after years of sparsely available coursework, a faulty system which graduated the mind-starved after, as was my case, five to seven-year tenures. But these girls I'd known had friends for me to meet who had friends for me to meet, and my exposure to each demographic proved to be cyclical, identical, and before I separated myself from them all, I had even slipped into a routine of talking about things that did not have any real importance, random suppositions about future cars to buy, expensive places to travel, things and things and things. I detested myself a considerable amount of time following, and then dove into the completion of school, voluntarily burying myself in anything but the thumbing through of high-end catalogues. I may have chosen, then, to shop thrift not from full necessity, but for a quiet reintroduction into the realest of my worlds I was surrendering for a more soulless, unwanted dream. The talk had been talking me, for too long, which meant I must have, no doubt, had no idea in any galaxy who I was, nor what was crucial against what was not. And what I had begun to learn upon catching back up with Knox, and from meeting Brody, was that no matter how much contempt I felt, in the past, that I had for those students apathetically handling the intellectual wealth that inarguably resided within the walls of both schools, at least, in their defense, they hadn't inserted themselves into the rut in which I was then lodged, selling myself to someone else's reality, someone else's American "dream," while ignoring the importance of momentary madness, in which all the better, more inspired risks were present and ready to be taken. I didn't detest the academy. Instead, it was just what those two in particular were allowing to happen with their progeny.

I sensed, as the recent days were becoming weeks, a gain in clarity on how the environment created around one's self is an indication of who a person largely is. The risks taken to arrive at this person, this quasi-Rattigan, what with all the Nothing I felt I had to show for it, included perhaps selling out long enough in the impersonal bottom-line business world to understand it wasn't where I belonged at all. No dealings with mergers and calculations and take-overs or negotiations, but I was, in fact, part of a machine that could have easily roared on, and likely would, without me. There was no justification underlying this thinking, as the former lesson learned had quickly become vital in coincidence with the lesson *being* learned. It was true that my basic nature required multiple perceptions, even unfortunate ones, in order to eventually function at its peak. I was getting close to satisfied in knowing it, a satisfaction that was becoming clearer by the split-second as I rode with Knox down Old Shell Road to the café, that feeling downtrodden by lot was irresponsible, and that glimpses of comparison were rife in my immediate environment, the one I'd unwittingly begun to construct around me. I'd been presented with a solid metaphor, days earlier, for how I'd been thinking with recklessness about my situation, desperately clinging on to some inevitable hope for resolution.

But the only problem, should it be seen as one, was in the metaphor. I'd wanted something more enigmatic, something hallucinatory and nearly inexplicable, not a lesson from a damned car. In hindsight, however, at least the revelation did come, albeit sloppy in form. And at least when it came I noticed it. Something too far out there might have skipped along forlornly beyond my scope or reach.

I was cleaning out my car on a warmer winter afternoon, the temperature in the upper fifties, while addressing the growing list of travesties occurring within the disheveled vehicle. And since I'd spent so many months alone, floundering in general loathing, I forgot Knox and Brody had suddenly introduced themselves to my life as adjunct characters, and quite plainly I couldn't fit them in my car should I be tapped one night to haul us around the planet. Their presence became impetus to tackle the jumper cables, at least ten beer bottles, soda cans, unimportant work copy I never read, a rock from Perdido Key which was the size of a bowling ball, two umbrellas, wrappings from cigarette packs, broken compact disc cases, a pair of old shoes, crumpled clothes and a Christmas gift I bought and had professionally wrapped but never gave my mother. During the resurrection of the car's cleanliness, I saw with great lucidity the very point, which matched the suggestions of Uncle Jimmy and his head's shaking at my rotors. I brought it up to Knox as we parked and walked toward the front patio. I'd allowed the car to become almost interminably locked in disarray before taking it on as a project of arrested ruin. What was being ignored was my ability to maintain its organization or hygiene, and maybe it was the effort to right this wrong that reared its head when I supplied myself with reason to change it. That was how I was living up to the recent weeks, dirtying everything with indifference, stagnating in various and fluctuating limbos, and then getting turned on periodically by the redemptive qualities of rebuilding, but not sustaining the energy.

"I know what you mean, man," Knox said as we waited to be seated inside. There were about twenty tables in the café, and the only one vacant was being cleaned by a busboy. We were shortly ushered to it, and my face lit up like a child's when I found a dime at the foot of my chair as I sat. *This is a good luck sign for me, man*, I told her while laughing and sitting down. *Lay off me.* She smiled as I pocketed it.

"Believe me, though," she continued, once seated. "I've done it, too. I've tried so many techniques to convince myself I was making mistakes, when in truth I knew I was doing the right thing. Like I was scared of the change that comes with improving the way I see the world, you know?"

"Definitely."

"But I think I got more frustrated at myself because I wasn't getting the results I wanted fast enough, even when I *knew* I couldn't speed up progress itself. Not substantive progress, at least. I mean, how fucking mindless is that? So I *do* know what you're saying. You're not upset about anything, are you?"

"No, no. I'm good. I should probably quit the paper. Other than that, I'm good."

"I like how that sounds, man."

"I think I do, too."

"Brody'll get you on at the restaurant. He says he makes more than you."

"When he shows up," I said. "But yeah, I don't doubt it."

"I wonder where he went this morning."

"I don't want this to just be about money at this point, though."

Knox studied the room with her lips pursed, her head tilting slightly at a James Dean black and white on the west wall.

106

"I didn't mean it like that. Sorry. And who has money these days, anyway?" She asked rhetorically, still studying the wall. "Nobody *I* fucking know."

The dining room inside was filled with similarly dressed women with similarly coiffed hair, women drinking similarly colored beverages with spoon handles reaching away from the rims of their similar glasses. This food, I thought, must be good. Knox was usually turned off by cookie-cutter *anything*, which was all I could see in the café, women in competition to seem more like their companions than their companions. I was the only visible man in the building besides the busboy and one server.

"So what do you think?"

"I'm not sure," she said, lowering her eyes to the menu. "I'd really like a cigarette before we order."

"I mean about quitting."

"Smoking?"

"*Work*, dickface. Where are you?"

"Oh, come *on*, Rattigan. Whose opinion do you really need? *Mine? Really?* And you know what Brody will say. He's probably already said it, in one of his languages."

"I must not have been listening."

"Yes, you were. Don't do that shit." She pointed at me as though she were holding a cigarette between her fingers. I imagined ashes falling on the white linens and I grinned. We were too just-from-bed-and-bar slimy, too half-awake to be anywhere so clean and well-lit, a place so terrified of itself, with chirping, rich, middle-aged and older, retired women under broad-brimmed hats, corsages on a few jacket lapels and clutching—it happened more than once—their pearls and trying not to laugh themselves into too much attention. It was an odd dance of theirs, how everything was just so *light*, so fluffy and *grand*. Oh, Bitsy, aren't we just *terrible?*

Our server came with waters and we bought time to look things over.

"Ok, ok. But the thing is, Knox, these last two years have been some kind of analytical tease for me, where I'd feel I was thinking too much, seeing too hard into something, if that makes any sense. But then I keep returning to a big fat No, you know? I'm *not* wrong in trying to understand my life as it's happening. But what we were talking about last night, I guess, is what I'd been missing."

"What was that?"

"That paying attention is different from worrying something's going to be missed. It's two different thought processes entirely. At least that's what I got from it. But at work, I don't do either. So, I've essentially been annoyed on a day-to-day basis because nothing was happening in my head at all. I mean, of course not lately. *Lately's* been good. It's countered the distance I'd been cultivating for so long."

Knox sipped her water.

"I want to fuck this glass," she said as she continued to read the menu.

"You're disgusting."

She looked at me with a surprised look on her face.

"I really don't know where that came from, man." She laughed. "I need food in me, pronto."

She looked around us, finally noticing who I'd been observing for a while.

"Holy shit, we're in the wrong place."

"I was wondering."

"Don't hold it against me, man. I forgot it was like this. I just like their tuna salad."

I shrugged and smiled. Our server came by, in more of a rush than earlier, so I ordered the same as Knox and our menus were whisked away.

"I'm sorry, Rattigan. What were you saying?"

I laughed.

"I doubt you'll be interested, babe."

"Why would you think that?"

"Because it doesn't involve coitus with dishes."

"No, seriously. You were saying something about lately. I was with you on *lately*."

"Then I lost you at *tuna salad*."

"But I'm back, you prick. You were saying *lately* has been good. I heard you."

I laughed again. She threw her rolled-up straw wrapper at me. A woman to my right studied me, and then Knox, rolled her eyes and went back to being miserable at her own table.

"Well, *yeah*. I'm talking about this time we've all been running together. I think I'd been waiting around for a catalyst instead of just creating one, and I'm kicking myself a little for that. But at the same time, I mean, I'm happy right now, at this moment, and I'm getting happier, daily. I'm at that point where talking about feeling happy doesn't sound so...I don't know...so..."

"So fucking cliché," Knox said, too loudly. The woman scowled. I'm sure I turned red, but Knox glanced over at her and then back at me, grinned a big Cheshire cat grin and lowered her voice to a whisper. "So fucking cliché. I know what you mean."

"I'm just glad I did something right by keeping in touch with you, rather than hole up inside myself and turn into, I dunno, *that* lady."

"That's the most sentimental thing you've ever said to me."

"Shut up."

Our lunches arrived. By then I was torn between wanting to leave the café, or at least, reroute to a patio table to speak more freely, *or*, continue to sit there and revel in the discomfort we were causing, as Knox would later dub them, "the Mobile cuntocracy."

"So as far as desire, man. As far as what my whole body's agreeing with my mind to want, I'm still fence-straddling, you know? The Dhammapada said something about cutting down the whole forest of desire, not just a single tree. But I don't think desire's all that bad, if well-managed. If that's possible. Or wait, was that quote from a Taoist text? I think it was Lao-Tzu. Do you know?"

She shook her head.

"This tuna salad's off the charts."

"I told you, man. Just pretend we're not here and it's a perfect meal. But yeah, I think desire shouldn't be considered such a villain. I also don't think you're on the fence at all."

"I don't know, Knox."

"Bullshit. What's it going to be?" Knox asked, drumming on the table's corner.

"Did you know that's called 'devil's tattoo'? That little drumming?"

"Who gives a shit?"

"It's the most important factoid in the world."

"What's it going to *be*, man?"

"Well..." I said, taking a deep breath and sighing out. "...I was think-ing it might be an awkward situation, giving a two week's notice and then having to deal with their probing into my job dissatisfaction, blah blah. What could have gone better, and so on. But if I just disappeared they might think I'm some child they shouldn't have hired anyway. And also, maybe it won't matter, you know? Maybe I'm not an asset in the first..."

"What they *think*, Rattigan? Come on. What about you? What would *you* rather do?"

"Put this conversation to bed, for one. I'd rather things be this way for a while. How it's been *lately*. I'd rather go to the beach and sleep in the sand. Or do something that would make old people scoff. I don't know." I looked around at the other tables. "It seems we're good at it."

"So, *what* then?"

"So then I'll *quit*, asshole!" I blurted, and again there was the nearby woman, a savage animal, baring fangs. "Sorry," I said, pointing at her.

Knox began to shake with ineptly suppressed laughter. I leaned over the table's wreath-like centerpiece, still from the holidays, and I lowered my voice.

"I'll quit, is what I'm saying. Happy?"

Knox sighed and, still smiling, put down her fork, crossed her arms at the edge of the table and leaned in to meet me in the middle. We committed to a whisper.

"This is not about what *I* feel. *Dickface*."

"I know."

"Is she still staring at us?"

"Yes."

"I want to stab her."

"I have a better idea, Knox."

"What's that?"

"We could put a hog's head in her yard."

Knox sat back in her chair, lifted her chin and squinted her eyes to study me.

"You're a strange, strange man."

CHAPTER 4

The small home that once belonged to Knox had somehow, suddenly, become our haven for escapism. Our telephones had gone on hiatus from steady ringing, and I familiarized myself with constant sleep, borrowing the idea of laziness from what I imagined others were doing when not living something similar to my more serious past life. Doing it, though, was not in itself a matter of laziness, and so hypocrisy, among other things, needed attention there, in my newer space, and then a chiseling down to sawdust, and then maybe something beautiful would come of it, a different idea, like its climbing upward from the ground to construct its own parameters around something more useable. But I'd have to wait and gradually learn what it was that occurred with the ghosts of old habits, self-modifying for this updated way of life. That included, without question, the embracing of dust and earth, other natural occurrences, the laughter of the hidden guesthouse walls that lived in the shadow of its own quiet frame, off Westgate in the heart of Springhill. Knox was dividing her time between writing and finalizing her thesis proposal on campus, swearing a lot about it and smoking a multitude of cigarettes on the thin granite stoop outside the door between the kitchen counter and the antique, dusty, inherited desk that slouched woodenly in the corner, where I would write, my hair bed-disheveled, eyes confused and somehow driven in the late mornings of hiding from the world, albeit in a new one, to practice using the mind for things that mattered, as well as the body, to levitate or dance or sit still as stone.

A solid week had collapsed into itself and passed like a car horn's blast before we'd see Brody again. I had passively disengaged from my job, and due to Knox's generosity with her school loans, supplemented by her part-time at a photography studio, I was afforded the luxury of living a series of days in a post-divorce-like stupor, the breakup not one of flesh or real investment, but that of a needed and divisive rift between me as my own establishment and that of the common grade. I had no plans as of that particular moment for the generation of revenue, and I even considered selling off my furniture in storage, but I still had enough residual in the bank to contribute to what copious wine nights we experienced, and how little food we ate. Even when I squeezed through the stubborn half-closed door of the bathroom and stood naked in front of the mirror that was blocked by rigged shelving systems we'd set up on the counter for our personal items, it seemed my body had at some point that week decided to shake off its outer layer to make room for the sudden thinness of my frame, to ready its untouched, uncared-for self for reinvention. Feeling healthy and emaciated and ebullient and docile, all of it, I was thrust into a commitment with the Westgate house, with the tangling vines on the outer north wall, the smell of coffee around many noons, the unplanned and welcome intrusions of Brody LaCoste on any particular Saturday morning.

"If God exists, he doesn't hang around here," Brody said to the backs of our heads, as the squeaky front door swung open across the small room from our face-down bodies. Something scraped across the floor, maybe a hanger, or music case, the sunlight perhaps, scribbling into the noisy panels of the morning. "The power of Christ just might need to compel you."

I tucked into a half-child of resistance toward waking, and nested into the frame of the large waterbed that engulfed the bedroom, an open space including a closet prominently demarcated by a divider behind the navel-high brown headboard, which had built into it a few cubbyhole-like open shelves. A shift from Knox's side sent me deeper into the pocket, and then her reluctant groan from her even more defiant and slumbering will entered my pores and shook my right leg over the bed's edge, and we simultaneously returned to stillness. Knox had forever been, in the limits of what realness *forever* might have embodied amongst the three of us, and for as

long as I had known her, one angry octopus eye in the morning, a grim danger—even in the first slight stir, in the moments where I would do as the
soft lovers of my old bed had taught me, and ran a light hand over her back,
and then whispered, informing her of the stranger infiltrating the kind and
gentle world of sleep. This, but to no avail, and so would I see the eye, the
crumpled set of fear-lips, then the mouth gone agape, and then my own
fear that who I had wakened had not yet loosened his, her, or its grip on
Knox enough to allow her safe re-entry into the not-so-non compos mentis
world of our mutual energy, our good, true, blue light of the waking hours.
I feared for Brody, then, and loved him in that I wished to protect him from
her, but would not move on behalf of that staid fear, that perhaps I would
lose him to her momentary wrath, that she would sit and rise and fly and
destroy, not him and his impeccable, exasperating human male venus, his
symmetry of kindness and innocence nor his good will, but just the voice
that represented, to her in the fog, a train, a bomb, a convulsing attack on
the delicacy of her prone and private silence.

"I've brought something odd. *Look*." Brody said, standing by the war
trunk that then had found its new place at the foot of our bed.

I shifted slowly from my position, meeting Knox's turn in the middle,
and there stood Brody, patiently, his hands cupped together.

"I swear, LaCoste. If that's a dead bird I'm going to fucking kill you,"
Knox said, rolling back to her side.

"I hope it is," I said, as she swatted behind herself at me.

"You guys collecting these corpses for an art project?" Brody asked,
kicking at a bent, half-crushed aluminum beer can on the bedside floor,
and then he sat at an uncomfortable angle on the corner beside Knox's feet.

"Movie night," I said, and sat up to scratch my forehead. The cans were
numerous, on both sides. I grinned. "Where have you been, man?"

"Working, babe. Trying to put some cash aside so we can go to New
Orleans. I told you."

"No, you didn't."

"Shut *up*, Brody," Knox exclaimed, sitting up quickly as the waves
rocked me askance and almost over the edge of the boat. "You were
working?"

"At least I thought I told you."

"I would have remembered New Orleans."

"Seriously, man," Knox said. "What did you bring in here?"

Brody nodded a moment, smiling, before realizing he'd been asked a question.

"*Oh*. Take a look."

He leaned into the middle of the bed as we crawled slowly to meet him there. On the sheet's merlot and wrinkled top, he set down a cell phone. Three heads converged over it, staring down into its face, an immobile mobile, Brody's sudden abyss, and we were silent.

And then finally, "I have no idea what I'm supposed to do," he said.

"I cannot believe you, of all people, have a cell phone," Knox said, furrowing her brow at the rectangular machine riding small crests atop the bed as Brody tucked in a knee.

"I didn't ask for it."

"Why do you have it?" I asked.

"*You* guys have one," he said, feigning injury from the inquisition.

"I need it for school, man. Plus, my stepdad's been in and out of surgery all year. I actually need to be easy to contact," Knox explained.

"Mine was for work," I said in self-defense, as Brody nudged the phone with the tip of his index finger. "Not that I need it anymore."

"Seriously," Brody said, distracted.

"Do you even know where your phone is, Rattigan?" Knox asked, stepping out of the bed and slipping on an open book that was face down on the smooth flooring. She cursed and then shambled across the house toward the kitchen.

"Nope."

"Wait," Brody said. "So did you..."

"Yes, sir," I said, lying on my side and resting my cheek over his knee as I faced Knox's rack of albums in the corner beside the television. "I thought it would be a lot more difficult than it was..." I continued, as my face smashed into the thick bone behind the curved denim. "...but I realized it was more of a worry that they'd single me out as some asshole. I don't know why I was suddenly so terrified of a blighted image, at the fucking paper, no less. Not like they actually cared."

"You *are* some asshole," Brody said, patting me on the temple before he began pressing his fingertips into the space behind my ear. "But your image, in *my* mind, just became significantly untarnished. Now it's time to heal. Time to *heal*."

"Why am I an asshole?"

"Because you didn't tell me you quit."

"I haven't seen you, crazy person."

"I sensed it was coming. That's as good as knowing."

"At least the phone stopped ringing. At least Richard stopped calling, slobbering into the phone, denouncing my lackluster inverted pyramids. I don't think I really followed rules as closely as he wanted."

"Your *what*?" Knox called out.

"Just rambling. Work shit."

"*Old* work shit," Brody said as he gripped my shoulders and shook me. "Gone, done work shit."

I groaned and slipped off the bed from beneath his hovering face. The sun had brought in with its levity a mixed review of the coming day's temperature fluctuation, and since the door had been left widely ajar from Brody's surprisingly soft entrance, the bend of rays from the courtyard past the three steps that led from our house to the pebbled walkway managed their own entry and glinted off a few of the beer cans that had rested, no doubt poorly, on their sides after indifferent tosses toward the small trash receptacle not close enough to the edge of the bed's foot. There was a mild chill outside.

"What time is it? You in the mood for coffee?" I asked him, popping the back of his arm on my way to the kitchen.

"I could do that."

"I wish I could be your humble servant," Knox sounded from halfway out the other door, the faint smell of cigarette smoke sneaking in from over her shoulder. "But your pal Rattigan forgot to tell me yesterday he finished what we had when he was up late working."

"Not a worry."

"I'll get more later," I said to her back, as she stepped further out into the late morning to discard her smoke in a bucket half-filled with water, bucket sadly tucked away in the shadowy corner of the stoop and the spider-webbed, sandy wood of the house. I shrugged at Brody.

"You were working last night? That's good. That's really good to hear. Prolificacy in your unemployment. A post-modern marriage," he said, smiling up at me as I passed him toward the bathroom to throw cold water in my face.

"You up for a store run? To quell her highness?"

"I'm good with that."

"You don't get to go, Rattigan," Knox said, picking up a pair of shorts from the floor near the base of a tall, glass bookshelf by the front door, and tossing them over the divider behind the bed. "I need to go for other things. For *woman* things. If I send you…" she said to me, "with *you*…" she said to Brody. "Fuck *that*. I can't depend on either of you to attempt managing my biology through your male-driven commerce, is what I'm saying. If you guys go anywhere, Brody, make him get a job. Plus we're out of wine. Make him get wine."

She pushed behind me in the bathroom and shuffled me out as I ran a cloth across my face.

"How about orange juice instead?" I asked him.

"Why do you guys have a rotting apple on the shelf by the door?" Brody asked. I looked at it, noticing it for the first time that week, and laughed as I stretched my arms into the ceiling fan strings. He lay out on the bed as I searched a cabinet for clean jeans and a shirt.

"I have no idea, man. New discovery for me."

"Oh, *right*, LaCoste. Like he's just now aware of it. Rattigan probably thinks it's romantic," Knox shouted from behind the bathroom door. Brody looked at me with convicting, inquiring eyes, and fixed his paint-splattered bandana before propping his palms underneath the back of his head.

"Who gave you the phone, Brody?" I asked, slipping into the jeans and throwing my shorts through the crack in the bathroom door.

"Hmm?'

"The one you're lying on."

"He thinks it's romantic, Brody, to have dying fruit in the kitchen. Like it's symbolic, I think. He's warped of mind, man," she continued.

"Some girl at work gave it to me. I don't know the back story."

"She's keeping tabs on you. What did you do to her?" Knox asked, the door swinging open, the shorts returning through the air, the door half-closing again. I plucked them off the top of a large candle and tossed them into a cabinet.

"Well, if dying fruit is representative of evolution within you, Rattigan, then I say let it turn black for all intents and purposes. Not that the fruit is actually *in* the kitchen."

"What are you saying?" I asked, changing shirts after smelling the one I'd selected. The house was already a well-oiled machine for one torrential individual, and with two of us, suddenly it was like being off at camp.

"He's saying..." Knox blurted as she re-entered the bedroom area with her hair tied back. She leaned past a thin chest-of-drawers by the headboard, flailing about a blind hand until extracting from behind the bed a white gossamer button down with short sleeves. "...without admitting it, that he destroyed some dumb chick's sense of reason with the tease of a lifetime guarantee of him and his penis, and now she wants to use the telephone as a hangman's noose to choke him into at least the occasional surrender fuck."

"He's saying all that?" I asked, returning to the bathroom to brush my teeth.

"Maybe the pending blackness of dead fruit itself is some kind of antithetical explanation of your energies together," Brody surmised, blowing fake smoke rings toward the ceiling, flicking unseen ash on a pillow. "You're beautiful when you annoy each other."

"What are we picking up again?" I asked through foamed teeth and lips.

"*Rattigan*." Knox screamed.

"Maybe you're both realizing what I've honestly been trying to tell you all this time," Brody continued. "That we're all just basic somethings that grow *into* beauty. Which could imply that your keeping that carcass up there as a reminder is a strong indication you've..."

"Hey, LaCoste," I called out after rinsing my mouth and wiping my face on a hanging pool towel. "Maybe Knox shouldn't talk so much nonsense about me thinking rotten food has some sort of metaphysical importance. Your thoughts?"

"Maybe we should discuss the plural of *carcass*," Brody said, laughing as he rolled to his side to leaf through a thin notebook in one of the cubbyholes.

Knox paced to where I stood over Brody, extending myself to pull him from the sunken depths of the waterbed, and she patiently leaned in like an

117

oddly deposited mother in the child-strain of our boyish swirling. She removed the notebook from Brody's custody. Once emptied, his hand found my hand and he stood as I kissed Knox's forehead before heading off into Saturday. She shook her head at Brody before swatting at his ass, grabbing the right half of his face with her small, aggressive grip, and then shaking his chin.

"I am not awake enough..." she began, "...to have you bastards start my day with talks of spiritual apples."

"Where are you...I thought we were supposed to..." I yelled after her as she opened the front door.

"I don't know."

As the door rattled in its frame, and the quiet returned, Brody and I turned toward one another from having watched Knox shuffle in her usual out-the-door haste, his hands in his back pockets, my eyes suddenly scanning the room for a hat. I found and put one on backward.

"Never saw you in a hat before."

"How did you even get here?" I asked as I led us out.

"I've had my car back for a while," he said, stopping at the top of the steps. I pushed him forward and down into the courtyard as I locked the door behind us.

"I can't believe the tide's turn, man. You, with a cell phone, and I finally get rid of mine. I'm not sure of the lesson hiding in that."

"Hey," he said, pulling two cigarettes out of a pack in his pocket and lighting them both, passing me one. "Twenty-first century, baby."

"When has that mattered to you?" I laughed. We walked through the heavy black iron gateway that was partially open from Knox's recent exodus.

He laughed, too.

"It seemed appropriate for the moment."

"I should put on another shirt."

"We'll be fine."

"Where is your phone, anyway?" I asked while keying into my car.

"It's not my phone."

"Ok, man. Where is *the* phone?"

"On your bed, maybe?"

With tired eyes slowly growing more alert, I reversed around his car which was parked at the mouth of the guesthouse's driveway. A small breeze out, it felt as though Spring had changed its mind, deciding to put off arriving any faster. The sun made the trees overhanging Westgate and Country Club Road seem crisper and more clear-cut against the backdrop of what was behind their trunks, the roads and restaurants behind them and the interstate somewhere in the miles past.

"Dead fruit." He smiled. "That's great."

———

Almost two-thirty in the afternoon, Brody recommended we forego a timely return, citing Knox's unspoken doubt that we'd arrive at all, evident in the dismissive wave of her shoulders as she was leaving earlier, and also, that we'd come back to more of a headquarters than a home with any of the items we'd discussed. Agreeing, I drove us to Bit and Spur Road, hooked east down Old Shell Road, Springhill a yarn ball within a yarn ball, to a small wine shop owned by a cute and ordinarily lubricated woman whose name I'd known during the time I'd worked in a nearby restaurant in college, a name I'd since forgotten. Brody almost climbed out of his seat to the music he'd fingered beneath the dash to a loud roar, half an arm crippling the lightness of the thin passenger window, an anti-hipster, run-of-the-mill soccer dad sneaker with a hole above the right big toe sprawled across the air vent, drumming playfully in the air to words of being carried home.

Traffic was congested in front of the small strip mall that housed the wine shop, a drug store and some high profile trinkets joint for wealthy women of the area. I'd once gone inside the latter, to thank the owners who'd allowed me to attend one of their parties with a girl enrolled at the Jesuit school across the street, a tall, lanky, freckled, conservative puppet of the academy, a girl I'd been seeing because I was willing, then, as with the others, to overlook her social deficiencies so I might not feel left out of even something I despised. As we pulled in, I wondered about Layla, about where she eventually turned up, if she still had such frightened eyes, and where she stashed her heart on her desperate dart to the middle.

"See, that's too good, Rattigan!" Brody shouted as he leapt from his side of the car and met me at the front bumper, throwing his arm over my shoulder as we made our way to the entrance. "I can't even *think* straight right now."

"What do you mean?"

He pulled the door open and shoe-shoved its heaviness far enough to my left that I could catch it as he skimmed in before me.

"I don't know, babe. Proof that one song can *enable*. I dunno. I felt like we were in an airplane."

"I love the smell in here."

"Ok. Like *I* was in an airplane." He slapped my arm and looked up into the dim eggshell lights, optical preludes to the ensuing ceiling reds that dangled just behind them over two lengthy aisles of other reds, those trapped in bottles along the wall.

"I'm listening, man. I dig that song, too. I just had an odd flashback about this part of town."

"You need into your heart and out of *this*," he said, pointing to my forehead while slapping my chest.

"I'm deaf again."

"Hey guys. Good afternoon."

An unrecognizable woman greeted us from behind a wooden post connecting the top of the sales counter to the ceiling. I couldn't make her out, yet, but it wasn't my drunk beauty from the past. I was disheartened by her absence.

"How are you?" Brody asked her as he stood in front of a chest-high rack of specials.

"I'm good," she said, at last delivering her face into view over the counter's open space. "Ya'll let me know if I can help you with anything."

"Will do. Thanks."

"Can you convince him he's not in an airplane?" I asked her as I lifted a bottle from the end of the blends. Her face, along with the older couple across from me, paused in confusion before they craned their necks at LaCoste, who was grinning into the back of a bottle of white. And then they smiled. We were in a good place. Every day was Saturday.

"You should check this out, Rattigan. I learned something the other day about a ladybug on the label."

"What I was trying to *tell* you..." I began, after replacing the red and joining him at the wall of whites. "...was that sometimes we're victimized, if we don't outright victimize ourselves, by these overlooked associations in our thoughts. Like in the car on the way here. I had this flash of these memories that evidently come with seeing that stucco building out to the left. It reminds me of a girl I never really felt love for. Then I flashed into the party she took me to at the owners' house, a couple years back, and how drunk I got, and how she told everyone I was a bartender. Or maybe I did, and suddenly I had all these snooty, drunk CFOs asking me about Spanish reds, and someone went outside in the frigid weather, way colder than this year, and slid voluntarily down a water slide by the pool."

"Sounds like my kind of time," he said, tracing his finger across the label.

"That's not the point," I said, punching at him as he continued to grin. "I'm saying I wasn't in your goddamned airplane because I was sidetracked by something else, thinking about certain machinery in our heads that allows us to follow the moments as our moods change from one thing to the next, or our ideas shift, and then we get confused about why. I don't have any unpleasant emotions that spark from Layla or the store itself, but it was interesting to see where just looking at the building could take me. Which, in this case, is all the way up to you, now, maybe not hearing me at all. Right as I'm speaking, at this very moment."

He laughed and lowered the bottle.

"No, I am, babe. And I think you're right. That song reminded me of a couple of things, too. As though being in an airplane, for example, was associated with some soaring part of the guy's vocals, like being in flight, just listening to it. From there I thought of this intense band I saw downtown a while back. My thoughts were jumping, *too*, man. You've been consistently right about a lot, lately."

We walked deeper into the store.

"It's like with the ladybug. I can't think of any association I have with it mentally that could connect me to something else imaginary *or* concrete. Not even someone else's story of them, like fireflies when I was a kid. No connection there."

"I think there just was," he said after walking backward to replace the bottle he'd had in his hand.

"What were you saying about it?" I asked as we made it to a cooler of whites already chilled.

"Actually nothing. I realized I forgot entirely if I'd had a dream about it, or if someone was telling me some story about packaging one day at work. I must not have clued too deeply into what was being said. Isn't that wild?"

"What?"

"The not knowing?"

I smiled. His face was so serious.

"I'm pretty sure it means it's organic," the thankfully eavesdropping woman volunteered over the counter.

"Yes! I think you have hit the nail," Brody exclaimed and pointed at her and then me. "Maybe. I mean, I'm not doubting *you*. I'm doubting what I can't remember from this dream-reality thing about ladybugs. Ignore me."

She smiled and shrugged her shoulders in a resigned-to-not-understand sort of contentment. She was adorable and at noticeable ease. I decided to love her.

"What do you know about this vineyard?" I asked her, pulling my torso from inside a refrigerator and bringing closer to her a Sauvignon Blanc.

"Not a lot. I know that sounds sad. I do know we've sold a good bit of it, though. And that's actually rated a 92, I think. So, at that price it's apparently a good deal. You guys drink a lot of wine?"

"I don't think it matters what it is these days," I said, suddenly aware of Brody's absence. "We've actually been issued…" I continued as I strained my neck to see the top of his bandana, which jutted outward from beside a tall brown shelf near the front door. He was talking to the couple who'd made their purchases and wouldn't be able to, in any sphere of my imagination, make it out the door before some kind of supplication, from Mr. LaCoste, to challenge their own universe. He glanced around at us at the counter and held up a glass of wine from the tasting table before averting his eyes back again to the conversation. There was laughter. "…a direct order from my housemate to not return home without booze. So here we are."

"Is he the bossy type?" She asked, while ringing up both bottles I'd sat on the counter.

"*She* is," I said. "But only once you get to know her."

"Sounds like a big happy family."

"Too big," I said of the three of us, and then passed her cash. "Do you like it here?"

"Yeah," she answered, handing over the change and two carefully wrapped paper bags. "It's relaxed. Boss is cool. Works well with my school schedule."

She wore a nametag that read, "Becca."

"Nice."

Ten knuckles, then two glasses, then wrists and then the rest of Brody appeared, slowly encouraging a wine sample.

"Hey, Mr. Manners. Bring her a glass," I said, nodding at Becca.

"Well, *indeed*," Brody said, pointing both index fingers at her and disappearing again.

"I can't drink," she said, almost convincingly.

"Oh, she can't drink Brody," I yelled across the empty store, and proceeded to inquire about her collegiate pursuits which, like mine and Brody's had been, and Knox's still were, seemed a defeated foray into voided confidence in the false utopia of the world outside the walls of promise. Becca said she'd likely do graduate school and hope, thereafter, for something in her field.

"I tried it. The attempt was really unfortunate. I mean, I think it certainly yielded a great result, but…"

"What was unfortunate?" Brody handed her a glass and raised his own against mine. "Come on, Becca. This is a team effort."

"I really can't."

"I was saying working in your field, well, not *your* field, particularly…" I nodded to Brody.

"What field is that?" Becca interrupted.

Brody shrugged his shoulders and sipped.

"…isn't all it's guaranteed to be. We're told to stick it out, pay dues, and then it inarguably becomes worth it. But that's not the full picture. I sold myself short, *sold out*, if you will, to finally get it." I downed my glass.

"Sold out in the sense of surrendering his self to achieve some higher good that turned out to just be lies benefitting strange pockets," Brody added. "Not trying to sound anti-establishment."

"You are, too," I said.

"Not at all."

"It sounds anti-establishment."

"It's a case-by-case thing."

"It still sounds like it."

"Well, I reject the label."

"Then what other options are there?" Becca interrupted.

Brody and I looked at each other and laughed.

"Not sure, yet."

"No idea."

Becca shook her head after looking to her left and right, and then took a deep sip from the glass that Brody had slid closer to her. We made smaller talk as she finished the wine, and when we left, three pieces of stemware sat naked and empty and well-loved and laughed over on the counter.

"Knox is going to have our skulls."

"Becca was a stunning little light," he said over the roof of the car.

"I think we bummed out that poor girl," I said as I climbed in. "Where are we drinking this?"

"Oh, it's like that?" He sighed and tossed his palms in the air. "Knox *will* kill us." He thought a moment. "Let's do Langan."

I started the car and pulled west back on Old Shell down to University, the longer route than the cut to McGregor, in order for Brody to use the wine key he'd bought from Becca. He had a bottle open by the time we reached the road's split around Langan Park. We turned left, curled the car around and past the old, defunct train sitting newly painted in the shade. The wind had picked up, and I shot us down a narrow, winding trail toward the water and settled the wheels in loose rocks and sand beside a concrete table, on to which we climbed once the engine had died.

"No." Brody sipped from a bottle. "I think we might have emancipated that girl. Come to think of it."

"I guess so."

"Why do you guess? I'm not convinced you're sure she's all right."

"No, you're right, I think. I do agree. It's not as though we came at her with some gloomy bent and said the world was this soul-sucking machine or anything."

"Exactly. And who knows? She might break a few more rules if armed with the knowledge that a little caution on the path to fulfillment might just strengthen her. *Man*, it's gotten cold again."

"I *told* you I wanted to get another shirt."

124

"When?"

I sighed.

"Never mind, Brody. You're uncomfortably close to me."

He laughed into the lip of the bottle, took another sip and moved with dramatic labor to almost on top of my leg before retreating across the table as his feet dragged on the bench below.

"You know, on the contrary, maybe she'll give up and grind until retirement. Maybe she'll work at the paper," he said, elbow-nudging me as a few geese shuffled past en route to the water's edge, where a family was dispensing bread.

"Ha. Yeah, maybe. But that's interesting, what you just said."

"What was that?"

"When you mentioned fulfillment. I've kind of been mulling that this past week, especially once I quit my job. My first thought was, well, it *still is*, that it's a subjective occurrence. At least, much of me wants to keep thinking it is. But then I think of how disappointed I get nowadays when I hear people talking about how happy they are, but only when their happiness is challenged, as if it's otherwise untrue until someone calls them miserable."

"Yeah, that used to be a concern of mine," he said, wiping a wet palm on his leg and then sitting on the hand. "I mean, concern for myself."

"But it's not now? Because, it's been kind of elusive to me, the meaning behind it."

"Behind what?" He asked, passing me the bottle.

"Behind the conflict of trying to inform someone for *their* betterment versus our *own*, you know? I mean, who the hell am I to tell someone else what their betterment is or should be? Is it ok to stand by while somebody avoids the reality of their own "happiness"? Is it ok to interject? I mean *you* do it endlessly, but at the same time it's not *preachy*. I think that's what offends people. Especially depressed people who talk the happiness talk but don't believe it. I guess it still means fulfillment is subjective, but it changes, in my mind, what subjectivity means. Does that make sense?"

"Absolutely, man. It's a tough situation. A tough line to walk. Do you play humanitarian or philosopher? Either choice, you still have to understand how you define those things before becoming them for someone else. And you have to be pretty willing to be called those things as insults sometimes, too, which is unfortunate. And we could subscribe to Boethius or Aristotle or Seneca or Aurelius or, I dunno, any take-your-pick sort of modernist, *Chopra*, even, and get dismissively labeled as being part of only one school of thought, like that's a wholly bad thing. Or we could just go with the essence of what we have in common as people. But then there's the risk of being considered a half-wit and not helpful. It's more than either-or, which makes it fun, I think, and challenging, to just try to help people with what you've got. But it's good to know your limitations, too. It's crazy. No, actually it's just athletic."

"I should have rephrased the question," I said and passed him the bottle. I drew my knees to my chest. I reached for the pack of cigarettes Brody had brought from the car and I lit two.

Langan Park had once been another park, another name, a park where I had many things in association, tissue-like, infighting for connectivity. Across from where we sat, as the sun readied its fierce dip into the invisible horizon behind the small houses, past the pavilion and the street, I saw my young legs running to my mother's van, I heard Coach Goff's laugh, saw him do a back-flip when George Naylor caught his first outfield fly. I saw a smaller me kicking pine cones. I saw an old man sit next to my mother and expose himself to her on the bench that, like the Berlin Wall, had been deconstructed, fortuitously, as though the danglings of a grotesque man would be removed to resurrect the sanctity of what once was a playground of fantasy and not one of fear. The children had returned though—the college students, the Frisbees, the animal lovers and the little girls with curling blonde locks, shoulder deep in popcorn bags, running alongside the waddling ducks. In Langan Park, no longer called Municipal Park, I saw myself for the first time in history. It was disturbingly, crushingly beautiful.

"No, you shouldn't have. It's one of the things I love about you, Rattigan. I don't want to be around you because you 'get it.' I'd rather have someone who's chasing after 'it.' Comrades, you *know*? Not that there's the guarantee of any radical discovery. Just the rush involving..."

"The chase."

"Exactly."

"So you're saying, really, that the essence of what we experience is more important than the literal? Because...and this may sounds nuts...maybe full subjectivity in the literal is as impossible as full objectivity in the abstract? Or is it the other way around? I don't know."

"I'm *saying* you shouldn't go to graduate school."

"What? Where did that..."

"Come *on*, babe. You really want to get deeper in debt you can't shovel out of, just to have someone teach you what you already know about perspective?"

I sighed a long sigh and took the bottle from him. He scraped the last of his cigarette against the concrete tabletop and dropped it into the metal trashcan beside him. I did the same to mine and passed it to him to throw away, and then I laughed.

"You know, man. You have no idea. I really fucking *don't*. But you might have at least a *small* idea how relieving that was to hear coming from a different voice than the nagging shit in my head."

"*Good.* I mean, just look at Knox going gray over her thesis. There's a point school stops schooling, and I think it's when the student learns how to school the self. Don't get me wrong, man. It's necessary groundwork for right thought, but even the academy shouldn't be taken *too* literally. The essence of that, too, is more crucial than the inevitable letdown of having spent four, or in my case, six years building up to getting a piece of paper to hover over our heads, paper meant to indicate achievement, but really, in the end, is just a testament to stamina that translates into societal apathy the longer we avoid entering the roles our coursework discreetly suggests we should pursue."

"No doubt. No *doubt*. And hey, it's crazy you mentioned Aurelius."

"Why's that?"

"Well, because I..."

"Did you know he persecuted Christians? As in, had them *slaughtered*? See how Stoicism is viewed today, versus then? Now people think being "stoic" is almost nihilistic, or at very least cynical. But really it once was almost in step with..."

"Buddhist thought."

"I thought so, too," he said, nodding and lighting another pair of cigarettes.

"*I* thought, speaking of thinking, that I met you as this clean-lunged, soft-livered specimen, LaCoste."

He passed me a smoke.

"Hey, I saw scraps in your back seat."

"What?"

"Your back seat. What was that stuff piling up back there?"

"Shit, who knows? Some new poem notes. But just notes. I'd like, and this is in theory, to try to finish a collection and send it off and get it away from my body so I can start seriously on one of these non-novels. I need to stay with one genre."

"Yeah, don't bounce around too much."

"That's what I want to avoid."

"That's what you *should* avoid."

"I *know*, babe. I'm getting there."

"And you should show me some of it. I've got a mountain of shit like that in my car. I let it all go on purpose, I'm pretty sure." He nodded across the grass. "*Yeah.* I've definitely made the attempt already in my mind to see if I can fill my car with absolute drivel, right up to the ceiling, and then machete through it, maybe find another book in there."

"You're straying."

"I'm in an airplane, baby."

"No, man," I began, laughing and finishing the first bottle with a reckless splash on my chin. I handed him the second bottle which sat patiently, or perhaps in fear, beside my right leg as we huddled in the increasingly cold dusk. "Something you said reminded me of Aurelius. That's the goods I was going for. And I'm not trying to, honestly I'm not...stop making that face...I'm not trying to bend to too much influence of someone else's ideals, because while I do agree with essence being the nurturer and all, I was reading a couple days ago through an old printout of 'Meditations' I kept from work, and it came to me, man, what we might have actually been saying to that girl."

"She was lovely."

"And it's involved in context, *our* context, in *this* moment, in this collective now with you and me and the fucking geese and Knox and the silhouettes before the sunset. It's a statement of purpose, not just of emancipation."

"Then it should be something simple."

"It is, Brody. That's exactly it. It's what I think of as the basic pronunciation of life's activity. *Dying or doing something else.*"

After a while longer of sitting in the chill, we muscled through the next bottle as the language of our bodies agreed it was time to leave the outdoors to itself. And so, half-smart, we followed bread crumbs to the little slumped house in the near-woods, only to find a note taped to the outer pane of the front door, in Knox's script, which read that she'd given in, had given up on us and had decided to surrender her body to the imagined precept of night, urging itself into her to be obeyed. She'd had a recent run of fairly productive, carnal luck with some shamefully young collegians who'd stayed in town for the holidays to work, rather than return home momentarily to kiss mothers and salt old adolescent wounds with junkie pals in, who knows, St. Louis, Philadelphia, Flippin, Arkansas, or the Vatican. "Young" in this instance not only meant youth of mind, but also of body—one eighteen year-old in particular who'd even brought her lunch one afternoon at her studio job in Midtown, after an especially profuse evening of bourbon and orgasms. Another was a sound man for the Saenger Theater downtown, a man with yellowish teeth but confident smile, trout arms, fidgety energy, quasi-into-the-bad, an off-brand of intellect I thought was fully unrelated to the breathing brilliance of the penetrating world of Knox being, in her wanton lust, penetrated. I told Brody I hoped it wasn't him. He hoped it wasn't either of them. Adventure was deserving of the human attention, we agreed, shivering like idiot boys on the front step beneath antique gas lights humbly blazing behind glass, free in the cold of the future spider webs that would engulf the lights, soon, when the faux winter of Alabama's coast sauntered back, unloved, into the sea. But the human attention, first, needed to learn the valuable serendipity of adventure, and then, and only then could adventure, abstractly, sexually, fundamentally or in the raw be freed to touch the shoulder of a busy earthling of the night and put in its own special request to go insane.

Not knowing where I'd stay for the evening if she did in fact let her legs go agape, and artfully unconcerned about it, I keyed into the house to find it hadn't been locked. Again, associatively, I stumbled through the comparison of my old home with the current one as I pointed Brody toward a cabinet which housed a few light coats and long sleeve cotton shirts to cover us both as I looked through the refrigerator for a pair of beers hiding on the bottom shelf behind Knox's pan of asparagus lightly covered with the last of our foil. This is not an ordinary home, I thought, and then, why is it not? A deviation from the norm is vicissitude, yet also chance. But when an erstwhile norm is no longer the immediate, it becomes redefined against that which has replaced it. The guesthouse was someone else's norm until I became a part of it, and then for Knox, the norm evolved with my entry, even if temporary at first, as was my approach, too, evolutionary. And then when not permanence, but prolonged temporariness had ensued, when I decided to stay and not return to Azalea Street, our norms again changed to where we found ourselves performing semi-deceptive behaviors, like hiding the last beers behind the small foods that staid us. We found ourselves climbing over one another in the dark, two platonic bodies of such perdurable dark, cursing against the backdrop of our mock grievances with shaken equilibrium, and purpose for the future reassessed as not one, not two, but with Brody, three stunningly abrupt manifestations fortified by the power of not love, not the construct of forever, but just the vital and incontrovertible Now.

I tossed Brody a beer as he thanks-babied me across the room and returned to thumbing Knox's dusty vinyls beside a player in need of a new needle to bring us back to that small slip of memory where we had remembered collectively, and on our own, the real scratch of that authentic sound when we were children, when our parents were kind of blue or, at very least, still getting their ya-yas out. I was still somewhat engaged in what Brody and I had and had not said on the park table an hour earlier, ruminating hopefully with good reason on the loam of what was once my norm and what had become the newer version of it, in its better body. I'd heard a man talking on the phone outside the floral shop beside the wine store earlier, telling someone some kind of crucially important truth involving that which is ahead, that it can be accomplished, and if not at first, it is no sign of weakness, but rather, the need for building strength to face the necessary conditioning for growth. And from that, I was stuck on essence as I entered the bathroom and lifted the seat, while Brody asked aloud for the whereabouts of a record store that no longer existed in Mobile, one that could provide for us a needle and a mental vacation to the connective tissue of the past, with maybe different Laylas. I didn't have a computer, none of us did, and I'd been fending off an upgrade from my old word processor that was inevitably nearing retirement, but could still work, and even seemed to want to. And Brody, I only know he managed to get his manuscripts typed and sent off in the time before I knew him from his mentioning several infiltrations of the college's business school computer lab, armed with the student ID of a kid he half-resembled.

Was I thinking of the practice of life ahead, of reasonable health—the need for the exploration of multi-faceted questions, and what were they—was I concerned for crippling simplicity, the debatability of good and bad men, the importance of the present moment being the only thing truly owned, and was that quixotic, did I believe someone could convince me it was quixotic—was it the commitment of observation, being wowed by sensation, was it action and purpose with no specific desired result, was it that worry—was it what pain can teach or how long might be the peregrination from humanity to human morality before we potentially regress to our pre-ethical selves, was it goodness, tranquility, definitely the frustration at devolving language, boundless time and Unhappiness—was it challenging with ferocity the superfluous act, the duty of a person to endure, but then, how to define endurance, and then there was objectivity, subjectivity, still that lingering apprehension that the voice on the other end of these mental happenings would be complacent, apathetic, still out of my control, was it about patience with the self, was it pursuit and coming to wisdom—was I concerned with the machinations of destiny, did I feel plotted against or did I think someone could convince me I was plotted against—was I dying or doing something else or doing both, was it relief that I would suffer no more from bad behavior toward myself, was it the power in what we create to demonstrate our power, was it rebellion, dichotomy, motive motive motive in thought and action intertwined with pain and compassion—was I concerned with the pending letting go and accepting, easiness, difficulty and imagination, was it perspective and rebirth, of course it was, was it forgiveness and the end of the tether and the eradication of chagrin from being ignored, was it that marionettes were unaware of their strings and I'd discovered I at last had no strings—was I concerned with daring myself to dare myself, and where was death and the management of pleasure and the involvement with the soul, the soul's window, was it the Hand the Eye the Breath, was the self all-powerful on the road to peace, was it honor, and who could tell me of honor—was I concerned with common elements and getting to care for them like children as the elements themselves climbed in and out of the vast temperatures of strange hearts, was it fairness and fault—yes, I was pissing a long time—was it bearing the unjust and was it voluntary acceptance and was it forgiving others to dispense favor instead of the clean slate, was it ever a clean slate, was it resolution, was it just one fragile thing in the silly tiny sky that could make a difference in this exhaustive ground-run of finding light?

"We really need a needle for this thing," Brody repeated.

The answer is yes, I suddenly thought, and gave out a great laugh. All we need in the world, right now, is a needle.

So instead, per Brody's suggestion, we left a conciliatory note for Knox and then took his car to do something we didn't think we'd do that night. We heeded her voice and, drunk on a Saturday night, went out, saddled with notebooks, to procure myself a job at his restaurant, a campus hangout three miles west down Old Shell Road, in the opposite direction of the wine store and the struggling, hopeful Becca.

————

The young woman behind the bar was a petite, pale-skinned wild animal with large, beautiful and lustrous eyes, a tattoo sleeve from the top of her bare shoulder to the spare breathing inch above her elbow, dark dark reddish hair more the color of movie blood than the real, and she was half-leaning against the long metal beer coolers at the lambent trickle of light across her half-exposed waist line when we approached and climbed on to seats below an air conditioning vent and a television set to a channel on world surf. She was in mid-conversation with a heavyset bearded man, likely in his late thirties, who looked older from an improper balance of abuse and revival. His beard was red, his arms furry and meaty, thick-thumbed at the tips of his hands, a near-intimidating snarl on his face until you heard the two discussing something educational rather than egregious such as Libertarian this, my-favorite-gin that, and she looked past the man's shoulder on down to Brody first, then scanned my foreignness, and laughed while shaking her head at Brody.

"You have no idea how glad I am you're here." She turned to the burly fellow, Roger, he would soon become, "I mean, of course I'm glad you're here too, don't get me wrong." She batted her eyelashes at him playfully, and then waved her hand for us out in display of the bar itself, stretching neglected and unattended down past the soda machines to the other end of the restaurant. "I've had nobody all night long. Just me, Roger, and you know that douche bag who comes in with his wife, Brody, the one we think beats him? The doctor? He came for some togo, chugged three glasses of wine in less than ten minutes. Big fat fucking zero on the tipline."

"Ouch," Brody said.

Roger laughed. "I tried telling her I'd take care of her, but..."

"So I started drinking. I keep forgetting how slow Saturdays are here. But, honestly, am I not the least bit fucking charming?" She furrowed her brow in forced, fake self-doubt. "And I had to lie to the servers that we're out of this syrah so customers don't buy up what little is left for me tonight. I'm such a bitch." She laughed, and then, "Who's your friend?"

She broke from her crooked position to realign herself in front of us, placing two bar napkins down.

"Rattigan, Sonya. Sonya, Rattigan."

She waved a half-wave and continued to dry her hands on excess napkins she'd lifted along the way down to us.

"Oh...is this? Are you the one Brody's trying to get me to hire?"

"Probably so," I said, smiling. "I don't doubt he's made a fairly severe case for it."

"When is he not severe? You must know him pretty well. Nice to meet you." She said, grinning at Brody. "What are you guys drinking? We just changed the Sierra Nevada keg."

"Sounds ideal."

"Perfect."

As she poured two pints, Brody began straightening papers which dangled from inside and halfway outside a thick notebook he'd brought in, while I kept mine to my side until seeing him place it on the bar. Brody had told me Sonya was an abstract artist who got high on pick-your-chemical and designed unconventional pieces, like Howdy Doody being noose-hung in an old television, and lately, several of her husband's own paintings had been of her in the nude on a wooden cross. So having Brody as a different sort of artist, coming in and out of responsibility and accountability seemed a comfortable fit for the small sit-in pizza joint, known mostly for its immense beer menu and odd, interesting human marginalia that worked there to avoid any mistaken inclusion in the body of the outside world. Brody had brought several stories to light, already, about sitting naked on her front porch with her husband and a couple other employees after shutting down the store and drinking the profits, caravan-cruising the few miles to Airport Boulevard and the Pinehurst neighborhood behind a sofa store for various talks of most dire matter, much to the disappointment of neighbors walking their dogs in the early morning.

The staff size seemed limited for a weekend, with two others working in front and what appeared to be two in the open kitchen in front of the door as we'd walked in. Soon it would be revealed that there were others on the clock, not at work, per se, but on the clock, playing tag on cigarette breaks out back while others took turns walking down the short hill to a dive bar at the corner of a university strip mall to buy discounted liquor shots to bring back up to appease the employees who felt and exhibited feigned disdain at the night of work which seemed to preclude their premature forays into the downtown Saturday hours. But the party, it became evident, would nonetheless persist there.

"Thanks very much," I said, as she set down our beers.

"Thanks, babe," Brody said.

"You got it. I'm actually about to start smoking on this side if it stays this dead. Will that bother you, handsome?" She asked me. I shook my head as Brody set his pack on the bar beside his beer and she reached for her glass of wine, which hid below the counter. She climbed into a tucked-knee crouch on the cooler again after glancing over her fine-china shoulder at Roger's half-full pint, and then back to a quick study of me. "I don't think Brody has any ugly friends. Sorry." She grinned and shrugged. "So what are you doing right now?"

She draped her arm over my notebook.

"My bad," Sonya said, lifting her arm. "He told me you're a writer, too. What are you guys up to tonight?"

"No worries."

"This is it, lady," Brody began. "Came to read over some new bits, and bring your beautiful body some love borne of what productive members of society might call laziness." He grinned and sipped his beer as she smiled. "But we did hit that wine store near McGregor earlier and took it to the park. Just kinda whacked out a bit. The weather wasn't too bad for being out."

"You liar," I said.

"No shit. It's too cold," she said. "But I get cold easily. I'm all skin and bones. Besides these guns." She lifted her tiny, gaunt arms and flexed and followed it with a laugh, a shrug and a sip of wine. "But that sounds like a better day than I had."

"What did you do?" Brody asked.

"You're gonna think I'm crazy. Well, I guess I *am* crazy. Sorry, Rattigan. No, I take it back. If you're friends with this guy, I doubt I can shock you. But just so you know, if I hire you that means I'm your daddy, which means I can be as offensive as I want."

"Sounds exciting."

"What is?"

"To have a girl as a daddy."

She one-eyed me for a second, smiled and continued.

"So I get off last night. I don't know if you realized how shit-housed I was, Brody."

"I could tell," Roger said.

"You could? Fuck, I'm a lush. Anyway," she kept on, turning down the television with a remote control near my glass. "So I decide I want to bathe all three of my dogs after not going straight home like a smart person, but after leaving Stan's brother's bar across the street, you guessed it, at four in the morning. And Derek had to get up for work at six, right? Because he's been pulling these ridiculous ten hour days. So we get in this HUGE fight because I apparently decided to try to straddle him with all this dog shampoo and water all over me, and he was half-asleep, had no fucking clue what was going on. So I told him I wanted a divorce. I'm not kidding at all, guys. I'm sucking at life at this point. And then I thought it would be a good idea to pass out on the rug in my bathroom so he'd have to talk to me before he left for work."

"Nice," I said.

"That's wild, man. What happened this morning?" Brody asked.

"I guess he just stepped over my snoring ass and got ready and went to work. So when I finally got off the floor around ten, I realized for the most part what happened and spent the day cleaning up the house, making this avocado spread he likes, trying too late to be the "good wife," worrying if I threw anything at his head like our last fight."

Roger laughed. Brody, too, while lightly slapping the bar top.

"So the point is, well, I didn't really have a terrible day," she said, a grin preceding another laugh. "Since that's a pretty standard day at my house. Maybe I'm just exhausted from all the guesswork, if I was going to be married or not by the end of the week."

"Have you talked to him today?" Brody asked as she looked left and right, then past our shoulders and shrugged, lit a cigarette and placed it in an ashtray on the bar.

"Yeah, he's stoned right now. I told him I love him and if he comes up I'll pay for his beer. Still want a job?" She asked me.

I laughed.

"I think definitely," I said, nodding my head and smiling. "I'm seeing what I've missed out on."

"What is it that you do? Have you told me?"

"No."

"Right. I think I have ADHD. Or maybe it's the pills," she said, resting her hand palm up on Brody's wrist, dipping her nose into the top of his beer. "I don't see how you can drink an entire one of those. It's too strong a taste for me."

"I used to work at the paper."

"Oh, ok. Doing what?"

"I did some features when I got lucky, but mostly stuck to my byline in metro. It was all right."

"It was eating his soul," Brody interjected before throwing an arm over my shoulders.

"I can't do a nine to five, man," Sonya said, shaking her head.

"I've never done it," Roger added. "I bounced at bars a few years, and then got turned on to this tree service company. I make my own schedule. I don't think I could handle regular hours."

"It wasn't really like that," I said.

"No way, man," Sonya said, eyes suddenly terrified. "I can barely make it here on time with these later shifts. I have no idea why Brad hasn't fired me yet. Been here four years though. So who knows?"

"I've worked in a restaurant before," I told her.

"Oh, who gives a shit?" The phone rang. "Great. *Now* it starts. Just when I've surrendered all motivation to do anything," she said slowly, melodramatically, sliding off the cooler and walking to the phone by a beer cooler on the counter. The heater turned on fairly high and woke me up at the bar's edge with its intrusive blast, and Brody took Sonya's direction toward the taps and brought both our glasses around the bar with him and refilled them, as Sonya made a give-me-a-break face about the person on the phone.

"This place..." Brody said as he returned to our side of the bar. "...is exactly what you need, Rattigan. I'm not *trying* to tell you about your need. I'm *telling* you. It's good for getting out of your head, make decent money, pretty much come and go as you want. I just pick-up when I'm getting low on cash. And it's five seconds from your new digs. Are you in, babe?" He asked, rocking me back and forth in my seat as I began to laugh. "Say yes. It's the only real answer. Say *yes*, Rattigan. *Say* it."

"Absolutely, man. But you had to know I'd be down before we even got here."

"I love this guy," he said and kissed the top of my head. "Love this guy," he said to Roger, and then we all leaned in to touch glasses in the dim light of the small bar as Sonya massaged a middle finger against the receiver of the phone.

Hours later the final customers left, a pair of mid-forties gentlemen who, as the story would be revealed, were well-off lawyers in town, but members of a radically conservative church—Baptist, I think—but conservative enough so that they always came in well after the dinner rush and sat in the north side dark of the restaurant and drank the freshest taps out of tall, red plastic iced tea cups. Once they waved goodnight about ten minutes after eleven, closing time, acknowledging even the kitchen guys by name, I ascertained a couple more things about the new job that was and was not quite mine. Primarily, it would be unlike the former restaurant at which I'd worked in college, for inarguably evident reasons, but most captivating in my quick assessment during the mounting laughter at the bar, as the full staff had set down their brooms and paperwork and grill cleaner bottles to put Sonya to work at the taps for shift drinks, was the unconventional family-by-design that was not restricted to just employees, but the respectful and therefore respectable financially successful men that came there to break free, if even temporarily, from the bondage of traditional behavior's choke.

And then there were the stories, the sublime cacophony of voices well off their throats' tethers. I grew only momentarily curious if I were entering the situation for reprieve from previously withheld wants. But I recognized that of course, that had to have been part of it. It almost needed to be. And then the rest came, that I wanted to connect with Brody's energy and language, as much as I could, as suddenly over the last few weeks, the comprehension had set in, or had been as fully embraced as much as anything may be fully *anything*, that life was and is and will be fleeting. Maybe not indefinitely, but for as long as time seemed lengthy and too extended in all directions to lasso and contain, I wanted to be a part of some other real and unbridled roar until I had managed a generation of my own. And I could already feel the rumble. But as it seemed in the transition between one version of the self to the next, I supposed that night that an awareness of the transmogrification was all that was necessary, and then patience, and then maybe just one eye open to view its coming on.

The entire count on the Saturday staff was seven, down one girl out front who'd had what seemed a typical non-emergency about a lover, with Sonya the on-duty manager behind the bar, Mason, a short and stocky motorcycle riding boxer with an irrepressibly sweet disposition and an exorbitant marijuana habit that didn't seem to affect his work serving tables. The other server, Kathy, a naive young beauty who laughed comfortably at herself and never turned down an invitation to a party, and then the few in back—Mica, the one responsible for the surfing on the television out front, as he'd often peek a free eye out from the shadows behind the stacked white dough trays, between where I was sitting and the open area before the office, to watch a few clips. And then Blain, a tall, multi-piercing, bearded anthropology graduate who spoke in slow, carefully-considered sentences, always sharp and relevant, always interesting and said with a smile, a guy I immediately hit it off with intellectually. There was the dishwasher, Rigg, a self-proclaimed DJ from the clubs in Pensacola, an hour away, who had a ruddy face and elfish grin but good energy, a bit of a twitchy chain-smoker. And then a boisterous, engaging creature named Dawn, furiously quick with sound laughter and a very confident tactility, a graduate student in philosophy at campus across the street, ever laden with a bandana like

Brody, and a good drinker, I'd soon discover. And with the exception of the one gay chap and one lesbian, both of whom were off that first night of my eventual acceptance, and apart from those married few, and strangely excluding Brody, a sort of in-screwing was occurring and had become so much a spectacle that it, when brought to my attention, had become laughable and almost laudable in its wild spiral off the tether, a sort of key party without keys, a sexual fusion that all but guaranteed future chaos.

Then the doors were locked, ashtrays were out on the two large tables across from the bar, Sonya's sedated husband and his tattoo shop mentor were seated at the bar, smoke filled our entire occupation, and Brody and I had been coerced with little difficulty after a day of drinks to climb atop the bar stools, after they'd been dragged into the center of the aisle, and deliver an impromptu reading of that which we'd carried in beneath our arms. *These are good people,* Brody had whispered to me at their first request. He told me since he'd gotten the novel published with a small press in New England, friends at work had rallied more behind his other efforts as well as the bizarre, almost secretive novel he'd told me about that was still being tossed about in New York, a book I had not yet read but wanted to, deeply and emphatically, though I was apprehensive about the sale of my curiosity toward it to him for two reasons—I was afraid I would love it and emulate its style if that, in fact, was what would work to assist my engagement in the publishing world. But I still needed to learn what it was I was doing on my own pages. And also, I was afraid I would enjoy it so much I'd begin to value Brody less, which meant I still knew too little about my own powers. It never occurred to me once that it could fall short of what I had suspected of his abilities, not after this cherry-breaking night at the summit of the bar stool mountain.

———

"Chicago hotel rooftop," Brody began, having first warned everyone, for which I was thankful, that what we'd brought was a pair of collections of rough and unedited scribblings, still in need of voice and clarity which, if I remember correctly, in psychology, that kind of disclaimer was called handicapping. Lowering the expectations bar. But I didn't give a shit. I just didn't want to be awful in front of strangers—but I had Brody's energy, and mine. "...we lay on a thin ply board, nailing..."

"Oh, shit," Mason laughed into his cigarette.

"...the wind was apparent and her name was Norah, from Charleston, I wished to move there, in her throughout and then after, downstairs through the cracked light from inside the cupped-palm moon to the washtub filled with beer, into our musicspeak, the sidewalk woman with lesions on her tongue, babies to feed, out shaking hands for milk, and I found her, in Carolina, with a letter the next year, and how a good lay stays in the mind, but was it good, oil, sand beneath sandals, one dangling unused off a splinter of the groaning wooden corner, two quiet thieves of learning hearts heaving toward the park, the cab ride and us, almost headless by the greased yellow hinge that coughed us toward the dark to walk..."

"Yeah!" A few shouted. Mica raised his pint. Derek clapped a hand on the bar and lit a smoke.

"The bottom of the rose cap," I started, "smells like dried fruit..."

"You and dead fruit, man," Brody whispered.

"He said *dried* fruit, asshole." Dawn yelled.

"...my back aches, the woman at the market says I still look like I'm in college,

I said Double Bag Me, Won't You?"

Good laughter from the wall.

"Me in your service, the kind eye above your collar...Mother taught me to talk to everyone, even home asleep smelling smelling salts of the petal, the gift of water and the vase, I think the warmth in me does not die, I think it was the Bible telling me so..."

"Not to punish the young thing, only twenty, hates her body, feeding it tin cans,

longing for touch, the hunger that is killing her, killing the spirit of growing up and strong..." Brody sipped his beer and wiped his lips. Our heads were ten feet in the air. "...I want to ask if she cartooned as a girl or believed in the power of spinach..."

Sonya dropped her head to the bar and smiled widely. I laughed, too, almost fell off the stool. The ground looked hard and far away.

"...or believed in her mother's love..." He kept on. "But she spends too much time getting dumped on the phone to take on my silliness, declaring that she listens, but how can she with such loud, exhaustive tears...a Buddhist, tonight..."

Mason, I heard Dawn say and watched her rub his shaved head.

"...told me she broke down before the new schedule at work, posted on the wailing wall like a shifted brick, a hanging vine..."

"When was this? Do I suck that bad at making the schedule?" Sonya asked across the bar, clutching invisible pearls, and even Brody laughed before going on.

"She did it to herself...the vine is not to blame for being a vine, nor the mortar or clay or crusted rock to slide amidst a quake...he smiled but didn't say much..." Brody was blindly pointing in Mason's direction.

"...and paranoid me, I felt judged..."

Everyone laughed. Rigg was behind me in a shadow, a cigarette close to his smiling mouth.

"...like he knew I'd tested her weeks before as she plotted in silence against me...I said go your way and seethe, it will eat you like cola or cancer...the Buddhist knows this...if he cries it is for maybe the brick, the drooping, prickly vine, the ocean crossing the face of the sad...that's what this whole thing is, really..."

"Is he talking about my roommate?" Kathy asked, whose roommate was a girl who'd recently been fired for an attitude not conducive to the nature of the controlled Stone apathy. Brody grinned and people kept with laughter in the smoke.

"...the big, sad ocean's canvas, painted immobile on a pre-woman's cheek...sometimes it moves, sometimes it drowns her other parts, breast, vagina, the tattoo not yet inked on her toe..."

"That's totally my roommate!"

"Like a wet, hatched duckling he lay on the floor...matted hair from a shower, shaking and nude, a blackout drunk at twenty-five..." I began as Brody pivoted slightly toward me on the thin cushion of his bar seat. "...someone had hit him as child or maybe poverty had put him there..."

"Or maybe he went through Sonya's pill bag," Blain added through a cloud. Even I choked and laughed with a look over to Sonya who had shrugged and nodded affirmatively. Brody passed a cigarette across the thin ravine between us in the stratosphere.

"...could see the ground through the bathroom...tucked into himself, not used to light, I stepped over him to piss..."

"You're a jerk," Sonya giggled.

"...this was how I came home when I lived with John, sometimes leaned to one side, his face tear-soaked, in just underwear, soliciting the barely legal on the phone,

never spilling his whiskey...the spare room given me before I went mad, took a shower with a stranger, or after thrown in jail in college, lying drunk on the floor beneath the bent shadow of an inmate dick..."

"Holy shit."

"That's disgusting."

"You can't know, guys," I said, laughing, "I'll explain later... *anyway*...'like the creatures of my future home, one of consequence and reminder, I stepped again over his soaked bird body, not thinking something wasn't right, this was not normal at all..."

"Hell, yeah."

"That was fucked up."

"Part of me says we have already met..." Brody didn't miss a beat. "An obese conference man, eyes growing at my wine gulp, tea tree chapbook from Chris, a lingering index finger, this is all shit I wanted to tell him, but I couldn't say just to tell him to leave his tongue in his own mouth..."

"Whoa, wait a minute LaCoste," Sonya interrupted. "Did you *french* a dude?"

"No baby, but he was aiming toward it."

"That's awesome," Dawn belted across the tiles.

"He wasn't my type," Brody winked and laughed and bent to stub his cigarette in a nearby ashtray. "But this really happened...'and in the picture of Andre somehow they converged into one, nodding at Robert and his tagalong trick, consummate smiler from a suicide college in Texas, Andre and his mackerel arm draped across the serving tray, but Chris sagging from the chair..."

"Ew," Kathy said, and then snorted.

"...both with tilted black hat, squinty eyes, losing the fight of differentiation between analytical gaze and one of desire..."

"Nice," I said.

"Nicely done," Mason added.

"...I'd met thinner versions of them all, hanging from terraces, starved toward the earth..."

"Right on!"

"...a cat I once found on the ditch side of a fence..."

"Huh?"

"...younger, it had been a marvel, the maggots at work, the bloated exposed tongue, not something someone had loved, but loved incorrectly to its demise, just a stiff memory unmoved on rusted chain..."

"I'm gonna puke..." Kathy said.

"Are you fucking kidding me?" Dawn asked her before thumping her arm.

"...it was no horror at all, not until I grew to a man and first talked about it..."

"So *now* he's grown up?" Blain asked the overhanging lamp above the table where he'd sat.

"...these days I might vomit at the sight..."

"Thank you!" Kathy inserted.

"...I look at the dead animal in everyone now..."

"Damn, Brody," I said, as he folded down the page and grinned at me.

"That's the line, man," Mason said.

"...the thick middle finger, unfurled into a Fuck You when I say with my eyes I don't care for tea tree poems, dry heat coitus or the longhorn, the heavy lip of Andre in any body who tells me one thing, as if I can't detect the other..."

Everybody had swollen into the night, a woman's womb rising up from inside itself to assume custody of the air before it. Life was good, life was very, very good. Scattered applause broke out as a few passed empty pint glasses over the bar to Sonya.

"I hope for your sake, LaCoste, you're not knocking fat queens. My brother's one," Sonya said, looking up the skyscraper facade of Brody's pant leg and then giggling.

"No baby, not at all," he answered as Derek looked up from his wife to Brody and smiled. "I just felt lied to about his motive is all. I love everybody. Right, Mason?"

"Peace, brother," Mason nodded from the table. Blain had a heavy forearm rested on top of Mason's head.

Brody turned to me and held out his arms and mouthed, *save me, babe.* So I flipped a few pages to something out of a dream from weeks earlier.

"All right," I said, "I'll go gay with Brody." Everybody clapped and a few raised their glasses. "Tentatively this is called 'portrait of me as untouched girl.'"

"Nice," Brody said, nodding his head as he dipped down to bring a full beer back up from Sonya's extended hand.

"It's from this vision I had of being one with my sister, but kind of in a historical sense, and it was really hazy...anyway...'from here she looks like a ghost, but maybe she was painted that way, to look like coming fear, brushing on her heels the top of that boudoir, stretching over its roof, its belly if supine...she looks insane...straw-haired girl, some kind of woman, late in the morning, one shoe...my first thought is to hurt her...I want to hurt you, I keep thinking, before I understand what I mean...I want her to stop what she's doing because it is hurting her...you love more to compete with love, and so with pain...but I catch myself, so I am not that human...no one has to die...I can remember she's only a child, still talks to her mother in baby voice...reversed role now, but still the airplane entering the hangar...still the allegiance and half-words dribbling down the chin."

I realized I was gone, because I hadn't noticed the silence until I stopped reading, and suddenly there in my mouth after recognizing the tone of the piece I wanted to apologize for the violent one-eighty, but then Brody spoke up and brought me to the truth of what was occurring.

"Ain't no way I'm following that," he said, shook an open palm down at the floor and slid down the chair to the ground. And then there was small laughter and everyone began to clap. I quickly became nervous enough to shrink from my elevation and the unexpected attention and I dropped down as nimbly as I could to the floor.

"How was that gay, Rattigan?"

"That was intense."

"The *title*, jackass. Did you *listen* to him?"

"Right on."

"I'll touch him."

"Pervert."

"Are you kidding me?" Sonya asked me as she stepped around the bar. "I got spun out with that, man." And then she punched at my ribs. "I thought you assholes were going to be playful."

Brody was at my side with his beer and a smile.

"They're just notes," he said.

"Yeah, half of what's in here..." I said, shaking my closed notebook. "...I can't even tell you what condition I was in when most of this stuff was written."

"Well," she said, one-eyeing me again as Blain clapped my back and maneuvered to my right, lit a smoke and set it on one side of the ashtray beside Sonya's empty tip cup. "Lushes are welcome here. But that surprised the shit out of me. Not that you're good. That doesn't surprise me. Not that I know you. Do you know what the hell I'm trying to say?" She asked, dropping an elbow into a wrist, inhaling from her cigarette and lightly shaking her head at me.

"I definitely do," I said, grinning. My face was a little red, not from the honesty or the seriousness of the scratch notes that had somehow, suddenly become something on the oddest stage of my young life, the most welcoming stage, but the accident that had happened, and then the survival of it, and the reception. I thought of Knox in some strange youth's bed, strange because he would not be Brody or me or moments like the concurrent one, and I wanted to un-thrust him from inside her and pluck her from the sheets and enter her into this scene of pregnant blue light. But with the stage deconstructing itself to a wide, Socratic drinking hour, with the inquisitive blending in with the additionally inquisitive from the tables across the bar, and all of our bodies becoming a concoction of other bodies, I gave up on her invisibility as I stood firm behind my smile at strangers, thinking again that something definitely was happening. But without her our powers felt reduced, and so, individual power would have to prevail until I collapsed again on the rocky ocean of our shared bed.

Before we'd eventually leave well past midnight, I grew to know with immense fondness the crew with which I'd soon be working. Sonya had made her way toward me in the swath of giggling skeletons, telling me to call her by Sunday night before she'd finalized the week's schedule to post Monday morning. Training, she said, would last a day and night to learn the computer system, guaranteed to be easy, she told me to my relief, as

I'd managed to swim through college without even knowing how to do something—I'd eventually admit to myself at the newspaper—as simple as a slideshow presentation. And apart from basic word processing programs I'd used for various classes while at university, if it wasn't as simple as the processor I had and worked on at home, my mouth was agape and stupefied at the prospect of convenience in the developing world that just might, I feared, cripple any creative process I was, like the digital world itself was, speedily trying to nurture. But there were no other worries—I'd be paid and fed during training, and drinks were on the house. Eventually I would meet Brad Baker if, she said, I felt like getting up around eight o'clock to stop by and introduce myself as he opened the restaurant each morning. And *then* things would at last be properly connected, would be set in the motion I think Brody sensed would transpire from the first time we sat and stared each other down over coffee, in the wake of Margaret and marriage and the wild, flapping bird wings of someone's damaged little love. Winter had already climaxed, the warm weather would soon come, had already managed a minor entry into the sporadic chill of the southern winter, but the world at the moment was truthfully, madly ablaze.

"You can crash at my place if Knox is tending to her..." Brody started as he slowed the car to a sharp turning speed.

"Animalistic desires."

"It's good she's letting loose, though. It'll only help her work once she rids herself of this thesis business and picks up a pen again," Brody said as he turned us into my neighborhood and pulled up to the house.

I sat forward in my seat to scan the driveway for an unfamiliar car. Nothing out of the ordinary. "Wait. You have a place?"

"Yeah, babe. What was the confusion?" He asked, beginning to laugh.

"I have no idea, man. For some reason I was under the impression a while back, maybe from Knox, who knows, that you just had crash pads all over town. Like you were a flight attendant or something."

"Nah, man. You should come by some time. It's this completely microscopic mouse hole in this larger house in Midtown, off Mohawk, by the train track pretty much due north of that antique store at the Loop. I have a little fire pit outside the steps I fill up some times, sit out and pretend to play the harmonica when I can't sleep, or I'm high on a good set of pages

I've been working. Really do come by, man. I think I broke the bathroom door. It might have been subconscious."

He put the car in park behind mine.

"Besides, why would *you* want something that functions normally? But yeah, let's get Knox involved and do up a night this week," I said, punching his leg and climbing out of the car.

"Give me a call."

I waved and began to step away from the car, but returned to the passenger window as Brody started reversing out of the drive. He reached over and rolled down the window.

"What about your phone, LaCoste? I'm pretty sure it's still inside somewhere. I don't have a number to reach you."

He grinned.

"I don't think I could call myself human with that device glued to my face all the time. And come on, man. It's not like we're going to be strangers."

"You're right, you're right."

"Great night, Rattigan. I think we're on to something really good. Be well. Give Knox love."

"But what about your phone?"

"See you soon, babe."

I laughed.

"Ok, ok. Loud and clear. Good night, man."

One light was on in the house as I let myself through the perpetually unlocked door, and Knox was sprawled on the bed with a glass of wine on the highest part of the headboard as she held a book against her stomach, a book she set down as I entered.

"Hey you," she yawned.

"I'm surprised you're home, man," I said, setting my notebook beside the dead apple and kicking my shoes toward the base of the tall book shelf beside the door. "I thought you were going out."

I took off the long sleeve I was wearing and dropped it in the corner of my side of the room and crumbled on to my half of the bed.

"I did go out to that bar behind Brody's job. Shit, I can't even remember what it's called. Total dive. It's the only place the kid can get in."

"You took your son out for cocktails. That's cute."

"Fuck you."

"How old is he again?"

"Eighteen, asshole. You know, I know, *everybody* knows he's eighteen."

"How does his fake ID look?" I asked, rolling over toward her and sipping from her wine glass.

"It was actually all right, you know? Nothing too crazy going on because of Dauphin Street having so many bands tonight. But I got a headache from him talking about some type of fantasy sport something-or-another, and when I asked him what the hell he was talking about he started defending it like you or I would Gandhi's position on peaceful resistance. It was pretty sad."

She shook her head as I flipped to my back and exhaled to the ceiling.

"I mean, we're not that much older than this batch of kids coming in nowadays, but I swear it feels like we talk a completely different language."

"We do talk a different language."

"I'm talking about how we communicate, Rattigan." She hit my arm. "You know what I mean. What do I really need to do to get back the young lay these days? Is it some sort of sick sign from the universe that I need to start going to martini bars instead of college shitholes? I don't like what Fate's got in store, man." She was still shaking her head as I turned toward her and the incredulous look on her face.

"I think it means either you sell out and learn their language, or stick to your sense of intellectual constitution and observe as they crash and burn. You can't save these kids from what they're walking into."

We were quiet a while before she asked about the night.

"It was good, babe. I'm kind of high. They gave me a job. I don't even think they need me, but they gave me a job." I exhaled again, my body sated, mind well-fed, my every fiber thankful for the availability of the bed. "And we need to go to Brody's one night this week to read. He wants to build a fire. Did you know he has an apartment?"

"It's probably all that charisma of yours. And where did you think he slept? His car?"

"That's funny stuff. I just thought he shacked up a lot. What are you reading?"

"What I'm doing is not reading Kundera. It's more like I'm holding it in my hand like a dog with a dead gopher in its mouth."

"That's exactly what I want in my head before sleep."

"Why is the restaurant called The Baker's Stone?"

"Owner's last name is Baker, and apparently they cook the pies on a hot stone or something."

"That's not very clever."

"Forgivable kitsch."

"They have good spinach salads there. Tomorrow I might..."

"What were you saying about the book?"

"Hmm? Oh, I've read it before. I think I'm avoiding being frustrated at leaving Matt at the bar instead of just eating shit and bringing him home. Just allow the mid-coital talks of touchdowns or homeruns. The book's just my way of convincing myself I'm not sitting here drinking alone."

"You were."

"Shut up."

"But you're not anymore. Daddy's back."

"What's with this daddy shit? I heard you say it at breakfast the other night out."

"I have no idea."

"It's creepy."

"I'm a horrible person."

She sighed.

"Maybe, Rattigan, I'm just getting old."

"Nah, babe. You're being yourself. Although I'm sure the next thrill ride you bring home will just be getting his learner's permit, so it should balance out." I rolled to my side and closed my eyes before she kidney-punched me. "We have messages," I said, looking at the blinking light on her machine which barely protruded from beneath a white blouse halfway draped over a wicker basket filled with magazines and sunglasses.

"I haven't checked them. They might be him."

"Pining over his gone mistress. I can't blame him, Knox. Knox the Fox."

"Please go to sleep."

I heard her throat process the last of the wine from her glass.

"I'm on my way," I said, my mouth sandwiched into the pillow.

She turned off the tall standing lamp on her side.

"Night, Rattigan."

"Dream important dreams."

A quiet minute passed in the pre-sleep air.

"Some little girl was blowing up Brody's phone ever since I got home. I turned it off and threw it under the bed," she said to the dark.

I fell asleep smiling.

The next morning Knox had beaten me to wakefulness, moving around the house quietly and in casual motion, which I could sense from the tiny seismic pulsations from the floor each step she took in our wafer-sized home as I edged away from sleep. She was sitting at the corner desk where I usually wrote, and she was flipping through the book she'd been reading and not reading the night before, as though rest had not secured her a place in the emotional suffrage she'd endured at the hands of her libido's imagination, as if young Matt could have freed that oppression of the night's curse on her body—or maybe none of that. I was half-asleep and watching her shake her head at the pages, convoluting her neck to a U-turn in the road from myself to her, her neck barely exposed behind the fall of her morning hair. I whispered *good morning* across the room.

"I'm glad you're up," she said, spinning in the nearly broken swivel chair and planting her bare feet on the small carpet beneath her, leaning forward with the book tightly gripped.

"I'm not really," I said, looking around the room for whatever it is confused eyes seek when letting go of a dreamless, deep entanglement with the previous night.

"It isn't that I don't grasp what's happening here," she said, shaking the book. "And if you ever pick this up after me you'll see I've underlined all of what I consider to be the goods. But what bothers me, firstly, is…"

"Am I smelling coffee?"

"What?"

"Be my senses for a minute. Can you tell from there?" I asked, sitting up and smiling, eyes half-open.

"Yeah, it's almost a pot. Want some?"

"Nope," I said, shaking my head. "I just want to smell it right now."

She looked at me and my half-eyes and softly laughed.

"Sorry, man. Good morning."

"Go ahead. I'm listening."

"You sure?"

"I'm not like you when I wake up. Go ahead."

"That's pretty funny."

I smiled and said nothing.

"Ok, so what bothers me is that I want too much out of this book. I want too much out of myself reading it, I guess. I mean, it would be great to *just* be a story of their relationship, or *just* a story of changing political systems, but both? I'm doing too many comparisons to those themes in a modern context."

"It's ok to do that."

"You think so?"

"It means you're flexing your mind to understand cycles in history, maybe at both group and individual levels."

"Well, what I'm thinking is, is it *that* worth the concern? Can't I just enjoy a fucking *novel*? But an interesting thought's been swimming in my head this morning, and so I wonder if maybe what's going on politically these days is affecting a broad range of relationships."

"Are you saying the government affects how we love?"

"Maybe. At least how we treat one another, yeah. As though when things seem personally destitute, we take it out on others, even people we love. Or *especially* them. Not that that's what I'm getting from the book. But the meaning seems wholly different when you take the same theme and, I don't know, change time and geography."

I sighed.

"Don't sweat it, Knox. That book's a mask anyway," I said, stretching my arms out in front of my body, fingers linked, palms out.

"What do you mean?" She stood and walked over to the kitchen. "Hey, I've got English muffins ready to toast, and some jelly out. Was thinking about egg white omelets. They'll be small because we're almost out of eggs. So maybe not really an omelet. We're almost out of English muffins, too. But of course they'll be the same size. This book is spinning me out of control."

"I think it's *you*, babe. Do you work today? What's today?"

"Not usually on Sundays. I don't even know our hours on Sundays."

"How long have you worked there?"

"What did you mean by mask?"

"Hm?" I asked, standing from bed and stretching again. "Oh, I think he was using those characters to talk more about the historical situation in his country, and to talk his philosophy of the body and what he feels is associated with the mind throughout our carnal processes. It probably wasn't his intention to look this far ahead and assume we'd all get pissed at the White House and stop fucking."

"Rattigan, that wasn't what I was say…"

"But I think it's well done. Don't get me wrong. It took me a while to commit to it, but when I finally did I enjoyed it. I certainly didn't take it to the extreme you…"

"Should I put a little basil in these eggs, babe?" She interrupted.

I pressed play on her answering machine, hovering over what would inevitably be a young man's pleading to be treated like a boy in the den of an experienced lioness, a prowling poet woman with talons for a heart. He would be begging through the night for continued education.

"I like the idea of basil in everything," she said to herself as a voice crept up and outward from the player.

"Peter, this is your mother. I don't know how else to say this, since you're not answering your cell, and apparently you've made a few life changes without telling your family. I see you've moved out of your house, and when I called your boss, Richard, or *former* boss, I should say…and I can't begin to imagine what that is about…he had this number from your contacts. He seemed…well, *regardless* of what happened, it does pain me to tell you like this, as I'm sure deep down you really do care about your family…but your grandfather died yesterday. Yesterday being Friday. Lord knows when you'll get this. *If* you'll get this." She sighed. "And everybody was there. Even Carrie Anne is in from Alaska. She asked about you."

There was a long pause on the machine. Knox stood beside me with a plastic spatula in her hand, staring down with me at the speaker.

"I didn't know what to tell her. Or your sister. She's disappointed in you. You can't, just this once…well, anyway. We have to bury him quickly, so his funeral is Monday. He's being buried next to Nana, same place in Magnolia Springs. Everything starts at eleven in the morning. The music's already picked out. I expect you there."

There was a click and then the message ended as Knox turned to study my face.

"Shit, Rattigan. Are you…what can I do?"

I ran my fingers through my hair and blinked a few times before putting my arms around her.

"Get a new answering machine with time limits," I said, smiling at her once we'd pulled apart. "She'll talk forever."

"I'm serious."

"She calls me Peter. Pretty silly of her to be so usual with her sternness." I said, still smiling as I sat back on the bed. "You know my grandfather's name was Dick? My old boss, Papa and me. We're all penises."

Knox shook her head and tried to return a smile. I felt awkward for her.

"Do you need me to do anything?"

"I don't know," I finally said to the sound of eggs popping in excessive, invisible heat across the house. "If you could tell Brody. So he can tell work."

"Of course I can."

"And then, who knows? I guess I'll…I guess I'll see you in a couple days."

She nodded, her lips turning downward.

"*Man*," I said, propping up on my elbows. "I thought I wasn't tired just a minute ago. But suddenly I'm exhausted."

CHAPTER 5

I had four suits, gray and navy and black and brown, all post-graduation gifts, or more accurately, four nonverbal, maternal suggestions that I go do what I eventually would, get a real job and comb my hair in a style that said, *Yes, I am the straight man's son*, only to be taken to task by the animal. But the suits were in storage with the rest of a sorrowful pile of goods that, if they were to anthropomorphize and invite me to a sit-down, would berate me over my neglectful manners and etiquette. These faithful, inanimate objects would glower at me, as if to say they had been committed to our strange world together, them the sheath and I the sword, the house master, the confused and self-abasing man who talked to himself in the late hours, in a coffee cup or bottle of Zin, a man who pulled his short hair and did knuckle push-ups on the wooden floor of his bedroom when drunk and flustered and running out of ideas. And I owed these objects something, I thought, as I flung the thin tin storage door to the ceiling and began skimming through and over the small sofa, the book shelf, the smashed television boxes filled with old collector's cards, trophies, drunken haiku notebooks from when in Mexico, pictures of friends who had gone on and done from the onset of post-adolescent life exactly what they said they would do. What I owed my belongings was a toss in the street. Someone I revered was dead, without explanation, and I was bleary-eyed, very much in the mood for renaissance, even if it involved a complete disregard of those reliable, tested goods without voice.

I muscled through the bits of bed frames and tied plastic bags of screws and nuts and bolts, almost tripping over them and falling into the hanging cart of my coats and slacks and leathers and vintage handovers, the latter mostly following the deaths of grandfathers who'd once belonged to friends who no longer belonged to me. I slipped out of my jeans and into black pin stripes and threw the same style coat over a gray t-shirt I'd worn in. I decided to stay in sandals, even though it was still undeniably cold, until making it across the bay to Magnolia Springs, past where I'd eaten lunch with Jerry in Fairhope, twenty minutes from Gulf Shores and the water. A storm had swept to the west of us a couple days earlier, but Mobile was still getting slight winds from it, and I imagined a procession of my family's cars, the cell phone commentaries, the waving on the highway when playfully passing, the poorly masked fear of smiling on such a day. I was thankful for the exclusion, for the distance and the voice machine.

At first glance when leaving home on the way to locate my suit, I thought it was going to rain. I grimaced not as much at the sky as I did the cliché of funeral-day rain, a day of rediscovered mortality made more gravitational and imperfect by the infrequency of those doing the discovering. But once cutting through town to the major interstate entry off Airport Boulevard, I saw a significant amount of sun poking through the long gray and white clouds stacked on top of each other over Dog River and Dauphin Island, and then the Caribbean past. I stopped at a gas station for smokes, deciding that since it was early I'd stop by a friend's house off Montauk in Midtown, maybe stir her into a coffee and some fortifying talk before the trip over. She was a former co-worker from the restaurant at which I worked during college, a girl who'd been around for the manic moments of my indecisions and capitulations, a girl who shared a lot of good energy with me, a girl who knew my family and would have cursed me for not telling her about Papa. But the front door to her complex was locked, and since it was just at sun-up and no one was remotely present on the pre-bustle streets, I concluded from the unmovable antique knob that it was best I be alone, rather than continue to fill all my available solitary moments with static and distraction. This was the same thing I'd sought to accomplish by relinquishing the cell phone, but I forgot, until that locked door, how capable the mind is of becoming its own disruptive machinery. I lit a cigarette and headed east on Government toward Water Street, through a morning just deciding whether or not to begin itself, beneath the overarching oaks on the edges of homes in the Historic District, past the opening farmer's market off Joachim Street, a few theatres. I couldn't tell if the RSA Tower had been finished, as I'd not gone downtown during the day or, definitely not, picked up a newspaper in a while. It was supposed to be some prodigious new world creation of height and port city power for the coming age, our huge Dick, our Big Peter, but to me it looked limp and skeletal and sad.

I turned the heat on low to the floor as I cut toward Pensacola and entered the Bankhead Tunnel, as my feet were catching the brunt of my mind's indiscretion regarding the outdoor chill. A song from some movie that had energized the marijuana demographic during the previous summer was on the radio, and like most of the other selections playing it seemed relevant, as if I were more deeply invested in each song to deter my thinking from what was ahead. And even recognizing that, I sped up through the tunnel, driving below the water just to spit myself out like a surfer on the other side and catch the end of the interrupted song, itself deterred by my smothered antennae. I was getting acclimated to the quiet behind the radio, the small, barely detectable noise in my mind about the bigger glimpse of things. I thought of Brody playing the last two strings on his guitar beside his bonfire, I thought of Knox escaping slumber in bed and finding only empty space and unoccupied sheets beneath her palm on my bed's half, and then I sunk deeply into natural trepidation about the funeral.

Over the Bayway I could see clearly how choppy the Mobile Bay waters were, and how appropriately they were to match such trepidation as I drove, but it seemed so much more than mere anxiousness. It was as if the dread of my family's histrionics and the negation of Papa's spark and my own swelling heart weren't enough, but had to be married with some feeling of a year's passage, of revisiting it metaphysically as if it had already happened and had somehow found a way to happen again once it was comfortably thought passed. Maybe I remembered Nana's funeral, how I had stayed up the entire night prior, drinking, shaving small fractions of my face at a time, and driving over to have my sister explain to Aunt Carrie Anne that I was simply redolent of my night out, that I hadn't drunk breakfast. Maybe I was considering how I was and was not my mother's son that day, considering her arched eyebrow and all the speculation circumnavigating the coffin room that I was *creative* and was *attempting life as a writer* and therefore was loose and bound by nothing to speak inoffensively. Or maybe I was looking forward to watching them squirm, again, in such speculation and I felt a moment, because of my Catholic upbringing, that I was letting down the honor of my grandfather. But the truth was, he was a secret smoker and delighted, in addition to his ability to keep secrets, in the occasions where he could do *anything* in a clandestine manner to keep at least half his middle finger extended to the matriarchy of the family, or the "vaginal oligarchy" as Knox called them—forceful and self-involved and competitive women who always kept him quiet and dutiful in the kitchen.

Also in process, a needed counterbalance was the final thrust of satisfaction derived from having finally sent off pieces around the country—to California, Missouri, Washington, two cities in New York, Tennessee, Louisiana and Massachusetts. A few small presses, some distinguished awards, but ultimately they were sent off to assuage an inner conflict that had somehow been stitched upon their sending. The act itself was gratifying, the chain of acts, including licking the envelopes and driving them to the post office and formatting the silly cover letters, readying my mind for the wait and the rejections and the education from both. The motivation had once been there, a few years before, and had gone on hiatus, hibernating, lying dormant until recently, and it was a success, immediately, that I had returned to performing on behalf of that unnamed nexus of my life where *need* at last converged with *want*.

In thinking these things, and seeing them as extinct concerns, finally, remarkably, by virtue of Brody, fire-breather, and Knox, acid-tongued—both saviors—and by additional charity from the gray-green waters of the bay, I hit ninety miles per hour toward the Daphne exit as the music stayed loud and good.

It was only after I arrived at the beach that I realized I was at the edge of the immediate world.

My plans had changed on their own, at some point, on the drive down 98 through to Montrose and Fairhope, past the unfortunate up-growth of commercial chains and massive discount retail operations, the latter of which, I remember, had been loudly protested by the affluent Eastern Shore citizens who, not really about their own money, I don't suspect, wanted to maintain the integrity of small town America without the intrusive vices set upon them by the corporate fist. But everything had changed since I had grown up somewhere in the middle of Mobile and Daphne. I even found myself allowing out the undesired voice of supposition, asking, Where did that kid go? The kid who was daring and took risks, or created them and then took them, developed philosophies with Nate and Paul on the Winding Brook pier, wrote songs, hallucinated, learned the harmonica, drank cough syrup highballs and smoked cloves. I wondered how that recklessness had mistranslated itself into what I had nearly become. But the trepidation was nearly gone simply because it was in the past, like the street through Fairhope where Jerry and I had lunched, the pecan farms with their new signs, the boat storages along Bon Secour, like the funeral home I passed on the way to the Gulf, housing a landscape where my grandmother slept, where my mother wanted to be buried, and then didn't want to be buried, where my grandfather and comrade in the familial war of tolerance and survival would be buried, along with his laugh. So, as Brody would have wanted, and as I apparently wanted, not for story, not for me, I went to the beach because it was early and I wanted to keep driving.

But once I arrived and discerned the bleakness of it, I remembered it was January, and that I was somehow still in the right place, sun behind the gray clouds or not. I didn't want to go to the beach, I didn't want to say, *I am standing in a half-suit on the cuff of the universe.* I just ended up there in coincidence with natural progression. A few people still staggered drunk-enly around the margins of the roiling surf, pacing the sands after napping in their cars, while newsmen photographed the ten foot waves and both whipping red flags over the empty lifeguard stands. I parked facing the water and smiled a tired smile and, below the pedals as I killed the engine, I slipped out of my sandals and cracked the door.

The sand was cold on my bare feet as I tucked into myself with a lit cigarette and crossed over the boardwalk toward the water. The sounds from the shoreline were deafening as I got closer, and I demurred a bit in the shuffle, thinking, if I were an Indian, my name would be Young Man Stares Into Sea, and then I began to laugh enough for my eyes to tear up in the exhaustion of my arrival. Things, more things were becoming evident, were *becoming* in their own rights. My education from Brody and Knox was surfacing as I traversed the salty, frigid line of the Gulf, but I was think-ing again about just my grandfather, just his implication by example that dying would continue, in no specific order. I thought of Morrison, writing how we can't rival the dead when it comes to love, and so I determined if there *is* soul and spirit and energy, Papa was hurting for *me*, and there was therefore no room, and no necessity, to be trodden and cast and low. And then I thought of my family, overcoming nothing, and I thought of Frankl as I walked the waters, how he suggested we stop inquiring about the meaning of life and start thinking of ourselves as people questioned by life. It was all making sense, I began crying in the weakest of the waves, and laughing still. I thought of Baldwin writing that confusion was a luxury only the extremely young could afford, and then I realized I was stepping away from confusion, and how Baldwin was further right, that beneath joy was amazement, and beneath amazement, surely there was fear, and I had been living that fear, at the base of amazement, and I put out my cigarette in the sand and dropped it into my coat pocket, and then I was Ferlinghetti, I was a word in a tree, a hill of poetry. I was awake in a suit in January, not on the cuff of anything, but rather, just a grandson in cold sand.

After a steady diet of threshold thoughts and staggered steps in and out of the surf, I realized my pants were wetting at the tailored lines, and I decided to make way to my car and drive through Orange Beach just east and visit Perdido Pass briefly so I could let the pants dry and drop off something I'd carried with me a very long time. And due to the most recent move from Midtown to Knox's, I still had it in the car, the large rock I'd acquired during a skim-boarding-excursion-turned-drinking-bout in high school, a near-decade prior, where I'd fully had that first good fleeting love in a moment with a girl named Tate Bonifay, a memory that was so sweet for such an extended time I couldn't enforce even the rules of my own heart, to let the past be past, but it was time to forget the patience and allure of that young flash in time, to put the sign of such memory to bed back across the jetties where it had lain for a long time before a heavy youthful heart like mine had come along and told my hands to take it and keep it and maybe later sublimate my resolve.

I drove over the Key bridge against the tumid sun and crept into the narrow parking strip alongside the sand's reach down toward the rocks' stretch into the Gulf. The dunes, I could see from the bridge, had blown down from worsening storm systems and beach erosion, and had turned into something only recognizable to locals who had been around enough to see its demise for what it was. I jumped them when they were once twenty feet tall, as Bonifay sprawled up top with Billy and Patrick. She had sat like a football player, confident in her wear, sipping a beer like a mother emancipated from child watch, staring into the sun, curly long hair, a boarder's attitude. Where had I, that kid, gone, too? The dunes were leveled like tables after a decade and were still beautiful, but lacked the luster of young people sweating in nascent love onto the sand that soon might forget them. I took off again alone on the beach and made it through the seemingly horizontal wind tunnels which tugged my lone body toward the result of what was cresting and crashing down at the shore. If I remembered correctly, the rock had been about ten yards down the rock row in the water, and so without self-doubt and a cigarette stub in my pocket, I negotiated the moist rock pilings down to a fair estimate, and sat on a heavier, dryer monolithic entity in the shade of a generous cloud between me and the sun. I was freezing at that point, but not confused, not in any mood to deliver a eulogy for that which was defecting from my custody, a memory of a beautiful girl I had carried around too long.

It was as I leaned forward to set it down at the edge of the splash that I fell face-in to the water, an uncomfortable, almost slow descent that included the top left of my head and my left shoulder. And so, on the walk of shame to my car I felt empowered by irony and the silliness of what had happened, that I might see Tate Bonifay in a store one day and say, *Yes, I gave the earth back our rock*, and smile, and she would feel awkward for not knowing why I smiled, and she would feel awkward on my behalf for her constitution of no longer loving me, or not having allowed me to keep her at bay as I learned about love and then its application. A younger, more tan, smoother-faced fellow and what appeared to be his little brother were working on their truck in the lot as I ambled on toward my car, trying to nod good energy their way but forgetting the mess I must have seemed. It was almost quarter-past ten and I had to get moving, so I took off my pants behind my open door and hung them out the barely-cracked window top behind me and drove, right-handed, northwest to Magnolia Springs, holding the thin shoulder of my suit coat just out the gape in my window as I fumbled into a pair of sunglasses and drove away from the sun.

———

I parked a couple hundred feet from the funeral home and slipped into socks and a pair of coordinated dress shoes to go with the half-dry suit I wore, and I checked myself in the driver's side visor mirror before climbing out and pacing up the one-hundred seventy-ish degree slope toward the building's front door. The wind had picked up, almost as though the bravado of the Gulf's waxing waters had called inland the salt and breeze and silence to Magnolia Springs, but the sun was back out and beautiful and, as I approached Oak Rest, the burial manor on sarcophagus land, I found it too difficult to feel sad anymore about Papa. The earlier, temporarily avoidable moments during driving had returned, those of feeling bad *for* him and the inevitable morass of lunacy that had evolved itself into my family's communal goodbye to him, and they, the feelings, were sweeping in like dried nettles of an old, dirty, frayed and disintegrating broom. Much of the illusory reality of my relatives' grief, as far as I'd experienced it, was steeped in their confusion by it, which ultimately led to its misapplication. And so not knowing who would be down and who would be in outright hysterics for the mere sake of hysteria, and not knowing if I would manage serenity or give in to petulance, and more over, most of all, really wishing Brody and Knox were there walking the verdant slope alongside me, the three of us one tilting pillar of indignation and ecstasy, I made my way to the entrance after a brief study of the long, metallic-gray of the front's façade. I imagined gargoyles.

The first and only person I recognized was my sister, Leah, standing across the glossy-tiled lobby at the mouth of the wake room where my grandfather, somewhere past the thick line of people near her, was stretched out pallid and interminably asleep. She did a double-take before letting her eyes recognize me, a half-smile of gratitude and sobriety on her face, and she waved from her hip as I crossed to her.

"Hi, sis," I said and kissed her cheek.

"Hey." She stood back to glance me over. "You look…almost handsome."

"Your herpes is less apparent."

We quietly laughed after a moment of reading each other. I broke the silence.

"How was the drive from Atlanta? When'd you get in?"

"Did you get dressed *before* your shower?"

I grinned widely and reached for the soaked spot on my suit coat's upper arm, noting its undying wetness and then shrugged as she combed her fingers through the front of my damp hair.

"I had an accident. At the beach."

She laughed a little too loudly, caught herself with a hand to her mouth, looked through the door in the direction of our family and then back at me before slapping at my arm. "This *morning?*"

"I needed to air out my head and slipped on some rocks."

"Rocks that were actually out in the Gulf."

"Right."

"You know she'll seek a way to destroy you."

"I'm sure," I said of our mother. I adjusted my waistline and scanned the thin hallway to my left that led toward the chapel.

"And she said you're *unemployed* now? Hi." She whispered the latter at someone I did not know, likely someone from the small community that had known my grandparents and worked with them in some capacity in their efforts to keep fed the local families suffering from layoffs in the nearby industrial plants.

"Hello," I nodded as the older man passed between us. And then back to Leah, "Long story. No, not really a long story. Bottom line is, I was tired of my job and tired of disappearing from myself and so I got on to something better. She said on an oh-so-uncharacteristically eternal voice message that you're disappointed in me? What's with that?"

"Don't worry, little bro. She tells me all the time you think I'm a sellout for trying to procreate."

"That makes no sense to me," I said, grinning.

"She's playing sides."

We stepped out of the way of two more people who waved at us while brandishing two identical *I'm-sorry* faces. Again, people I didn't know, and I experienced a sudden rush of relief that the distance between myself and the Rattigans was so vast that I had not fully become of their grade, and then in followed the rush of imagined accusations from those I did not remember, as if they nonetheless wanted to be remembered, regardless of our limited times together or things in common.

"I think they go to Aunt Josephine's church in Mississippi," Leah whispered.

"Oh, wow. How's she behaving?"

"I caught her by the vending machines speaking in tongues."

"Nice," I said as Leah's face reddened from suppressing the laugh. I nodded at the room with Papa. "Our cousins here?"

"Yeah," she said quietly, suddenly serious. "Hannah's taking it pretty rough. And Celie's taking breaks between fart jokes and crying. I think her medication isn't working."

"I didn't know she was taking anything."

"It's new."

My sister looked distracted suddenly, almost guilty for our whispered levity. But to those who may have known us there, it should not have come as a surprise that we were still somewhat connected by the bubble in which we existed in childhood.

"Well? How are you?" I asked, putting my arms around her shoulders and bringing her in for a hug, a genuine hug once our territories had been analyzed, and who we were in our very different worlds, wet or dry, employed or on skid row, could converge to a stable sense of humanity against the backdrop of defining loss and resurrection and rightness and harmony, in a building of not-gargoyles. Her eyes had small tears.

"I'm good, I guess. I don't know." She shrugged. "But you look..." she said as she straightened my lapel. "...you still look good." She sighed. "I'm never disappointed in you. I just want you to have a steady job and for you to stay in one place. You're not in college anymore."

"Well, I certainly don't think you're a sellout for trying to have a baby, sis. That's not a term I would ever attach to you. What I told Ma is that you and Matt *shouldn't* have kids. Because of your faces."

"He's around here somewhere," she said as she slapped my arm again and laughed and wiped at her eyes.

"Come in with me, babe," I said. "I can't look directly at her when we walk in, so I need you to tell me later about her reaction. I probably look insane."

"No," she answered after shaking her head, clearing the moisture from below her eyes a final time and then nodding. "You just look like you." She took my hand. "Let's go."

I first saw Uncle Jimmy, perched on the side of a small sofa in back of the room and talking with his hands. He stopped to lift one arm along with his eyebrows and wrinkled forehead in a salute toward me before returning to a discussion with a pair of Episcopalian preachers I recognized from forced attendance several Christmases past at the Springs. I waved and suddenly felt the rumbling return, the roll of cowardice that comes with second-guessing what people might think of a person they really wanted to know years ago, before realizing by his absence that he didn't wish to know them, people who still whisper in small circles, wondering what "that boy" is up to. Is he is married now? What has he done with that gifted brain? And I also felt on display from this, as if finding that enigmatic but false memory of spinning with my sister on a carousel in the safe recesses of our parents' vision, in a theme park, everything blurred except Leah and me holding hands, oscillating like mad and important, tiny people. But the pictures I remember were different of the past, with different environments, very stark and clear images of our mother smiling like a retired supermodel, and our father, before his fast death as we were growing, standing unmoved in his paternal posture, grinning and hoping the automatic switch on the camera had been properly set and we'd not be immortalized for what we really were, a family of people incapable of paying attention to one other. So instead of returning to myself, in that moment, I did what I thought best and became Brody in the airport on the way to New York City, giving blue light and love to those bereaved of Papa and those who couldn't, on their own, look back at their pasts and not be wounded by them.

"Hey, you," I said to Hannah, who stood in front of a lamp and table about five feet behind the backs of my mother and her sisters—Beatrice left, Josephine right and Barbara to Josephine's right—women crowded into a fortifying huddle, bestowing their last look upon their father in the long, handsome oak box at their fingertips. Leah had moved on to find her husband who was indubitably eating in the secret place where there was food to be found.

"Hey," she said, moving her folded hands from below her waist and wiping at her eyes. "I was hoping you'd be here. I mean, you better not have been planning on missing it."

She leaned over and into a side-hug, the standard greeting of most Rattigans, about which I was reminded when first seeing Leah at the door—as an odd matter of human protection, my family's sense of touch was almost unforgivably repellant, like reacting to the smell of a wet dog.

"Why would I not show?" I whispered as I broke from her embrace and bent past her to kiss Celie's forehead after she'd reached a hand around her sister and pulled at my coat.

"I don't know. I'm sorry I said that." She smiled and turned fully toward me. "I didn't think I'd be this upset." She wiped her eyes again. "It looks like you missed your mirror on the way out this morning."

We smiled.

"Yeah, I already got it from Leah," I said, looking around the room, which was much more empty than first appearances had suggested. But considering the time, I assumed most people had taken to the chapel to leave the family to do what we didn't need our own private space to do, and that was embarrass ourselves. "But I'm here."

"Did you know he lied?"

"Did I what?"

"Papa," Hannah said, tears welling again. "About being better."

"No. Who says?"

"He made Jimmy swear not to tell."

I thought a moment, running my index knuckle across my lips, but it was too quiet in the room. The music of human reaction to loss was beginning to embed beneath my skin, not for the matter of loss itself, but the source of the sadness, the sisters, minus my inexplicably disengaged aunt from Anchorage, how they had conducted themselves in the months leading to his sure death, and then the dissipation of their clash when he "recovered," and then their unity once he'd passed and they could stop the wild finagling over future monies and at last get down to mourning. I began to feel inhumane in looking at them, from knowing of the petty behind-the-scenes behaviors and largesse of their hypocrisies, so I cut loose from Hannah's near-miss at warmth, as I enjoyed her better when she was drunk and distracted by the luxury of things going well in the world. I stepped around Aunt Beatrice to exit the room and find a cup of coffee. The picture of Papa's face I afforded myself was a convenient blur, from childhood, maybe invented by my mind to see him one final time as I had always seen him, not the frail and tenuous body lines and bones, but a man I was certain was enjoying himself thoroughly wherever he had gone. I could feel my mother's eyes follow me out, but I kept busy with the realistic notion that

166

Papa was good, and that I had tried with him, had taken from him what I should have tried to take, and I had given him, in return, all my light.

I found Aunt Carrie Anne in the coffee room after having snuck eyes into the half-filled chapel at the end of the thin hallway. She argued with a machine her supple body obscured from my view, so I lightly touched her shoulder as I moved beside her to see that she lorded over the coffee maker.

"There you are," she said after sipping from her cup and setting it down on an old brown microwave. She suddenly, uncharacteristically became the feared aunt who grabs nephew cheeks, and then she kissed my forehead, declaring my handsomeness in a voice that had not lost its southern inflection even after nearly two decades in Alaska. "I wasn't sure I'd see you since your mother was saying earlier how…"

"So the coffee's fresh?" I interrupted, sensing a subliminal theme had manifested itself in more overt conversation. I was thinking of the beach, still, and Bonifay and old sunsets, and Knox swearing at work and Brody discussing the merits of green tea with strangers.

"Yeah, I just made it. I couldn't take it in there anymore."

"I know what you mean." I poured a cup and took it with me into a lean against the counter. "This room is tiny. One of us should start hyperventilating. Make a scene."

"Oh, listen to you," she said, pawing at my upper arm and reaching for her cup before returning to feel the fabric of my upper sleeve. "Did it start raining?"

"Sort of."

"Look," she said, serious in the face and lowering her voice. "I've been wanting to send you an email, but your mot…I was told you don't have one anymore, so now that I'm here. Well, now that *we're* here, I want you to feel like you can talk to me about anything. Funeral or not."

"Why. What's up?" I asked, blowing at the coffee's steam.

"Is that coffee?" An old woman asked in a shrill voice from the door.

I took my eyes off my aunt, who'd taken to a facial expression toward me as though I'd hidden her car keys, and I looked at the woman who had entered and managed to insert a hand in between us for a Styrofoam cup.

"Absolutely. Help yourself."

Carrie Anne and I stepped apart.

"You know, Eric," the old woman said to me as she smelled the coffee. "Your grandfather helped me out at the Conoco on Sundays. *Every* Sunday. He was there for bent cans and extras we needed to take over yonder to the Mission."

"I bet," I said, smiling at my aunt as the woman paced to the door and talked over her shoulder.

"He was a good man. A *good* man, Eric. I'm sure you already know."

And then she was gone.

"That was definitely something I needed to experience before going home." I turned toward my aunt, but she'd still maintained the look. I grew curious. "What?"

"I know we don't talk that much. But I want you to know..." Her voice broke to a whisper. "...that even I was known for experimenting a few years back. I know what your culture is like. I was in several three-ways."

Mother, I thought. And then, Carrie Anne, please don't continue.

"And I admire you for being who you are, no matter who that is, because I have always loved you, and I don't agree with the position your..."

"This *reeks* of my mother. Fucking incredible. Ma told you I dig guys?"

Carrie Anne looked suddenly confused and I began to laugh, almost spilling what was left of my coffee.

"Well, not in those exact words."

"That's fascinating. I mean, shit, I love *everybody*, if that's what's she's alluding to, or deriving from my personal philosophy or something. Not that she reads my...wait...did she offer you any theory?"

"Why, Peter? All of a sudden I don't..."

"No, I'm actually curious."

"She thinks..." My aunt sighed and crumpled her brow, formulating the thought into explanation with evident fear for offense. I suddenly wanted to go kiss the nearest man on the mouth to spite, who knows, everyone. "She thinks because you think you're a writer, and you hang out with all those artsy people, that..."

"*Think* I'm a writer, huh? That's Ma." I sighed my own sigh, thinking there would be no room for escape in this death house, this house of deaths on so many maniacal levels.

"So you're saying..."

"I'm *saying* that's Ma. I guess that's all I'm saying." I held my hands up in the air at my sides after throwing my cup in a nearby trashcan. "What else is there to possibly say?" I began to laugh again, with incredulity, and then ran my fingers through my hair before lowering my arms and straightening my jacket. "I'm heading to the chapel. This has been illuminating."

"Peter," she called to me once I was in the doorway. "I wasn't trying to...*look* at me."

I turned to face her with as much positive energy as I could, affording her my full believable face of forgiveness, as she was after all part of the female force which comprised the chaos that would trickle downward through more than just my generation. She was a product of some other culture, some foreign language. I told myself it was not entirely her fault.

"You're not going to tell your mom about the three-ways are you?"

I grinned, I hope devilishly.

"Oh, you can count on us never discussing it, sweet baby," I said, winked and returned to the quiet hall.

It wasn't until fully through the swinging wooden doors of the tiny chapel in back of the building that I heard the sisters' opening musical number playing overhead, *That's What Friends Are For*, that I burst into an uncontrolled laughter, laughter I wanted to ravage my insides and keep me sick for days. In front of my family still collecting at the last minute in the front pews, I pivoted and made it through the lobby and out the front door. I took a deep breath and stared toward Mobile Bay, hidden by miles of trees below the western sky.

———

"I thought I'd have to make the first move to even hear your voice today."

She tongued the inside of her cheek and rested an arm on my car's open door, following the graveside service, once I'd moved my vehicle into the back parking lot of the building. She eyed the sky above my head. "He couldn't even hug his own mother, which was all she needed today."

I looked past her shoulder toward where the casket had exited and then been loaded into the hearse that led us to the northwestern edge of the pruned gardens. The service had been short, refreshing to be ministered by someone who actually knew the deceased. I had nestled into the middle of the crowd next to Jimmy, who'd begun to have a difficult time with the understanding of his ended labors to not revive my grandfather, but to keep him from suffering as much as possible until an odious death-hand plunged into him from an unknown, elevated space of repossession and beat him with last minute struggles for air before he and his finally ceased. My Uncle took my offered palm and stood with me gently, letting go months of with-held tears in a solemn, delicate way that forced me into the recognition of his own beauty and sensitivity and love. He was an outsider of the family, too, which meant for the Rattigans that when he did come around with Barbara, he was loved so attentively by those who'd missed him that others grew jealous. We had some of that in common.

"I wish you wouldn't do that, Ma," I said, leaning a hip into the steering wheel before stepping out from the shield of the door itself and stretching my arms over my shoulders. I slipped my hands in my pockets and tried not to squint too forcibly into the bright sun.

"Wish I wouldn't what?"

"Talk in third person about me in front of me. It adds unnecessary drama to all this," I told her, waving my hand at the back of Oak Rest.

"Well, I'm being serious, Peter. And you're being sarcastic."

I laughed with quiet resignation. "I'm really not."

"And you look like you did at your Nana's funeral. I'd ask to smell your breath but I don't even want to know."

"I just got a little wet is all. I'm here. I *want* to be here. I'm struggling with my supposed apathy you've spread around, but I'm not angry at you. So what gives?"

"What *gives*," she began, "is you're unemployed and not answering your phone, and I had to embarrass myself calling after you at your job wondering why on God's green earth you've quit. And you brought your little writer friend to Christmas and hardly talked to anyone, and I dropped the cheese dip and Hannah climbed on me like I was a Shetland pony, and Todd thought he heard you call another man *sweet baby* on the phone? Do you know how hard it was for me to stay there after you left? I was glad you didn't come by the house much to spend time with your sister and brother-in-law. I'm sure it hurts her when you ignore her, though. My God, what kind of things you wouldn't have held back from them. You know your sister is disappoint..."

"Eileen? I need you to stop for a..."

"...and she is *not* impressed about your life choices, whether or not she..."

"*Ma*."

Her eyes switched in to first a bizarre and heart-breaking surge of hurt, but as I was allowing her humanity to reify itself in my mind after its vacation since her voice message and the very moment, her stare flipped from that of a person's to that of an angry cartoon villain who had suddenly had its number checked and would then up the ante for revenge by all necessary means. Or maybe she'd become some angry astral wildlife with which I was unfamiliar, as well as she. Or maybe, just maybe, she was still human and was angry at her own hurt. So as I moved toward her to hold her, there was an evident resistance embodied in the heat of her muscles tightening, and then tears denoting her desire to be held by the only man left in her life, and I then felt a sense of power for not doing what I usually did years earlier, turn away from anyone's misdirected transmission of emotional pain—there was a spiritual pain in there, too, not quite the color of light inside me, and so, since my grandfather was gone, I gave what I could to this equally frail thing still breathing and still, in her own languages, wanting the confirmation of love.

After we separated, she ruffled my hair the same way my sister had and then let her hand slide down to the side of my face, and then she wiped her eyes and looked me up and down.

"You know I wanted you to be a pallbearer but I wasn't sure you'd show up."

I looked at her with my head tilted to the side. "I would have said no."

"I thought so," she nodded, and then, "Well. *Why?*"

I shifted in my stance and draped an elbow over the top edge of my car. "It's that I already said my peace to Papa a while back. My *own* peace. Will you ever allow that to make sense to you? I wanted *our* specific form of parting ways. Not your view of it." I touched my chest. "It was only my relationship with him."

My voice cracked, but I rebounded. I couldn't give her that.

171

"It would have been nice for you to have done it. You did it for your father."

"I was younger, Ma. Different and sidetracked. I ran my fingers along the casket. I didn't even help. Gum fell out of my mouth. I might have been skipping."

"I know," she said.

"And I don't like how I break it up in my head, 'bearer of palls'. Like it's a profession. There's that gloom of it I don't like."

"Well," she sighed. My family was a small nation of sigh-ers. "You could have...couldn't you have at least *tried* to wear a button-down? What does that shirt say?" She opened my coat to view the graphic of a large belt buckle-looking object with the word *manifesto* written across it. "You really could have tried harder."

"And you could have foregone telling your sister I put cocks in my mouth, Ma. So what if I..."

"See, there's the son she expected would come," she said again to the sky above my head.

"No, the point is *so what?* So I'm wearing a t-shirt and I'm damp and don't look the part anymore because I quit my job."

"So vulgar."

"So what if right at this moment you can't reach me by a cell phone or tell your office I have a career label?"

"So disrespectful to the dead."

"So what if I'm reassessing what it is that contributes to my happiness? Eileen, listen." I continued as she shook her head at, who knows, God swinging in the trees behind me, covering his lips with an index finger as if to say, Don't let him know I'm listening. *"Listen."*

"Honestly Peter, that was uncalled for."

"Look at me." I put my hands on her shoulders and lowered my body to meet the horizon of her eyes. "I need to know you're processing what I'm saying, Ma. I need you to stop victimizing yourself over something I'm doing for my own improvement. We don't have to define my life similarly, and we're not going to, probably ever, but I have to do what I'm doing. I tried your 'real world' and let it almost empty me. The bouncing back and self-doubt were horrible. You can't know how even recovery can turn a person into a monster."

172

"But those friends of yours, they don't care about anything but living for the moment. They have no plans to..."

"Those friends are my family, too. You need to understand I'm not replacing you guys, I'm just adding them. All right?"

"But what'll you do for money? You can't live off of Amber. She'll get tired of you so fast your head'll spin, especially when it comes to money."

"I got a job with Brody at a restaurant near campus until I figure things out. I'm good. It's good people there. I'll be good."

She rolled her eyes. "Oh, that's wonderful, Peter. A *restaurant*? I thought you said you were giving that lifestyle up when you graduated." She slapped her legs and waved her hands in front of herself. "I guess things never change with you. Do you ever have plans to get serious?"

It was my turn to sigh. Others who had remained at Papa's grave had finally trailed in to let the burying men do their work, and their car engines were roaring to life, and their bodies conforming to the seats within were steering them back to more tangible life beyond the grass and stones.

"I'm more serious now than I've ever been, Ma." I kissed her on the cheek and began to step into my car. "Give the family that number at Knox's. Anyone can call anytime."

Dissatisfied, and seemingly defeated, she rested her hands on the edge of the inside of my door after I'd shut it and fully rolled down the cracked window.

"But what I think you should tell them...honestly...if you tell them anything about me, don't make it up simply because I don't give you a play-by-play of my happenings. Tell them to call with good energy and love. Or don't call at all. I can handle my type of madness. I just don't accept our kind anymore. Ok?"

She exhaled and reached in to scratch through my hair a final time as I kicked on the engine.

"I guess that's not too much, son. And I'm sorry. I worry. May I at least worry?"

"It's fine to, Ma. Of course, but you don't need to is my point. And I have love for you, I really do. So much. And the world. But stop thinking that's so utopian and let me learn how to use it. Please."

She tapped the car door and stepped away.

"I'll try, I promise. Your car smells like smoke. I love you."

I set the car in gear and waved a short wave over the wheel as I aimed toward the right side of the building, then the meandrous thin drive away from the west side, then north of Oak Rest, and I slowed to let two people pass who had stayed with their vehicles longer after the ceremony, or maybe had walked the breezy walks through the other rows of hopefully remembered people, had seen the fallen wind chimes slightly storm-covered in the dirt, or imagined walking through banana spider webs soon to come with the eventual heat. I turned right on to the country road and reached for a smoke from a pack in the console between me and the air of catharsis in the seat beside.

The drive to Mobile after such hours was a contemplation on performance and countenance, of what was then past and what was ahead. I thought of being in motion and still being alive enough to capitalize on ability, how to determine what matters and what does not. I turned at the same gas station that had been my signifier for where to turn on the way back from the beach many times before, when I was too exhausted and sun-red and booze-beaten to attempt 59 North through the small towns and speed traps that led to I-10 and the westward crawl home. Then I headed north, still, back through the tiny farming areas and random signs with arrows directing the lost to summer camps, and it began to feel like a better winter. It was bright, no longer bleary, and I was glad to be left alone on the highway I had driven nearly ten years and even then could not recall its number. And the largest curiosity didn't stem from the freshness of the leaving, of my family in the rearview or who again had been taken away—when someone dies the removal is one, then the wake, two, then the funeral, three, then the rest of the lives of the living, those carrying on what in fact was taken, are countless removals again when the dead is revived in conversation, anecdote or the lull of not mentioning the dead at all.

I felt already the prospective wrangling of nerves Knox and Brody may or not have been preparing to experience themselves, upon my return to our tiniest of castles in the estates, amidst the silly grandeur of other peoples' money. And I didn't even know the time, as my clock on the dash was set some eight or nine hours in another direction. I never wore a watch, I didn't know their whereabouts, and I thought of Brody's cell phone still beetle-like dead on its back below the bed, and I wanted to call them at home but had no coins shifting noisily per turn on the bending highway road. But suddenly I wished not to, anytime soon, need again that exact moment, to reach out to someone in advance, to sense them out, warn or relieve them. I was unsure at the notion of reenrolling in the school of our growing habituation, our new addiction to one another which involved, from its development, learning how to talon-down on each others' arms and refusing to leave, refusing to push away. For in real sincerity, it was not a return from anything, but more a rush back to. Surely a sense of compunction existed as well, that I had treated so quickly the funeral as not a goodbye, but rather, an obligatory hello before dipping once again into an inarguably mindless life of conflicting tethers and freedoms. And in thinking of the latter pairing, I lifted a knee to the base of the steering wheel and wriggled from my suit coat and draped it over the back seat, revisiting the main highway section of Fairhope, the hospital, the up-growth near there, too, the gas stations with the same products and the same prices but with different colors, different mascots and logos, the same drug stores with same brick, same thing aisle after aisle, same light drooping from the ceilings as if aware of their baseless originality. And then I felt saddened for them, the ceilings and the lights and the people who walked into and under them each day, just to look up and objectify their meaninglessness and be grateful they could at least afford the gas being sold at that yellow station down the road, or was it green? Through Montrose again, through Daphne and the recollection of drag races and sleeping with Erin in her parent's bed in high school, Katie's militant college football drunk of a mother, Hagan living on the soccer fields, Ray and his efforts to grow a beard, all small elements of a world that mattered differently then. And in terms of what did not, they still somehow did, in that when passing these ghosts and thinking ahead about the new ones oncoming, the shiver of memory was that of closeness to how beautiful even the seemingly nonsensical and superfluous were and would be. And that cohesiveness, with the confidence behind it, was not the warmth about the future but rather, an odd excitement for the past.

I finally arrived in Mobile after bypassing the Bayway jump-on ramp in favor of the causeway, a thin strip of connecting highway that didn't hover bridge-like over the waters as did its counterpart, the bay bridge, but instead was the elevation-equivalent of a putting green above the still choppy waters from the morning, the more docile of the two on low-wind mornings. And though the causeway was more prone to flooding, it had held its ground during the recent wind gusts from the earlier storm, and only presented to its passersby a smattering of bodies alongside the thigh-high embankments, bodies that held fishing poles and sat on coolers and had taught themselves over time and experience to wait with patience and steadfast hunger for what the inlet of the ocean would provide. I pulled over briefly past a small family of three, a father and boy and girl and thought nicely that Papa might have been saying he would see me around, the family's collective vision another excitement of my personal history, thinking of Papa's Lake Guntersville hat, the usual fish hook on the bill, his *own* patience, his dependable arm on the rod when the largemouth proved too much for our own allowances, how we would have, had he let us, jumped right in and wrestled the catch to shore. I sat about a quarter hour on an embankment's edge, my sandals back on and half-hanging from my feet just inches above the water, and I had a book in my hand I'd extracted from the back seat beneath my then-dry coat, but I wasn't reading it. I was holding it close to my hip as though osmotically it knew on its own how to climb inside and flourish as its own thought in another body. Or maybe, again with the *just maybes*, I was unwilling at the moment to admit I was alone by choice, because I was in love with the solitude of that one exact day and I could not create within me, not until I made it back to Brody and Knox and the creaky old brown bed, the further admission that I was ready to teach myself the balance between self-governed quiet and the roar of those surrounding that a person direly needs. I imagined the sun going down prematurely, and stared at it a bit as it refused to submit, and then I spun off the wall as though it were an office chair and kicked up a small bit of dirt and pebbles when my feet hit the shoulder, just to climb back in the car and put a tire track in the leftover dust.

———

"Come on, Rattigan," Knox said as I groaned and put a pillow over my head. "It's the new millennium, babe. *One* of us had to jump."

I lifted the pillow and cracked an eye at the laptop she had sitting across her knees in the bed. I'd been home a half hour or so before she'd delivered the news of her morning purchase, after brief talks of her skipping work to surf the tech aisles below indubitably drooping lights and ceilings. And after an overview of the beach, the fall, the funeral procession, the competing shades of graveside greens, the howling and the muted sobs, my insides, Jimmy's hand, the omnipresent Eileen glare and as ever, the desired update on Josephine and her work with prison ministry, and most interestingly, how God had changed his mind and told her after five days of starvation to not *completely* fast, but rather, just eat vegetables and only a small amount of water. *That's pretty much a diet, right?* Knox had asked as I laughed.

"*No*," I said, reinserting my face into the shadow beneath the pillow. "No one *had* to do anything. How did you afford it? I haven't even started working yet."

"Credit."

"Oh, come *on*," I said, rolling the sham corners into my fists. "Brody's gonna flip when he hears."

"I think he'll recover. Besides, I thought you'd dig this."

She slapped my left shoulder as I stabbed a hand out toward the headboard in search of my wine glass.

"How did that possibly enter your brain?"

"But it's so *new*."

"You dig it on your own, man."

I sat and sipped and smiled at her, slightly tired spiritually, and on the outside I don't doubt my face was half-hearted. I looked at her machine the same way I remember looking at my mother's dog when she'd first been brought home from the pound, how sorrowfully the puppy's eyes had peered upward as I studied her, how they seemed to say, *I'm afraid you won't like me.*

"I'm happy with what I've been using."

"I know, Rattigan. I'm just saying one day your processor's gonna die. And then what?"

"I'll figure it out when it happens. Maybe learn the stand-up bass. Did you say Brody's at work?"

"Yep," she said, her eyes returning to the machine's screen. "I think he's giving up on New Orleans because he got a letter today about his book. Maybe needs to shift focus. I told him to take that girl's cell phone in case they need to talk to him, but he refused. Of course. So I think he's giving them the house number."

"Giving who?"

"Somebody in New York, I guess."

"Good. We can be a part of what's happening."

"Well," she said, slightly turning her chin toward me but keeping her eyes on whatever light was flickering against her face and changing colors. Not blue, I thought. Definitely not blue at all. "That's just it. They want him to reconsider some transitioning in the entire first half, and I shit you not, pretty much change the entire fucking M.O. of his narrator. At least that's how it sounded to me. I don't know. I tried to tell him it's his golden ticket, if he'd at least listen to them and try it out."

"Golden ticket?"

"Yeah," she replied, her face still glowing, still not looking at me. I took a deeper sip and reached for the bottle atop the board and added the rest of it to both our glasses and then handed her hers, for which she said thanks and blindly set it back up top to return to the puppy. "I mean, there's first and foremost the issue of integrity. I'm not challenging that, because I think...hold on...I think he could..."

"Where are you right now?"

"Hm? Sorry. I'm still trying to install all the crap that came with it. Sorry."

"Do you need to do it now? Let's go see Brody and get a drink. I need to see about a schedule anyway. I'm getting low on funds. It's hard to enact dreams when you're penniless."

"Yeah. You're right, I'm sorry. It's just so unfamiliar. Plus I'm a little overwhelmed by the expense, so I've been all day trying to..." She waved her hand at it and closed it after a few clicks. "Nevermind. Sorry."

"Or, you mean you're overwhelmed by fears associated with the expense."

"Ok, Doctor Assho..."

"Anyway, you were saying about Brody?"

"Oh. Yeah, I just think he should give them a listen. We talk about balance all the time, and logic and passion, and I think maybe now that the actual draft is done and he's looked it over and actually brought it up there, maybe he should sit back and let professional eyes help push it along to being sellable now. Or *more* sellable. I'm not sure what to make of it. I haven't seen any of his book. Have you?"

"Not yet. I don't think he's trying to be mysterious though."

"Me either," she said, climbing out of bed and setting down the computer on an empty office paper box and beginning to open drawers, searching for pants to replace the sleeper's pair she'd been in most of the late afternoon. "I just don't think he's too concerned, honestly. With what happens, I mean. The press that put out his novel? There's still time for it to get picked up by something larger. Couldn't that help later? I don't know how all of that works yet. I don't know what kind of market there is for the short novel anyway, since I don't write it and don't follow it. I'm still trying to get the poems from Fall organized to send out before April's shot to shit."

"I know how it feels. I'm kind of in the middle of that, too."

I finished my glass and stretched before throwing a leg off the edge of the bed to get dressed all over again, after coming home and dismantling for split-second respite. I yawned.

"For some reason I can't shake the reflection on today. Not that I need to shake it, but I guess I'm confused if I want to or not."

"What do you mean?" She asked from behind the half-open bathroom door as I saw one of her legs kick into a sleeve of jeans through the crack.

"I just wonder..." I said, and laughed briefly as I armed into a long-sleeve t-shirt. "...if I really did act like a jackass, or if everyone else did. I doubt myself when I'm around those people, so militantly insistent on their normalcy. It just felt like everybody stood around like, it's hard to say, nervously compacted molecules or something, not knowing what to do or say, as if it's wrong to feel happy at a funeral. It was bizarre."

"They should have had a wet bar," she called out.

"I was almost worried someone would spontaneously combust if I accidentally caught them up in a wax on teleology or something."

"I would have brought a flask."

"As though the undercurrent of their group thought is laden with real fear I might not let them get away with being ridiculous. Yeah, a flask would have been good. They expected it anyway."

"When you've got a hit show..." She said, grinning as she exited the bathroom, stopped, threw back an arm and flipped off the light. "...no need to change format. You ready?"

"Yeah." I grinned as I put on shoes in the corner. "I'm good. I definitely think I'm good."

We stormed through the process of initial departure from the house, from the inside heater's warmth and down the few steps into the chilly courtyard as Knox lit two smokes and passed one over before offering to drive us to see Mr. LaCoste and perform a series of tasks, which included assuring him the world had not capsized on me in the interim. *That*, in and of itself included the fullest embrace possible of everything I could recognize experiencing, whether it be destitution or remorse or content-ment. And upon entering the pre-dinner rush front doors and being met with sympathetic energies from all those he had informed, the three of us traded hugs and dealt out kissed foreheads like cards, and Knox and I sat at the bar for the next hours with Brody, mostly ignoring his customers and tapping his leg at our sides.

CHAPTER 6

Spring, at last, arrived with its Alabama usualness, first a week of warmth, then a chill, then a rain that brought humidity and steam. People in grocery lines became people in drugstore lines. Sick strangers grew resistant to the enthusiasm of the healthy. Knox found herself ensnared by a cold and turned pensive about the world for two and a half pharmaceutical days, recovering only after passing me a less severe version of it, which fortunately didn't preclude a busy schedule at the restaurant. And Brody, naturally, was unaffected by it all. He'd taken to what I thought was a salutary self-distraction, laboring to induce an out-of-body experience, a labor I suspected had nothing to do with the increased phone calls from New York City as he bantered amicably with a woman from Bombay who worked as a trade editor for Viking Penguin, a woman he described as "generous with unfamiliar cigarettes." The effort to resurrect the creative energies toward his novel, rather than those of an editing nature, seemed to be something that didn't worry him inasmuch as it seemed silly to do, and so in concession he went about with projects such as flying in and out of himself, or at least trying to, until the momentary urge to cooperate found him and sank in.

Work was going well on both accounts. Financially, I was saving some of what was being brought in, due to the shared expense at home. Knox had accelerated work hours on her graduate thesis, her job and the collection of poems I thought would surely die a quiet death for a long while in late Winter until we'd finally adjusted to the pancake-stacking of our lives in the little house and readied to get on with spending appropriate time in our various corners, scribbling and doodling and drinking wine, laughing sporadically at the barrage of epithets escaping our mouths when the motions had become heavy for the night, and what was left was our communion on the heavy, immobile bed for final palaver that preceded the battle of our nighttime sounds.

A microscopic groan was transforming itself inside me into something larger and less controllable, even though the afternoons by the pool were frequent and stretched into lengthy occasions of the three of us, when agendas aligned and overlapped, engaging in necessary discourse on items from spiritual thresholds to what we, after much analysis, dubbed "logical, unfettered hindsight." But the groan wasn't from the leisure, for within it was the true work of its not being leisurely, as it included the generation of important ideologies to replace if not disseminate old, unworkable ones. What was spinning out of my control was another vital something, a kind of space to either more or less—I couldn't yet tell—get out of my own body, too, and look, from a different promontory, down or up or laterally at the space from which I had moved, to assess the work I was doing on someone else's clock as well as my own. A tree-hidden coffee house was a couple miles through the winding streets adjacent to the golf course across from the front of the main house, and embracing fully the cliché of it as an artist's escape, I nonetheless determined when the inside of the house was pulsating like a heart, beating not out but into itself, that the coffee house was a fair place to partially victimize myself alongside the unpredictable noise of commerce, surrounded by identical women who, with their husbands' credit cards, labored to outspend each other at the counter. Or there were the young who'd walked up from nearby houses, pre-teens in need of an as yet undefined escape of their own. The objective was to sit amongst the confusion of their attendance, likely similar to mine, and stare at printed pages from my thickening novel, maybe some old poems becoming new poems once the expository function of my brain had shut off for the afternoon. I had already received a few rejections from several editors of reviews, and was surprised by some with handwritten suggestions for future contests. No disdain existed for any of them, even those who'd dropped standard cards in post on the way back to me, as I had taken off the fear suit and sent for exactly those expected cards, those unexpected handwritten offerings in order to learn precisely whom to pursue again when the work began getting really, really good, to my standards and not theirs. The first received, I had brought to show Brody at work, which we'd taken turns tearing up after Sonya's suggestion to wrap a used condom in it and mail it back. "This'll be good practice..." Brody had said, each rip a new song on the soundtrack of the painless rejection. "...to go ahead and tear up the ones that even accept you. If you shred them, too, then it's an equal reaction toward either response. You'll be balanced. I mean, all you need's a yes or no, right? *Right?*"

A unique family dynamic was developing at work, too, which by association seemed to turn Knox into devoted denizen in training when Brody would follow me home after a night on, and we would powwow on the floor in a moat of sarcous and amatory possession, as she would laugh and gawk at some of the stories of human behavior and madness that occurred nightly, behavior that was becoming far too ordinary, yet still triggered the surprise grid in our brains. We'd sit with cold strung-together beers on the creaky wood around the bed and look up at her, saying we swore to all that was and wasn't holy, *that really happened,* and *what is wrong with people.*

And the boisterous, alive Dawn who helped run the kitchen, a girl who smoked inordinate amounts of cigarettes and was in the final throes of her philosophy degree, had become an indisputable comrade in the thinking wars. And in coincidence with that groan, so did she have an insatiable urge to get out of herself with a familiar sense of multiplicity to which I magnetized myself. I fell instantly in love with her various crescendos and daring, anti-feminine panache. Our forays into other nights apart from Knox, who was handily maintaining her own missions and credos, and apart from Brody who was immediately and importantly surrendering to the avocation of loving his latest girl with his newest might, were of their own prestige and salience, and they thankfully were of our own design as well, rather than occurring on their own in some mystical confusion we'd be comfortable with putting up to fortuity, rather than owning their outright claim. Dawn lived almost centered between my old place in Midtown and the guesthouse, and so in times of needed disappearance, we capitalized on such desire and took, together, our interpretations of what the night could do, and we began taking to downtown to spread them out like blueprints for earnest study.

This particular escape was also due in part to Brody running out his lease off Mohawk and moving not only his small fold-out sofa into our ever-shrinking digs, but his body as well, but only sometimes, when either we were up drinking together or no one at all was home. He would slip in for a shower and a few uninterrupted hours of pouring over the manuscript, to quietly ask himself his own versions of questions the Bombay woman had dispensed regarding his book. He endlessly carried it with him and never left it out even when the three of us filled in between the walls. It isn't to say he was unwelcome, and I cannot say with accuracy that he had officially moved in, but he was suddenly a child of nowhere. Protectively, I thought the migratory nature he'd assumed was unstable if he wished to work, which meant, in at least *my* reality, I was thinking selfishly, as Knox and I both were elated to have him around more than just often, congestion be damned. But then, I suspected he viewed with romance his self-imposed limbo. Regardless, it seemed the natural progression was to have him plop down the sofa and make a small space beside it for a clothing shelf, and then get familiar, fast, with his feet kicking to what was activated in his dreaming mind some mornings when he did stay and I managed wakefulness before him. Knox was the dominant advocate for his more indefinite insertion into the formula, and so, like three mice in a tied sock, maneuvering and getting settled and making do, I found it easy most days to pull up and out from a heavy night and see him dangling off the fold-out—when he hadn't stayed at Heidi's? Harriet's?—a guard dog of somnolence against the inquisitive winds outside the door.

One early evening toward the end of the week, on the cusp of two welcome days off to work in my no-longer-semi-isolated corner of the house, I'd surrendered the notion of plugging on at my typewriter after a procrastinating stint in the outside courtyard, with just a pen and several loose sheets. Knox had come home from a busy day of not working at work and her energy was good and athletic, so we went out into the crisp shade below the trees and had tea and a few smokes before returning indoors, at first, to review the pair of pages I'd done and the three poems she'd hatched at the studio. But then came the familiar cork popping sound, and then there was laughter, and then the more enjoyable extension of the process itself occurred, the not thinking about the new goods at all. After a quick vegetable sauté dinner, I took to a shower and she to her laptop which had somehow earned a position in the bed with us, rather than the box on which it had ordinarily sat, due to higher traffic to the bathroom on nights when Brody stayed. I had felt enough like a new boyfriend adjusting to his girl's dog at the foot of the bed, a feeling which propelled me toward the Stone to wait for Dawn to get off, to take her up on the previous week's offer to wash away her recent breakup with a series of damn-the-world liquids in a bar, or six, downtown.

"You know what's fascinating..." Knox began as I slid into jeans in what had become our mutual dressing corner opposite her side of the bed. "...is that these online communities actually do most of the work for you. You can find anybody."

I ran fingers through my damp hair and dropped a shirt from shoulder to waist on my thinning body, thin from so much rest and the anti-aging of proper sun and the sparse food supply, the healthy yet sparse supply. She had reconvened on the bed in her usual sitting position, prophet-on-the-mountain, with pillows stuffed beneath her as she angled forward and loomed over the keys. I felt a growing distaste for what the machine represented, but was as yet unwilling to determine with spoken word what that was, exactly. There had been no need for such vocalization, thanks to the multiple languages of the body. And Knox knew, mostly from what I did not say. But in at least partial concession, the fey wonderment of her entire face as it glared at the in-rush of newfound capabilities was endearing, *almost*, and I couldn't refuse myself at least a smile beyond my resistance.

"I don't even like the sound of the keys on that thing. It's too quiet-before-the-storm," I said, sitting on the bed's edge and tying my shoes.

"I think I like it," she said, closing one eye and peering at me. "I feel like a great white shark on this thing."

"Just keep writing like one. What's the point of those communities, anyway?"

"You can keep up with people you haven't heard from in a long time. It's actually a great way to sniff out new music and meet new people. I don't know. It's overwhelming in its limitlessness."

I walked around the bed and reentered the bathroom for a quick assessment in the mirror. It had been a long time since I'd left the safety of the guesthouse for the rage of downtown, and for some reason I suspected the rules of engagement when it came to strangers might have changed.

Looking in the mirror, I subconsciously thought an answer might be there, in a preparatory look before going out into the dark and either forgetting my self, or staying too incredibly aware of it.

"I understand their *function*, Knox. But what's the *point*? Wouldn't you have stayed in touch with old friends if they were really friends?"

I rounded the bed again, in search of my keys.

"I guess so," she said, looking up at me from the machine. "But sometimes you lose touch. I mean, look at Brody. He probably doesn't remember half his family. He should be on here."

I laughed.

"*Yeah*, babe. Good luck with that. He can barely dial a phone." She grinned and nodded. "Besides…" I continued, walking across the room to unplug my heavy, medium-sized processor and lift it, along with a stack of clean papers to go with the new pages I'd written earlier in the day. "… the sounds *these* keys make are more seductive. *Much* more seductive. And you can tell more easily when you've made a mistake without having to constantly look up at the page."

"But this has a spell check system with it. Where are you going?"

I stopped by the door and cocked my head to the side and stared at her in disbelief.

"What?" She asked, without shame or suggestion.

"Where on the globe has your accountability gone, babe? You gonna have it write your poems, too?"

She laughed. "No, it's just that it helps when…"

"*Oh*, no. What it helps you do is…it *helps* you eradicate all that beautiful knowledge you've stuffed in your head."

I supported the machine on my left knee as I reached for the doorknob.

"Isn't that part of, which is it, Buddhist teaching? That intelligence is how much you get *out* of your mind, not *in*? I thought you'd be all for it."

I turned around to her blinking eyes.

"You're right. You're right." I nodded and laughed. "But I'm going to pretend you didn't say that. No, I'm actually telling Brody. You'll pay."

I winked at her, pulled the door shut and headed for the car.

———

"She's actually a cool girl, whatever that tells you. It's not gonna last. *Obviously*. But I think she can at least hold her own," Jena said, one of the other managers who ran the bar at night.

"How do you mean?"

"She just seems to have her own thing going. Seems pretty connected, pretty intelligent. So there's likely to be less of the usual when they don't work out. Shit, I don't even know what to call them. They don't seem flirtatious when they're together. Another?"

She pointed at my near-empty pint.

"Yeah, thanks." I slid my glass closer to her side of the bar. The store was fairly full, but the bar as usual had its regulars, and the crew in back had already been drinking for a couple hours. Jena had switched from some type of high-energy drink earlier in the shift to the same wine Sonya normally drank. "I haven't met her yet, but Brody digs her. Wait, of *course* he digs her."

"Hey, kid," Dawn said, rounding the corner below the bar's television. She leaned into the side rail and lit a cigarette. Jena, who was trying to quit, took it out of her mouth, lit it and took a single hit and passed it back between Dawn's extended fingers. "I'm halfway out the door already. I should be out pretty early." She gave me a kiss and propped an elbow on my arm.

"So LaCoste says he's living with you?" Jena asked, after thanking a woman who left with a take-out order.

I grinned. "That's one way to put it."

"What's another way?" Dawn asked.

"What?"

"What's another way of putting it?"

"Give me a minute to think of something."

"I don't know how you all do it," Jena said.

"Me either," Dawn said, and exhaled.

"Taylor and I pretty much growl at each other over personal space, and we've got a two bedroom," Jena said.

"How's he doing?" I asked.

"He's good. I don't know. No offense, Rattigan, but..." She looked at Dawn and smiled playfully. "...men suck sometimes."

"No shit," Dawn said, handing me the rest of her smoke and pushing her ashtray toward me. "I'm pretty much at that point where I'm ready to go back girls. I thought it was a phase, right? But who knows now?" She patted my arm and promised to be back momentarily after breaking down several machines in the back and getting another beer from the walk-in cooler.

"And *that*..." Jena said to the drinkers at the bar, spreading her arms outwardly as though showing a car in a display room. "...is why we love her."

"It would be wild to watch her work out front," I said, smiling.

Dawn preferred the particular type of hours spent in back, which is where most debatably foul-if-not-just-simply-honest mouths were relegated. And though she and Blain had never consummated a sincerely animalistic longing toward each other, ever since she and Troy had broken up, the possibility seemed oncoming, as well as with Brantley, the other girl, coincidentally the other philosophy major, albeit undergraduate, who worked in back with them.

"How goes it, sir?" A voice said, followed by a strong grip on my shoulders, the hands belonging to Mason.

"Hey, babe. It goes, it goes." I pivoted in my seat to clasp my palm over his freshly razor-shaved head as he lit a smoke and eyed the television over the bar. "How's the night?"

He sighed and gave it a quick thought, looked down at the floor and deposited his lighter in his pocket. "It's all right, man. I got nothing," he said, pointing to his section on the far side of the front door. "People say it's too cold over there. So I'm basically here for show."

"Did you move that sign over the main air vent? Doesn't that usually work?"

Jena heard me and started to laugh, along with a couple regulars on the other side of Adam, a personal trainer who sat beside me.

"Well," Mason began. "I'm glad you said something."

"No, he's not," Jena said, laughing harder and shaking her head. "He definitely is not." She had a wonderful laugh, full and worth joining, regardless of knowing or not knowing the story behind it. I smiled and sipped my beer.

"I climbed up a stool to do exactly that," Mason said. "But let's call this thing what it is. The design of the bar pretty much makes it impossible to kneel on the edge without a good sense of balance."

"Oh shit, Mason. You busted."

"Well, *yeah*. And not just a fall, my friend. I brought the sign down with, so you can just imagine..."

I was working into a soft roar with the rest of the bar and I slid my beer to him, which he picked up and sipped and set back down.

"Cheers," he said and forearmed his lip. "So anyway, you can just imagine my short ass with this shorn dome of mine bouncing off the railing, at the same time a few tables were eating, and then this thin metal beer sign, about the size of my body, right, landing on and then around me on the tiles, just how noisy that was. Good thing there weren't any elderly people. I would have feared for their pacemakers."

"It was probably the funniest thing I've ever seen happen here," Jena said, and then paused to stare into the sky through the ceiling, and then she returned. "Yep. Definitely the funniest."

"Are you hurt, man?" I asked.

"Nope," he said and stubbed out his smoke, walking around the bar's edge toward the back of the kitchen. He turned before disappearing past the doorway, making claws with his hands. "Cat-like reflexes."

I sat another hour until Dawn resurfaced and declared her shift completed, telling Jena that Blain had the line under control in back. Jena thumbed us up and I set down cash for her and the beers but she refused it, which I left nonetheless after stepping bar-side for a hug and, offering to meet Dawn around the back of the building where she'd parked, I followed her to her townhouse. She quickly showered upstairs and changed while I drank a pair of her beers and set up my typewriter on her small round kitchen table, in preparation of the days ahead, of working through the end of morning while she slept, and then our pre-planned late lunch, more work as she studied and I danced my continuous dance alone on the keys, and then another night out before coming back to the other world we would then be pressed to recall. Being that it was later in the week, more bars were open for the choosing, and so we took her car down Government to Conception Street and turned left toward an upward-sloping, free parking lot and made an unmentioned pact to walk Dauphin Street from east to west until each of our curiosities had been sated. The first we chose was the brewery across from the old Saenger Theatre, the same place Margaret and I had failed at lunch. As Dawn and I passed the bar where Knox had taken Brody and me months back, I regaled her with details of the sparkly drag queen at the door, the sharp sounds inside and the all-night labor of going hoarse from laughter.

The beers were unique and good, and the array of shoe types clopping on the shiny wooden floor behind us was a welcome drinking rhythm. We had the occasion to converse with the same kid from the long-ago lunch, the psychology student, as well as a homeless woman who'd been picked up for pending sexual favors by a slimy old man, standing instead of sitting, near the microbrew taps about six or seven seats down. A different woman had managed a good bit of vomiting in a neighboring stall while Dawn had gone to the restroom, and I was offered sex in a whisper from the homeless woman in Dawn's absence. An old classmate of mine from college came in to pick up keys he'd left at the bar the night prior, and once the homeless woman had begun to solicit Dawn for a between-the-sheets romp, we paid out the attentive bartender, a sweet young fellow who'd just had a first child with his wife, and then we hit the street for a different sort of mayhem, the night already auspicious.

"Not a lot of people give Ortega credit because he isn't French or German," Dawn said as we received a fresh round of beers at a small blues jukebox bar down Dauphin past the Cathedral. "But I'm hoping to focus more on his particular use of metaphor whenever I get off my ass and start thesis hours."

"What's keeping you?" I asked. "Money?"

"No, I'm actually lucky in that I've got an assistantship. I just don't want to finish yet. I mean, what the fuck is a philosophy Masters going to get hired to do?"

"Maybe you could do more school. PhD? Teach?"

She leaned her head past me to eye the new people who'd entered the bar past the lone pool table near the front windows.

"This new crop of kids coming to college makes we want to stab myself. Spoiled little bastards, thinking the world owes them something. It's crazy how different they are with just seven years difference between us, you know? And you're one to talk. Why don't *you* go?"

190

"I thought about it, babe. But there's the money thing. And I talked to Brody about it and I agree with him, that it's a real risk on the writing side to go into some costly school on loans, because you need a lot of time to write in those programs, so it's hard to work and do it. Believe me I tried, and it seems..."

"But you work a lot now."

"I know, I know. I'm saying it's hard risking a job that's not conducive to that mindset, because then you're fighting against one thing to have time to fight for another, for what matters. It's a tough sell. Look at LaCoste, man."

"He's an anomaly," she said, shaking her head at the mirror over the bar as she held her glass to her lips. "This is good stuff."

"He really is."

"And besides, I can hide as long as I want. Or at least I can hide until Dr. Mohler finishes his novel. He's mentoring me, or so he says. Oh shit, Rattigan!" She slapped the bar after turning toward me in her seat. "You can help. You *should* help."

"With what? I don't even really know him."

"Me. You should help *me*. I'm getting some crazy assistant editor credit or thank you of some sort for Mohler's novel. It's my excuse for not starting thesis hours. It's ideal."

"But what about your own research?" I asked, spinning my pint glass on my bar napkin as though it were sticks rubbing together to start a fire.

"Man, I've been buried beneath Ortega since I started the program. Troy even used to say he was his competition, that asshole. But I'm good on material. It's just a free semester of organization once I register for the hours. But Mohler's got to sign first, so as long as I'm working for him, he's working for me. Good to have protection."

"He sounds fantastic."

"He's just glad I haven't become a complete cynic," she said, shrugging.

"What, from being a philosophy major or from viewing the world through a realistic lens?"

"I think that's asking the same question."

"That's funny," I said and lit a cigarette. "But I think you're right."

"About the latter, definitely. The cynic part's still in the air."

"I guess that's interpretive. These days, you're over-analytical if you talk things out, at least to those who want to conserve mental energy. And you're an apathetic prick in the eyes of academics if you choose to dumb down or, I don't know, refuse to embrace an awareness of your limitations. I don't think you're cynical."

"That's probably because we've got homogeneous worldviews. I bet you a beer someone in this bar right now would *hate* talking about metaphor in existentialism, or shit, even foundational ethics. Even a little good baby-bad baby."

"What are you talking about?"

I laughed and briefly surveyed the room.

"Fuck it," she said, shrugging. "The prospect of human stupidity eats away at my tolerance."

"I hear that. I miss the language of school, man," I said to my beer.

"It's all I purport to know, like it's a safeguard, although I know that's a mask, too. I know that pretty clearly. It's tough to know teaching's the safest route, because I think it's a deplorable notion, to go the safest route, even though in saying that I feel like a fucking coward, like I can't or won't want to try subverting from within. Being out of school's the danger these days. You've got to be willing to work for Daddy and sell your soul, or stay in school and run up debt and cross your fingers for a tenured gig later on, which pays dick. Or just, I don't know, move to a non-extradition country, say c'est la vie or au revoir or some shit and then plan on never coming back. Maybe The Netherlands, if that's one. I have no clue."

"You say stay in. Brody says don't go back."

"I think you've got it pretty easy comparatively."

"I have no idea," I started to say, caught in a good laugh as I set down my drink. "I really have no idea what you're talking about."

"You have *talent*, Rattigan. I mean that. You can afford to take a year or two or three, play with Brody's crazy ass, learn from him, teach him something, who knows? You can write a book at your own speed, and if it gets taken up and acclaimed you can teach workshops at some cozy university, and then you can be as eccentric and unbalanced as you want and no one will fire you because you're quirky and bring in student dollars. It's a master strategy."

"Right. A strategy drummed up by a philosophy student." I laughed again. "That's not my theory at all."

"You're just saying that," she said, turning her head and adjusting her eyes to align with her chin in a joint expression of doubting me as she again looked past me at the door. I looked, too, and watched the homeless woman from earlier pace past the window after a short stare inside, slimy old man unseen. "You're saying that for your own creative reasons. Take it." She waved her hands in front of her as though she were dusting the counter. "Take it. But it's true. If you're good, which you *are*—I devoured the limited amount of shit you've shown me—but *since* you're good, you specifically don't need more school. Unless, of course, you can find some institution that won't pervert what you do, but pay you instead to go nuts and get better at what you've been doing. But even then it's just a fucking title chase. Kind of soulless. So do the former, man. Definitely."

"That almost sounds romantic."

"What does?"

"The whole going-nuts-to-improve thing."

"You *would* think so."

I took my turn with looking past her at the bearded old men to her right as I hugged the corner of the bar and stacked my feet on the railing below. Dawn's language, as well as maybe mine, too, slightly differed from when not at work. When on the clock I was busy with accommodation, even temperance and peaceful co-existence with customers for whom I danced, a different dance than when alone, when no one knew me. And she, in the kitchen, took to shock-speak and loudness to hide, in the high volume of the heat before the ovens, who she was when no one knew her, except for during the limited moments when, as a brilliant and alive and lunatic wonderer, she could reveal, she *would* reveal, the intensity of someone who has seen so much in tangible texts that every *body* afterward seemed trivial, maybe lovely, and maybe, maybe definitely easy to pick apart. I leaned forward and kissed her forehead.

"And don't fucking think I don't know what you're into. What you're sitting there *doing*," she said, slugging my arm and then finishing her beer. "I know your kind, man. I see it all the time with these affected kids coming in to the department trying to seem super fucking deep to even the secretary. You're the perfect opposite, which makes it easy to spot. They're just a cluster of jack-offs, trying to seem like something they aren't, in hopes it will better their position in other peoples' perspectives. And as philosophy students you'd think they would know better. Who gives a *shit* what people think, right? But since they do it anyway, it means the degree for them is all flair and pretense. But *you*, Rattigan, you do just like Brody does and you don't even see it. You *sweet baby* everybody into thinking you're all honey and balloons and good fucking times just to keep them simultaneously nearby and at a distance, when you really just want to be left alone to get high on staring at the page and feel privately inventive until you begin to lose it and need someone else's company for temporary release, and *seriously?*" She said, looking around again, wilder. "I have *got* to get laid."

"I think a fly went up my nose."

"Man, fuck Troy."

We sat a moment, steeped in the whirl, as laughter volcanically teemed from the upended side of the bar opposite us, a younger group in ties and dresses from some sort of debutante ball it seemed, people younger to us because of our own behaviors, sitting there watching other more nonchalant energies undulate in their own brand of birthright stasis. Dawn looked at them, stuck a finger in her throat and ordered another round and a pair of shots I'd not heard of, something Jena had mixed at work earlier using the juice odds and liquor ends of what hadn't been drunk already by the day crew.

"How is it..." I started, post-shot, post-wince and post-thank you. "...that your mentor's

writing a novel? I mean, it isn't *ridiculous*. It's actually wonderful, but I thought..."

"He said he's tired of writing tenure work. That's another thing I've found to be a turn-off in academia. We come here to sate mental hunger, we aspire, we even fucking achieve," she said, talking with a cigarette in her mouth as I lit another of my own. "And we see these supposed intellectual champions are just people who aspire, too, but get beaten down by putting off their own desires just to secure a steady cover on their mortgage payments. Like I said, Rattigan, you've got it easier."

"So he's writing a novel now, as in a damn-the-depraved-machine novel? Or just to get his rocks off?"

194

"Rocks," she said, nodding and exhaling. I was getting off, too, in the spoils of being away with only minimal guilt from the guesthouse and perhaps the dwindling guarantee of its internal constancy, with Knox's distractions and Brody's fluctuating vanishings, of not knowing where Knox would go with what seemed on its way, as I was concerned for her works, and also, Brody saying with his not saying that he simply didn't have it in him, hadn't created in him, for the moment, a desire to assess what New York was asking him to assess. The spoils of being able to have the old conversation in the new, apart from all my guessings and loves for them, was all-encompassing, intoxicating to stand on a different precipice and watch someone else shake a head and bark at the reality of the mad world. "I got drunk with him at some going-away party for a professor who got inexplicably terminated and went off to work non-profit, and he said screw it, time's apparently here and now and way too fucking short. He told me the premise, which is why I think you should help."

"What's the premise?"

"It's a long story. It actually doesn't sound like a novel. Up front, it sounds like discourse, some kind of altered Hegelian aggression with an added middle finger in there somewhere. If I show some to you, don't tell anyone...he thinks this'll make him famous."

"Gross," I said. The face I made was noticeable because the bartender, a thin long-brown-haired fellow with a dimpled chin and generous smile, even in the face of the old bearded drunk men and the young never-going-to-dies, never-going-to-run-out-of-old-monies, came over to ask if I disliked the beer selection Dawn had ventured off into after our ales had become too familiar. "I'm good, brother," I told him. And then to her, asking, "In what way?"

She saw my face and laughed.

"Not like that, babe. He thinks it will make him famous because it really could. The idea is insane, the expression and layout, they're both insane. But what's insane? Really, if you say *nothing*, you're right. Because new theory, if even through the mask of the novel, usually happens and sticks and works when people are willing to be called insane. You should see his eyes."

I imagined what I could of him from my memory in seeing his shuffling body in the erstwhile academic halls, my memory of what I had heard—spectacles, crazy hair, too many cigarettes, long nights, the acquisition of diabetes in the face of ignored health warnings. I imagined growing into that identity later into my older life, if I made it, same as Brody had said, same as Dawn was thinking about herself and maybe Mohler.

The night was getting louder.

We were uncharacteristically thinking about the future, and future bars, the old night getting young in knowing that we saw too far ahead, or did not see, or would not. I thought of what Dawn said about Mohler and the novel, and I considered the sudden resistance to become something I once and recently thought I might have wanted. I tripped over the word itself, *might*, and then as its own indicator, I recognized that without an awareness of our limitations, embodied largely in our target-less seductions borne of roles and false identities in a culture that didn't necessarily want us to white-picket-fence ourselves to death, but certainly took issue with people like Dawn and LaCoste and Knox and myself not falling somewhat into predictable tow, I recognized that I had been considering what she was saying on both ends of the spectrum and that I had already made a choice. I instantly lost where it was in the past I'd presumed I would ever be what I *might* be, and in so becoming, I would need to be something else entirely in the meantime. A sickness shifted in my stomach from the newly seen imbalance, and then it lent itself to an external levity, as if something in the noisy, smoky talks with Dawn had exorcised more of the ash inside of me, not smoldering but not blown away, ash which in its own repulsion against not being wanted had floated up and out and went on to settle in the hair of someone else less interested in themselves.

"Man," I said, nodding and then tapping my hand on the bar. "Think of how much frustration there must be in being so involved in your career before realizing you haven't been doing what you want. How old is he?"

"Mid-fifties, I think. I'm pretty confident he's still at university because of his commitment to life in the classroom. But it's been tough on him. He went through a couple wives and cars this summer alone. Seriously. You up for a change of venue?"

"Yeah, let's walk," I said, standing with her to finish our beers and unfold cash to cover the tab.

It was early out, an earliness in both our bodies, mine for drawing yet another conclusion, and hers for holding back from what was really on her mind, her future direction, her separation from what had seemed one constant in the melee of work and thinking, some fellow named Troy I'd never met and didn't want to, having already caught a glimpse of him in how she offered insight over the booze, seemingly to cut her own self a break. I threw an arm across her shoulders as we reentered the swelling street and it occurred to me, Ortega, yes, I read him in a beat up old existentialism book still under my driver's seat across town, the man of Madrid who had known what she and I were getting on to know—that in this very moment, what it is that's happening to us is the *not* knowing, at all, what the hell is going on.

"I know what you're saying," Dawn said as she pointed a toe toward the dart line and readied an unsure hand to throw. We'd passed a pair of cross-corner bars with collegiate children spilling into the street from the opposing sidewalks, and we'd opted for a shotgun house of a pub across from the symphony entrance just beyond a loud music hall which advertised bands of the digital age, both of which didn't interest me or Dawn inasmuch as they, the bands and the age, confused and worried us. The pub we selected likely had elements of such progression, but they were hidden by the ability to still hear one another speak and hear strangers laugh. The beers were cold and I was getting heavy. "And it's applicable to me, too. It's an unsafe time to be too caught up in dreams." She threw the dart, scoring nothing with a high toss off the board. She cursed. "But if we get *too* logical...does that make sense?"

"Of course," I said, leaning on a nearby cigarette machine.

"It just becomes muddled, trying on a new hat and not liking it, but wearing it because someone else says it looks good. It's best to go to the extreme of passion rather than logic. You ever thought about it?"

"More times than I can remember, babe." She handed me the darts she'd pulled from the board and I stepped to the line after sipping my beer and passing it to her to set on our small, high table. "You go too far experimenting with logic you might end up like Mohler. Go too far with passion? Without just enough survivalist reason..."

"Brody," she said, shaking her head.

I laughed.

"Perfect. Yeah, because without the bare minimum of how*ever* you'd describe reason, maybe a person goes all the way to their own freedom.

I don't know. But the true crazies in the world who are self-endowed with 'normalcy' either simply think the free should be contained, or actually try to have them locked up. They can do it a million different ways."

I finished my turn and we traded places as a server brought us another round, a busy, kind-looking girl to whom I whispered to only let me pay the bill, come time.

"There's a guy in our department who talked to me about that kind of freedom, you know, in terms of logic and passion. He's gay, so his reference point for the sake of brevity was that it was like coming out of the closet, in a way."

"How so?"

"*Shit*." She swore at the board. "Well, I think he was talking about asking the right questions of the right people, but first discerning our own versions of 'right' defined, then avoiding the normative example."

"Like stereotypes."

"Exactly," she said, flipping off the board and leaving the darts imbedded as she climbed into a seat opposite me at the table. I could see it was getting later in the night because less people walked with confidence by the window outside, but instead had begun to swagger or look repeatedly over their shoulders, afraid to forget what they'd stirred up, trying to nonchalantly walk it off while passing the police precinct a block west. "He said it was spiritually and physically detrimental to all involved parties if we entered the work of the passion-logic balance without analyzing those we know well and how they'd done it, unconventionally or otherwise."

"That makes sense. I think those who disagree actually don't think of that at all until presented with it as some subliminal reminder that they haven't challenged themselves. There's a lot of panic involved in the labor of avoiding it."

"Mohler, man. *Mohler*," she said. "How nuts do you think you and I are gonna be in twenty years? If everything in this country stays exactly the way it is? Which isn't to say it…"

"Well it seems to depend on so many things. But even then, I don't know. It's not a dreary prospect, thinking that far ahead. And at least we're not talking about expectations."

"No, I agree with that. But where I'm going with the question isn't for an answer, really, because it *is* that far away, but at the same time it isn't, right? I was in junior high five seconds ago, and I looked in the mirror last week and started eyeing grays above my ears. From *what?* Natural progression, or making quick work out of not thinking about the future?"

"Yeah, that's still technically thinking about it," I said, smiling and shaking my head. "Knox and I talk about it sometimes. Actually, pretty often lately."

"What, talking about the government or the future?" She asked, pulling hard on her beer and shifting in her seat.

"No to both. No to either," I said. "We talk more about not talking about it. Then there's the curiosity of cowardice, or strength. It's pretty funny when you add LaCoste to it, because we all piled up for a drive last week over to the Spanish Fort side of the causeway to have a couple drinks on the water at that new seafood joint—which was lame by the way—but the musician was really good. Anyway, the entire time we're talking about the conflict within the conflict, Brody's mesmerized by the conversation in his own head. And when Knox shot him a question about the election, he finally looked up and said he didn't like drinking green tea out of plastic bottles. I felt hopeless for myself."

She started laughing, and resigned, so did I.

"After just a short while, though, you should admit being confounded by him is a stark impossibility," she said, laughing more.

"It really is, because I wasn't in the mood to get into politics or any of…"

"It's all bullshit."

"I think so, too, but then you get entangled in the worry that…"

"…you're not playing the role of concerned youth."

"Absolutely. Cowardice or strength, again."

"You know, Rattigan," she began, as I lit a smoke and pulled the ashtray closer to my elbow as I rested my cigarette hand on the table's edge. "That's this country still affecting you. There's no such thing as spiritual doom if you're in constant pursuit of what's best for your mind. We've talked about it."

"*I* know, for sure. And I don't even think I'm worried about doom. Well, I *know* I'm not, so doom isn't it. Doom is too romantic a punishment for the confident. I suppose it's more a…"

"Nicely put," she inserted, lighting a smoke of her own and exhaling to the ceiling. "I guess I'm a little gone to say that clearly. But no doubt, that's it."

"It's just this stop-and-start worry I have."

She cocked her head to the side, looking puzzled.

"As though it's best to stay a certain way, own it, develop and nurture it, and forget trying to come up for air and be noticed. It fits with what you were saying about taking a couple years. A couple years I *can* take, if it means getting conditioned to commit to just doing what I feel I should do."

"Rather than worry you don't care about your life because you don't care about your country?"

Not expecting it to be phrased in such a way, I hit my cigarette, thought a brief minute about it as her eyebrows did an odd flinch independent of the rest of her face, as though she'd managed to say with them, or ask, rather, don't you agree? Or, was that too far? I began to laugh.

"No, baby. That's not it. I think being single's turned you angry."

She let out a breath and began to grin.

"I was talking about writing," I said, and we both started to laugh. Heads turned our way. It was very good, suddenly very good to be serious and be laughing and be high off Dauphin beside a window, looking out at the walking lost and found of the city. "I'm talking about focusing on what really matters, immediately, for me, while not fully blocking out what's going on around me. Definitely not. But not investing so much into it that it damages what I'm doing. I'm talking about not feeling compunction. Because…" I shrugged my shoulders, put out my cigarette and threw up my hands and smiled. "…otherwise I've stepped in what I thought I'd stepped around."

"*Ameranoia*," she said, pointing at me and nodding.

"Say again?"

"Mohler's book. That's the working title. He's writing about exactly this conversation."

"He seems like a pretty inspiring person to work for, partially broken or not."

"The funny thing, no, the *beautiful* thing is this," she said, leaning forward and kissing me on the eye. "He's writing the book to reclaim himself, to save himself, because of our generation versus his. He's watching *us* not give up, Rattigan. We're inspiring *them*."

———

The many hours after posed as a collage of blurs and redemptions in the subtle light sliding halfway through cracked blinds in her kitchen of late morning, where I'd sit unbothered for a brain stretch at her table, waking with a slow high from the cold coffee made the night before, the early morning before, feather-fingering the keys so as not to force her from her heavy rest upstairs. I could hear the frustration in her quick steps to the bathroom when she'd wakened herself and was physically and sleepily furious with the requirements of her body. I felt inextricable from the inside of the townhouse and spent smoke breaks on the patio lying to myself that I could stay there forever. To warm up once fully alert, I wrote a few junk pieces on forever and infinity just to play with the notions behind the words, and I grinned to tears in the stillness of both soundless mornings, the requirements of my own body insisting I missed the proximity of Knox and our romantic semi-squalor. And in thinking of Brody I imagined him, too, at a table somewhere across the house from a sleeping stranger, bending a propped elbow to house his chin in a hand that climbed around his jawbone as he stared down the progression of his book. Dawn and I had neared exhausting ourselves from what we were eluding, her with what we'd discussed during night one below the war canopy of flying darts, and me, the appeasement of the groan as if I'd been a child in a tribe wanting not to leave the village, but just to walk to its edge and make determinations on my own about the growth of the circle itself—to watch the world get bigger below my feet, to study its happening with wide, ready eyes.

The novel was becoming exactly a novel, but I'd somehow forgotten whenever it was I recognized the small truth of this, in that it was at the same moment, I assumed with Dawn the night before, that I stopped with concern that it would. "Oh," she'd said, slapping me on the upper back as she took in a sword of olives from her martini glass at a restaurant bar where we'd begun our second night. "That's a young person's luxury. To get blown away by the discovery of small truths. To quote Mohler." And after a late sleep-in for her and another characteristic long morning for me, we parted ways as I tucked the typewriter under my arm and the rolled pages in my back pocket as she walked me to the door, kissed the side of my face and said she'd terribly needed them, the nights. I returned to the guesthouse in mid-afternoon to find Knox on her machine in the bed, her hair wet from a shower and the smell of laundry drifting through the courtyard and through the cracked window on our north side.

"Hey, you," I said as I kicked out of my sandals and slid into bed beside her.

"Hello, traveler," she said, furrowing her face at the screen.

"I'm so glad to be home." I buried my face in a pillow and tucked inward and curved my back up to the ceiling as if to force my stomach into my spine and my entire self into the bed's memory, fearing maybe it had forgotten me or was silently calling me a traitor. "These last couple days have been intense, man."

"They've been that way here, too. Completely unexpected."

I rolled to my side and faced her before closing my eyes.

"What's been going on? This must be how rainbows smell."

She smiled.

"Maybe so. I let the window so I could smell the laundry from here. I've actually been on some new pieces, which I like, but usually I handwrite them first, so it's strange using this computer for..."

"I'm relieved about the poems. Tell me I can say it," I said, smiling and opening my one exposed eye from the pillow.

"Say what?"

"I told you so."

"*No*," she said, punching my shoulder. "It's just an adjustment."

"It might affect your style."

"Well, at least I can read my first draft for once."

"Your chicken scratch is pretty wild."

"What have you been up to?" She asked after finishing some business and closing the laptop and setting it at the bed's end by her feet.

"Crashing Dawn's. Worked a little. She's been needling through a breakup and she's been too unwilling at work to admit it's messed with her."

"That sucks, man."

"She's good though. I think she's good."

"Not the actual breakup that sucks," she continued. "Just the process of, I don't know, *processing* the new reality that comes after the bullshit. Identity shifts and all that."

"Yeah," I sighed. "I think that's what's really nailing her right now, how she'd found herself allowing her personal definition to change a little by having him so involved in her day-to-day, you know. Like her powers had been diminished from the sacrifice. But once we talked it out, there was just that struggle with trying not to kick herself for being vulnerable to it. Who knows? We've all been there. But I guess it helps to realize you're not the only victim in the history of the world when it comes to taking a stab at sacrifice. You seen LaCoste?"

"That lovely man is MIA. I think between the rigors of ignoring Penguin and being into this girl and his new body infatuation, who *does* know, man? If I've seen him at all it's been a ghost of him encouraging the neighborhood kids to rebel and toilet paper houses."

"I noticed that," I said, laughing, having driven through the east side of the estates on the way home from Dawn's, spying the wind-whipped 2-ply snakes dangling in their own mischief from multiple limbs of the opulent landscapes. I thought of Pied Piper Brody in the breeze, invisible, teasing teenagers on their bicycles to resist, resist in any manner, resist at all (la) costs.

I was suddenly struck with a worry for Brody in that Knox might have been partially right that he hear out his editor. And from not talking to him, not getting at least a partial read on his face when he shrugged off if not ignored what he was being asked, it presented a very unbalancing feeling to latch on to, which I did, in that I knew I was allowing the worry if not inventing it in his absence. On the other side of the worry wasn't worry at all—same as I'd been feeling over the impromptu weekend with Dawn, the good nothingness of doing a very real something—that Brody wasn't shrugging off anything at all, wasn't taking time like I had endlessly needed to in terms of letting an answer come on its own, nor would he pursue the correction of such struggle because he usually stayed busy with the new. I thought, after lying in bed next to Knox and hearing the guileful whir of her laptop putting itself to sleep, that maybe he was getting out of body by entering another, that he was not getting laid or falling in love but disappearing into the activity of either possibility. And then it became clear, clear as the air between Knox's elbow and my left eye, that I had unknowingly wished to be the only one of mystical disappearing acts that week, and LaCoste, of course, had floated out of the realm, again, of his usually unpredictable self, and I had wanted him to come home, too, and spin with me on a wheel of just my own discovery. "When's the last time you talked to him? I miss the kid."

"A while. I'm not sure exactly," she called out from the kitchen after having pushed from bed, declaring renewed energy from someone else at last contributing to the fullness of the house. An odd confession I thought, but one for which I was thankful after fearing for that pair of days alone but not alone, removed from one world for another without having really left either, that I was unsure of their sameness. I wondered when the onslaught of Knox's laptop would replace the purpose and fervor of me tugging her out into that sameness, to share it, to prove it was one real thing. "He taped a note on the door after you left the other day. It's with your mail behind your head. It's great. Read it aloud."

Folded, crumpled pieces of notebook paper sat atop a few white envelopes I ignored when I rolled over and selected it from the pile, opening it and returning to my back to hold it overhead, to split my body from the ceiling to read it.

Sparring partners, it began. *I no doubt feel your energies across the city. Something's decided to swim into me and I'm rolling with it, or turning in the wild surf, I can't even know right now. But I miss you and here is a gift of that recognition. Words, right? Always words. And I've been in this ocean like a pirate or raft-riding madman or solitary lover, it's all so bizarre, or maybe I'm not anything in it other than just In It. A wonder, an utter and genuine mystery being unraveled... you both dig into many of your own so we can share later. I've been thinking about the body lately, as you know, and somehow grew tired of my own a bit, which turned out a miraculous exhaustion in that I started studying vibration states and sleep bordering and almost drum now in the air to a song both parts of my being seems to experience when "asleep." It's crazy! I've come back to breathing—so boggling that we forget it, or say we forget it, but we're ignoring it, aren't we? Aren't I? Are both of you? I'm so interested in where you're breathing! Rattigan, I hear you're taking to a bit of evanescence, which is great. Knox slipped some of her new stuff under a wiper blade yesterday when I was "working." Why you didn't stop in, woman! I think timidity has no room even if the work is newborn. Knox, read it to Rattigan! Hold each other accountable! Start talking of pulsation and methods of calmness, if you feel like it. We can't talk now, as I'm on the rise, if even trying to shake this desire for levitation, but I'm thinking we're all in the air all the time anyway and the best we can do is determine how to get back on the ground. Does that make sense? It better. We'll get on with it soon. Heidi's been a mad enabler with all this, got parental money and a good terrace, no real interest in anything but pursuing answers. And she seems pretty involved in a nearness with me I find inviting. Crazy. No You, soul friends, not at all comparable! Be blessed and well and hang out here on the earth and I'll be there in a flash. But don't wait for me for a damn thing...Rattigan, I'm taking off at the Stone a good while. Knox, talk to this man in stanzas...be well, be well, be well.*

I smiled and set down the letter on Knox's side of the bed. She sighed loudly from the kitchen and I belatedly followed her there.

"You sold me out, Knox," I said, passing her to the refrigerator. I removed a pitcher of cold tap water from inside, reached over the sink for a plastic Mardi Gras cup, filled it and looked at her over the brim. She rolled her eyes and shook her head as she cut an apple on the small cutting board slid sideways between the coffee maker and old knife block with too few knives versus holes for them.

"Not really. I told you I worked a little when you were gone."

"But it's good," I said. "It must be good, on both accounts, if you slipped it to LaCoste and he mentioned it. So you know what this means."

She handed me the first slice and I crunched on it with fake, theatrical frustration. She laughed.

"There's a self-addressed stamped envelope in your mail. Did you notice that?"

"It means you owe me a read. No, I didn't look. It's just another rejection."

"It's from Tennessee, I think. Isn't that one of your contests? It could mean money," she said, turning to lean her lower back against the chipped countertop beside the sink, briefly chewing her tongue's tip at the side of her mouth.

"We're both off tonight," I said, returning to the bed and leaning across it for the mail. "So start thinking up somewhere we can go so I can see the new goods. It's gotten cloudy out, but we could still go to the park. Not too hot. But I'm a little beat. It's up to you."

"I'm into being a hermit today. But I'm down for a co-conspirator."

She raised her eyebrows a few times and bit into an apple slice.

"That's good, too." I shrugged as I stood at the edge of the kitchen, continuing to pry open the taped-shut envelope. "They're determined to make you work to find out how irrelevant they think you are. I need a shower."

"There's a couple of library movies by the player. See what you think."

"That definitely sounds good. Maybe I'll get some real rest for a change before tomorrow. Or attempt it. I could certainly use…"

I paused over the unfolded letter in my hand, a typed letter, a galaxy apart from Brody's lustful script.

"You look confused," she said.

I took a deep breath and exhaled.

"I might be."

"What's it say?" She asked.

I shook my head.

"*What?* Is it harsh?"

"No," I said and began to laugh. "I won, man. At least that's what it says."

"Shut the fuck up!" She shouted, bounding to my side and pouring over the letter as I read it a third time. "Holy *shit*, Rattigan."

"Yeah," I said, still laughing. "I guess so. Holy shit. And I don't…" I quickly looked around me as though an answer lay at my feet. "I don't even remember what the first prize is."

"We can look it up."

We stood in place a short moment, grinning at one another before racing toward the stack of magazines across the room. We flipped through the one I'd dissected two months earlier and from which I had pulled a few dates and deadlines, half-committed to them before going about the business of forgetting.

"Eight hundred dollars," she said, staring into the page with me. "As in almost a thousand bucks."

"For a short poem I wrote two *years* ago?"

"You can buy a laptop now, Rattigan."

"Fuck you."

"I'm just saying."

"And they want me to come to Nashville to read? This is crazy. Too crazy. A month from now."

We stood beside the lifted window in the fog of laundry and we hugged, dancing a partial dance of victory against, I'm unsure still, perhaps the self-doubt about which we rarely spoke. And we missed Brody. We stood in the dance and laughed like maniacs and we missed Brody like mad, agreeing to send him back his offered energy across the city, doubly, triply, even though I hoped I'd cross paths with him down the street some time soon at the Stone, or he'd come by when either of us were home. And though he was off flying above the roads and avenues and trees and rooftops, looking for the ground, we had all just done something remarkable together, unwittingly, from just one of us having opened a wrinkled letter.

"Get your shoes," Knox said, pacing around the bed and walking into a pair of jeans. "Let's get out of here. We're celebrating. We *have* to."

"What if it rains?" I asked, smiling large, still confused at the letter in my hand.

"Oh, I *dare* it," she said, shaking her head.

"Then bring your poems. We're not going without them."

"And you, my friend," she said. "You're not going to Tennessee without me."

CHAPTER 7

The ensuing month of anticipation toward leaving was rife with uncomfortable responsibility, though if it were a song it would have seemed euphonious and even catchy, worth singing, with Knox and I humming along in some determined synchronicity aimed at eventually landing on the highway north. New protocol was that we would conserve money by living only in the guesthouse, bringing in our food and mild but steady misbehaviors from outside our world's walls. Around our work schedules, she took to organizing the floor for easier navigation over what had become its own blockade to prevent maneuvering to and from the kitchen, and even the bathroom mirror seemed to have begun to forget our faces. I attended to making clothes disappear into rightful cabinets, and as our money built into a readiness for evacuation, my novel grew closer to completion as Knox worked a little apart from the fascination with her laptop. She wrote response pieces to old poems of mine I'd unearthed to assemble along with the piece that won the writing award in Nashville, in the event I'd be asked to stay longer and disrupt the audience with more of my reading style, *our* reading style, and then the themes of body and bare motion inside the languages that the body itself spoke when the mouth could or would not.

Her poems needed attention I didn't foresee her giving them, no time soon, as her dedication was understandably split between finalizing her thesis on the Beats and minimal work at the studio. What seemed unsettling to me was Knox's quiet joy from just having gone through the process of segmenting her vigilance into creative expression and staring at the clock—unsettling only in that I saw the coming award ceremony, still, as a win for us both, an opportunity to meet others in the field and get our feet wet and quickly into the process of drying. Unrealistically lusting after her zeal to pair with mine and wishing her labor would continue uninterrupted, I was even so content with her poems' births. I wanted us to go north and get weathered with identical ambition, but I wouldn't share this with her in fear it would thrust her into a rush of forced prolificacy that left her winded but unsatisfied. So we sat around like a grumbling elderly couple, yet familiar, understanding various groans in the silence we provided ourselves, not knowing how to wait and unwilling to admit to the angst of having chosen to. We were at least cognizant enough to recognize we had no alternative, which meant our conflict then became just a game.

I'd taken to working a full forty, and was relieved to see Brody in and out of the store, still touching strangers at the tops of their arms as they passed through our bizarre bubble of commerce, still involving himself very much in what he was doing while there. He stayed after for drinks most nights, his palm stayed at my neck and there was much laughter, but he rarely contributed to the traffic of the guesthouse. His couch in front of the door soon became a neatly designed landfill of my clothes from the floor, as well as a box of Knox's albums and several of our ratty notebooks, half-filled with sketches of older thoughts from just a few years earlier, lines and furious erasings that would, at some point, either die a necessary death in the trash or be revived for the sake of exercise before reaching out to the matter of the new.

"Are things well with Heidi?" I asked him one night, just before midnight, as we stood by our cars parked in back of the restaurant. I lit a smoke and handed him one and we turned our backs to lean against my driver's side.

"It's good, babe. It's quiet. I think she's doing something for me but I can't figure out exactly what it is. Maybe I haven't been paying attention."

"What do you mean?"

He exhaled toward the sky over the roof.

"Well, first off, Rattigan, it's not even a physical event between us, which is odd but very, very good. You know? I've spent so much time with some personal vision of, well, I guess *pursuing* a sense of planes, meditating, trying not too hard to place an emphasis on the stars or the ground. And she just sits back. We have tea sometimes, sit knee-to-knee and, it's great babe, just sort of touch. I guess that's the physical of it. The almost un-physical-ness of it."

"It sounds important, Brody. Very necessary, man." I thought a moment and flexed my brow. "I think I've entered a similar space lately. Been strange, too, but intensely good. Knox and I have established a sort of routine of conversing through unmentioned urges."

"Such a small place. The energy there, especially between you two, doesn't seem to require many words. It definitely makes sense."

He tossed his cigarette to the road beside my front tire and stretched his hands behind him, over his shoulders and on to the top of the car.

"And I definitely concede there's a palpable anxiety working at home, too, but a right one. It's been a minor challenge to wait for Tennessee. It's not even about the award or the money. Honestly. Not at this point. It's about being in motion again, and sending out some strong light in unfamiliar environments."

"I'm glad that's how you're seeing it, babe."

"How else should it be seen, right? There's a good opportunity out there, somewhere, to move someone toward what we're doing here. But without manipulation. Knox says she doesn't even want to talk to anyone, but just sit in the back and try to...this is her word...shimmer. And just let me do whatever it is I end up doing."

"That's the point I've reached with Heidi. But I miss time with you both. I mean, this has been a necessary departure. An evolution, really. And I don't know if I'm even communicating it with her very well, but thankfully she either gets it and keeps a fair distance, or she doesn't understand at all but is just enthusiastic about watching someone else's process develop itself."

"What are you working on?" I asked, stepping back from the car and running my foot over a flattened soda can on the pavement.

"At first I thought it was confusion, and then I laughed it off when I realized I was disturbed at the confusion itself, instead of just letting it do its thing. Then I saw it, pretty clearly, that I was studying this out-of-body labor, and wrongly calling it labor, and then going over the levitation idea, which turned out to *not* be what I want or need, once I defined it. And then it struck me like, I don't know, a water balloon to the face. Like I was bracing for pain or shock at its onrush, but it was more a surprise, and then I got the facetiousness of the planet handed to me."

"In what way?"

"I'd been resisting Penguin in terms of where to take the book, not as some sort of rebel or defiant lit kid. Nothing like that. But I saw I needed to evolve along with the next direction I was taking after finishing the draft, at least before I could assess what they were asking me to do. Who I was when I finished the book was already on its way out, so really I needed to focus on what was coming, pay attention to it, stop giving it, I don't know..."

"A label?"

Brody took a deep breath. His chest lifted high toward his chin before the air escaped and his shoulders came back down into themselves.

"Yeah. Yeah, man, that must be it. I was cheapening what was happening by trying to prematurely name it. Exactly."

"I know what you're talking about," I said, scratching at my forehead and grinning. "I was in an obvious stage of that when we first met."

"Yeah, but you were fine, Rattigan. You were lovely and kind of spiritually unkempt, but the energy was there. It was in your face. Pretty fascinating to see. I'd forgotten that look."

"And now I'm into what's ahead. Just immediately, though. No rush for what might happen after Nashville. There's still a good bit of reviews with their juries out, and a month or so left until their deadlines close. I'm guessing it'll be early June before I find out the rest, including that fellowship in California. Maybe it's better to enjoy this kind of evolution at home, too."

"That's where I've been, babe. It's what I'm doing now. At some point I reached a really strong comprehension of the changes going on, and the conclusion I drew was that I couldn't adhere to the suggestions in New York if I didn't complete what I was off doing on myself. And what I learned, what got me back into the book, wasn't the silence necessarily, and it wasn't the departure from our thing with Knox at home."

"Yeah?"

"Yeah. Instead, I think it was from learning, after some really serious letting go in the evolving, that the investigation of being out of the body actually leads, well, not inside the body, but it seems to have erased a disparity with the two. As if the line's gone. I feel I've really accomplished something important these last weeks."

"I think you have, man." I reached toward his shoulder and gave it a firm squeeze. "It's been good to have you gone, then, in knowing you've been well."

"I have, Rattigan. And I've also worked out some crucial objectives in the book."

"I haven't read a line of it, you know. Knox is curious, too."

He laughed and nodded.

"I think most of me knew it wasn't completely right. I was definitely hoping the transition to the big market would be as seamless as my other book. The book no one's ever heard of." He kept laughing.

"Well, who do you think's going to give a shit about one small poem of mine in Tennessee? It's not about that, right?"

"Not at all." He grinned. "I mean, the stakes have changed because of the requested increase in effort. Same with you, now that you're beginning to win. We're both going to have to reconcile with that."

"I wish you could ride up with us, Brody. The invitation still stands."

He pulled his keys from his pocket and faced me.

"I can, Rattigan. You *know* I could. But I'm working this thing out as fully as I can. You guys sail away, get wet, whack out in the mountains, and then when you get back you'll find me."

"I know, I know. It'll still be a good, good thing."

I pulled him into a hug and patted his back, and then laughed him off with a push.

"Of course it will, babe," he said, jiggling his keys beside his ear and stepping backward toward his car. "*Of course.*"

We disappeared into separate geographic nights, but similar in spiritual aim, his car turning right down Old Shell past the college's sporting arena, west toward Hillcrest Road as I lefted through the parking lot to stop in for a bottle of wine at the nearby package store where an old friend from school worked. But Raj was home prepping for a presentation for a graduate class, the cashier told me, and I made small talk over the importance of such work, but without having much stock in my belief system behind it. The earth had its reasons for the work we chose, sometimes choosing us for it, and I knew I'd never fall in to more educational time in the academy. But for others in the fray, to find their own evolution and become a part as naturally as they could bear, the movement needed to be done. It was with that sense of celebration of continuity that I passed well-wishes to Raj by way of the timid fellow at the counter, and I bundled the cold bottle inside my arm and made my way back down to the fairy tale cottage in the trees where, in the dark, it seemed possible the guesthouse was made of children's candies. There was a chimney, the small glow inside was its heart, and within breathed a girl who wrote of burgundy. And on top of Nashville eventually coming on, I'd forgotten to tell Brody that Knox had contacted an old friend who lived in Chattanooga, just two hours east, and so our escape to go talk about a poem at a festival had become something else entirely, including additional pulses and voices in what the weatherman, three days before we'd take off, predicted to be "a weekend worth staying awake for."

———

I packed the night before we left, after pulling a final shift at the restaurant, and I did so just tight enough on wine that multiple reviews of my clothes and accoutrements resulted in a surfeit of items I wouldn't need but still kept. Knox went against instant reason and forged into the early morning without sleep as she faced off with her computer and caught up with old school mates from times I did not know her. And as she was called to open the studio at eight o'clock, our departure was shoved into mid-afternoon, which heightened my want for leaving, leading to drinking beer and self-sputtering to past noon before realizing I'd be driving us up in her car, and then I finally caught up on sleep, waking to her shuffle across the house and the smell of coffee around three-thirty. After a quick room survey on her behalf, and the group lugging of our bags and hanging shirts, the disconnection of old appliances and the cut of the air conditioner, we made the car just under an hour later and hit the gas station down Dauphin past the Springhill golf course for cigarettes and headache pills, pumpkin seeds and a pair of sodas and, with Knox on the phone with her incredibly pregnant friend Cora, who lived in Chattanooga, we could confidently recognize we'd at last gotten on the way. The sky above the road ahead was beautiful and forgiving.

Around forty miles up I began to finally feel out of the familiar space of home, the highway offering occasion for me to redefine it, even if temporarily, as something else. As much as I'd anticipated Knox's exhaustion to consume her, and my empty stomach to respond to the remnants of the beers I'd had mid-day, I wasn't hungry and she couldn't fall asleep. It was an elation I could call the night before Christmas, or after a soccer game's victory, but at the real expense of telling the truth as adults, no longer children in the regard of effusiveness that comes with no longer having to wait for an outcome, I was high on fluidity set forth by all our foreign planning the weeks earlier. And it was manifest in Knox, too, as she hung out the window as we crossed a bridge I couldn't properly name, monikered by locals as "the Dolly Bridge." She snapped a pair of photographs from a disposable we'd bought with the pumpkin seeds before leaving Mobile. The girl at the counter had made a face when I threw it in with our assemblage of odd unpredictables, and when I inquired about the look, she waved the small disposable in the air with facial dissatisfaction and said, "You should really look into getting a digital camera. They're not too pricey these days and..." I felt the quake of Knox's internal groan and saw her shift where she stood as she gripped cash tightly in her palm, and then she put her even bigger penis on the counter, saying, "I actually have a very expensive one at home. We just chose not to bring it." An infinite moment of palpable awkwardness followed before the girl shrugged her shoulders and gave us the total. On the way out the door I asked Knox if she had, in fact, purchased a digital, if she had done something additionally unfortunate against her credit. As we slid into the car she said, "No," while lighting a cigarette and exhaling out her descending window as I dropped us in reverse, "but fuck her."

The conversation up I-65 glided around her contempt for the inefficiencies of her work mates, the sublime dysfunction of those at my job, with little guessing at what lay north beyond a few sureties regarding Chattanooga and Cora. My stomach began growling more noticeably, and so we decided we'd stop halfway to Birmingham in a town called Greenville, a haven for fast food joints and gas stations just off the exit ramps. But we were over an hour shy of it, and the music of the radio seemed unimportant as anything but backdrop to the building energy in the car. It wasn't until the conversation pivoted into the political that I knew without sustenance I'd become pensive and spiritually out of reach. So Greenville took a mean-faced eternity, even when beautiful Sam Cooke came over the airwaves as the sun first considered its vanishing.

"I really don't want to talk about that shit."

I sighed, massaging the vinyl wheel with my palms.

"I don't either, honestly," she said as she propped her bare feet on the dash in front of the passenger seat. "I just need your input, man. Not even on politics. How about not-politics? Can we talk about *that*, angry person?"

She had a serious expression on her face when I studied her briefly, which forced me to smile.

"Not-politics it is. I'd rather talk about me."

"Of course you do, Rattigan. How silly I get."

She grabbed my right arm and shook it.

"You're putting us in severe danger."

"*Anyway*. I've been trying to tell you I've kind of grown apathetic toward the whole process."

"You rarely tell me. What's been up?"

She pulled her left knee into the seat and turned toward me while looking past my ten-and-two hands, off through the windshield and over the outstretched landscape of greenery spreading west.

"Nothing wild. Nothing out of the ordinary, I don't think. I just don't care anymore about it."

"You worried it means you're an asshole?"

"Yeah. Well, sort of. I just don't want to seem like what's at stake lacks value, but the ride to get there's so exhausting, even as a spectator. Does that make sense?"

"Definitely, but it doesn't make you a coward."

She nodded, and her face had taken to stern, almost inquisitive.

"I wouldn't feel bad about being frustrated. Was that a hawk?" I pointed out the windshield past her.

"See!" She slugged my shoulder. "You seem fine with not talking about it."

"I've already talked it out with Brody a good bit. I really think that was a hawk."

"What did he say?"

"Same simple Brody stuff. At least we've all got a good thing going, and we work with people that tackle the world the same way, that could-be-worse sort of talk."

"True," she said, lighting a pair of cigarettes as I rolled down my window. "Why does it not sound dismissive when he says it?"

"I don't know the answer to that, babe."

"His comfort on this planet boggles me."

I laughed and changed to the lane beside the highway shoulder.

"I'd go nuts if I didn't work with the people I've got at the Stone, man. You should have seen my family at Papa's funeral. Their eyes when I said I was in a restaurant. My mom conversed with God a lot."

Knox rolled her eyes.

"But I was *in* it, man. Don't forget. I was miserable at my old job."

"I know," she said, laughing. "Every time I caught you at home I thought you were, pun absolutely intended, headed for the oven."

"Maybe so. But I'm not completely out of touch now, you know? I step in and out of the conversation with customers watching the political ticker at our bar, but they all usually come at it from good places, because really there's no direction to go if we snarl and hiss about shit you and me can't affect with a notebook at this point in our lives. That's what I'm hoping…"

"That's what might be getting started in Nashville. For *you*," she said.

I looked at her and she was staring at me with one eye tightly shut, and I laughed again.

"I hope. At least, I'd like to hope so, but I don't need to be illogical about it. What does a hawk sound like?"

"How so?" She asked after throwing out her cigarette.

"I'm asking you."

"About what?"

"Does a hawk 'caw'?" I asked as I grinned and sped around a truck pulling a filled horse trailer.

"Seriously, Rattigan. Enough of the fucking hawk. I meant the illogical part."

"Ok, ok," I said, laughing. "This award could just be one thing. I've got a lot out right now that could lead to something huge. And I think age leans at least a *little* more in my favor, since I'm not right out of college and won't seem desperate and inexperienced. The collection in New York will take up to three more months to hear back about, and believe me that I threw this Tennessee award at the top of my accomplishments page I sent to Rochester. The short fiction thing in NYC, too, would be a prestigious start. But the fellowship in California's what I'm really, well, yeah I'm definitely hoping for it."

"How much was it again? How much is it? I'm talking like you've got it already."

"Over fifty *thousand*, man. For two years of just writing and doing workshops. You want to use campaign language?" I thumped her kneecap. "That would be a game-changer."

She smiled. "I'm coming with you out West. If you win it, man. I can't stick this out in Mobile, not after seeing what you and Brody deal with."

"It's just about the maintenance of integrity. For as long as we can hold out. I don't want to be fifty and still shadowboxing over a book I'm too weak-willed to send out."

"Even the writers I knew in grad school went off to either more school, or another town with a better cultural thing going on."

"Hey, at least you'll have your M.A. That's good for marketability. But for what, right? Adjunct comp. teacher, with a side telecom job because you don't get paid crap and can't afford PhD? Or you do entry-level copy? Let me go ahead and be the beacon of that failure for you. It led to minor promotion, insulting pay and a lot of slobbering alone on my pillow on the nights I was heavily considering some other life entirely. Who knows? A Nepalese Sherpa. Full-time alley cat. There's our exit."

"'Bout time," she said, readjusting in her seat and inserting her feet into sandals on the floorboard. "You know, when you don't eat you prove you're still fluent in 'real world' language. You're almost unattractive when you speak it. Best you become a Sherpa."

Knox chose a greasy sandwich spot to the right past a few traffic lights and we pulled in, parked and stretched. It was as close as possible to being dark before becoming it. I threw an arm around her as we made it inside and toward the bathrooms as some of the locals looked up from the dinner tables, unsure of the two maniacal deposits from the road wearing wrinkled t-shirts and looking slightly dazed.

I came out first and waited for Knox in the slim hallway as a woman jiggled the handle on the single-use women's room.

"There's a crazy person in there," I warned.

The woman was middle-aged and quietly backed from the door and stared at the tiled floor. Definitely a local, I thought, and sent her good blue light. Knox, in natural form, bounded out soon enough, her widely agape mouth poised to say something I inwardly hoped would be terrifying, but she caught herself uncharacteristically when she spotted the woman.

"You're right," the woman finally said to me, smiling, as she moved around Knox to step inside the bathroom. "She is a crazy person." Knox's eyes grew wondrous and large as she aimed them at me. The woman, almost fully immersed within, stuck her head out and said, "I know 'em 'cause I live with one." She winked and shut the door. I beamed.

"You're hilarious," Knox said, pushing me toward the front of the restaurant and the ordering counter.

Once we'd gotten our packed tray of food and had assaulted the condiment counter for multiple and unnecessary acquisitions to go with the road dinner, we found an ideal seat beside a window which looked out on to the street. It took us both sitting before we noticed a large piece of tape-stuck signage was thwarting our view, unless we chose to duck our heads below its lowest border and study that which we'd not be able to see clearly, anyway, by the end of the meal, as the darkness of night was coming on strong. A lone diner sat hunched over his food behind Knox, a family of three beside us, and as I began spilling things on my entire body, a quiet couple planted themselves at about one o'clock past Knox's shoulder. After a brief moment of collective analysis, we determined it was local high school football night, hence the burgeoning, bustling mob of the famished. And after conversing a few more minutes we realized two more things, that we were heartily out of place and that, at the end of four weeks of clock-staring, we were traveling and away from "it all" and were precisely where we needed to be.

"Now I know..." Knox began once we'd swapped sandwiches. "...that we quote-unquote agreed not to talk politics, but..."

"I think your sandwich is better than mine. And please note that what I ordered isn't a *real* Reuben. I'll find us the goods when we get home."

"But I'm really kind of talking economy."

"I'll have to think of where to go."

"I was thinking about a cool job. Might be just as cold as Sherpa work."

"Oh yeah, there's this neat little joint in Midtown. Uses the right bread, homemade sauce for it."

"It might require we buy more intense jackets," she continued, squinting her eyes into the not-Reuben, ignoring my not-desire to talk her imminent talk.

"I spoke with a chef once who said Jewish Rye is best. I don't know."

"And a heightened tolerance for chattering teeth."

"Personally I dig on pumpernickel."

"*Rattigan.*"

I picked up my drink and pursed my lips over the straw, sipping and lending her a big set of curious eyes, celebrating how far out we stuck in the building, and getting off on it.

"I'm trying to tell you about the fucking Iditarod. Don't look at me like that."

I laughed and noticed the small family beside us looking over, and I could almost hear the whine in the little boy's mother's arms wishing to stretch out and cup palms over his ears. But he was lying in his cushioned seat, making odd noises and attending to the distracting works of his own mind.

"I thought you wanted to talk politics."

"No. *Economy.* That was just my official segue. I read there's some guy who sells hot dogs at the Iditarod, and because he's got the balls to stand out there and freeze, he rakes in so much money he just tosses off the rest of the year. Incredible, man," she said, shaking her head and diving her sandwich she'd reclaimed into a spilt vat of spicy sauce on the tray between us. "See? Not-politics."

"I know someone who lives in Illinois who said some guy by her college sells hot dogs outside a busy bar downtown. Makes a killing."

"We're in the wrong racket," she said, head still shaking in disbelief.

I sat in silence, having found rapture in the sating of my stomach. I was motivated, too, by the continued exodus to an unclear elsewhere between "here" and "there." Knox closed her eyes during the last pair of bites, with a concomitant understanding paired with mine that it was possibly our last involved, big meal of the ride. Once we agreed the driven discussion of hot dog economy had whorled madly like a leaf tornado into palaver, we decided it best to give after-the-fact relief to the nervous couple at one o'clock who'd already shuffled toward the door. Once back at the car we noticed the two of them were parked beside us, were still sitting inside their vehicle and were likely, according to our theory, realigning their driving chakras before more highway. I saw on their bumper a Mobile Symphony sticker. They were dolefully heading to the coast.

"Oh," I said to Knox as we climbed in and cranked up and rolled back toward the exit. "They weren't frightened. They're Symphony aficionados."

"And that's its own distraction," she said as we lit smokes and rediscovered 65.

We stopped for gas after reality overrode my inattention to the tank light, in Gadsden, a town in northern Alabama. Before finding a station, and after much doubt about our ability to succeed in getting back to the interstate, we found a small, tucked-away spot on a side road, a place offering the cheapest gas either of us had seen in over a year, and as we hailed the find as triumphant, neither of us were too interested in using the facilities there due to the unsure locale, opting instead to play paper-rock-scissors for who would go in to pay. I won my way out of it and was subsequently accused of cheating, which perplexed me. When Knox reengaged the air between the building and me at the car, ogling three obese children yelling in the parking lot, she reached in the car for the camera to snap a shot of me pumping gas. She commented on my smile's authenticity, which I suppose had been a rarity during the time we'd been waiting to break town.

Surprisingly, we got back into our thrust northeast from Gadsden with ease, on toward a rest stop before she got on her cell and called our hotel she'd booked over the computer, as she was confident we were on our way to being lost. Her exhaustion was wearing on as we successfully pulled into the front of the hotel and parked, as she'd been babbling on about turnips and mastodons for a solid pair of miles.

We checked in after an odd joke from the security guard about how he was "dying of cancer, but at least the weather's nice." And once in the room on the second floor, which was also the top floor, as I went to the restroom again, Knox stood by the window past the two queen-sized beds, promulgating the layers of the mountain that housed our hotel. Once out, I joined her and wished aloud that we could have had a balcony to sit on and have smokes and watch, even if just for a small while, the stars do their business of sitting or darting or blazing in the sky over the hotel above us and the mountain, and then the looming haunted house of an apartment complex at the very top before the sky began past it, pointing toward South Carolina or an invigorating, undisclosed other.

"I forgot to tell you," she said, pushing off the glass and into the guts of the room to begin digging into a mid-sized bag in front of the television. "Surprise."

Knox pulled out an insulated lunch bag with a bottle neck protruding from the top. She ripped at the Velcro and displayed just the top wrapping of the bottle, in brief demonstration of her forward thinking, her applied wherewithal prior to the trip.

"I thought..." she continued as she walked toward me, bottle behind her back. "...since you've won, we should celebrate with champagne."

She pulled out the bottle and flashed the label.

"It's total shit, Rattigan. But I know you're into symbolism."

I laughed and took the bottle from her.

"Plastic cups are behind you, babe."

She laughed, too, and took a large breath. Then her eyes illumined, a crazy person again coming suddenly not out of a bathroom in mid-Alabama, but a person alive on an eighteenth wind who'd come up with yet another idea to stay the unfortunate work of sleep, somewhere in the new Tennessee dark. But the room buzzed with light.

"We should take our drinks for a walk and have a cigarette."

The popping sound ensued beneath one of my thumbs and a protective palm, as I'd been purposefully shot in the back with a cork once at a bar I worked in only briefly, but still recalled its implications and potential havoc, and we galloped in wildness toward the elevator for the fleeting ride down. Going through the lobby I noticed the confusion in the eyes of the guard and the desk fellow, as Knox and I had changed into different shirts to pair with the weather we thought would be cooler when getting ready for the drive, his confusion also at our tiredness we'd claimed at check-in would keep us in for the duration.

I followed her lead around the building toward a concrete and maybe fortifying uprising against a dirt wall beside the menacingly narrow road leading up to the haunted house. She chose seats for us as we lit cigarettes and drank our plastic bubbly in opposition to the flood lights of the hotel's corner. But it only took a pickup to whiz past, carrying a belatedly Mardi Gras-masked crowd of noisemakers to ignite in us a want for the inside again, a small crowd dangerously hurling themselves in the direction of the chaos we agreed existed at the top of the mountain. We stubbed our butts and took our quickly emptied cups down to the leveled parking lot, around to the front door and endured the staff's stare as we went back up. We somehow became hungry though, after refilling our drinks, and as I could see in her drooping lids while we sat in the floor and played with the TV channels that she needed even the most insincere stab at her own fortification, I nominated myself to procure necessary snacks from across the narrow road, from a gas station that would surely offer more wine.

"You know what I like," she avowed as I shut the door behind me and descended again.

I was almost hit by a car on the narrow road, but weathered it with what I teased myself into thinking was aplomb, even after being cursed for being a pedestrian. I thought that if we didn't push out of the place by just after sun-up, we'd die horrific, film-worthy deaths. And then, in an odd marriage of the two thoughts, I suddenly missed Brody and wanted him there. But in his absence I considered what he would be owed from our drive up without him. I wanted to jump on back of the next ascending truck and roar at their calamitous energies just to go home and tell him our lives had been well-represented on the road. But I made it over the gravel and into the station, as LaCoste was somewhere sleeping or not sleeping, with or without champagne, hopefully for a night inside his own body.

"They don't sell forties in Alabama," I told the clerk as I set two towering malt beverages in heavy glass bottles on the counter, along with impartially selected snacks to bring back to a withering Knox. I didn't imagine she'd be awake when I stumbled back across the lane.

"They don't?" A fellow asked behind me.

"Just thirty-twos, brother," I answered over my shoulder after turning to study him. "The world's a mad place."

I paid the smiling clerk after mild chatter with the man, on his way with work mates back to Kentucky, telling him with minimal devotion to the story of a short stay over in Paducah, years earlier, when driving through to help a friend move to Illinois.

"Yep," he'd asserted as I made out the side door. "Lotta them damn Pentecostals in Paducah."

Unsure of what it meant but pleased with the transference, a sense of unity was almost visible in the air during the short walk back, a walk precluding any real fear I'd be pancaked in a poorly lit area of darkness which hid the surely nearby mountains. The glue-eyed guard and desk attendant had seemed stuck on their interest not with, but at me as I traversed the small lobby and turned left back to the elevator for the jaunt up to Knox who, once I keyed inside, was sitting on the floor, still before the television, gripping her champagne cup and fumbling with the buttons below the screen.

"I'm surprised you're up, babe," I said, after handing her a drink and setting down the bag of sundries.

"I fucking love these things," she responded, extracting the pizza-flavored chips and decapitating the bag's head. "Did I ever tell you I considered auditioning for an acting school in New York?"

"You most certainly did not." I sat beside her and cracked the lid on the heavy beer. "This is really disgusting," I said, after sipping. "Thirty-eight more ounces to go. I was trying to fit in with the natives."

"I think that's stereotyping."

"So acting, huh?"

She looked at me, perplexed, before regaining the conversation, and then her eyes widened.

"It was a sad, sad day, Rattigan. I was supposed to audition in Atlanta for these reps from NYC, and I was told to memorize a monologue."

"Cheers," I said and clinked her bottle with mine.

"So I'm thinking, how intense would it be to memorize the Hannibal Lecter piece from *Silence*, right?"

"You're kidding."

My breath caught and I began to smile. Her face was sagging, away from her usual tough youthfulness, into an old ghost of a girl who had died and become translucent from sleep deprivation. But Knox was like a car that could only drive in second gear, still moving along, and she was doing all she could not to go face down into the carpet.

"So here I am, when I was living with Celeste off Catherine near your old place. This was freshman year when I realized I loathed the disrespect that comes with being an undergrad, right? So the natural progression for me, somehow, was to become an actor and fly off to fame and money. Anyway, I'm at home all hours and practicing this crazy, I don't know, *death saunter* toward the mirror and prattling on about 'the barn' and 'the screams' and fucking fava beans, man. I even had that inward, swift sucking thing down that Hopkins does."

The imagery was too much, matched with her seriousness about her labors to convince herself she was a cannibal. I shook with a laugh too afraid to fully come out, in that it might have muted the rest of the coming details.

"But then two days before I was supposed to drive up to do my read, I actually read the fucking application, and it said I was required to do something gender specific. Gender *specific*, Rattigan. What kind of shit is that?"

"I don't know," I said, beat and then out of control. "I don't know at all. But what did you expect?"

"*I* could be a killer, man. You think I should have just done a Sally Field and danced their stupid monkey dance? I want a cigarette."

"No, I don't think that at all. I've thought for a long time you're more of a man than I am. But maybe you could have..."

"Read all the forms? I know. I *know*."

We laughed a while on the floor, in full comprehension of our mutual fuel depleting. A lawn care commercial filled the screen and I thumped the off button.

"Needless to say I didn't go. And by the way this jerky is *horrible*."

"All right, kind sir. More snack my way comes," I said, swiping her uneaten beef strip and flattening out with it on my bed closest to the window. "You can go smoke. Those guys down there are too eerily fascinated with me."

"I could definitely hear a banjo somewhere when we checked in," she said, slowly lifting herself over the foot of her bed and army-crawling toward the pillows.

"I don't think you're a nice person," I said, shaking my head with forced shame at the visible side of her face, which barely stood out against the pillow in which it was buried. My hunger was gone, the beer was nearly finished and doing unfortunate work on my taste buds. Considering the day ahead, and Knox's suddenly enacted immobility, I clicked off the one lamp over the nightstand that divided our beds, and beyond the fan there was no noise.

"Nobody," I heard her say, maybe to herself, in the dark. "Nobody gets us. It's nice."

———

I woke just over two hours later with an unforeseen alertness, maybe mysteriously due to how aware I'd become in sleep of the presence of the looming mountains in the black quiet. Over the wall fan purring in the corner, I could barely hear Knox moaning in her own contract with slumber. I flicked a lighter in the dark and thumbed through compartments in my carry bag, which sat in a cushioned seat at our small table, and I pulled out a notebook and pen for the haul downstairs to the lobby. The clock on the nightstand read that it was after five, so assuming coffee was on I made it down after quietly pulling our door shut behind me. I met a middle aged man in the elevator who turned out to be from Chicago, and with the resurfacing of my Illinois friend's geography, after brief talks he told me that where she lived was "really, if you think about it, the true heartland of America," a town about two hours southeast of the city. I saw the sun had crept through the sliding glass doors of the entrance once he and I parted ways with a mutual traveler's blessing. The desk attendant was nowhere to be seen, nor was the guard, so I sought and found a cup of robust and went to work a good while on a poem about a woman I'd worked with at the paper, a sad woman, and I used words like "frailty," "cogs" and "disavowal," even borrowing from the wide and horizontal mountainscape spreading visibly across the road and then the valley, finally and obviously below the same sun around my bare toes on the thin carpet of the lobby's couch. I was hoping to be looked upon as exactly how I felt, a loner in wild silence. I wanted to look insane. Knox had told me recently about her own foray into solitary writing, how she'd driven, a pair of weeks back, over the bay and plunked herself in an uncomfortably bustling book store in downtown Fairhope, how she felt the eyes on her were judgmental eyes—not because she was a poet of the moment, but because she was a young poet, not old enough to have paid her dues by their own assessment, not gray enough nor remotely wistful-looking by the eye. Knox had wondered if the eyes watching her belonged to people with opinions that perhaps differed when they were not influenced by others who also watched and opined. Or maybe they'd been envious that she had subverted their guidelines to become one of them. And so I wanted that, the appeal to strangers without daring them to call me anything but native.

Time beat itself out and the poem concluded with something on the woman's daughter, something on a mirror and a quivering lip. I went outside by Knox's car for a smoke and saw that somehow, the drink Knox had emptied on the downward-sloping hill behind our back tires hadn't seemed to have fully dried, leaving as just more than temporary evidence that we had been there. The liquid had shaped like a spread of friendly talons assailing the soft blacktopped pavement, like talons of a hawk, of course. Maybe one that cawed. *We wuz here*, I thought, like my childhood friend Martin had knifed into a tree off Dog River back home, or like in bathroom stalls off the highway, *call such-and-such for a good bj*. Passing back through the lobby after falling in love with foliage ascending the mountains, I noticed the clock over the counter announcing in its quiet tick-tocking manner that it was eight o'clock in Chattanooga, which meant no possibility for extra winks for me, and definitely time to get serious about stirring the un-stir-able Knox into at least a mock-excitatory state, so we could hit the road across town and see what we could get into with Cora for a good half day before rocketing west to Nashville.

But upstairs the room clock read seven, so I tiptoed toward her large book-stuffed purse and extracted her phone, pressing random buttons until the face of it illumined and agreed with the clock by the bed. So I returned downstairs, not wanting to confront Knox's wrath if I were to phone down and noisily talk to the staff as she continued to converse with abstractions behind her eyelids. A distracted-looking woman stood behind the desk.

"Our clocks are saying seven in the room, but your clock there says eight," I told her and shrugged, while looking at her wall clock as she stapled papers. "I just don't want to disrupt my travel mate if it's too early."

She looked past me as if I stood elsewhere.

"It's eight o'clock. They didn't tell you?"

I felt suddenly awkward as though I should have been standing behind myself, or at very least wherever it was the woman gazed. And whoever "they" were, ostensibly I should have known them, should have paid better attention to their message.

"Who?" I asked, looking behind my shoulder.

She sighed.

"Our property is on the line of the time zone switch. What half are you in?"

"What?"

She rolled her eyes.

"Ok, what *room* number?"

"231."

"Mmm-hmm. That's technically Central. But really you're in Eastern. It's eight o'clock."

"Wow," I said and nodded. "Is there a note in the room that I missed? Because we've got this thing in Nashville later that..."

"No," she said, blinking. The absurdity of her reaction was too entertaining, but instead of laughing my skin went warm. "They should have told you."

"Oh, ok. So I guess I should just..." I began, pointing back up to the room, past my shoulder, where apparently I still stood. "...go let her know that we..."

"Mmm-hmm."

I made the room after a more pronounced and hurried shuffle, still keying in quietly, but cracking the curtains half a foot for the sun to hit the wall just past my pillows, inches before her face that had turned upward toward the top of the window. I sat on her bed's edge and lightly ran a palm over her upper arm until she moved a little.

"Knox," I whispered. "Hey babe, I need you up in a bit."

"Marbles," she groaned and tucked her face into her pillow.

"*Knox*," I whispered louder. She cracked an eye. "Our clocks are off. It's actually an hour later. We need to move if we're not going to be late for Cora."

"What time is it?"

She turned her face toward the clock.

"Time to get rolling. I'll shower and then get you coffee downstairs. Then our destiny is on you."

"Ok," she sighed, and then I lost her.

I took a quick shower, cleaning my hair and body with what house-keeping had provided tub-side for us, and then hopped out on to the wet floor to conduct the most fastidious speed-shave of my adult life. I threw on everything but the semi-tattered button-down I'd slide into prior to the reading in the city, a shirt Knox had said in Mobile looked like what "a poet would wear." Downstairs, yet again, the continental breakfast buzzed with a maddened crowd, and I wore a pair of heavy-heeled business type shoes that clopped like stilettos on the tiles leading to the coffee, the sound much different from the basic slap of flesh from my previous visits of the morning. A few heavyset men in torn T-shirts dressed me down with their eyes as I paddled noisily through the bone-sea of travelers in motion around me. Back in the room, yet again, as I was getting profoundly good at com-ing and going, Knox hadn't deterred from her immutable mission to go on un-paused, so I set her coffee down, dragged her hand to it in the dark and re-embarked on the journey of nudging her gently into the morning. After ten minutes of nothing—even after reading her the poem I'd written earlier and lying to her, beforehand, suggesting it was by Sharon Olds, even after she said it was amazing, and even after I confessed ownership, to which she said, "I feel duped"—I turned on the lamp over her head. In the transition from one kind of waiting to another, it had become quarter to nine.

"So has Cora called yet?" I asked, then stretched back on to my bed, my bags organized and overlapping my right foot at the edge. Knox was at last sitting up in her bed.

"*Rattigan*," she said, looking away from me, suddenly angry. "I told her we'd call her once we got up. *Shit*."

"I wasn't on the phone when you guys made plans, babe. You told me eight was our time to get going so we could meet her at that brunch joint. I'm already showered up so you can take what time you need, so..."

"But we have plenty of time, *man*. Is this some nervous energy thing? You're gonna kick everybody's ass, man. Stop *worrying*, you fucking *tod-dler*." She ran her hands through her hair and found her cup after double-checking the clock. "Thanks for the coffee."

"It's not that," I said, laughing. "I just thought we were supposed to meet her by ten, and you always take an hour. It'll be time to check out when you're ready."

Her eyes got big for the first time of the morning.

"Wait, are you saying it's almost nine o'clock?"

I laughed harder. "*Yeah*, Knox. I tried telling you about the time. I've been trying to save this whole thing from implosion. But when you're in a coma, you don't..."

"*Fuck!* I'm so sorry, man. Let me..." She looked around as if extra time was scurrying around the room and, if caught, could be bottled and used. "Let me get this process started. *Really*. My bad."

She jumped from her bed, collected a few things and disappeared into the bathroom as I yanked back the entire curtain and pulled my own coffee to my chest and admired, really taking time to admire, the cerulean blue teeming over the haunted house on the hill past us, which only looked slightly defeated in the light, not as daunting a breach as my imagination had assumed the night before, the few disarrayed hours before. The shower ran heavily across the room, and I met with my exhaustion and told it, as if it were someone else entirely, to go far, far away and come back when I was ready, on my terms, to concede.

"Holy *fuck*," Knox soon yelled. "Pete. *Pete*, really. Come here, I need you!"

I stood outside the bathroom door.

"What's up, babe?"

"Come in. It's ok."

I walked into the steam infiltrating the small space of the room. She yanked back the shower curtain, and as she did so I imagined more of the blue sky showing itself behind it, through the steam, but it was her wet and frustrated face. I smiled.

"What is *this*?" She asked, handing me a small, white container from beside the tub. "Is this conditioner?"

"I don't know. I thought it was."

"It says moisturizer on it, Rattigan. I think it's lotion. I can't...you don't *know*...I can't do anything with this crazy fucking mop without..."

"You have a dirty mouth."

She glared at me.

"Right now, Rattigan? *Really*?"

"Ok, ok. Do you have to have conditioner?"

She looked at me studiously a moment, half-smiled, and then said, "Yeah. You just don't...yeah, it'll be a bad scene. If I give you money will you go across the street and buy some?"

"I can get it. I'll be right back."

In the hallway, though, I ran into a young housekeeping employee who looked as though she were part of some broken child labor law. I asked her and her beautiful olive complexion if she had any conditioner. She went to her cart a room down and handed me another microscopic bottle that said "moisturizer" on it.

"Is this conditioner?"

She kept trying to hand it to me, and then I realized she spoke little-to-no English, so I flagged another employee several more doors down. The similar result was her pointing at the bottle and then rubbing her arms, which confirmed Knox's concerns and jump-started my own recognition of what I'd scrubbed in to my scalp earlier. So I said *thank you* and headed to the elevator, which seemed to groan at the sight of me, and I made it down to the lobby, stopping first at the front desk to remark on our debacle.

"I've probably got some." She rooted around in an unseen drawer by her knees. "This enough?"

"It should be. Thanks very much. You know, I actually used the lotion for conditioner earlier, so maybe the housekeepers..."

"Mmm-hmm."

Back in the room I peeled into the bathroom and passed over the conditioner, after noting the time across the bed. I was growing pensive at the moment's aggressive pace toward noon, the churlish haste of time, like us or not.

"We're going to overlap checkout time, babe. So look. Let's just be tired together and say to hell with it, ok? We'll call Cora on the way," I told her as beads of hot water pummeled her cheeks. I closed the shower curtain, stepped away and then returned to it, patting it to announce again my presence. Knox slid it open. "And also, the staff might think you're my hooker. I called you my 'travel mate.' *Sorry.*"

"I'm so over this place, Rattigan," she said, laughing at last.

We regained composure once making our final departure, ready to get on to the next unacknowledged road ahead. Knox took quick pause at the hotel computer to print directions to Cora's, not trusting the unsteady hand of her traditional script on a notebook sheet from the most recent time she'd visited Chattanooga on her own. She made her point, also, in saying,

"I'm telling you Rattigan, technology helps out sometimes. Even though I know you revel in your distaste for it."

She met me at the car as I reinserted the luggage we'd assembled for the trip, and I stood alongside her awe at the design of the spill she'd given the parking lot, her amazement much like mine, that it had outlasted the night.

"It looks like an angry hand."

"My hair's all slime," I said as I lit a cigarette and climbed in the car.

"You're such a chick."

I pulled us on to the connecting road that led to the highway across what Knox had taken to calling, with forgivable affection, forgivable because we'd soon be leaving it, the 'Nooga.

"Do you know where we're going?" I asked once blending with the small number of cars on the interstate.

"Normally, no," she said, cracking her window with one hand, a smoke in her mouth for breakfast, the coffee long lost on us both. Her other hand's fingertips massaged the radio dial, finding Vivaldi, there, in a mountain range of near-death and forties.

"Marbles," I said to myself.

She didn't know.

———

We found Cora's house without confusion, as Knox recognized the streets once we arrived in the district. The getting there, however, included a combination of highway links and project housing, opulent neighborhoods and a waterway around which we zoomed unsafely as she crawled over my seat to snap a picture of it to our left. I'd craned my neck to see it as well, but the road around it curved like a semi-circle against the favor of my driving eye, so for me to see it required I test death personally. And with more mountains to our right, we were pinned down in a pond-sized shade overlooking the calm water that was fully immersed in sunlight, near noon then. Boats were out, people were in their own moments, and as I gave up on the view and took to the management of the wheel, I thought of the fellow in the elevator, I thought of the heartland and realized just how big everything, each thing even without a name, actually was. Life on the coast gave a different glimpse at the world because of the presence of the vast water, which I had surely taken for granted until that precise moment of trying not to get us killed on the highway around boats making mid-sized waves across the surface, understanding as close to fully as I could that everyone does what they can to insure their version of beauty, regardless of locale. The sun was suddenly everywhere in thinking it, and I thought of Brody again, wanted to send him good blue, but wanted more than that for his own energy in the back seat, his fingers drumming on the console between Knox and me and calling every stranger we met his sweet baby.

"Damn, it's nice out," Cora said as she opened her front door and peered over our heads to squint against the light. "If I weren't such a fat ass right now we could..."

"You're so *pregnant*," Knox said as she kissed Cora on the cheek and bent to run palms around her belly. "You look beautiful."

"Hey there," I said, and pulled my hands out of my pockets to follow Knox into the house after entering Cora's outstretched arms.

"Good to finally get you here, man," she said, shutting the door behind us.

"You too. Definitely. Sorry we're late, though. Rough start."

"Eh." She waved her hand.

"Rattigan, this is Clark." Knox stood across the coffee table beside a fellow with his arm across her shoulders.

"Whoa, no shit?"

"Hey, brother!" He said.

Knox's eyes flashed. Cora had quickly gone back to sitting, nine full months in and prepped to be induced that actual weekend before her doctor decided to go on vacation. But even armed with this information before arriving, and battling my imagination that she'd be the same as my irascible sister had been at the end of her final trimester and rope, Cora was still smiling.

"Wait, you guys know each other?" Knox asked as she stepped around the coffee table toward the sofa, but without sitting, a pre-sit non-crouch downward, as if the answer had to come before she could collapse.

"Yeah," we said. Clark looked at Cora and smiled shyly.

"You tell them, man. Small damned world."

He laughed. "This guy..." he started, gripping the back of my neck with his left hand, "...was doing some kind of, what was it?"

"When I was at the paper," I told Knox.

"This guy was at my grad ceremony, I guess almost, what, two years ago now? And we were both trapped in the back of the auditorium. Remember, baby? How late I was getting there?" Cora's face brightened and she mouthed *no way*.

"I was late as hell," I added.

"Yeah, Knox," Clark continued. "We decided after fighting the crowd that it was all ridiculous, pretty pointless to walk since they mail you the diploma, anyway. So instead we went across the street and drank beer, and I gave him a bunch of nonsense to put in his article about the program."

"Coincidentally, it was the first feature I'd been assigned. No mystery, in hindsight, why I was rarely assigned more."

"That's completely nuts. That you guys have met, I mean," Knox said, finally sitting. "But how did you make up the commencement stuff?"

"I have to pee," Cora said, standing, and Knox rose to follow her toward the bathroom in the hallway.

"You need anything, babe?" Knox called through the door.

"Just food. I'm fucking starving."

Knox turned toward Clark and me in the living room.

"Is she mad? I know we're late. Our clocks were wrong. I tried getting Rattigan's ass out of bed, but he..."

"As you can see, she's a really bad liar," I told Clark. He smiled.

"You guys want something to drink? We have caffeine-free soda. That's all she drinks lately besides water."

"I'm good. Thanks," I said.

"Ok, so how did I not know you guys knew each other in Mobile?"

"Cora kept saying you were bringing your roommate 'Rattigan' up for some festival," Clark told her, and then turned to me. "As much as we ended up drinking, I didn't remember you even having a last name."

"Hey, I forget sometimes, too."

"That's wild, man." Knox shook her head.

"Did I hear you say your clocks were wrong?" Cora asked, waddling baby-heavy across the wooden floor of the hallway back into the living room. "What exit were you off?"

"I think 174," I said.

"No, it was 172," Knox said.

It was quiet a moment.

"It ended with an even number," I said and shrugged. Clark laughed, Knox nodded and Cora furrowed in thought.

"You know that section of the city's on the zone change, right?"

"We dig the hard lessons," Knox said, looping her arm in to Cora's and pulling her toward the door. "I'm stealing your wife," she said over her shoulder to Clark as he and I embraced and laughed at serendipity. "I'm sorry I'm sorry I'm sorry," Knox whispered to Cora, kissing her again and bending to help slip her feet into sandals.

"You guys have fun," Clark said as we filed out.

I eyed the clock on the dash from the back seat of Cora's car as we drove more into the center of things, knowing we'd face another time change and lose an hour once headed to Nashville. I wasn't, in any capacity, apprehensive about the reading because I was too tired to think about how it would transpire. But I was privately adamant about being as punctual as we could, and not throw an unnecessary middle finger in the faces of people who'd selected my work for the award. We were good on time to enjoy a solid lunch, and fifteen minutes of motion dumped us out in the daytime pulse of the Nooga's downtown. We circled a few blocks before parking in a drug store lot, which sat opposite a neat and buried little dive restaurant and bar off the main strip. The traffic was thick. We waited at a pedestrian crossing next to a shirtless collegian holding a car wash poster for his fraternity.

"Vomit," Knox said after smiling to him and reading his poster. We followed a determined Cora across the street once the electric crosswalk man turned from red to white. "My ex was in that fraternity."

She shook her head as I squeezed her shoulder.

"*You* and a *frat* guy?"

"I'll shoot you in the face, Rattigan. I'm not even lying."

"Come *on*, assholes," Cora called behind her.

"We're following you, babe," Knox said.

"Hmm?" Cora asked once we'd made it over to the bustling sidewalk that ran from our low point on the street's hill, up a slight incline to even more restaurants and shops for almost a mile. "Oh, no. Not you guys." She laughed and turned to study the chalkboard menu in the window of the place she'd suggested during the drive, a real life potpourri of foods and alcohols, perfect for people like Knox and me, who weren't selective and had grown accustomed to rarely eating, and Cora, pregnant lovely Cora, who was the exact antithesis. For some reason, and maybe because of her self-image problems from having gained the baby weight, from her sweet humor over it—even if masked in some anger-prone foreground—I felt I'd known her a long time. "I was talking to myself. Or the cars, actually. I wish one would plow into me and make this little kicker pop on out."

Knox smiled and put her arms around Cora and crossed her arms over her chest as they discussed the menu. She'd pressed Cora back at the house to agree to a trip to a salon for a pedicure after lunch, which aroused my trepidation as I added in my mind all the minutes we'd need to shave from our visit to make, in a timely manner, *the Nash*. But, in citing her "fat feet," Cora said she'd already gotten one earlier in the week, and so I predicted then, in front of the restaurant door, that we would still be fine. I wasn't equipped to play the role of my old boss and micro-manage the day, even in my own jittery brain. And with a growling stomach, I was glad their energies were solid and that they'd amiably agreed on the same joint.

"This place really looks so much like..."

"The Stone, I was just thinking that," Knox agreed as we followed Cora to the counter in back to place our order before sitting outside. The staff was all young, like my work family back home, replete with visible tattoos, bearing no evident aggressions nor any sort of feigned drive to overly please anyone but themselves. "Great vibe in here for sure."

"Clark loves this place," Cora said into the menu.

"Order whenever you're ready," the cashier said. He was a tan, good-looking fellow who would later let on that he was from Nepal. *We should talk about a Sherpa gig.*

"How are you doing?" Knox asked, smiling over the right shoulder of Cora, a woman ablaze with sudden resolve.

"Howdy," I added.

"I'm actually really good, guys."

"I'm ordering for all of us, by the way," Cora turned to tell us, and then pivoted back to the cashier, named Distance. "This is for all of us. Cool name, man."

"Yeah, it's ok."

"But I've got the ticket," Knox said, regretting it when it came out over fifty dollars, which wasn't too dire considering Cora scored us three waters, one tea, two double-shot bloody marys—"they're fucking brilliant here," she told us—a large Thai pizza, a highly involved turkey wrap, a mammoth burger near the size of a small Frisbee, and a rich cream cheese and spinach dip to start.

"If you could split that bill, babe," I told Distance.

"*Ah*," Knox sighed. "You're a beautiful man."

We took our drinks once they were ready and found Cora outside, since she'd wearied from standing and wanted to secure us a spot with a good view, a view which faced the waterway Knox had photographed an hour earlier. The weather was a friendly tepid, with low-to-no humidity, and the music playing overhead was forgettable but not revolting, perfect for talks. A few sunburned female tennis players sat opposite us on the porch and took turns glaring our way when we erupted in too loud, too inexplicable laughter. Mainly, though, through the course of the meal, which was incomprehensibly kind on the taste buds, and a beautiful discovery if I planned on the Nooga again, my main objective was to keep Cora refilled with peach tea and water while they fortunately overlooked my existence to play catch-up on the roils of their old lives which were suddenly colliding back into the now. It was very, very good to be ignored. I needed to level out mentally from the furrowed mug shot I felt I'd been casting at others while off in my own pre-panic about time which hadn't yet worked against us since we left our hotel.

"I know," Cora began, in response to Knox's talks of recently feeling, as she put it, uncomfortably untouched. "It's a little different for me I guess, being married, right? And I feel so bad..." She set down her napkin and hid her eyes behind her spread fingers. "I feel so bad for Clark. He's been so good about the hormone flair-ups."

"How so?" Knox asked.

I continued to eat.

"I've been such a crazy person. I'll get horny and then when we're getting started it just turns right fucking off sometimes. *Most* times. And right in the middle of it. Then it's, *don't touch me, I'm sweaty.* If *my* lover decided to get pregnant? I mean, if I were gay, then I'd absolutely leave her. I have no idea why he's still around."

"I've always thought he was good for you."

"He *is*. No doubt. But I miss the other stuff before all this. Not being single, necessarily. I mean, I love my husband. *Shit* yeah. But I don't know, maybe it's not even our older days. You keep me updated with what you guys are up to in Mobile, and it doesn't even seem like you live in Alabama the way you talk. Congratulations by the way, Rattigan. I don't think I've told you that yet."

I didn't hear her and kept eating.

"As in, way to fucking go?" Cora said.

Knox laughed and I looked up.

"This pizza's doing things to me, man. You can't know."

"Where'd you go?" Knox asked, finishing her vodka drink and pulling close her water cup, which had perspired a small lake through the napkin beneath it.

"I'm emotionally invested in this cheese dip, too. So watch your fingers."

We lingered a bit and then made it through the increased flow of bodies by the counter as Distance flashed us a peace sign. We exited the door back on to the sidewalk, waited again at the corner and then crossed toward the car to seek out an ice cream joint across town that Cora was craving. "I look forward to it every week," she'd said. But it took a solid twenty minutes to get there, so by the time the mint chocolate chip cones were bought and dispersed, my energy was throwing off Knox's because I'd slipped into silent. She would occasionally glance back at me in the car on the drive to Cora's, but I found it difficult to look at anything but the clock.

We alternated turns in the bathroom back at the house, trying not to disturb Clark who was studying for medical boards. I threw on the shirt we'd selected hundreds of miles south, a shirt to represent me as something I didn't feel I yet was, a serious and published writer. "So, are you ready?" Cora asked as we stood in her new nursery. The time was dangerously against us. "Always," I joked, but I was ready for a smoke and to get going.

As it turned out, the interstate connector was only a mile from Cora's front door—we'd taken the long route in—and as we took her directions toward it, we called out from where we'd parked by the mailbox that we'd phone her once awake at the hotel in Nashville the next morning, that we'd drive back over for the afternoon to give her real, unbothered time without schedule, to rub her feet or make her late breakfast or put together a puppet show. And then we were off through the neighborhood, up the on-ramp and careening around the boats still at play, driving west toward a city in which neither of us had ever had a glass of wine. Ten miles out, just before the series of "falling rock" signs off the road's shoulder, Knox had fallen asleep with sunglasses half set across the bridge of her nose. I turned the national public radio down to nearly inaudible, lit a smoke and took a deep breath, really considering for the first time of the ride what it was I was in Tennessee to do, which was begin. I'd need the full two quiet hours to determine how.

I'd stuffed myself with an odd amount of additional trepidation around the midway mark, knowing already with full confidence that I could talk all day long about the journalistic elements of the winning poem, of all my poems, the who-what-when-where-why and the ever elusive *how* of them, but my concern grew and boiled and almost took to volcano-angry when I understood I didn't know what I wanted to say versus what I'd be able to say. And then the conflict detoured. The next progression was why, if at all, it mattered. The answer evidenced itself shortly thereafter, that I *wanted* it to matter. I remembered it was still *our* win, not mine, and whatever I said first would, in my mind, be representative of what would come for all of us, would set the tone somehow for the trinity of our coming authorships. And so that was the pressure, *that* was the unresolved mania.

The car had begun to smell of the rotting banana I wouldn't let Knox throw out during the drive north the previous night, and I was even letting that goad me. I was thinking far too much about the incorrect concern, and I knew it. I wanted the ceremony over and the two of us walking like released convicts into the light of freedom. And I would have kept on, no doubt, internally pulling my hair had I not noticed a break in the hills north of the highway where, about forty-five minutes shy of Nashville and beside the road about twenty yards into the valley, a couple splayed out in the golden yellow grass. The man was on his back, knees bent into a cone as his arms crossed his chest. It was wild, driving eighty miles per hour and seeing a still-shot of his closed eyes as if I were crouched beside them and not blurring past. The woman with him sat upright but dipped her head down and into the book she'd had open in her spread-out right hand. The easiness of it, the who-gives-a-damn-about-how-we-look of it was such a sudden, gentle rush of some indefinable kind of love I almost wanted to waken Knox and say, they get it, babe. They *get* it. But I let her sleep, and would later tell her about it not as something she necessarily should have seen, but something she should know was going on in the world, people slowing down their lives enough to rest when rest called, be patient when patience asked, and to generate the good color of their natures, no matter the tint or hue. I had it planned out by the time we struck Nashville, had it in storybook form for her, but the conversation would have to wait once I entered downtown and got summarily lost. She woke on her own as I circled the city blocks, and she apologized for having fallen asleep. But I was good from the education of the road, and she was good from the education of slumber. As she was tugging at a pair of boots which jutted from beneath her seat, I spied a huge banner over a massive business building's colonnade two blocks past a major bus terminal and found, somehow, one of the only available free parking spots behind us after looping the block once more.

We didn't know at the time the meter was free, so as Knox scrambled to shove her feet into her uncomfortable dress boots, I was face down in the floor seeking loose change to feed the meter—I'm sure to passersby we were an unabridged expression of lunacy—and once she had conducted her own search, and we'd checked the time and realized we were miraculously ten minutes ahead of the ceremony's start, it was then we noticed the red-blinking meters beside all the nearby cars, as well as the sign over our own that announced weekends were free with the exception of thin time frames that had already, like the meters, expired. We shuffled up the slope toward the obstreperous bus noises and passed the people in wait outside them, people standing below the tinted glass houses built to keep inner-city travelers from the rain. At the end of the street we saw tents for the book show portion of the festival propped at the top of marble-looking governmental stairs, yet made of basic concrete before being painted, and scuffed, no question, by the dress shoes of legislative bodies of the local legislative body. We stopped at the center tent to ask a blond fellow around our age where we could find room 31.

"What you're gonna wanna do, is you go back down the stairs and hang right, take the sidewalk all the way until just before the corner. If you go to the light, you've gone too far. Ok? It's through to the plaza on your right down there."

"Very cool, thank you," I said as Knox smiled noncommittally at him and readjusted the purse which sagged at her hip.

"Right before the corner light, now. Watch for it, ok? It's tricky. I'm just telling you."

I took back down the stairs, with Knox at her best speed behind me.

"This is extra-terrestrial," I said. "All they told me was room 31. How buried could it be, man?"

And then I recognized the coincidence in our hotel room of similar number back across the state, tried even to revel in some possible meaning behind it, and then realized Knox was not in the mood for mystical musings and was ready for a seat, post-nap, in my audience so she could get fully awake and turn on her own blue light.

"There it is," she said.

"Nice. I think we're good on time."

"That guy was *intense*. I have to piss."

I laughed.

"Me, too. Let's get this over with."

I stood in wait outside the women's bathroom door once out of the men's, glancing to my left at a sitting crowd along a row of wooden benches. As I engaged a quick-study of the group I noticed a fifty-something leaning forward from his seated position, watching me. Since I'd had to mail up a picture to go with my biography, I assumed he knew more confidently who I was than I did him. I guessed quietly as Knox reemerged that it was Ronald Halpert, the editor of the magazine publishing me in concomitance with the award. I pretended to read a small series of plaques on the wall until he approached.

"Peter?"

"Hi." I turned to him as Knox joined my side.

"Ron Halpert. I'm really happy you could make it up."

We shook hands.

"I'm glad to be here. Very much so."

Knox smiled, more invested in his evident warmth.

"This is Amber Knox. She's a poet, too."

He shook her hand, but he seemed distracted as if he'd undertaken too much with too little time.

"We'll get you started pretty soon. There's been an overlay on readings in our room. I can't win today."

"All's well, man."

We followed him toward the door and stood, with those who'd risen from the benches, in a moment of silence prior to the emptying out of Room 31. He stepped away to talk festival shop over the event's program with a short disheveled woman in flowered pants. Once the crowd had thinned and thickened again, from people trying to leave and enter the same narrow door, Knox and I made it inside the auditorium and found comfortable seats in the back near the exit. Ron was quick on the microphone after the fifty or so of us had tamped our bodies down to the theatre-styled cushions, and to my surprise he began with the poetry winners, calling up the woman who'd drawn second in the competition, as the third place poet couldn't make it to town.

"Is this how all these things are gonna go?" I whispered to Knox, assuming suddenly we'd continue to win as then the winning had begun.

She put her fingertips on my knee, already committed to the moment, and she wasn't looking at me, but whispered back, too loudly, "Beats the shit out of me."

The woman who took to the podium was about sixty by our later and agreed upon estimations. Knox and I rifled through the magazine copies Ron had given us so we could linger momentarily at the second page of the publication, that had my judge's review and poem and snapshot, the picture of me on the steps outside our guesthouse, in the dark, with a bright light from the flash that "makes your forehead too shiny," Knox had said, before saying it was a keeper. We read along with the woman after her brief and awkward talk on daffodils, a talk that ruined my illusion of the audience. I realized with a fast horror that instead of just reading my piece with passion, and bowing out, I'd have to talk, too, beforehand. But what I wanted to discuss of my work had nothing to do with flowers, nothing on sepals or a calyx or a thorn, and I turned 31 shades of timorous as her poem ended.

"And finally," Ron began, "our first prize winner of the poetry competition, author of the collection, *Standing On You Like A Grave*, which is pending publication? Is that right?"

I nodded as a few people turned in their seats to find me in the back.

"Ok. And also, for those of you who follow fiction, a working novel entitled *The Hamiltons*. Of his winning poem, this year's judge Garry Nadal wrote, 'What drew me to this piece was its succinct economy and voice that both rewards and bothers.' Welcome with me, please, Peter Rattigan."

I carried a folder that encased the poem, as well as others, up with my tired body toward the front of the audience, and I shook Ron's hand amidst mild applause. I'd brought more from sheer inexperience, wondering if the listeners would bite and want more, if that even ever occurred at such events. But feeling the heaviness of the pages, married with the understanding of my sudden place, apart from Knox's good glow, I realized it wouldn't happen and that I was preempting a real joy at leaving the auditorium alive.

"This poem…" I said, entering exhaustedly into my unprepared speech. "…isn't typical of my recent work, as lately I write about the thrill of touch, the musicality of the body, the sexual voice…"

I paused for a quick scan of the faces facing me. My voice seemed loud and penetrating, and I could feel the tension elevate itself above everyone's heads. I was in unfamiliar territory with them, and they, for sure, were the same with me. I felt powerful.

"But this poem is about the conflict of two passionate people's minds. Usually I don't enter the area of mental supposition when I write poems, since I think the time for it has passed," I continued, finding Knox's porcelain face in the back and thinking, fuck it. If Brody were here he'd say, *they just don't know*.

I read with what strength I had while gripping the podium's edges, as if it would take off had I not given it the confirmation of myself as its master. By the time I tried to round off the sharp point of the poem's ending, I was fully done and ready to rediscover Knox by the door. Half the people applauded. Maybe less. Knox grazed my knee again once I returned to her side, but my body was electrified by what had happened, as well as the analysis of it that had begun already, and I couldn't look at her. For the duration of the fiction winners' readings, we flipped again through the magazine and pretended we had no idea that the other had multiple thoughts begging to be shared once we were emancipated.

Knox and I stayed in our seats after a last round of ovations for all the winners. As the unenthused muscled out the door, there were several who wanted to talk to me and shake my hand, which defined the ceremony as slightly less than a loss. A board member of the festival said I was one of the best poets he'd seen there in years, but I think he was mostly flirting with me which, to me, altered the truth in his compliment. Other audience members, due to the content of the poem, were evidently nervous when trying to shuffle past me toward the exit. Knox made her way out to the plaza to have a smoke while I briefly conversed with Ron about staying in touch. By the time I found her, on a concrete bench in the diminishing shade of the coming night, I was ready to shed my skin.

"If I didn't tell you, your check is in the mail," Ron stopped by to say as I took a lit smoke from her.

She grinned at me as he walked off toward 6th.

"You do realize..." Knox said, after exhaling gray fumes toward the colonnade. "...that you just challenged their idea of God's gender."

"It was just a poem."

I grinned back.

"I've got to talk to you about the insanity in that room when you started talking about the body."

"I felt it too, babe. That's why I decided to shut up about it and move..."

"I could *tell*," she said. "I saw you read everybody. Backwards thinking fucking assholes."

"Easy, tiger."

"I'm just saying."

I crinkled my nose at the sky dipping in between the surrounding stone. A woman walked by and touched my arm in passing.

"I like your work," she said.

"Thanks very much," I responded to her back as she zoomed on. "Very much." I turned to Knox, still sitting on the bench. "Let's get out of here."

"See, she even seems nervous," Knox said, throwing her cigarette butt in the cylindrical tray beside the bench's edge and taking my hand to lift her up, and definitely, to lift us both away.

We locked arms and guessed correctly about the direction we should take toward a sporting coliseum, and as I marveled over just how unimportant the reading had been, at first, and then how enlightening its actual significance was—having inappropriately deemed it superfluous solely based on its tornado-like brevity—Knox angled us into a shadowed street that somewhat reminded her, she said, of Bourbon Street in New Orleans. But nothing was going on in the bars of Printer's Alley, with a few early drinkers visible from out on the bricked road, sitting in dimly lit spaces before mirrored walls, behind the poised and ready liquor bottles and cash registers. We aggravated traffic with our newness to the streets, and even took a cue on maneuverability from a fellow who'd deftly skimmed through the cars against the command of the little red stoplight man, who refused, for us, to turn white, our new green.

"I'm from Manhattan," he'd said in passing. "No time for this shit."

We paced slowly in the pre-hectic shuffle once on what turned out to be the main strip of the downtown scene, after I followed Knox into a pair of touristy joints selling signed guitars and Tennessee thimbles. I tried not to be too distractedly dazzled by the potential of the city, trying harder to keep my face down and looking local, so someone could look at us and think, *definitely locals*. I was redolent with the odor of being in the gone new now, and took in the encompassing smells of the restaurants firing up around us as we ambled on.

"Where are you thinking?" Knox asked, facing away from me and in through a window of a bar from which a loud rock-country mélange exploded.

"I don't know yet," I said, after side-stepping a man outside a pizza parlor, offering us dinner vouchers, maybe to get bodies in early before the overhead-paying swell of the later night bodies. "I'm waiting to see what leaps out."

My mind was depleted and beaten, and I wasn't interested in the music venues until we could laminate ourselves against the top of a bar and talk. We crossed the street like lovers with no agenda, or a strange pair of thinkers with big weird souls encapsulated by what Knox called "the mind vernix." My awareness of our possible appeal to people passing on the opposing sidewalk fed into an easiness similar to the earlier valley couple off the road, who'd taken in stride a bit of calm before more ardent going. Knox could see, she later told me, a beaming sense of golden yellow attachment to that valley in my face as we walked in defense of our energy together. I was tired and so tired and so ridiculously tired, but I still felt a sense of performance was necessary. We were in the *here*. We were gold.

"This looks good," I told her while pausing to look to my left into a window of my own choosing. "They might not sell thimbles, though."

"That's pretty funny."

"Seem good to you?"

"How do we get in?"

"I think it's down that way."

We stepped further on the walkway and pushed through the heavy wooden swinging doors and got flagged immediately by a hostess in the back by the restrooms, but we were intercepted by a server who said we could place ourselves at the bar if we were there just for drinks. The place was fortuitously a wine house with its own good flailing hustle, and we cornered ourselves off to the left of the entrance against a vertical and reaching partition that divided us from the majority of the dining area. A hyper-attractive trio of bartenders bounded around guts of the curved countertop that leaked into both eating rooms, and a twenty-something girl with dyed red hair greeted us with a sense of anxiety over something we couldn't see, so we bought her time by skimming the wine list until she could come back.

"She's responsible for what happens," I told the girl, trying to emit what kindness I could, thinking even in my weariness that kindness in that place could have been an unusual and fleeting trend. Knox chose a bottle of cab, wishing along with me against reality that we were there in winter and a heavy dry was the obvious and only option.

"No," Knox said after a second sip and studying the wine's turn in the glass as she cradled it in her palm. "No, you're right. It *was* palpable in there. I was thrown off by the audible groans when you started talking about writing the body."

"I thought I imagined that."

"Oh no, I heard it."

"It was like I could *see* the groan, more than anything else."

"It was definitely there."

"But it was so strange from *my* vantage, Knox. Their faces numbed out. I don't know."

"I'm proud of my choice, Rattigan. This wine is fucking great."

"I mean seriously, I don't know that what we talk about when it comes to our poems is so bizarre, but I guess the type of writers that get into this certain scene..."

"How's your wine?" Our bartender asked.

"It's perfect," I said.

"It's really great," Knox added.

"Maybe they would rather get off on daffodils, babe. Kudos to them, I *guess*, but..."

"But boring," Knox said.

I studied her a moment.

"I think I'm really awake suddenly," I told her, part of me still pulling back toward the car in my mind, where our leftover tepid Thai pie sat unattended in the back seat, likely reeking of banana.

"You don't know, man. I'm so happy right now." She scratched lightly at her forehead. "*Wait.*"

"What's up?" I asked, swabbing a wine dot off the bar tile past the base of my glass's stem.

"I just realized something about your reading. Of *course.*" She slapped the bar. "When I was doing my exit interview, which usually, by the way, I thought was supposed to come *after* the thesis defense, the asshole who conducted it was some prick I never even met. Did you know Dr. Collins from your classes? He might have been new when you were graduating."

"I think I spilled beer on him at a bar but I never had him for a class."

"Ok. But you know the wormy little bastard, with the dark-rimmed specs? Bald head?"

"Yeah. He wasn't happy when we met."

"I'm not saying all bald men are wormy bastards."

"Yes, you are," I said, smiling into the edge of my glass and then sipping. A table full of serious men sat in a booth behind us, serious men who'd seemed to take the night off from at least excessive seriousness, to get a friendly and boisterous kind of loud. They exploded behind us in cheers as their server brought a new tray of poisons. Knox smiled at them, about the *idea* of them, and then looked back at me.

"*Anyway.* He had me, for some crazy fucking reason, read him a poem by, shit..." She snapped her fingers. "The Irish poet. A woman."

"Boland?"

She thought a moment.

"Yeah. Boland. And at first I wondered why he got so detached from what I was doing when I read it..."

"How so?"

"What? Oh, I don't know. He seemed to want to be out of the room suddenly, and after your reading it all finally came clear."

"I'm completely stumped."

She started laughing, took a drink from her glass and sighed.

"It's because of how we read poems, Rattigan. *Out loud.* I think now that he was trying to prove some point to me through the content of the poem that I was too much a rebel in the program and..."

"That's stupid."

"It actually isn't, *now*. Because I'd never read the poem and didn't even have an idea what it was about. So that was the department's final send-in to let me know they disagreed with how I played the role as grad student, and he was some patsy shoved in to convey the message."

I understood, finally, and began to laugh.

"It was so far removed from what you should have actually been talking about."

"I *know*," she said.

"And it backfired because you made him uncomfortable with your own interpretation, or what he thought was your interpretation. What a load of assholes."

"So when I saw how awkward it was for your audience at the plaza, I realized the same thing happened with me on campus with Collins."

"And it was just you being you."

"*Yes*," she said. "Same with you back there."

We sat in silence for a while.

"I miss Brody," she told the inside of her glass.

"Same here, man."

———

After a needed lesson on parking off the strip—Knox and I had a theory regarding our near future, of going on for the car and bringing it in toward the pulse—we learned from our bartender, Rachel, that it would be best to patrol the area after a local hockey game let, which sent us on to our better agenda, provided the eight o'clock time that had sprung upon us. We would drive to the outskirts of Nashville and check in to our hotel and plant ourselves in different clothes before hopping a taxi back into the city. We paid out after leaving a note of cheers to her on our receipt, and we made our way with more familiarity back to Knox's car which thankfully had not absconded, or been absconded, from our neglect. Once the engine came alive we began infiltrating our bodies with the leftover pizza. Then we got lost again. But on our way momentarily out of town, we found the right connection to the interstate in the fully realized darkness and motored on toward what seemed a shamrock design of crossing highways, found our exit and descended the ramp's slope and then the hotel's entrance after Knox had called the front desk from her cell, passed me the phone and allowed me, in my abstract detachment, to refer to the man and his high-pitched voice as "ma'am." Twice.

Our room embodied our collective view of paradise. We were elated to be inside after enduring the wedding crowd in the elevator, spilling beers on the carpeted floor. One woman declared how bad a person she was as she hiccupped back her ineluctable puke. Knox tested her bed once we'd dived in from the hallway, beds as good as the ones in Chattanooga, we agreed, as I dropped my bags on the floor at my own bed's foot and collapsed into a capitulating nap after calling downstairs to request a shuttle into Nashville. I warred with what exhaustion Knox could see in me on her own, and so she took to the bathroom to get settled before the mirror as I stretched out. Once she stepped nearly soundless into the space of our bedroom, I lifted just one eye, and then my jaw.

"I really think we could just walk over to the cafe behind us. It's a famous joint, right? And how long, really, do you think this taxi cat's going to take? It's been almost an hour."

Because Knox was incapable of preventing thoughts from expressing themselves in her face, and happy to know a kindred bad liar, I watched as she reared back to call me names. And then the phone rang.

"Mr. Rattigan, your cab's arrived."

"Thanks very much," I said, and then added a well-intended, "sir."

I put down the phone and looked at her, curving an eyebrow upward, half-expecting the barrage to nonetheless begin.

"Let's go," she said, beginning to laugh.

"I know, man," I said as I rolled on to my back and hung myself over the bed into the space between hers and mine, under the lamplight shining much brighter than the one east under which we'd slept across the state. "I don't want to hear it."

"No worries," she said.

I stood and followed her toward the door.

"Your Indian name, babe..." I began as we reentered the hall of lurking bridesmaids and cacophonous men behind starched lapels, "...could easily be Never Tired Due To Frequent Naps."

She smiled and nodded and threw her arm around my waist as our elevator door opened and we took it down, a few beer caps at our feet.

Down through the lobby and then the front doors, a van idled in wait about ten feet off to our left, and as we approached it the older fellow behind the wheel looked up with a start and gunned the engine forward to a position more central to the door, so Knox and I grinned at each other as we paced back alongside it and opened the sliding door to get in. But suddenly I felt guilty, as if we'd disallowed the enactment of the driver's protocol, since he'd hopped out of his door and sprinted around the front squared jaw of the van to let us in in a sort of welcome ceremony, as in *here's my livelihood, let me let you*. He was a very endearing man from first scan, someone I assumed would care little about my poetry's take on God's gender or Knox's vernix of the mind. But from his hand's firm presence over my knuckles as we shook and made eye contact and followed his lead into the spacious seats awaiting us, I felt we'd landed the best carriage toward town, and I happily hopped in behind Knox.

"He looks like a man I used to work for named Reza," I whispered to her as she buckled in and watched him jet again across the van's fore.

"He's adorable," she said.

He offered apologies for a tardiness Knox hadn't noticed, a tardiness I'd celebrated in that it provided me time to downgrade my thought processes to a meandering neutrality, necessary for a survival in our vampire's night ahead.

"No, we're good," Knox told him as he lead-footed us on to the freeway.

"We're never in a hurry," I added. "What's your name, my friend?"

"Reza," he said, looking into the rearview, and then he threw on a signal indicating our declared presence in the heart of the high-speed night. I felt Knox's study of my face as I smiled wildly and satisfied. I didn't know he was from Iran, which he'd eventually tell us when talking of his family and his work hours as we made it five minutes later on to the exact and long street that would lead right into the colonnades from earlier had we not cut left toward the bowels of where we'd been earlier. I'd once worked for the man he favored in college, eerily similar in the face, to the point I thought I had not aged and had not in fact gone to Tennessee. The Reza I had known, too, had been beautiful and kind and rife with blue light.

He deposited us in front of the wine stop we'd made earlier and got out, damn the multi-lane traffic, to open our doors.

"She's got your card. Can we call you later when heading back? Will you be on still?" I asked.

"Yes," he said. "Just give thirty minutes and I'll meet anywhere."

"Because we want you if possible," Knox said, smiling as he took her hand in his and looked across the street past us.

"I know most of these people. Where you went? Martin is the manager. He sends me business. But I tell him, I hope your restaurant is good, otherwise I cannot recommend you. So they let me try them sometimes, and trust me." He nodded assurance. "It is very good."

"If this guy gets hungry, we will," she said, swinging his hand lightly beneath the bar lights across the sidewalk.

"How much is the fare?" I asked.

He studied me quickly, as my Reza had before, questioning my young and amorphous energies as an undergrad.

"Is twenty dollars fair?" He asked.

I gave him a twenty and Knox added a five to it, and as I thanked him and told him we'd call him later, he kissed Knox's hand and patted my cheek and instructed us sternly to have a "wonderful night." And then he sprinted around the van again, threw on his blinker and joined the traffic that, from where we stood, seemed nothing like New Orleans anymore, but faster. A different *New*. "York City," I said aloud, finishing the thought.

"What babe?" Knox asked as we stepped up on to the curb.

I shrugged my shoulders and smiled. We kissed at each others' temples and were finally *off*.

The crowds had predictably developed into the sea of bodies Rachel had suggested would surge, following the emptying of the area post-game before refilling again, and we spent a rich amount of time slipping in and out of them, pocket-cashed vagabonds, and we curved our shoulders around the more rigid of them on the pathway. Knox was ahead of me, then in proletarian pacing shoes, having surrendered the Senators off the outer pike at the hotel, and occasionally she'd turn to monitor my whereabouts, but I was injecting into my body the molecular collisions of passersby and didn't want to lose out on some education of their presence. So when I stopped to light a cigarette Knox fell back and joined me for one beside a row of locked bicycles near a car whose owner or renter I guessed had paid a hefty price to park there. Her eyes grew large and lit and lovely and kept growing over my shoulder. I turned to look in to the bar entrance below the sign she'd been studying.

"What do you think?" She asked. "That rockabilly shit sounds good, man. Kind of crowded though."

"Definitely packed," I agreed, watching people barely making progress past the bouncer taking cards at the door. She raised her eyebrows a few times at me. "Yeah, let's do it."

"I'm sold on that guy's pompadour," Knox said of the singer we could see through the window as we stepped to the bouncer at the door before shoving ourselves into the chest of the joint, having to touch knees and elbows and drop a few I'm-sorrys until we hit the bar and caught a round of the cheapest house suds.

Knox took over a lone bar stool at a table at the edge of the small dance floor, and I stood beside her as we recognized the mix of age brackets and spiritual agendas in the place, which included a group of sixty-somethings from England across our table. The singer was mad and beautiful, built into his zoot duds and manic tie with purpose, and Knox and I were getting off on the stand-up bass player hiding behind his own dark shades. Around the time the lead man broke from a set to order beers off the microphone, I took to the bar for another round for us, having to sandwich in between a girl with long reddish-brown hair stretching below her shoulders, and a salt-and-pepper-haired man askance over his tightly-gripped lady to my right. The barkeep was busy, so I stood a while, allowing myself more welcomed time to take the place in amidst the torrents of neo-swing permeating the space between the walls.

"Maybe you should shake your money at her, man," the long-haired girl said to me.

"Nah, I'm good. She's busy. *Life's* good."

The barkeep made it down and I asked how she was doing, which knocked her off balance, and then I ordered the beers, and when she returned change that I slid back her way she said, over the music, "You're the nicest person that's come in tonight."

"Be well, yeah?" I said, or something equally terse but joyfully felt, and she got it, she understood, she nodded and smiled and wiped at the counter. I lifted the beers and nodded back a good smile and moved on through the thick bodywalk back to Knox.

"I want that guy's tie, man. Thank you," she said, nodding toward the highly illuminated singer, so placating of the masses with his bright grin and sweat and literally *sound* labors.

"Some interesting people at the bar," I told her.

"Really?" She asked, turning her head to look behind me. "Let's go up there, then. I need to pee anyway. It's messing up my chi. Hold my beer."

I followed her toward where I'd stood previously as she angled around the thinning crowd, thinner the farther people were forced away from the stage, and I reinserted myself in the space I'd been before which surprisingly hadn't been filled. The same girl from just earlier continued smiling my way, so we struck a short talk on the bar vibe and then she, Angie, went on the introduce me to her three friends, one girl whose name I couldn't catch, a young man beside her whose named was Jerrod, which I had him repeat a few times over the volume, and another young man beside me named Brian who was straddling Angie's knee in a desperate attempt to avoid the carousing bodies that filtered up and down the walking path in front of the bar. We were sudden and old friends by the time Knox returned and sat on the stool over which I loomed while leaning against the counter's edge. After a good read of Knox's face, I could tell she agreed, too, that they had a good energy. It was a no-brainer to follow Jerrod and Brian to another bar, as their lady friends wanted to stay, as the two men had immediately taken on the responsibility of showing Knox and me some of the goods on the strip we may not have discovered in basic wandering. We said "so long" to the girls and took back to the street and had a smoke while waiting for the guys to make it out, and then they led the way to a piano bar nearby, equally as packed, and Jerrod knew the door man who waved us in.

We navigated with mild frustration through the bottom floor of the place, but collectively agreed once in the middle to bail and head upstairs to some dueling piano area that was supposed to be the real pulse we were looking for. I could see Knox scoffing at the fraternity boys within and understood it was bringing her too close to an old life she'd probably exhausted with her ex, an old life she knew for what it was which, based on her shaking her head, I couldn't imagine it being something too terribly thrilling, so I was glad to participate in a decision with the boys to get her and me and them and *us* out of there. The upstairs was choice, with room to maneuver our small herd, and we found a low-level table available in front of the stage and seated ourselves around it, with some incredibly nice blonde women behind me saying "no I can still see the stage" as I conversationally regretted to them the invasion of their space and view. Jerrod reversed his chair into an older fellow who fell short of a roar at the surprise of the marriage of chair and body, but once we got settled and Brian jetted off to the back bar for our first round, I was finally alert and happy amongst interesting strangers. Jerrod kept telling me across the table he'd seen some celebrity in the back on his way in when scanning the joint, kept telling me I needed to go with him to check it out, but I wasn't interested and kept saying "No worries, babe, it's not my thing." Knox laughed and explained to him I didn't watch television and was turned off by cell phones.

"So she's a comedian, right?" I said to Jerrod as he took a beer from Brian who'd returned, and he gave me a salute with his bottle from across the table.

The two men opposite each other at their pianos turned out to be brothers and had an intensely experience-able chemistry as they bounced from pop culture jam versions to standard and crowd-rousing Joels and Johns and some mad, hyped up Waits that Knox and I were heavily in to. And the brilliant and curious moment arose when they began to add to the show friends who'd seemed like audience members, a pair of guys who jumped on the tiny drum set in front of the huge mirror behind the key boxes, and a guitar no one could see until it was lifted off a stand in back, and the sound took toward more a duel than a real, palpable collective, and the night enriched itself with their bantering and mid-song jokes. And then they'd switch instruments to heighten everyone's interest and definitely illuminate the vastness of their abilities, and as the crowd of a hundred or so began to swell and drop cash on the piano tops, as well as handwritten requests, the security guards at either side of the stage began communicating in aggressive body language worth the price of a movie ticket. But as gruff and rigid as they seemed, it was still an endearing testament to their involvement in their jobs that no matter whose skulls needed an occasional thumping, they could sing along with the band and not take the world too seriously. Knox and I were tossing each other wild stares and grins.

Brian and I got entangled in a great talk on what it was Knox and I had come to Tennessee to do, talking most of the hour there once I discovered he taught speech and drama at a local high school, while the other two of our group occasionally threw us preoccupied eyes of their own. I found myself occasionally inquisitive as to their discourse, but beneath the canopy of roaring music and laughter in the bar, my guess was snuffed out by the wind of harmless apathy, because the moment had finally arrived, after a wealth of days waiting for it, and the now had proven to be good enough for my resolve to not know. I stood and ran a finger around the table at everyone, they nodded and I swept to the back bar for my turn at a round, dipping first into the hallway past it to use the restroom. Having only twenties in my pocket, I felt real sorrow a moment when the eager young man working the cologne counter hosed me down and scrubbed my hands and nodded at his tip jar. And even though I didn't know it was that kind of joint, I wanted to be a part of such grassroots commerce and throw him some good blue even if it were in cash green, but I couldn't a twenty for a knuckle massage.

"All I've got's a twenty, but I can hit the bar and come..."

"A twenty's fine. You can just put it right there in the jar. I won't mind."

I made him an empty promise to return and then redistributed my better energies into the noise outside the door, scoring four beers from a friendly brunette girl behind the bar.

I found my seat after handing out the beers, but Jerrod was whispering into Knox's ear when I lifted my bottle toward him. He looked across at Brian, who stood and bent down to me as Knox made a strange face at me.

"We've gotta take off," Brian said.

"Really? That's no good, babe. What's up?" I asked.

"J's gotta work early. Sorry, man."

255

"All right," I said, looking over at Knox who had taken to a deep pull on her bottle. "Pass me your number, man. Stay in touch if we come back up. Who knows?"

I passed him a wet pen and a dry bar napkin from the far side of our table. He wrote down his number as he kept looking over his shoulder for Jerrod, who'd jaunted off toward the door leading downstairs to the street.

"Take good care, brother," I said as he shook my hand and patted my shoulder and then was gone.

Knox looked at me a brief moment and was shaking her head, smiling into a real laugh after watching to make sure our boys were gone.

"You are so fucking clueless, man. Let's go to the balcony and have a smoke."

I took her hand after gesturing a goodbye at the women still sitting behind me, and we made it out on to the packed balcony that once again took us back to New Orleans, minus the copious bare breasts and cheap shiny beads of Mardi Gras. I lit us two. A trim-bearded fellow came out and stood beside Knox and lit his own. Her eyes undressed him too apparently and I started smiling.

"You really aren't good at concealing what's on your mind. Not at all."

"Damn, he's beautiful." She shook her head.

"So why am I clueless?" I asked while examining the loud drinkers around us, people emitting usual party sounds down to the street.

"Oh come *on*, Rattigan. Those guys were into you."

"Hmm?" I asked. "Wait, they were gay?"

"*Hello.*"

I laughed.

"I had no idea, babe. I don't look for that sort of thing."

"I didn't say *I* was looking for it, asshole. But it was completely obvious. Are you kidding? I was wondering in there what was going through your mind."

"I was telling Brian about my book and your poems." I hit my cigarette. "I didn't know. Who cares?"

"I couldn't give a soaring shit, *Rattigan*. I'm saying I thought you knew."

"My mind wasn't there."

"Ok, when you went for beers, Jerrod told me he thought you didn't like him because his hair was messy. Can you believe that shit? *And* he thought you were more interested in Brian."

I smiled. "I was."

"That cat was nuts, man. He kept going on about how beautiful he thought you were."

"I'm flattered. No doubt."

"I just don't think he had to work in the morning, is all. He just wanted to get Brian away from you. Brian even asked if you were gay."

"He and my family have way too much in common." And then I thought a moment. "What'd you tell him?"

She smiled a huge smile.

"*What*, Knox?"

"I didn't want to burst his sweet little bubble, man."

"Holy Buddha on heroin," I said theatrically and then laughed. Knox's crush stubbed out his smoke on the ground and studied the two of us a short minute. "Let's blow out of here, man. You're complete chaos." I threw my arm over her shoulders and we headed downstairs. "Let's go find you a girlfriend."

She punched my ribs as we flushed out, sans boys, into the human tide. And after the fact of the piano bar, we decided a gay bar would be a kick to experience, so we hit up a cool-looking girl running a late night hot dog stand and asked for directions, figuring there was one amidst the flurry.

"I dunno," she said. "But hang on."

She got on her cell, phoned someone and then gave us directions up the street about three blocks. We thanked her and, armed with a new mission to find ourselves imaginary lovers, we cashed in at last the cue from the New Yorker we'd crossed paths with earlier in the evening, and skimmed the fervid taxis off the strip and ignored the blinking white traffic man, making it across the road and up a hill as onlookers finally thought, I sup-posed, *locals*.

We hit close to the top of the joining streets which was to bare the bar we sought, but no such place was tucked into the buildings saddled against the sidewalk. We saw a group in similar shirts, a group of some men but mostly women, two of which were playing an unexpected game of piggy back, with one of them on all fours rather than the stand-up versions we

257

both recalled from childhood, and I told Knox after reading them that we were at least close. But we couldn't find anything once the ascent had ended, after Knox made note of decent music coming from a small bar we passed, so we stopped and asked for further directions.

"Hey Donna!" The woman we asked yelled out at a woman up the road with the group.

"What!"

"Come here! They're looking for a gay bar!" Then she turned back to us. "We're all gay, well, he's not and...she's not, that one there. We're doing a scavenger hunt down here."

"Right on," I said.

"Nashville's not very gay friendly. Donna!"

Donna approached.

"Where would you say the closest gay bar is around here? They're looking for one."

Knox was grinning at the interest we'd sparked. The majority of the crowd had pivoted and come back down to stand nearby and listen.

"We want to do something different from the strip," Knox said.

"Everything like that's a cab ride from here. Maybe twenty bucks. We don't really go that much," Donna said.

"And the nicest one, *I* think, is like a shotgun house. Way outta town. *I* think. It goes straight back." She pressed together her palms and made a piercing dart with them into the road away from us. "Not very big."

I talked it out with Knox. We agreed it wasn't worth the cab fare to spend our final and diminishing hours in an area that closed their bars at three a.m. So we thanked everyone and wished them a blast, making our way back to the bar Knox had mentioned earlier, and we shot toward the back of the place. We sat long enough before recognizing we were pressed for bar time in the late hours and needed to get food before heading back out to our beds off the pike. And besides the burgeoning hunger within us, the music in the place was offset by the noisy silly drunk of a singer, not giving his female counterpart enough microphone time to do what she did better than he. But being there mattered, watching the twilight clowns flail about with more fervor and bravado than we possessed, dancing with little concern for strangers' eyes that crept in and out of the joint. We downed the drinks and stopped on our way out to chat up the inviting bouncer who half-sat on a stool by the door, a guy who was working the downtown scene until he could "make it, like everyone else around here's tryin'," he'd said.

Back down the street we rediscovered an Irish pub and grille we'd been interested in earlier, before the wine, and the doorwoman told us they were closing in fifteen minutes but that we could still order food, so we bounded in, suddenly famished and happy. Perhaps people could see in our eyes we were around with no other agenda but to, I suppose, just be.

"We know we're pushing time," I said to the bartender, a glitter-faced beauty with blonde hair and tired eyes. "We'll make it fast, no doubt."

"It's cool," she said and shrugged. "What are ya'll drinking?"

We ordered a pair of beers, with Knox still reeling from the speed of our intake earlier, thereby ordering a short draft while I opted for the larger, knowing it would be our night's last, the last drink of Nashville. A quick skim of the menu resulted in a big burger choice and two appetizers, which we got put in without mutual contest to the relief of our bartender, Katie she would become, as she celebrated our serious devotion to getting out of her way, although she was beautiful about it, and warmed into a talk with us about her shift's busy fluctuation pre-and-post-game. A couple of thirty-somethings joined the bar to my back, as I'd shifted in my seat toward Knox as we sipped our beers and made on with topics analyzing what was happening, and what would come clear on the road back to the coast, knowing what was going on would change and get more or less true in hindsight as does all reality. After a while, I could tell in Knox's face that yet again more was occurring than what her speech was letting on. I spun in my seat and noticed the fellow next to me, in cowboy hat, Irish beer t-shirt, as well as the woman to his right, both of them drinking short drafts and eyeing the menu. It suddenly felt less romantic that Knox and I wouldn't be the last starved transients in Katie's hindsight.

But after a minute exchange between myself and the cowboy, Knox interjected an opinion across my chest, into the talk, after he'd said something to me—not necessarily derogatory—about Alabama.

"Wait, we're not all like that," she said, shaking her head, and I could sense she wanted a cigarette. I perked my ears to learn more of what she was seeing in the conversation that I wasn't. One of our appetizers came and we fingered into the potato skins below a mountain of cheese.

259

"Yeah," I added. "I stopped screwing my cousin months ago. Found a real woman." I nudged Knox on the knee for emphasis.

The strangers both fell into a laugh, along with Knox, and it suddenly turned good.

"Where are you guys from?" Knox asked them.

"Fort Collins, Colorado," Cowboy said.

"Oh, right on. You guys bleed camo. That's sexy," I said. More laughter.

"What are you drinking?" He asked, looking at his smaller beer compared to the exorbitantly tall one I nursed. I picked up on what he was asking.

"Mine's bigger than yours, man. Sorry. That's how we grow 'em in Alabama."

After that, and all that followed, I can't remember a moment in my history more overflowing with hilarity. Good people, they became. They got it. Knox was spewing a different mountain of confidence in the stereotype of our hometown, throwing me off, too, with what she'd noticed about Mobile but never articulated around me. She even called out Cowboy on his ironic t-shirt once we learned he detested Irish stout. We laughed with such body-aching complication we decided to ask Katie for a couple of boxes for the rest of our goods so we could vault off to the hotel and eat slovenly on our beds and allow a deterioration of wits to overtake us and muscle us into sleep.

"You guys have been the most fantastic people I've had in here all night," Katie said when dropping the bill. "Really."

"You've been so sweet, babe. We were nervous about coming in so late," Knox said.

"No they weren't," Cowboy said. His lady friend had been too quiet apart from the laughing. I wanted her take on things, on Colorado, on Tennessee. I wanted more of their story.

Katie shot him an uncomfortable glare in protection of us, not understanding our established rapport.

"It's all right," I began, as Knox and I dug through our pockets for cash to pay. "He's got a fetish for in-breeders he's finally realized tonight. He's projecting."

On our side of the bar we ended up in hugs after paying out and downing our beers while standing, with Katie thanking us, us thanking Katie, the night in its denouement the way a colossal night should go. And we emerged for the last time into the street of downtown.

"Pass me Reza's card, I'll call him," I said as I juggled the takeout boxes and accepted a smoke from Knox.

"No," she said, almost wistfully, studying the street before us as I noticed the stumbling crowd had thinned to a state of worry-free manageability. "I want to hail a cab. I've never hailed a cab, man. It's a must-do for a poet's repertoire. Come *on*, Rattigan."

We shuttled off to a sidewalk corner after she wisely rejected my idea to do it in the middle of the road, and we caught one on her second wave. Our cabbie was a sweet South African man.

"Where am I taking you?" He asked.

"Funny thing," I began to say, not knowing how in the curse of foreign geography to tell the man where our heads were paying to lie. Knox squeezed my leg.

"We're off the pike, off 45, I can call and..."

"I follow," he said, looking in the mirror. I missed Reza's comforting presence. I slumped against my seat, finally enthralled by my exhaustion and Knox's handling of our arrow-ing home, our part-time home, a kind of home I thought then, as a nascent national poet, *recognized* and celebrated, if even on terrifying terms, that I wanted to interminably call home. But Knox, out of, yes, the blue, generated some unforeseen composition of freeway numbers to our driver and got us on the accurate way, along with his familiarity with the terrain.

"Pete," she said, patting the vinyl seat between us as I stirred and looked at her, her eyes not distracted, not analytical, but filled with near-tears, a gloss of understanding. "I am so happy right now. This, this is really..."

"What we're here for," I interrupted. I put my hand palm-up on the seat and she took it. I readjusted my body, understanding, too, the gravity of what we were doing, away from Mobile, and felt obligated to collapse into an affection for it with Amber Knox, as my sleeping in motion, I thought, would have been an insult.

We spilled from the taxi in front of the hotel after paying our man and giving him blessings for his night ahead, and sauntered tiredly across the quiet lobby and up to our room, the hallway at that hour emptied of the wedding herd. Knox and I both sighed through the door as we set down the food and took turns at the john, after agreeing we should rent a movie off the hotel TV system. "Can we?" She asked. "We should try, anyway," I said. It worked out, and we stripped to basics for sleep as we piled on her bed and ate the crab-cake sandwiches and burger and fries along with the leftover skins, laughing at the indulgence before climbing into our own beds and, twenty minutes in to a film with a title I can't remember really even wanting to watch, falling into the few hours' sleep we'd need to make it home, to our hidden home in the woods, alive.

———

Knox and I shook ourselves out of the hotel with what I considered admirable hastiness, even after Knox called Cora to find she was feeling sick and didn't want to test herself in her late stages of pregnancy in terms of niceness, meaning we had no schedule. So we made our way to a local coffee shop and I bought us both hot cups, and myself, a pair of juices which I spilled on the floor by the counter. Driving out of there, it made sense based on the stares of the patrons, the middle-aged well-dressed, that we didn't belong, as driving up to the on-ramp we noticed the opulence of the area, evident in the light we didn't have for analysis in the erstwhile dark. Again, I got us lost a while before we saw I-65 South and jumped it, ready to be going as Knox fingered the radio dial and found a station playing subtle independent tracks our nerves could take in the exodus.

We both stayed wide awake during the follow-down to the Gulf, for a few hours, the only pauses in our talks of what we thought had occurred in Nashville coming from Knox belting out toward the window that she saw goats or donkeys or cotton fields, even begging me a moment to let us step out and run through the latter, but she fell back on the suggestion as we hurtled south and she grew sleepy, and then I lost her for a few hours until I got hungry and, as she put it when she snapped alert, noticeably disgruntled. We stopped north of Montgomery for a humorously mutual desire for country food. Our server was an Army girl who told us we talked and sounded like aliens, and we ordered too much and ate it all with coffee that propelled us to a rest area where I knew, after leaving it, we'd need to change seats before I ran us off the road. The reading was gone, Nashville had been done, and my basic fuel source was depleted, which Knox could sense. I surrendered the keys after hovering over a toilet and reading what I'd predicted in my mind before, right across the stall walls. BJs, someone loathing both white and black people, an awkward progression in the country, even if an angry and nonplussed approach to equality, and a penciled haiku above the one-ply roll that said, to some effect, that the government was a whore with a mouthful. Who carries a pencil? I wondered. I couldn't be the only one who wondered.

I awoke just south of the Dolly Bridge to the sound of Knox's driver's window rolling down, after she'd lit a smoke, and I leapt into an apology for abandoning her for so long.

"No worries, babe. Honestly," she said. "I actually needed time to process everything. Well not *everything*. But the trip. I think Cora's pissed off."

"Really?" I asked, looking around to get my bearings and grabbing a lighter from inside her passenger door and accepting a smoke she passed over the car's gearshift.

"I shouldn't have...I dunno." She exhaled through the crack in her window. "I should have outlined a better schedule for all of us. It's no huge thing."

"Do we..." I started, looking around more, at the trees buzzing on past the shoulder of the road. "Wait. Sorry, man. I'm still waking up."

"No, I'm not bummed about it. This drive's been almost surreal. I was just thinking about that when you woke up. How was your sleep?"

"Let me be lame and say it was 'far out.' But it was, man. *So* deeply good. Years away from right now."

"Nice. I owed you anyway."

"No *way*. Let's go up again to see her when she has the kid."

She nodded and thought a while.

"I really need to get back to my poems," she said.

I adjusted my seat and leaned back, took a long last pull off my smoke and tossed it out the window.

"You're so good, Knox," I said. "Once you start listening to me, you'll figure it out." I closed my eyes.

"What?" She asked as she changed lanes and joined the line of cars heading into town.

"Your poems are better than mine."

"Stop," she said.

"I'm telling you, babe. Keep with them. Please." And then I fell asleep again until we showed up in the short guest drive at our house.

The lights inside were on. Brody's car was in the drive.

We dragged our bags, heavier then from their stories, down the walk to the steps up in to the house. I was ahead of Knox and tested the door like potential fire and it was unlocked, so I pushed it in with my fingertips.

Brody was stretched out across his couch, shirtless, a bandana pinning his lengthening hair back, jeans and socks on. He folded himself upward at us as we walked in. I nodded toward him as I piled into the small room, and Knox exuberantly called out his name.

"Hey," he said, finishing his move up to sit, dragging his feet off the sofa arm's end and placing them on the floor. "*Hey* mates."

Knox landed on him and they wrestled one another on the couch as I rolled her luggage piece to her bed's side and dropped my bags in the corner as I stepped out of my shoes.

"Come here, gorgeous," Brody said, waving me toward him, supine, and Knox on his stomach.

"LaCoste," I exhaled as I joined the flesh-fray of old and familiar bodies. We forced ourselves on to the couch, we confused ourselves, ignoring the night, suddenly charged. "There's so much to tell you."

CHAPTER 8

My shifts at the restaurant would seem less important once home from Tennessee, and since neither of us had overspent ourselves, my award check was on the way and Brody was back around, I planned to work just what I was scheduled in order to extend the pulse and exhaustion from the trip into our time at the house. I addressed the last swing of my novel's draft by designating certain hours a day in my respective corner by the side door, a less-than-rigorous schedule I followed a solid week and finished what remained of my final chapter—Knox had just under two weeks to finalize her approach to her thesis defense and Brody, while he still wasn't mentioning much on his own book, had taken a hiatus from his involved nights with Heidi and we all slipped on our family hats again. LaCoste was in great spirits, exuding real accomplishment from his time away, telling us over a series of late talks in our local bar down Old Shell about experimenting with "seats of his other self," discovering the layers of his unseen body, the inner eye, rich and important talks that spurred a good electricity amongst us as those students new to the bar who didn't know us watched from across their drinks and short straws, as we were back to being, collectively, on to something.

Dawn was a happy sort of busy, too, plugging away with ferocity and predictable shouting matches with her mentor as his book was at last having itself birthed after too, too much of a gestation. My co-workers had preserved their mania in my absence and I was regulating the high over my project's completion with joy excursions into work, not wanting to be there, compared to what was going on beyond its walls, but hungrily feeding on the moments when I was assigned to be.

"Heard you killed in Nashville," Blain said and squeezed my shoulders as he lit a smoke and leaned against the side of the bar, his forehead bumping into the hanging beer pitchers. He and I had closed the restaurant along with Brody, Sonya and Dawn and we were sitting around behind locked doors, profit-sipping and winding down a busy midweek at the Stone. Brody elbowed me.

"This guy tell you?" I asked.

"Nope," Blain said, pulling Sonya's ashtray into his reach as she counted cash out of the main register's drawer. "Dawn's talking you up to some eventual fame. Figured I'd drink as many beers as I can with you before you leave and forget us."

Dawn rounded the bar and took Blain's pack from his chest pocket.

"I don't think I even asked about your trip yet," Sonya said in the middle of her count. "27, 28, 29. I suck at friendship." She smiled at me and shrugged before starting in on the loose change.

Brody laughed. "I should have been there, babe. I should be the one apologizing."

She looked up at both of us, a handful of nickels in her right palm. "Oh that wasn't an apology. Shit, I lost count. Nobody talk to me."

"I'm beat, man," Dawn said from the other side of Brody.

"Brad tell you he wants me to manage the kitchen?" Blain asked me as Brody turned in his seat to massage the back of Dawn's neck.

"You gonna do it?"

"Don't have much else better to do at the moment. Nothing I can think of."

"Be more money," Dawn said between soft moans.

"If that's what you're into," Brody added.

"Make sure he puts you on our insurance if you take it," Sonya said after bundling the counted money and receipts into a green bank bag. She took the pint glasses from Blain and me and filled them with something we weren't drinking before, handed them back our way and lit a cigarette. "I'd have been screwed when that bitch broke my nose last November if I wasn't on our insurance. And ask for three more bucks an hour."

"That much more, huh?" Blain asked while studying the different beer in his glass. I grinned at Sonya.

"Brad can afford it. Totally. Don't let him bullshit you about overhead. Ours is through the roof because of what he starts new people out at, plus what we...what the fuck are you guys drinking? Did I do that?"

She laughed and shook her head.

"No worries," I said.

Blain shrugged.

"But you won't have any real say or control," she continued.

"May I have some of what they're having?" Brody slid his glass across the bar.

"You're a beautiful man," Dawn told Blain as she spun in her seat to face us and propped a forearm on Brody's shoulder. The air conditioner had surrendered its abilities earlier in the shift, to the chagrin of the guests, the malfunction likely due to the age of the building, the heat of the huge ovens and the amount of people filling the seats, but it had begun to cool again, the air roaring loudly out of the ceiling vent over the bar.

"He just double-checks everything. I mean, he *has* to, right? So whatever inventory you take, especially end of the month, he combs through. There's some management theory of his that goes with that, but I dunno. I majored in leisure studies."

"Really?" I asked her.

"Fantastic," Brody added.

"I don't even think they offer it on campus anymore. Oh well." Sonya bit a synthetic cork jutting from a wine bottle.

"What about liquor inventory up here? Am I responsible for that?" Blain asked her.

"No sweetheart. No, no. Leave that to Mama," Sonya said, patting her chest. "But he drinks this shit up, too, man. So we kind of ignore how little the profit is off the booze."

"Love to all you guys, but I'm hitting the road. I'm over this joint for tonight," Dawn said. She stood and downed her drink before heading with the empty iced tea cup, from which she drank because it held more ounces than a pint, toward the kitchen. "Adios." She distributed a few hugs around and gave Blain his cigarettes back, though he hadn't seemed to notice they'd been lifted.

"Yeah, let's get outta here. Knock 'em back, boys," Sonya said.

"Rattigan, come stay over tomorrow night. I found a first edition of *Herzog* at the thrift store in Tillman's Corner. We can drink wine and take turns petting it," Dawn called out from the kitchen.

"It's a date, man," I said, standing to finish my drink alongside Brody. We filed out the back door after Sonya hit the breakers and set the alarm.

"Just come by the department when you get off here. I'm there 'til four anyway," Dawn said from her car before firing the engine and following Sonya out of the parking lot.

"I was gonna see what you guys are getting into tonight, but I think I've had it," Blain said as he packed a single cigarette on the back of his hand and then dug out his truck keys.

"No worries, babe," Brody said.

"I'm pretty beat, too, man."

"It's the old man creeping up in me, I suppose," he said, grinning and backing into his driver's seat.

"Take care brother," I told him.

"Peace, guys."

Brody and I watched him drive off as we remained beneath the flood-light behind the building.

"What are you thinking?" I asked.

"I'm thinking I want to drive your car."

I looked at my vehicle we'd shared to work, snug with the curb. "Brody, it's exactly the same as your car."

"No such thing, man. Nothing's the same. Come on, you got to drive here. This could be the thrill of a lifetime."

He was smiling and had his hands in his pockets, his shoulders pulled up toward his ears as if it were cold out.

"Hey. Knox tell you her aunt scored her a room at that new fancy Marriot downtown this coming weekend?"

"She was on the phone about a hotel but I didn't catch what was going on. That's wild though. What for?"

"She said it's to clear her head, get away a bit before her thesis defense, you know, without being *extremely* away. Get pampered some."

"That's really generous," Brody said, nodding at the ground. "I was thinking about a road trip this weekend. Kinda the same thing. Keep it minor. I might not, though. I've had some left-field stuff on my mind I want to knock around."

"Things good, man?" I asked, trying to examine his face silhouette against the floodlight.

"Come on, Rattigan." He smiled another brief minute, eyes still aimed at the ground, and then he looked at my hand. "Keys."

I tossed them over and we hopped in. I suspected since we'd made money that night that we were headed to some place that might satisfy a momentary curiosity of his, but I was merely guessing. We ended up driving down University to Springhill by way of the same park we'd visited a while back, then cut through side roads toward Midtown, Dauphin Street, over to Old Government and took it down through a neighborhood past a high school, cut back to Dauphin and then made it back to the house about half past midnight. We didn't talk during the drive, and as Brody flipped the radio stations one after the other, and even drummed along to a few songs, he was distracted by something that was supposed to be out in the dark, darting across a street or hiding behind a column of a historic home in passing, hanging from a tree maybe, who knows, but whatever he was seeking out, unmentioned or even hinted at, I was silently proud he trusted me to be there.

But the next morning he and I both awoke to Knox's alarm, as she and I both had work during the day. As I passed him on the couch to put on a pot of coffee, he slapped at my leg and was all smiles as if he'd found what it was and either didn't tell me on the drive, or had engineered a better answer in his sleep. He sat up when I brought him a cup, but I had to muscle my way through the bathroom door to get a frenzied, hurried Knox to submit to at least a few meditative sips before an extended fill-in shift at the studio.

"How late do you have to work?" She asked me as she stumbled around the bed, looking for her work button down.

"Early out is by two."

"Shit on that, man," she said. "I'm lucky if I can break out by five."

"You guys are beautiful," Brody called out, having stretched out again on his back.

"Not now, LaCoste," Knox growled as she went back in the bathroom. I sat on the bed to get out of her way.

"Why do you even keep that job?" I asked her.

"Bustling around, so serious in the morning," Brody said to the ceiling.

"Because I'm naked without shit to complain about," she answered from behind the door.

"That's harsh for almost eight in the morning," I said, grinning.

"Is it almost eight? *Damnit.*"

She finished her dance and handed me her cup on the way out.

"Coffee was good. Will you drink it? I can't. No time. Gotta go."

"So stern and driven," Brody continued, his body lightly shaking with a giggle.

She stopped at the door and took a deep breath, exhaled, then walked over to the couch and fake-strangled him a moment before kissing him a few times on the forehead.

"So I'm nuts in the morning. I get it. I *get* it. Love you bastards."

"Be well," I called after her.

"Catch you tonight, *lady*," Brody said as she shut the door.

I showered while Brody sat on our front steps and had a couple smokes, and we killed the next hour talking out thoughts on what might be ahead. Keeping with his caution when I brought up his book, he was nonetheless genuinely interested in the fellowship I'd applied for, even interrupting me once to suggest if I were to go to California, I'd have to become a surfer, would have to grow out my hair longer than "this," he'd said, sliding back the bandana from around his forehead to show how much his had grown past his ears. "I could definitely go for that gig," he'd added.

"What are you up to today, man? I'm heading out," I said, stepping into a pair of sneakers by the door around nine-thirty, as he climbed back on the couch.

"This is it, babe." He closed his eyes and folded his arms across his chest. "Think I might take advantage of the empty nest until later."

"Do it, for sure," I said, patting the door with my hand before stepping out into the sun.

"Hey, *Rattigan*," he said.

I stuck my head back inside. "What's up?"

He looked directly at me, a mischievous grin spreading over his mouth, and he lifted his hand, contorting his fingers.

"Make your hand do this, and just one time, for me, say *gnarly*."

"Ok, later man."

I shut the door as he yelled, "Come on, *babe*. At least say something's *rad*."

———

"You're early," Dawn said as I entered the philosophy department offices. She sat at the front desk and faced a computer resting on its corner. "I take it we weren't busy."

"It wasn't bad. New girl Kennedy was crying all day, but..."

"Shocker." She looked back at her screen, and then over the top of the machine as a fifty-something fellow wearing khaki shorts, covered sandals and a short-sleeve button down with a shiny medallion dangling from his neck, partially hidden in a protruding chest tuft. His hair was shoulder length and unconfined by a band, and he had an unlit cigarette between his fingers, a mug of what I assumed to be coffee in his other hand. Big, wild eyes behind small specs.

"Hey Jack," Dawn said to him. He paused at her desk, looked her up and down best he could past the computer, turned to glance me down similarly and then focused back on her while patting his pockets. She reached in her purse and then handed him a lighter.

"Dawn, how long do I have you here?"

"Through the end of days," she said, shaking her head at him. "This is Pete Rattigan."

He pivoted swiftly back in my direction.

"Hello sir!" He said, vigorously shaking my hand. "How do you know this gal?"

I was into him instantly, as I'd learned the difficulty in discerning manias, bad from good, but inherently affixing myself unquestioningly to either kind.

"Work," I said, as he scratched his fingers over the medallion at his chest and studied me a bit longer. I felt my answer wasn't long enough. "But we..."

"Good!" He said, gripping Dawn's lighter and stepping off toward the front door. He turned inside the exit. "If I can have you 'til four," he said to Dawn. "Then you can skate. Cool?"

"I always stay until four, Jack."

He shrugged and said, "Good!" And then he disappeared out toward the courtyard dividing the two Humanities buildings. Now I recognize him, I thought.

"So that's Dr. Mohler?"

"More like a young son sometimes," Dawn answered. She made a few clicks on her keyboard and then set her elbows on the desk to prop her chin in her palms. "Today's been silly. How was work? Did I ask you that already?"

"When I was in school I remember thinking that cat was crazy."

"Genius is madness, man. You know he's got a J.D., too? I could use a beer, man. You need my key?"

"Yeah. I'm going to run home first to get out of this business," I said, running my hands over my work clothes. She peeled a key off her chain and stood to walk around the desk and pass it over after a hug and heavy sigh. "Are campus cops usually so militant about giving out a day pass to park?"

"They're just short of implementing cavity searches. No lie." She rolled her eyes a quick second. "Sorry babe. Look, I swear to be less distracted once I'm off."

"What's been going on?"

"Fucking students, man. Running late on papers, and Annette's out sick. So I'm two people today. And this one bastard, cocky little sophomore, in here earlier trying to, well, I *thought* he was flirting before I actually listened to what he was saying, some bullshit on modal logic and anarchy, maybe? Strange combination. Honestly, if Mohler wouldn't have bailed early from his last seminar I would've broken into his liquor drawer."

"Nice," I said, swinging her hand in mine. She finally broke a smile.

"He thinks he's clever, but I've got him down to a science at this point."

"Hey, if Annette doesn't work out, maybe I..."

"You don't wanna work here, Rattigan."

"No I think I'd be a perfect fit because..."

She started pushing me toward the door.

"...maybe I could be your bouncer for undergrads..."

"I've got that covered, man. Get outta here. I'll give you cash later for beer if you'll pick up."

"I'm a really fast learner," I said as we broke apart, standing on either side of the door.

"All love, babe. See you in a few."

"Be well," I said, and skipped toward a side door, trotted a few stairs down to the sidewalk level, pushed open the heavy doors and hopped in my car after pacing a couple hundred yards west of the building to where it snoozed beneath a row of pine trees.

No one's vehicles were in the drive when I got home, not even the main house residents', and I could hear the guesthouse phone ringing as I approached the door, so I jogged up and in and nearly splayed out over scattered t-shirts on the hard wood to get to the receiver.

"Who'd you kill?" I answered, thinking it might be Dawn calling from work.

There was a brief silence on the other end.

"Are you just waking up?"

"Hey, Ma," I said, and then let a sigh as heavy as Dawn's back on campus. "Just got in, actually." I exhaled. "Why, what's going on?"

"I've called for two days but no one seems to find it worth their time to answer."

"You could leave a message."

"*Right*," she started. "Like you don't stand around the phone and laugh when you see it's me."

"We don't have caller ID."

"Oh, I doubt that. Answering machine but no caller ID?"

"It's still possible."

"Get serious, Peter."

"Come on, Ma."

"Well, ok, I *will* 'come on,' now that I've got you."

I sat on the edge of the bed and slid off my shoes and lay back, stretching the chord tight across my pillow.

"I'm calling to tell you your grandfather's estate finally closed."

"That was fast. The land sold already?"

I rolled over and looked at the clock, then reached for a magazine half-wedged down the side where Knox slept. I wondered how my mother and her sisters had managed to end their fighting over money long enough to reach a resolution.

"The Episcopal church bought it. Everything was finalized two days ago, and you need to know there was a stipulation that involves you and your sister and your cousins."

"Right on," I said, as the phone dangled in my hand while I skimmed the table of contents of the magazine.

"Why are you talking to your mother like that? *Right on*. I'm trying to tell you something..."

"What is it, Ma? I don't have anything to do with Papa's stuff."

"Oh, I suppose you don't want the autographed Hank Aaron baseball he left you?"

"I already have it. That's silly. I'm glad to have it."

"Do you even know where it is?"

I thought a moment to myself in too much silence. But before I could tell her it was in storage, I'd lost the battle.

"That's what I thought. Listen, Peter. His will left five thousand dollars to each of you."

"Oh, shit," I said, putting down the magazine.

"*Now* do I have your attention?"

"You're being ridiculous, Ma."

"I can say the same for you lately, which is why I'm calling. I'll put one thousand of it in your account, but until you decide..." She paused. "Until you decide to move past this, I don't even know what to call it, *bum* experiment of yours and get concerned about your life, I'm not confident you'd do anything intelligent with the rest of the money. But you do need some extra in case of emergency."

I propped myself on an elbow and studied the headboard a short while. A perversion seemed to be taking place, and after a few deep breaths I recognized I was growing annoyed and knocked slightly off center from my good thoughts for the night ahead.

"I'm fine on money, Ma. If...if this is how you want to tackle disbursing it, just keep it."

"Sarcasm on top of indifference. Clever. Very clever, Peter."

"For rainy day money. Go shopping. Just quit..."

"Go *shopping*? Tell me Lord, what has happened to my child?"

"Gotta go, Ma. Truly great to hear from you."

"I should call your sister..."

"All love," I said and hung up. The phone rang a few more times before its final silence. I sat up and ran fingers through my hair, shook my head and stood into a stretch to the ceiling, and began to smile. Whatever world my grandfather had entered after his death, it wasn't one in which he was glued to some ticker that monitored who was getting what he couldn't spend in a wilder, better place.

After another shower I slipped into a pair of torn jeans and a red t-shirt with a faded picture of a building across the chest, and beneath it was an even more faded "Chicago." On the way to Dawn's I did think while laughing, the windows down, beer and a notepad and a few books riding shotgun, that a thousand bucks would buy a lot of t-shirts.

Her townhouse was quiet, unfamiliarly, as the times I'd been over before had been filled with conversational noise and laughter, with many of her lovely, vulgar railings against the university establishment spreading late into even later nights. The quietness was disarming as I passed the immense blood-red couch along the north wall and the torn-in-half college diploma she'd taped in plain view over the sitting chair just before the entrance to the kitchen. I placed the beer in the fridge after extracting one from the box and stepped out on to her small patio, as a cooler front had come in from the bay to stave off for a few days the oncoming heat that would move gypsy-like into the city and root down for its usual coastal endlessness. Inside was too sudden a reminder that I'd learned to write in organized chaos at home and had forgotten the fundamental human desire for silence, even if occasional, and then I recognized my avoidance of it, as many others in my experience were terrified of what it, in vast supply, could cause or bring. So I did a shuffling dance of indecision, between the patio's ledge and the door, as to whether I should reenter and sit once more at her table, this time without a typewriter to key-clack in distraction, and do something apart from both thinking and not thinking, maybe try to determine what, in the quickness of the quiet, that sixth sense, that third eye might be. But as I voted from the options and headed in, I heard Dawn calling from the front door.

"So it shall be," I said to myself as I crossed through the living room.

"What, babe? I got beer."

I laughed and met her by the coffee table.

"Just talking to myself," I told her and kissed her cheek. "You assigned me to get the drinks, man."

"Oh, *I'm* aware. But I thought about it after you left and decided I needed to keep thinking my job was too torrential long enough to convince myself to buy copious amounts. Is tomorrow really Friday?"

She handed over the beer as she removed her wallet from the back of her cargo pants and set it with her keys on the small table by the front door.

"I don't know what you're up for tonight..." She yelled behind her as she ascended the stairs.

"I'm last to know," I responded from the kitchen, returning to the living room and sitting on the couch with two beers in hand.

"...but whatever it is..." she continued. "...it has to include me telling you what they're trying to do to Mohler."

"I've got some nonsense that's come up."

"If you're hungry right now, you're screwed. I need time," she said, out of breath once returning in jeans to the downstairs. "But I'll make us a stir-fry later, if you're down."

I put my sandals back on, which had been momentarily kicked beneath the coffee table—her thick carpet was a must-feel for bare feet after so much time traversing hard wood floors covered in album covers and loose change—and I handed her a bottle as we hit the patio together.

"You're beautiful," she said once accepting it.

"No worries." I smiled. "And I ate at the Stone. I'm good. You just decompress, man. No worries at all, I can..."

"My day was fine, Rattigan." She lit a smoke and climbed into a crossed-leg seating position on a wooden bench across from her small laundry room. "I'm just keeping with the theme of needing a drink. Dramatic flare." She winked at me and took a long gulp. "What's your news?"

I laughed, shook my head and sat beside her, telling her of the phone call from my mother, about which Dawn had little positives, even interrupting once for a tirade, to call it a "fascist manner of retying the umbilical just to sever it again, a reclaim of power, mock-castration, full-on cowardice."

"I'll live," I said and continued to smile.

"Yeah." She sat forward. "Under a maternal threat blanket."

"So what's happening to Mohler?"

She took a minute to deeply breathe and exhale.

"They've demoted him to assistant dean."

"What? Why?"

"Because he's been spotted having drinks with students, and the administration thinks his alleged drinking problem is going to negatively affect America's youth to be apathetic and more self-destructive."

I took a thoughtful sip.

"Doesn't philosophy already do that?"

She laughed. "Yeah. *Yeah*, man. But this is like shooting the messenger."

"Sounds like it. Want another beer?"

She nodded and continued to talk as I stepped through the cracked door and scooped two bottles from the lower shelf in the refrigerator.

"They can't fire him, so they're trying to humiliate him. It definitely tests the theory that the academy is run by liberals."

"What's his take on it?" I asked as I sat again beside her.

"He says 'fuck 'em,' pretty casually at that, because he knows they're not going to do much more. He says they won't because of his tenure, and the fallout his termination would ignite. His theory is that they'd rather quietly castigate him for alcoholism than publicly address his bi-polar condition. They're into controlling worldviews at this point, and his teaching style says not to abide by it."

"Well, either way he's a villain, right? Since the students prefer him? I think that's what happened to Knox's first thesis advisor. Complete and utter..."

"Bullshit, I know. And what really smacks of political maneuvering is that the chair of Knox's department had a play in it. A totally different *department*, man. He used to sit in on her workshops sometimes and, I dunno, I guess he was too vocal about her academic discipline. Maybe she thought she was losing some false devotion from her own students. We should put together a protest."

"Sounds a little..."

"You better not say *risky*," Dawn said, finishing her smoke and dropping it in the top of a half-filled planter beside the low wall dividing her patio from her neighbor's.

"No, babe," I said, laughing. "I'm thinking of that cavity search I'd have to endure to get back on campus."

"Oh, don't be a pussy, Rattigan. It would be for the cause. Let's go in. Reacting to injustice makes me hungry."

I followed her inside and sat on the counter above the dishwasher as she talked out the implications of his demotion and how their workloads in the department would change, how she worried his efforts on *Ameranoia* would be halted by an assessment of altered responsibility, how she might be wedged into a spot where she had no other option but to dive into her Ortega text and face, as she put it, the man's fucking music. She sautéed in a small skillet huge blocks of tofu in an Indian sauce after cooking in a larger pan a series of snap beans and carrots and water chestnuts and broccoli, and after a makeshift picnic on the floor of her living room, involving a Vaughn album from the player beside a television she said had died a week earlier, the night came on and we found ourselves again on the patio, staring across the soccer field-sized lawn that stretched between her building and a long one beyond the grass. The stray cats of the complex had come out, darkly in the dark to saunter and crouch low and occasionally study us as we splayed our arms over the back wall.

Dawn said she'd forayed into poetry in the down time of her avoidance of the thesis, and she used surprisingly vulnerable terminology about its implications as well, how she'd written of climbing out of her mother, the push and pull of entering and reentering, something on responsibility of the flesh, colostrum, swollen breasts, the wail of a child. She looked across the yard, distracted with a half-smile at the cautious animals looking, stepping twice, looking again, as if she were using them to be her real voice for what she didn't wish to describe too intensely about the few poems once she'd begun analyzing them and realized what she was doing. It was beautiful to watch, to stand beside, almost wistfully, and I tugged my shoulders up around my ears as if manipulated by invisible strings and suddenly, I wanted to be known, too, as a philosopher, wanted to yank at my hair if even in metaphor, wanted to wear medallions before my chest and have wild, mad eyes.

From there, what we did and did not talk about shoved us into a late, ethereal pre-dusk gentility, and she began to sway at the first real front of exhaustion as I took to my own distraction about Knox and Brody and what they might be seeing or not seeing just a mile or so from where she and I stood, ignoring the light of the moon. It was just after three thirty when she announced with her own real shock that she had to be at work at nine, and we put out our final smokes and went inside.

"Just leave my key..." She said as she stood in the coat closet below the stairs. "...under the ceramic frog out back when you go in the morning. Afternoon, whichever."

She produced a blanket as she resurfaced from the closet and tossed it toward my feet as I lay stretched on the raft of a couch. I'd sunk into the beginning of abstractions prefacing a dream, and blinked sleepily at her and touched her face as she bent to kiss my forehead.

"Thanks for letting me crash," I said while stabbing a blind hand at the heavy blanket by my ankles.

"You did me another favor, babe. By coming over." She said. She stepped up on the first carpeted board leading upstairs. "Sucks that I still need it. Sorry I didn't ask if you like tofu."

I closed my eyes and smiled as she conducted her ascent after flipping the light switch at the base of the stairs. Night, morning, a black afternoon, sleeping on deep red, some shine from the street through the window, a tiny green light on the player, they all came together and I was gone. So gone in fact that I didn't hear her mad shuffle before work later in the morning, and I slept until nearly noon. When I woke I folded her blanket and placed it back in the closet, where she kept a vacuum cleaner, two heavy coats and a mountain of boxes filled with books. I pulled out a Nietzsche reader and carried it to the patio for a smoke before going home, identifying the location of the ceramic frog seemingly hidden the night before, alone and dusty in the corner by the door. But the day was too illuminated for thoughts of Zarathustra, so I finished my cigarette and went in for my sandals after placing the volume back in its box, telling myself that if I were a philosopher, ever, someone would have to call me one. I couldn't weather the storm of what Dawn had conquered and still, happily, produce any works of my own gravity. I put the key under the frog and took a deep breath to squeeze between the cracked patio door and the hanging tree limbs that dangled over the entrance from the back, and I paced around the south corner of the building and found my car, one of only few still in the parking lot at the hour, climbed in after stretching by the door as if I'd been on the road for multiple infinities, and drove home.

Knox was in a dash around the house as I stepped inside.

"Hey, babe," I said. I kicked out of my sandals and walked to one of my cabinets and changed shirts before lying down on the bed.

"Rattigan, *shit* I'm running so far behind."

"You guys have a good night?"

"Hmm?" She said while disagreeing with various shirts she'd pulled from the floor, draping them over the chest on her side of the bed and reaching behind the headboard for others. "Yeah. Actually, hell yeah, Rattigan, I wish you would have been here."

I rolled to my side to watch her entangled in the flurry.

"Stay up late?"

"Too late, man," she said, furrowing her brow before shrugging and dumping clothes into the same huge carry bag she'd brought to Tennessee. "Brody talked me down from thinking too far ahead about what I've got to do this weekend at the hotel. We drank way too much wine and wrote *way* too many ridiculous poems."

"Sounds necessary, man."

She stopped to consider, and then nodded while returning to her rush.

"It was. Definitely. I even think I can keep a couple. I dunno." She shook her head. "I really don't know. Too close to them right now."

"You heading downtown now?"

"Yeah," she sighed. "My aunt got an early check-in for me and I'll feel like such a dick if I'm late."

"Why?" I laughed. "It's your time, Knox."

"I've got coffee on," she called from the kitchen. She came back into the main area with a pair of dress slacks that had been hanging over the pantry door for two days. "Are these excessively wrinkled to you?"

"They should have an iron there."

She snapped her fingers and pointed at me and then partially folded the pants before jamming them on top of the rest of her things and squeezing the guts of the bag between her legs on the floor with her ankles and zipping tight its swell.

"Where's Brody?" I asked her as she entered the bathroom and shut the door.

"I have no idea," she yelled. "He said something about an agenda. No way to really guess what that means. At least not with accuracy. I look like a fucking monster."

I grinned and stretched across the entire bed to study the ceiling. A pair of glow-in-the-dark star stickers still clung to it, a purchase of Knox's she'd made a month earlier when, as she admitted, in an "odd moment of longing for my childhood." Unlike LaCoste, I had the night ahead to work at the restaurant and then a double on Saturday before having Sunday fully off to return to my nearly forgotten child-novel and begin its first edit. I was a good, solid kind of tired, from which an even better light shone on the other end of the next two days, composed of soundlessness and sleep.

Knox exited the bathroom.

"Do I?"

"Do you what?"

"You're such an asshole, Rattigan."

"I'm a confused asshole."

"Oh don't be such a fucking *man*. Do I look like shit?"

"Knox, you look fine." I laughed. "I think it's in your head. Tardiness doesn't make someone unkempt."

She took a deep breath and let out, rolled her eyes and then climbed on to the bed after pushing me over.

"I'm sorry, babe." Knox put her head on my stomach and looked up at me. She took another deep breath and blinked a few times. "I just suddenly don't want to do this, you know? Go burrow in and pull my hair and go nuts for the next few days."

"I was having a similar conversation with myself last night."

"Oh, I am such a *dick*."

"In what way?"

"How was *your* night?" She threw an arm over my belt buckle.

I grinned.

"You're not a dick, babe. But it was good. Really, really good. Stayed up late, too. Watching strays. Talking constant birth."

"You wanna come have breakfast with me Monday morning before my defense? My aunt's buying."

She raised her eyebrows up and down coercively.

"Absolutely."

"But don't you have to work? You don't have to come down. I mean, I honestly think you should and just go in late, but..."

"*Knox*," I said. "I don't go in until ten. I'll come wake you up at eight. I need to investigate your weekend digs anyway."

She sat up and smiled and nodded.

"That's perfect news."

"It's a date," I said.

She shoved off the bed and circled around her travel things a last time.

"You need a hand?" I asked.

"I've got it," she said, walking toward the door, hands full. She turned to look at me. "Hey, thanks Rattigan."

"For what?"

She sighed.

"For not letting me feel insane."

I smiled. "You'll be great. You *have* to know that."

"And tell Brody, if you see him...tell him the same."

She stood in place a moment before smiling and getting a better handle on her bag.

"And tell him he's expected at the defense."

"I will."

"If he bails on me..." She said, backing out into the open air. "...no amount of *sweet baby-ing* will save his beautiful ass."

"Hey, what's colostrum?" I asked as she began closing the door.

Her body had disappeared but the door held cracked a moment, before she moaned *not now Rattigan*, and then it shut.

I spent the next pair of hours before work lying in bed and listening to public radio. A comedy show host from television was on, talking about his on-screen persona and how who people project themselves to be these days has become more important than who they really are, and then sometimes, in a trap, they become it to survive the "scary work," he said, of proving to the world the difference, otherwise known as the truth.

"I get that," I said, and got undressed for a shower.

The rest of the weekend was similar, though my own work persona, unlike that of my old job at the paper, was fortunately the same as when I was not there. It had first been Brody's mantra regarding work, to choose something that doesn't change a person, a mantra among others I wouldn't be able to hear at all for the following days, as he was incommunicado and had likely taken off on the road somewhere as he'd said, to clear what needed clearing, or work to keep what needed to remain. But he wasn't there to stare down with me at my award check that arrived on Saturday in a handwritten envelope from Nashville. So both guesthouse nights were quiet and no doubt filled with less mania than a hotel room across the city, where Knox was letting her hair down, and letting it fly.

I slept long on Sunday after a late night at the Stone. Blain had accepted the KM position, which became impetus enough for us all to stay and drink after shrugging off an unusually elated Kennedy's invitation to caravan to hear her latest future ex's band cover songs in a small joint down Old Shell. Once up at just before one in the afternoon, I dug out the last bag from a box of earl gray sitting out on the stove and put a few hours' worth of eyes on the dissected guts of my manuscript. The characters were drawn from a deep affection, the environment surrounding their casual lives fairly seductive in the simplicity of the way I realized I'd made wealth seem so achievable, that in itself a projection from the opposite pole of our guesthouse and a roof that sometimes seemed to sag heavily under the weight of bills we fought less than was necessary to pay on time. In the quiet of home I endured the joyful palpitations in my chest involving what I'd at last completed, and as the sun went down I ate Knox's leftover pasta she'd forgotten days earlier and then took an unexpected nap to the sound of a Tchaikovsky scholar on public radio, ever on, a man speaking in a calming rasp about something I only remember sounded, because of his voice, beautiful.

For the second time on Sunday I woke, around nine in the evening, and after testing the weather outside, retrieved an old textbook of mine from inside and carried it with a glass of wine out on to the front steps to sit beneath the generous glow of the gas lamps beside the tops of the door and read in the still-cool air. The book was a compendium of famous writings, old and new, a book I'd devoured when in school, writing poem scratches in its margins and heavily underscoring the particulars of pieces with which I couldn't allow myself to disconnect. I found a Dylan Thomas piece I'd read with Knox once, a year prior, in a bookstore east down Airport Boulevard. We hadn't seen each other much around that time I was sputtering along through life in Midtown, and we celebrated the reunion by taking turns reading the poem back and forth as fast and loudly as we could muscle the words from our throats as we sat in a hidden corridor past the coffee station just beyond a stretch of magazine racks. It hadn't taken long for an employee to find us and tell us to leave. We retreated in a hazy sense of triumph, knowing no nobler a cause for ejection.

The glass became the bottle as I sat on the middle step and occasionally took pause to look up into the tract of silenced sky, or watch small flying insects tear upward from the surrounding bushes and zip across the specific path of lamplight which cut across the walkway toward the pool. As I neared the end of a long Corso poem, I heard the heavy iron gate groan open near the drive, and I looked up to make out in the dark what was Brody's body slowly moving into the light.

"Hello, sir," I said, facing the open book down on the step beside me and giving him a nod to join me. But as he got closer I could tell something wasn't altogether right. I stood and dusted the backside of my shorts with my palms. "What's up?"

He wore a plain white t-shirt with paint flecks across the chest, and a long solid black tie sloppily hung around his neck. Usual scarred jeans, also paint-filthy. Same bandana set on its standard roost at his hairline.

"I, my dear friend..." He mumbled, while pointing both index fingers at me. But he didn't finish the thought, stumbling instead to his right and collapsing sideways in the bushes.

"Brody?"

I stepped over my glass on the stoop and grabbed his one hand that stuck out of the thin branches. His other hand pressed flat against the vine-covered front wall, his body at several disagreeing angles at once. After righting him he draped a heavy arm over my shoulder and stood still a moment before turning his face toward mine, where I could feel his breath on my forehead as I slumped to prop him up.

"I do believe that was a plant," he whispered.

"Let's sit, babe."

He seemed to momentarily sober as I left him to stand on his own in order to clear the steps of my things, as if he'd snapped into recognition suddenly once I'd let go that he couldn't do it independently. But he fell heavily on to the stoop and swayed backward toward the front door, dug through his pocket and pulled out a cigarette pack and lit a smoke from it, and then he leaned forward to let his head drop to just above his knees. I'd never seen him so gone, and we sat in silence for several minutes before I leaned my own head down to the same level as his and I patted him lightly on the back.

"You good, Brody?"

He took a deep breath and let it out toward the ground before nodding slowly, and then he unfolded his torso into an upright position.

"Tonight, Pete..." Brody hadn't called me by my first name in so long I'd thought he'd forgotten it. He sighed. "Tonight I'm unsure, babe."

"Where've you been, man?" I asked him. As he breathed out, laboriously, a sudden old man, the smoke from inside his body met the dark air before us, orbited, became figures one sees in clouds--a floret, an animal, a wrench.

"I've, um...I've been," he started, and then paused, his chin drifted downward as his eyes slightly shut, and then he rebounded, head up, alert again. "Heidi's."

"I thought you were taking a drive."

I lit a smoke and lifted my wine glass, moving it over my legs to my side of the steps. The couple who owned the main house had a light on in their bedroom directly across the pool. Their thick, likely expensive shades drawn nearly taut, horizontally cracked, I could make out portions of bodies crossing the floor.

"That was a half-plan, babe. But she went to some music festival in New Orleans for the weekend. Gave me her keys."

"So what did you..."

"Think of it," he said without continuing. We sat a moment in silence.

"Of what, Brody?" I finally asked.

"All those bodies, crammed into one another. Moving the same. In sadness. Or joy." He paused again. It was a fast night of pauses. "But I've been painting." He nodded.

"I see that, man. I wish I could..."

"She's a good girl," he interrupted. I tilted my head, a physical manifestation of my confusion at the cadence surrounding our talk, but had he been fully there, or maybe less there, I couldn't tell, he would have picked up on it and turned in his seat as usual and corrected what I was thinking before I could say. "A good girl."

"Yeah?"

He exhaled and put out his cigarette between his sneakers on the brick. But he still wasn't talking. After more sitting, more watching the sliced bodies through the French doors leading into the main bedroom of the house, I was losing ideas.

"How did you get here?"

"Mason, man. Lovely guy." He nodded slowly.

"You were at work? I thought you were off."

I put the flat of my left palm on his upper back and squeezed inward a few times. His body seemed to fold beneath the push of touch, his strength depleted or regained by it. Again I couldn't tell.

"I filled in, babe. You have another cigarette?" He asked as he fished another out of his own pack and lit it.

"Is your car still there?"

He'd returned to the position of hanging his head down to his knees, and offered a thumb up over his head.

"No worries," I said. "I'll take you to it in the morning. It'll be early because I'm going to see Knox downtown. Oh *shit*. You should come down with me tomorrow."

"Her defense. That's right," he mumbled. I put my hand once more on his back and gently tugged at his shirt.

"Come on, babe. Look up."

He waited a moment before slowly sitting up again. With a cigarette in his right hand, he wiped at his eyes with both palms and shook his head to wake himself.

And then he said, quietly, "I'm sorry, Rattigan."

Skipping it, I continued.

"We can have a good breakfast, man. Prowl around downtown a little while. Knox can use both of us before she..."

"I'm off tomorrow," he interrupted. "But I can't. I just...I can't. I've got this..." He trailed off, and then returned from elsewhere. "I'll be at her defense, for sure. Wouldn't miss it."

He breathed heavily again, his body sagging. And as awake as I'd become, I was being put to sleep by my indelicate efforts of delicacy. But instead of moving past what confused me, I sat, more confused. He reached a hand over and patted the back of my neck, as if he knew. Then, I recognized he'd been buying time.

"So I tried to paint," he began. "All weekend. Something different to do, babe." He lit another cigarette and sat up, forward, turned in his seat and faced me. "I wrestled with structure, with color. I don't know. I *can't* know. Not now."

"About what, Brody?"

"About anything," he said, and lurched forward in brief, unexpected tears. Unexpected by us both. "About *anything*."

"Brody…" I said, extending my arm around him again, but he recoiled and leaned away before rotating back to look at me. No real flood, but his face had poorly managed the immediate reaction to the flush, and his lips were unsteady as his eyes surveyed whatever it was he was looking for in the black air.

"We do what it is we're doing, babe." He wrapped his palm around my knee as he kept looking forward. "And we seek out reason for it." He shook his head. "And we try new things. But when we write, what are we *doing*, Rattigan?"

"Brody I don't…"

"Celebrating the empowerment of language itself? Its nuance? Or is it something else?"

"I'm still trying to figure that out, man."

"Exactly. *Exactly*. Is it that there isn't any majesty anymore, behind the labor of creating, but instead there just *should be*, and that by itself is supposed to be enough?"

"What made you want to paint?" I asked, facing him squarely and sinking my chin into my palm.

The question froze him. I felt like a comedian who can't understand why a joke didn't work, a politician who concedes to a constituency that he or she has lost. But Brody's answer froze me.

"It's because I can't handle all these words anymore."

And he started crying, fully. His body shook from what I knew *he* knew was not a weakness, but a surprise that what becomes part of the mind stays there until it is noticed. I put both my arms around him and pulled him toward me, during it. I kissed the side of his head and tasted paint.

"I've been enveloped by some sort of *what-if*, you know? Rattigan, I did everything I could and would with the book, everything possible. And it's changed so much for the better, and I…"

"Do you think you cheated yourself by changing it?"

"*No*," he said, shaking his head against my chest, and then he pulled back to look me in the eye, with sternness. "No, I went to Heidi's because I had to...*shit*, Rattigan, I just can't *tell* you."

"I don't care about what you can't tell me, Brody."

"That's it, babe. I *know*. But look at this. Look at it."

He fingered the tie hanging toward his knees.

"Is *this* me? After everything? Do I strap this on and say I'm *now* part of society?"

"Do you think it's about..."

"*Yes* I think. I think too fucking *much*. About everything. You know... no, you don't know. I..."

"Know what, babe?"

He shook his head.

"What?" I asked, raising my voice.

He studied me a moment, that same bright flash in his eyes, and I grew afraid he'd walk from it, would walk from what I wanted to hear, what I needed to hear. But he took a deep breath, reached to touch my knee again, and separated himself from me on our stoop. We were two distant bodies, spinning in galactic light.

"It's that I'm terrified suddenly, Rattigan. Fuck my novel. *Fuck* New York City. I'm terrified that I push people too hard...I mean you and Knox, damn I wish I could..."

He paused and then continued.

"I'm afraid I push people so hard to reach their fullest potential, even the potential that disagrees with what I see in them, their capabilities, their *beauty*, man. But I've been thinking this last month, since you and Knox got back from Nashville, and what you guys talked about on the road, that maybe I'm just pushing people to be more like me, I don't know, for some falsely guaranteed continuation of what's fading from the modern era. Like maybe our independent spiritual movement is losing its voice if we don't keep screaming, and I'm afraid to feel as though I'm doing it alone."

"That's not the full..."

"Like we won't face that we're in some kind of, maybe there's no real way to describe it, some fucked up Molotov of paranoia and anxiety. Like there's too much psychology, like the market of our hearts is saturated with bullshit."

"Maybe it's that..."

"Like it's *wrong* to believe in our hearts, man."

Brody was still crying, furious at his self-imposed clarity.

"But we weren't *engineered* for disbelief, Rattigan. We don't come from a space of doubt. And we're not adults. We're not. We're not that construct, babe. At best we're full-time children, we're full-time *Other*. You ever have some old man come in to the Stone and tell you to just be who you are, do just what you're doing in the now, that the 'real world' is a basic entity of the post-graduate imagination?"

"Sometimes."

"Babe, we've got this immense play yard of very real possibility, that those out *there* who subscribe to the 'real world' call fantasy, or idealism. But it's only because to them it seems like too much work to give themselves over to the unpredictable..."

"Like it's *cute* to be all right sometimes with not knowing."

"So they shove themselves into structured patterns that really prove to be even more convoluted whorls of un-knowing and they lose their fucking minds, I don't know, in commerce and acquisition, and then they get self-cornered by want and bullshit *want* and suddenly they're telling a stranger for a hundred bucks an hour how miserable they are and how they don't love their partners and then they go out to dinner and mistreat someone like you or me because we were too awake too subscribe to their misery, too. And I really do think..."

"That makes complete sense."

"And I really do think, babe, out of all of this, that any of us, in *this*, are not in some impractical utopia. And I don't think the *other* Other is wholly wrong, but this?" He asked, fingering his tie again. "If this is supposed to *define* me, Rattigan. Not their world, but just mine is tested. And damn..." He said, sighing, spent, beautiful, true. "I can't just stop because it's difficult." He shook his head again. I lit us a pair of smokes and passed him one.

A few minutes elapsed, and we watched the motions between the blinds across the pool disappear behind a lamp turned off, a television powered down.

"You know we don't talk about love, Rattigan. Not here."

I hadn't thought of it, in real truth. I hadn't thought about love because when I was at work, I didn't think, *I am at work*. I hadn't thought, when I was at the grocery store, *I am at the store*. We just are where we are. We're in what we're in.

"I think of you, babe. I think of Knox..." He said, shaking his head, tears still in his eyes. "And I don't think about love, Rattigan."

What do you think of, I wanted to ask, but I didn't want to ask enough to ask.

"Damn," he said, still shaking his head. He stood and stretched his arms widely, palms facing the main house, fingertip to fingertip. "I think about..."

He turned to look down at me, still sitting on the stairs, straddling the line of my own stirred threshold inside.

"I think about vindication."

"How so?" I asked as I stood.

Brody took a deep breath. He took his time with it, his face moist, his eyes back to sober and eternally, forgivably blear.

"That what we're doing, being *us*. That it matters."

"It does, Brody."

"That it has strength."

"Let's go in, man. It's late," I said. "Knox needs us tomorrow."

He inserted his hands into his pockets. I still tasted paint.

"I think...I think, nah. I need to go for a walk," he said.

"Where?" I asked.

"Around, babe. I need to..."

He stepped away as if to go ahead and leave.

"What are you doing?"

He faced me, shoulders up in the high air. He shrugged and displayed his palms upward, and then fell back into the posture of a fatigued warrior. But after a short moment of it, he began lightly pounding his fists against one another in front of his stomach, pulling the balled hands apart and then repeatedly bringing them together.

"I've got this tug-of-war inside me, Rattigan," he said, his face contemplative behind the sad draw of his mouth. "I can't see yet how to cut the rope."

He shook his head, again, ever in the night of pauses, of the shaking. As I walked to him, he spread his arms forward, and he took me into a long hug. After we broke, before he let me go, he kissed my temple.

"If I ever talk about love, babe," he said, tilting my face toward him in the broken light. And then he glanced at the guesthouse to my left before looking back at me. "In whatever capacity you can know, Pete, know I'm talking about here."

I pushed him back playfully and smiled.

"I know, Brody. I know that. Go be safe. Be well."

"Don't wait for me," he called behind him as he made it to the gate. "Just wake me when you get up. We'll rescue Knox in the morning."

I watched him shuffle off.

"Brody?" I said. I wanted to tell him, against his own knowing, that I loved him. That he was owed something as simple as that, and that was what I knew at that moment, what he deserved.

"Yeah, babe."

"You good?" I asked.

His sigh found me across the courtyard.

"I'm good," he said, his tear-sparkle most of what I could see in the sidereal punch of night. "I think I'm good."

———

I woke to Knox's alarm the next morning at quarter to seven, having slept a relatively sound sleep after processing in silence the reality Brody had been facing alone, the concern that had almost ruined me leading up to the time when he and I first met in that restaurant. I didn't come up with anything workable, and found sleep because before it came I had found a contentment with not knowing, just yet, that in time the answers reveal themselves, that they stay in the mind, like conflict, and turn and moan and stretch until ready to be shown. It was this thought from the night before with Brody that had more than casually taken root inside me, and even though I had wanted to wait for him to make it home, I needed to commit to that feeling that time, though fast and sometimes impaling, can sometimes be even more generous when left alone. And as I shuffled from the bed, I noticed Brody hadn't come home at all, so I had a quick shower and threw on a pair of jeans with the least amount of holes in them, a gray t-shirt featuring the Munch painting, "The Scream," and I put on a pair of black sandals. Into a small black shoulder bag I folded a work shirt and sneakers and socks, as I was planning on ignoring my own advice about time while downtown, squeezing out every minute I could in order to give Knox the blue light, the insight, the attention, anything she needed that I could give before she at last could put the thesis and that program, that "guiltless criminal" as Dawn referred to our alma mater, behind her.

Time existed to make a quick stop at the closest coffee shop across from the Jesuit college, a store that along with wraps and bagels also sold cards and good teas in distractingly beautiful tin cans, so I drove to it first, bought Knox a congratulatory card and some kind of blueberry tea, and I cut down the service road beside I-65 and rode it south until I could connect by the huge Baptist church on the corner of Dauphin and the interstate, jump the ramp and roar south before connecting to I-10 and shoot east. The sun had been up at least an hour, but still hung low enough in the clear sky to be hidden during sporadic and blurry microseconds by billboards that stood off the road between my car and the shipyard by the bay. I took the Water Street exit and turned at the first light left on to Government, and I noticed the huge science theatre had new banners up for the coming summer season, something on mummies for the adults, cartoon fish for kids, or vice versa. I took a right on to Royal and found the hotel after looping the block once. A young valet fellow seemed reluctant to approach me, so as I let the car idle at the curb I got out and asked if I was in the wrong place.

"You need to park?" He asked. His nametag read Sam.

"Yeah, man. I'm visiting a friend for a couple hours."

"It's still ten dollars."

"Oh, that's fine. Just letting you..."

It was too early in the morning for Sam to take on a story. I felt I was in some marketplace haggling over the price of a blanket or vegetables, even though I hadn't really said anything. I started laughing, which seemed to raise the tension on the street, so I handed him fifteen dollars and told him to keep the change, said thanks and began to walk off.

"*Sir*," he called out as I stepped up on to the sidewalk.

"Yes sir?" I asked after turning to face him, my gift bag for Knox swinging beside my knees. He stared at me a brief moment with real consternation, but I couldn't stop smiling because I felt so completely out of my element. He waved me to him. I wondered if I'd broken a law.

"You can't expect to get your car back without this," he said, handing me a parking voucher with a few numbers on it.

"Right," I said, still grinning. "That's my bad, man."

"Ok."

Sam climbed into my car after what I guessed was a nod in thanks, as the nod coincided with his flash of the bills I'd handed him. He honked the horn to clear the entrance of other valets standing out in the middle of the crossway, and my car disappeared into the guts of the Hastings Hotel. I found the heavy glass doors off to my right, noticing a posh-looking coffee joint down the sidewalk with live music advertisements in the window, and realized how little I had learned about the city's development once I was no longer required to study it, and I nodded at a poster displaying the face of one of our regulars at the Stone before entering through the front.

I caught a closing, empty elevator nearest the door and rode it up to the fourth floor, stepped out and walked the long corridors but I couldn't find Room 421, so I descended in another elevator and asked an employee near the door how to reach it. Turns out I had to walk through the entire lobby to the back elevators, as the large hotel was designed around some kind of mind-bending grid that forced guests to interact with staff. The lobby itself was beautiful and decorated with antique-looking yet modern furniture, and the high ceiling strained my neck when I stopped in the center of the huge room to look up at it. A few men in business suits were sitting cross-legged and slumped to the sides of their big chairs, laptops across their upper legs, stern-faced. As I passed them, each one broke their gaze to study me head to toe as I made it to the back elevators beyond the front desk that was buried past the lobby. I assessed their looks once inside the carrier, thinking, sure, that I didn't fit in there, relieved I didn't live that particular kind of life, but I was also curious if they saw in me something they had disallowed themselves, the ability to traverse a foreign territory as completely who they were, stripped down into their basic comforts and not some multi-layered sartorial expression of power, or the pursuit of it. Maybe, too, I kept thinking as I stopped at the fourth floor and walked out, bag still in hand, maybe these were men in it for something other than power, maybe they had families they were doing it for, so that those they loved could broadcast themselves in *their* basic comforts, and the men, the husbands or fathers or lovers were willing to sacrifice a huge element of their own want to give with love to those who'd considered that freedom their need. I smiled about it as I found 421 and saw that the latch had been swung out to keep the door cracked for my arrival. I knocked softly a couple of times and pushed inside.

"Hey, you," I said to Knox. She was sitting at the desk with a tray of food covering its entire top. Her hair was still wet, and she wore a cloud-sized white hotel robe. Her face was of a peaceful exhaustion, and I could tell she had prepared, along with the defense notes, a significant amount of pride in herself, much-deserved after so much doubt.

"Hey yourself," Knox responded. She stretched her arms upward and smiled. I walked to her and set down the bag on the thin amount of empty space on the desk by the wall past the tray, and I gave her a hug.

"Nice room, man." I surveyed the dark stripes of the wallpaper, the mahogany furniture, the thick, comfortable bed linens.

"Isn't it crazy? I have slept so fucking well, man. Try the bed, it's insane," she said, spooning in a bite of something from a bowl.

I lay on the bed a moment and stared at the ceiling.

"This place really needs some glow-in-the-dark stickers," I said, lifting my head to look at her. She grinned.

"It really does. *Oh.*"

"What's up?" I asked and sat up.

"Come here, Rattigan. You've gotta try this."

I followed her to the closet as she fished out another robe and handed it to me, which, after accepting, she helped me slide into it. She returned to the breakfast as I tied the robe shut.

"And this food is so good. You don't know. Come here. I ordered tons."

I picked at some of the fruit she'd had brought up, and took a few bites of the oatmeal and waffles, the latter being covered in fresh blueberries and a thin, delicious sauce of some sort.

"Speaking of..." I said, handing her the bag.

Knox studied me a quick minute, giving me a what-did-you-do look before retreating to a bigger smile than when I'd entered, and then she pulled the two items from the bag.

"Cool tea, man. And of *course* it's blue. I've never had something like this."

"Me either."

"We should try it tonight to celebrate."

"Definitely."

She reached across the arm of her chair, and I sat forward from the bed's edge to give her a hug.

"This is great, Rattigan. Thanks so much for coming down."

"I'm proud of you, Knox. Really am. The card says so."

She slapped my arm before I sat back down.

"That ruins me reading it, prick." She winked at me and opened it and read aloud what I'd written. *"I'm proud of you, Knox."* She rolled her eyes at me and continued. *"Whatever comes next, we'll be there together. All love."*

"Thanks again, man," she said.

"So, judging by the scattered papers everywhere, the weekend was a hit?"

"Hmm?" She scanned the room and laughed. "Yeah, I got my talking points put together, not that I know what those bastards will ask. And last night I walked down to the wine store way, way down the other end of Dauphin, and brought those two bottles up." She pointed at one and a half empty bottles of red sitting in a small pile of their shredded wrapping on the nightstand.

"Nice."

"Yeah, I needed this time. Aunt Viv's my new hero."

"No doubt. What made her think this up?"

"She was supposed to be in town for my defense since my parents can't make it, but then she got called away for work, so I guess she felt bad. I dunno. I think she got her government rate, so maybe she wasn't put too far out. This place is intense."

"It really is." I laughed. "You should have seen me getting dressed down by these business cats downstairs. I'm sure I looked like a bum to them, face all puffy from just waking up, sandals, this..."

"Shirt, yeah man, I dig it."

She popped a strawberry in her mouth and got up to join me on the bed. We lay back and stretched out.

"What time do you go in to work?"

"I need to be there at ten. I told Sonya I might run behind. It's not a worry at all, babe."

"Wait." She sat up. "How are you going to make my defense at one if you have to work?"

"They said I can be early out and just come back after if they need me."

"Nice," Knox said and rolled to her side to look at me.

"You look so relaxed, man. I'm glad this happened."

"I think my brain's just gone to shit from over-thinking this thing. Plus the wine."

"I bet."

"What did you get into last night?"

Her question brought back the night before with Brody. I guess I'd set it up in my own head to not mention it in the morning of such a big day for her, because Knox had a tendency to worry about others to the point of near-mania, and in that it was just before her culminating afternoon, of those years spent for this exact moment, I decided to stab again at the delicacy I thought I'd failed at the night before.

"Brody was...he came home a little gone."

"Did he go out of town?"

"Nah, he'd stayed around. Just had a lot of stuff on his mind. We talked a good while. Painting and other things."

"What can't that kid do?" She lifted her eyes and grinned.

"Yeah. I dunno. I think he was trying to get at something deeper than the canvas, you know? Like in writing, too? What exists beyond the page, stuff like that. It was...he's good."

Her head tilted.

"Everything ok?" She asked.

I smiled and rested my cheek on my arm that stretched out toward the pillows that were in mad piles against the headboard.

"Yeah." I sighed. "Just stuff we all...stuff we all have running through our minds at one point or another. But he's coming to the defense. I invited him down this morning, but he's...he wasn't there when I woke up, so he's busy. Said he wouldn't miss this afternoon, though."

"Fantastic," she said, climbing off the bed and entering the bathroom to begin the process of looking temporarily professorial once thrown to the wolves. "I'll definitely be feeding off your energy, man."

"Why are you getting ready so soon?" I asked, still in bed, flipping through a few pages of her notes for the talk she'd give in a few hours.

"You have no idea, Rattigan, I..." I heard a series of exasperated exhalations. She stepped into the short hallway in front of the mirror with a brush entangled in her hair. "I still have to spend at least a whole hour at the graduate school before crossing campus. And that halfwit woman in charge of my formatting sent word that somehow, at the last minute, after it was approved to be bound, they found some stupid margin problem on the fucking abstract page. The *abstract* page, man. One page out of almost 90, and I have to..." She took another deep breath, let it out, shook her head and disappeared again into the bathroom. "It'll just be another fond memory of that place I won't have in my discourse when asked about the program."

"You think maybe that's why they had your exit interview so early?" I called out as I stood and disrobed. It was getting close to departure time, and I had no way of predicting if Sam had given up on life and driven my car through a concrete wall and down to the hotel gardens below.

"You know, I didn't think of it that way," she said, back in the hallway. "Bastards, man, I'm telling you."

I lifted my keys from beside the coffee maker, a sad and tiny machine that had been inarguably abused over the weekend, as the outside of it was stained with dried coffee, and grounds were scattered across the tan-colored tray on which it sat. I stood at the door of the bathroom, familiar with her morning process, but nonetheless still amused.

"Stop smiling at me, Rattigan. I'm ready to slug someone."

"That's no way for a lady to talk on her special day, is it?" I grinned.

She tossed me a serious look and then cracked a smile while facing the mirror and fist-fighting her long hair, her dryer roaring on high.

"I am in no way a fucking lady today. Ladies don't plan murders. Are you leaving already?"

I laughed, and she joined in, turning off the dryer and setting the brush on the counter, slumped forward with disbelief in her eyes and a recognition of her own humor across her lips.

"It's cliché, but just think, *one more day left*. I know it's not good to wish your life away, but..."

"No," she shook her head. "*One more day* is fitting. You're the best, man. I owe you huge for coming down."

"No way, Knox. I've been looking forward to it. Thanks for the eats."

"Did you get enough?"

"Yeah, it was all really good. I think you'll have withdrawals from this place soon," I said as I patted the doorframe and motioned toward the door.

"Be well, babe. I'll see you at one, right?"

"Definitely. I'm amped about it. Just remember to go slowly. You're an authority on this stuff by now. Remember that, too. And I'll bring good light."

"Ok, I'll try. Thanks for the tea. Have fun at work."

"I'll try," I said while backing out of the door. I flipped the latch back so the door would close behind me. "See you in a few."

I shut the heavy brown door and took the same elevator from earlier down to the back of the lobby, crossed through the space that had emptied itself of the business men, my sandals loudly popping in the quiet echo of the vast space. I couldn't find Sam at the valet counter, but a friendly heavyset man named Charles doubled his efforts to find my car by radioing someone upstairs on the lot, and as it zoomed down the ramp minutes later, I passed him five bucks for his kindness and attention and then hopped behind the wheel to rejoin the traffic on Royal. I was still in good time, having left time alone upstairs in the dark room of Knox's mania, and so I drove through the city instead of taking the interstate back to West Mobile, and I pulled up to park behind my boss's truck at the Stone with nearly ten minutes to spare. Sonya's antique Volvo was there, which was unusual because she had a fairly strict schedule that, in the beginning of the week, included Monday and Tuesday nights. And in front of her car beside our dumpster was a city patrol car. Behind that, Brody's car still napped in the sun. Shaking my head, I thought someone hadn't locked up the night before, so we might have had a break-in. As I stepped out of the car and changed shirts and put on my sneakers, I remembered Brody telling me that had happened before, about a month before I was hired. My suspicions heightened further when I tried the back door handle to find it was locked, so I knocked loudly a few times before Greg, our assistant kitchen manager, lightly pushed open the door and nodded me in.

The television the prep crew usually had blaring in back, during the hours before we opened, was off and not even turned in to face the kitchen, and no machines were running. As I walked through the kitchen toward the front I studied the inside quiet, ready to see once up front some massive destruction to the place that could have accompanied a robbery. Greg returned to standing in his usual spot below where the television hung and he looked at me with an emptiness in his face that, to me, bordered on confusion, and then he lit a cigarette. As he did, I noticed the smell of cigarettes heavy in the restaurant, something we only allowed at the end of business hours.

"What's up with…" I started to ask Greg across the kitchen, but he shook his head and pointed toward the front of the store. I walked around to the space between the bar counter and the well the servers used to make drinks, but nothing was out of the ordinary with the tables, and no glass was broken anywhere.

I saw Sonya with her face in her elbow, a lit cigarette between her fingers above her head. I heard male voices from the office, and I lightly scratched fingertips over Sonya's back as I passed her behind the bar to look around the corner into Brad's office, which didn't have a door. It was a converted old walk-in cooler that had been made into a desk and file cabinet area. Brad was seated on his swivel chair, and a cop stood over him, but leaned against the doorframe and was nodding as Brad fumbled with some papers and kept shrugging.

"Did someone serve a minor last night?" I asked Sonya as I walked to the front of the bar and moved a few stools out of my way to lean in toward her. She shook her head, still in her elbow, and then lifted it to take a pull off her smoke. A long funnel of ashes landed on the counter beside her arm. Her face was splotched, nearly all red, and her eyes were exhausted. She kept shaking her head.

"Where is everybody?" I asked.

She shrugged, and I realized everyone there had the same look in their face, the same shrug. We were over, somehow. Our illustrious bubble had been burst.

"What can I get started on? Are you…what's wrong, babe?" I asked.

She shook her head once more, as if to shake something away from her, and she put out her cigarette just to light another. She sniffed a couple of times and blinked her eyes, looked up at the ceiling, and then once her eyes settled on me, the only thing left in her, that I could see, was an indefinable sense of failure, as if she had done something wrong. As if everyone had done something terribly wrong.

"We're closed today," she said. She wiped her nose and shrugged at me again, but her eyes weren't on mine. They were located somewhere on me.

"What happened last night? Why is Brad...?" And then I lowered my voice. "Why are the *cops* here?"

She looked at me in real surprise for a moment and then began to sob. I wanted to reach over to her, but I didn't understand why I was reaching, or why I wanted to, why I *should* want to. She was crying, surely, but a person as strong-willed and aggressive as Sonya likely didn't want touch when shoved into a display of her own emotion. I was lost.

"Did...are you and Derek ok?" I asked, a question which I didn't think could explain the cops. Couldn't explain our being closed.

She wiped at her face again and then turned to pour red wine into a plastic take-out cup.

"You want something?" She half-laughed, before her mouth bent into a frown and her eyes teared up again. "Fuck it, right?"

"No, I'm good," I said. "I just don't understand what's..."

"Brody got hit by a car last night, Rattigan. On Westminster. He died some time this morning."

She began to cry again, shaking her head, amazed at having released the words to someone with perhaps the same, ironically whip-lashed gentleness as had happened to her. But I dropped what she'd said, a weight I wasn't prepared to catch. I heard the words, but what they meant to me, immediately, is that something horrible had happened to her and she still needed to be listened to. I stood still in front of her, dumbfounded by a relief that what was occurring in the building had been flushed, but the content of it, the *reality* of it, was not real. Not because of its offered handicap, suddenly, not yet, but because the information had come as quickly as I had wanted, right as I was growing pensive from the guesswork of not knowing. Suddenly, then, I *did* know, and I didn't comprehend fast enough what it was like to actually know anything. I recognized the clash of knowing and un-knowing weren't just ideas apart, they were immeasurable galaxies apart, before they could ever settle in the mind. And standing in front of

Sonya I knew, against my hastily redefined will, so many real things, about her, about myself, about *reality* and about what she had just said. She had said, without saying it, that nothing anyone ever knows can prepare them for the truth.

"The cops are here for his emergency contacts. They...they couldn't find anything on him when they..."

Her mouth crinkled again. She shook her head again. She looked over my shoulder toward the closed window blinds over the booths and she bit her bottom lip.

"I'm so fucking tired." She sighed into her hands.

I tapped my fingers on the top of the bar stool I'd previously draped an arm over. What she was continuing to say had its specifics, but carried less and less weight. I saw the street in my imagination. I saw his painted shirt, but I didn't see him yet. I could see only her, and that view of her wasn't telling me enough of anything.

"Rattigan..." She finally said, shaking. "I *so* fucking know you and he..."

"I'm not..." I started. I backed from the bar, looking for my keys suddenly, as if they were on the floor somewhere in a shadow and not on me. I looked at her, and it was my turn to shake my head. The first and only question that came was *what*, but it stopped itself on the way up my throat. I was out of place again, walking through the lobby of a four star hotel. Instantly the walls were judging me, for not being a wall, the tiles through the kitchen were capsizing and becoming new tiles. Greg had crossed the kitchen as Sonya and I talked and he leaned against a metal post marking the entryway back in, his cigarette done, a beer bottle at his lip.

"Is this how you..." I began to ask, studying them both. I backed into the edge of a booth table and only reacted to it slightly. I ran my fingers through my hair, attempting to pull my forehead back into not knowing. Again, the not knowing, and this conflict caused my body to surge, everything in it wanting out. Greg jogged toward me and put a steadying hand on my shoulder, but I caught my breath. Once I rebounded and stood, the look in my face, as Sonya would tell me later, asked, without asking, *why did you let this happen?*

"Hey, brother," Greg said softly.

I stepped from under his hand, looking at him briefly and then back at Sonya. Brad followed the policeman out into the dining area. He looked around the room, dazed, his eyes red and searching, and when he found me he elbowed past the cop and came just short of putting his arm on me.

"I don't....Hey, Rattigan, I don't know...shit, this is so bad. I know it's bad. And I know Brody's a good..."

"Shhh," I said. Brad had, from beginning to then, been a good man, a wild, lovely employer and friend, and I could see, even then, the strain in his neck, the wince in his eye, the how-do-I-do-this question in the face of someone who'd never before been thrust into the control of mass consolation.

"Sonya tell you we're gonna close? Today? Maybe tomorrow. Fuck... excuse me, officer." Brad turned his head toward the policeman, who shrugged with just his face. "Fuck business." He put his wrists on my shoulders. They weighed a car each. "We got this...I dunno, Pete. We got this family to take care of here first. You know?"

"I got it," I said, nodding. "I *got* it." I stepped out from beneath his arms also, feeling suddenly consigned to a conveyor belt of helping hands, of an unwanted presence on an assembly line of touch, and I looked over at the policeman, feeling uncomfortable for him, doing his job, one involving the occasional glimpse into something being prematurely torn apart. "I'm sorry guys," I said, patting myself down with evident nerves and confusion, as if I carried resolution with me, at all times, and it would slip from a pocket on to the floor and any of what was happening would make sense, if not be instantaneously reconciled. "I'm gonna..." I pointed toward the back of the kitchen. "...maybe go. Maybe. I don't know." And then I smiled, because I thought of him, not Brody at the moment, just a generic yet precise *him*, walking through the airport on the way to New York City, sharing what power he could. "Yeah, I'll go," I said, and kept pointing east toward the back. Sonya covered her face again.

"Hey," Brad called to my back as I shuffled through the kitchen. "If you need any...hey, we're gonna be around if you..."

I lifted a hand over my shoulder to signal a goodbye as a knock hit the door in the back. It was Dawn, with a lit cigarette in her mouth.

"I am so fucking late, man."

I pushed past her.

"But I'm filling in today, so screw it. They *owe* me, Rattigan." She took a last pull and tossed the butt in the outside mop sink. "What are you doing? Why's there a cop car here?"

I traded places with her as she stepped into the door and I moved out. An anger then found me, an anger that perhaps could have waited, no, it *should* have waited if not completely ceased to exist. People were still showing up, and the blind eye of it enacted a temporary, foreign rage, represented by an unrecognizable tongue.

"Fucking call everyone!" I yelled past her into the open air of the store. She jumped at the volume and growl of my voice. "Get fucking wise and think! You fucking *assholes*!"

I didn't take the time to observe Dawn's face, I just left. I fumbled confusedly through my right pocket as if my keys weren't there, as if somehow I'd changed my own symmetrical idiosyncrasies on a dime and had blindly put them in my back pocket, or sock. I got in my car and started it and watched a few college students shuffle past from the neighborhood behind the Stone, backpacks heavy on them as they slouched forward in their walk to campus. The sun was less beautiful, but no less bright. My radio was on and I grimaced at the sound of it and turned it off. I'd forgotten the use of the wheel, the shifter, the groan of the seat or the engine's purr. And then, as I pulled away from the back of the store and U-turned around the shopping center's grassy median behind our building, I caught traffic on Old Shell and drove against the sun, then much higher than earlier downtown. And then reality came, my immediate reality. Not anyone else's. Not him.

I remembered Knox.

Her clock read ten-thirty as I glanced at it while entering the house. She had been there, as her bags and a few bits of clothing littered the bed, a sign of frustration and chaos before racing to the university, and the sound of her invisibility was deafening. I was in need of an entirely different world, suddenly, consisting of her and not her, sleep and unrest, food and the cusp of starvation, but what I didn't want, this bullshit *want*, was to stand at the foot of her bed and stare into the deflating noise of her absence until silence did or did not come. Not for those hours until I could get to her, which in my head was the paramount duty, the only, to get my body in the space of her body and feel sustained. There was no way for her to know, then, what I would end up wanting from her. But what she *needed*, for an hour and a half of the afternoon, was a Rattigan who was there, in her space, not for himself but for her. Convincingly.

To inject a false sense of weakness into the power of the struggle, that tug-of-war of my own, I began to realign the house into some state of a normalcy I couldn't define, but was nonetheless pushing toward. The act was more important than the result, and the result would become unimportant quickly and be replaced with another act more crucial than its pending, disappointing result. I talked to myself, testing aloud what Knox would buy from my face if I tried to sell her anything but my confidence. I folded her shirts, emptied everything from her bags and set them in a row on her side of the bed, after making the bed, a first, and then I took to the albums in disarray inside the old basket by the phone, still asking myself questions only about the thesis defense, just about Knox, waving my hands at myself, and I cleared the floor of varied debris that had come to call the cold flat wood their home. Hangers reclaimed their space on the racks, the bathroom surfaces were wiped clean. I took Knox's things off the bed, re-made it and then put them back. I ignored the phone's ring, which came twice, one message from Brad, his voice was broken and apologetic, inviting me up to the store for an employee dinner and drinks, to "get everyone together on this." A second message brought with it a sharp, coherent devastation in Dawn's voice. Something apparently terrible had happened to her. I stood over the machine to listen, but the subject of her sadness was foreign and couldn't have had anything to do with me, so I deleted the message and returned to what I was ultimately doing over and over again, as the bed area and bathroom had been realigned and straightened and thrown back into the fray and then tidied again. Part of me allowed the theory of Brad's difficult position, but most of me wouldn't commit to the rest of the *why*, nor any part of Dawn's garbled speech. But I could only do what I was doing for a short while longer, because it was almost time to shower and head to campus, and although the kitchen was a semi-landfill, I had put it out of my mind entirely because, regardless of the newly discovered diligence, to get to the kitchen, I would have to pass a couch that belonged to someone who no longer lived there.

———

Without interest in defying the aggression of the campus police, I waited patiently for my day pass and pushed it on to my dash outside their small building and turned south on to University Boulevard to make a left into the entrance nearest the library and, due to finals week, I easily found a spot a short walk from Humanities in the barren lot. When I reached the second floor where the English department hid in the northern corner, I saw a few newer professors with folders tucked under their arms walking into a small seminar room at the far end of the hallway, so I assumed they were lining up for Knox's defense and I followed them in after taking a few deep breaths. Knox stood at the end of a long table, stacking and separating papers, occasionally looking up to smile and converse with her advisor, a serious-looking man with a shaved head and dark-rimmed glasses who sat at the table's corner nearest her. A few of what I supposed to be her classmates sat at the other end, just in front of a wide bookshelf covered in oblong glass pull-down doors, so after Knox smiled at me, I gave her a quick wave and nod and side-stepped past the professors who were getting settled in their large, black rolling chairs. I tried saying Hello to my new neighbors, but the atmosphere was one of odd, hushed reverence, which I recognized as being well-deserved, considering the efforts of the speaker finally coming full circle. It was as if even though the instructors were there to test her mettle, they brought with their academic pressure a sense of awe. And this collective respect for her sparked in me a swift, surprise despondency, made it difficult to see her.

Once the department chair entered and was met with a little less deference than Knox, which was palpable, a feeling in the air that reminded me of what Dawn had said about Dr. Mohler's attack crossing academic disciplines, I thought maybe the bellwether of embracing the chair was more just of basic tolerance, knowing it was out in the open that she had been jealous of someone else's passion and had gone for his jugular because of it. The room quieted and the shaved-headed man introduced Knox. She did a quick scan of the room and found my face. *Go slow*, I mouthed at her, standing beautifully beneath the boring bright white bulbs at the ceiling. She nodded with a quick smile and then began taking questions. I felt I had done most of what I could by simply getting there on time, maybe looking tired, best if not cracked or fully broken.

Knox was meek at first, because the questions were those of bland ass-kissery and therefore unchallenging, but it became apparent that the graduate coordinator, a fat and bearded inward-thinking mental dilettante was baiting her, the motive behind it coming more clear as he probed through Knox's theoretical analyses, that he hadn't read the thesis at all, but had signed off on its approval to hide his guilt or lack thereof. And Knox was thrown off balance. He discredited one of her sources, a book written by a Beat literature scholar with which the graduate coordinator was admittedly unfamiliar, and I even heard one of Knox's school friends groan, two seats to my right. The reactions of the more uncomfortable people in the room gave me all the information I needed to usher in the anger I'd developed from the late morning. When Knox would glance at me, I'd alter my face to a smile and forced wistfulness in my eyes, like that of some kind of journeyman who'd returned from seeing something inexplicable and could only tell it with his eyes because there were no words. But at some point her kindness drained, and she caught on to what the department chair was allowing to happen, this lynching, because I would later find out from Knox that she'd been viewed as a notorious smoking partner of Mohler's, out in the courtyard, friends with him, too, and this relationship, innocent as it was, inspired, even, disrupted the shaky balance of their hubris, or as Dawn would say, the powers that fucking be.

Knox wouldn't have it. We were forty-five minutes into the defense and she'd permitted the escalation of nonsense long enough, and so, even against the kind attempts of her advisor to distract the department chair and graduate coordinator, she took control of the moment, as she always had with me, and doubly so I found myself enthralled by her strength to be herself, a trait of hers I would soon come to count on.

"No, actually I think you're wrong. No," she said, contemplatively tilting her face toward the ceiling lights. "No, you're completely wrong in your research." She told the fat man.

Caught off guard, he blinked a few times and sat forward. I watched the chair look at him as she folded her hands over her crossed knees. They both looked old, confused, obtuse, a different kind of sad.

"Well," he said, leaning forward, drooping his heavy arms over the papers before him on the table. "When you've, um...when you posit in your second chapter that the Ginsberg-Kerouac relationship was beyond platonic, and simultaneously maintained an undercurrent of irrational anti-humanism capped by an overtly verbalized Zen-like human equality—and I understand the use of multiple theories here—but you seem to overlook the theme of personal revolution in terms of behavioral change, regarding, um...regarding..."

"I've overlooked nothing, John," Knox said. The sound of pins dropping, like her earlier absence, was evident and deafening. "In fact," she continued. "The second chapter is a full lead-in to not only three, but the following two, as well as the conclusion, where I state, *repeatedly*..."

"I think we could somehow..." her advisor began.

"...*repeatedly*, that the purported anti-humanism—which you're misusing contextually and apart from my other sources where personal revolution is discussed, a term *not* used by even Snyder or Ferlinghetti, either—was correlative to the unimpeachable sacrifice to maintain their own selves, even while being perceived as subhuman, a sacrifice which *is* revolution, small scale maybe in the moment, *John*, but in history, the person or people of sacrifice under the auspices of power white male literary domination embodies revolution, behaviorally, because what the person knows, *John*, is that the managers of marketed language don't own mind or soul, they don't own one's *power*. In what way is my position unclear?"

The entire room was silent, minus the soft giggle of Knox's female friend who'd moaned earlier. It was then that my first desire to cry surfaced. About everything. About it all. The chair straightened her purple lapels and sighed in John's direction. She looked like a clown, a clown selling poisoned juice in a sandbox.

"Well," he said, stumbling through his thought process, looking through his papers. "When you say 'repeatedly,' what I take from it is that there's an element of insecurity behind your argument..."

Knox's advisor shifted in his seat. He looked miserable. John noticed, and redirected himself.

"Which is not to say the entire argument. Just there, the nuance of that word itself, to me, means..."

"Oh, this is *bullshit*."

All faces slowly turned toward me, the guilty, though I hadn't realized I'd yelled it out until the condemnation of their eyes. I looked at Knox, who'd turned red. From embarrassment, maybe, or maybe she'd been mad-red before and I'd not noticed. Either way, I needed to leave. I shuttled past the shit-eating smirk on the chair's face, shook my head in apology at Knox as I reentered the hallway and sat on a bench below a framed wall hanging that had, behind glass, national MFA program brochures. Knox's classmates joined me shortly thereafter, sitting on the longer bench across the hall from me.

"They called the defense," said the girl who'd giggled earlier. Her name would soon become Shelley. "Knox should be out pretty..."

As she said it, the loud door opened and Knox met us in the hallway as someone closed it behind her. Knox was shaking her head and looking directly at me. I became angry at myself.

"You."

She walked toward me.

"I'm sorry, man," I said, sitting forward and resting my elbows on my knees. She reached out her palms to the spaces above my ears and kissed my head.

"I first thought I wanted to punch you, but..." She thought a moment, looked over at her friends and then back at me. Shelley was grinning widely. Knox lowered her voice. "But what a bunch of *assholes*."

My eyes teared up.

"What's wrong, Rattigan? Are you stoned?"

I laughed and wiped my eyes.

"No, babe. I'm just proud of you. I'm really tired. And I'm proud of you."

"That was crazy, guys. They probably won't pass me." She sat beside me. "But I'm so glad you all made it," she said to the three people on the bench across the hall.

"They better not try that shit with me," said the thin brown-haired fellow next to Shelley.

A few students quietly passed between us.

"So what happens next?" I asked Knox.

"I don't know. They deliberate and probably call me a rebel bitch, and then they call me back in, I think."

"This is kind of a juvenile process," Shelley said.

"It really is," Knox agreed. "I had no idea."

The door opened and the department chair walked out, alone, faking magnanimity in her stride and smile.

"Amber," she said. She looked around at all of us, and then back to Knox. "Congratulations. You're through."

Shelley sighed and sat back. I studied the woman's face, which held within it defeat and a disregard for reality.

"Thank you," Knox said, shaking the woman's hand.

"We need you back in for a few minutes for follow-up." The chair turned to us all again. "We'll have her back out in just a minute."

I waved a positive thumb up, half-heartedly trying to conceal my scowl. Knox looked back at me as she followed the chair inside, holding an index finger out as if to say she'd be out in no time. I motioned toward the courtyard and made a smoking sign with fingers at my lips, and she nodded as she disappeared again into the seminar room.

By the time I finished my smoke, Knox had descended and was digging through my pocket for a cigarette. She looked years younger.

"What was that about?"

"Ancillary crap about the program. Felt like another exit."

"At least you're done, right? Finally done."

"We need a drink, man," she said, while adjusting her shoulder bag as we made the steps down to the parking lot. "Where the hell is LaCoste?"

"Hey, do you want to change first?"

"Do you need to go by work first?"

We stood in the middle of the parking lot, our cars resting in spaces on opposite ends.

"No, I'm good."

"*Nice.* Yeah, let me get out of this nonsense and then we'll figure out something."

"See you at home," I said, turning toward my car.

"I'm gonna choke that man when I see him. He would have loved that shit in there," she called out. My back stiffened, and I lit another smoke.

The drive, following Knox's car, was an infinite three miles in process, too short once we pulled into to the driveway. What to say, and how. Given her elation, no sense of timing seemed workable. The confusion was wearing off, but not the anger. It was becoming more evident, more appalling in its aggressive onrush, and from it, because of one thing manifesting itself inside as something else entirely, my stomach felt knife-pierced and some-how, also, filled with rock, a pain borne of the coming motions and what I would have to finally say aloud.

Knox waited for me by her car door as I heavily slid from my seat. The sun, in monstrous and unavoidable radiance, shined a thin-striped glow atop her dark hair, and she tapped her leg with a childlike excitement as I put my arm across her shoulders, feebly attempting a smile to match her own.

"You look so worn out, man. You need to nap a bit?"

"I don't think I can sleep."

I pushed open the door and walked inside behind her.

"We don't have to go do anything too involved," she said. "But you have no idea how good that feels to have behind me."

She exhaled loudly and set her bag down beside the edge of the bed, and she sat in her usual seat after kicking her shoes against the wall by the bathroom door, having noticed the neat arrangement of her clothes, the organization of a usually destroyed bed.

"I think you should lie down, Rattigan. I feel bad now, asking you downtown so early."

"That's silly," I said softly, sitting in front of her crossed legs. A small wave broke out across the surface of the waterbed, crested against my half and rolled back into us. "I'll be fine, if I could just..."

"I'm really curious as to what boulder Brody's hiding under. Especially after our talk the other night, man. I thought he'd be there."

"Don't be mad," I whispered, looking at her shoulder. "Don't be."

She turned her head to the side and looked at me with studious con-cern, pausing long enough for me to force my eyes toward hers.

"Something is really not right with you, Rattigan. I'm worried."

I felt my face gain weight, as if all its muscles had given up on false animation and forced on display the honesty of the previous night.

"Don't be," I said again, almost inaudibly.

She sat forward, her eyebrows folded inward, her lips pursed together in curiosity, first, a motion to speak but suddenly unable. I was some-how relieved when I could see in her face an understanding that might have saved me from speaking, but instead she slowly began to shake her head, almost as if she doubted I would tell her the full truth behind my exhaustion. Something in her already knew.

"Brody, um…" I shrugged my shoulders and blinked my eyes, and then I moved my hands around my upper legs, over my knees, locked fingers in my lap, unlocked them and clenched my fists as Knox shook her head faster, her body tense as though she were readying to spring from the bed. "*Knox,*" I said weakly.

She had a few fingers over her lips, and from behind them I heard an even weaker, *just tell me.*

As I spoke, I could see each letter of the sentence spell out in the air between us, I could count them, I could finally know them, but once they were there they could not be made to disappear. I mouthed them.

"Brody died last night."

The rock in my stomach shifted as I watched her body begin to tremble vertically, building in its own force, and then her face understood what the rest of her body had recognized a few seconds earlier. Exhausted and sick, I couldn't stop looking at her mouth, opening into a horrified "o," and then crumpling downward. She leaned forward slightly, her eyes pleading, and then swayed backward as she began to sob, began to push toward the edge of a scream before receding into a breathlessness that scared her. I realized a sudden inability to touch her, and so I sat with a pale, expressionless stare as she reacted to a pain I was still in the process of naming. After a few minutes, her experience became unbearable to me, and in this I felt cruel, I felt empty, but still under an extreme and unseen weight. As Knox stretched out on her side across the pillows, still crying, burying herself deep into the sheets as if trying to put her whole being behind the muffled tears, deep into the ocean of the bed, I quietly slid off the side and walked to Brody's sofa, lifted the thin blue blanket that draped over one of its arms, and I slid under to lie facing away from her. I watched the unwavering sunlight through the cracks in the blinds on the front door, and once Knox had relinquished her powers and fallen, drained of sound and strength, into sleep, I finally closed my eyes.

CHAPTER 9

The tone inside the house changed, the cadence and content of our speech, as we drifted in and out of the amplified rigors of our sudden, unwanted work lives. But Knox and I consumed every hour available that kept us away from more than just home, and in the process, we unknowingly prepared to do ourselves a tremendous disservice that would prolong what was still too fresh to be anything but imaginable. In an unspoken agreement made by simply performing such independent acts of strained preoccupation, too much work became the only pursuit in the following week that could insure our coexistence. I assigned her a role in my own periphery, which weakened us, first by my viewing everything askance, secondly by my awareness of my doing it, thereby ushering in latent guilt, and thirdly, by the quiet admission of her body's language that she knew what was happening but couldn't bring herself to attempt a break in it, if not altogether make it stop.

My anger, at the very moments it began to feel puerile and able to be let go, went on to become other forms of itself, and from the frustration to which it gave birth came a contempt for frustration, a child that hates its parent, and when I looked at anything, anything at all, I felt disheartened by its unquestioning continuity, as I'd wanted so many things to come to a conclusion for at least a small fragment of time, on their own, but nothing would comply, nothing to which I'd ever felt connected would take pause in conjunction with me and exist in a stupor. So I made even the simplest things invisible. The not-knowing from that first morning had left my head and found the high end of my chest, and I grew to deplore the transitions occurring, with intolerance one hour, erratic thoughts another, then focused, elongated bursts of clarity that attached itself only to the components of my emotion, but not an understanding of the point at which they met, not how one confusion became a surety, not why one confidence became disdain. It was as if I'd stolen the last and maybe only night of his doubt, elevated it to an improper height of lunacy and stared down at the world alongside it, so far up then in the dark clouds, my view so muddled by the black and tenuous tree limbs and swishing leaves that although I couldn't hear at all, I could still barely see. And though dissatisfied, I would not descend to better light.

Some nights, when I could bring myself to come home when there was still a lamp's glow on inside, I'd pretend to read a book on Brody's couch as Knox kept busy on her computer in bed. We weren't strangers—our agendas had simply shifted without discussion, without any question given to the direction of our own wants, and during the nonexistent conversation, we were inversely selected by our own paths. I thought more about my grandfather's funeral that week, purposefully, in the event Knox were to ask my thoughts, or someone at work, as if devising a plan to offer that lie would satisfy anyone who had grown to know me in the context of what was there in my midst, in *ours*, and then not. On a more distant moon there was rumored to be a sense of unity in loss, and I could see the efforts of my family at work, striving harder behind the counter, beyond the store hours, to grow closer from having something removed. But the opposite was happening with me. Because I was concerned with a perceived lie behind the unity, that people would improve their lives momentarily, out of fear, and then violently return to destruction and arrested conciliation between each other, the world seemed to have less love than it had at first let on, and so I sought a readiness to absorb what loss would eventually be discarded by those who called themselves *strong*, those who could deftly move on, those who, in reality, were forgetting prematurely. I wanted to possess all general failed attempts at unity and I wanted them intact within me, unbothered, where they could either implode along with loss, or redefine themselves and through some bodily kindness become clearer in my mind. An organic corrosion was welcome, too—anything that could be more easily identified.

But on other nights, when the simplicity of our diversions in the guest-house became pressed, and Knox and I edged toward mutual clemency, or at very least when things became not so simple, *or*, when I craved exposure to a different sadness, a less nonverbal articulation of it, I would stay at Dawn's just to watch her kick at the thickening layer of ash on her patio as she lectured against the black blank sky. Her sadness was an anger, too, but it was many things at once, not a crossover between things, but instead, mostly a direct fury at a spate of universal principles she could not bring herself to discuss with me regarding her consideration of personally rel-evant death. I was not especially content there, either, but I was content with the listening I could do outside with her in the slight dark, occasion-ally looking up at one side of her face as she shook her head and vocalized determinations I knew mostly excluded me. And I think Dawn didn't want me there, specifically, as much as I didn't wish for stasis or philosophy, so we did our dance perfectly, fearlessly as junkies who tell junkies they love one another, beneath a freeway bridge, as they continue to light up or inject. We hinted at one another, we invited and accepted, we showed up and moved our lips and kept each shared evening in some kind of forward motion, but our authenticity was on hiatus, leaving us to speak in echoing auditoriums with little to no one listening. Brody's death engaged the liars inside us.

The movement between buildings, from one home to work to another home, was a steady current of neutrality, regardless of the weather—gray with rain or a lucid, dry blue—and remaining in such motion turned down the volume if not the power off, completely, on our differing accountabili-ties. The mandate of unity in loss was agreed with by its ignorance, as we all married our jobs. Nights were disgustingly still, the motion of our bodies therein delivering groaning bellows of our bones and molecules and bloods upended like a schooner on a hurricane wave. Any movement at night had to be calculated, and because I was then alternatively defining sound in the voice of my body, and not defining it in the searching of Knox's eyes, I spent many nights after work at The Blackbird, where the music was good and loud and I knew people well enough there to feel comfortable with seeming aloof, or if nothing else, just a basic distant. And I couldn't, even in the later, less amicable hours after these quiet, loud nights in bars, force my tires and eyes onto Westminster to cut more quickly through to home.

So in returning to what I was continuously leaving, I avoided, too, what had already left, the site of what had been taken, as if chalk still might bruise the blacktop there before my headlights.

A couple of days after that Monday, I enacted a passive listening regiment at work, doing what I was to do with a tundra separating my usual self from the present. I learned subsequential facts this way, that Brody's father was a stern man, terse and to the point in his dealings with Brad and Sonya. She had assumed a post-loss role of ambivalence toward everyone, that she and he and they and we should do what our hearts desire, do it patiently, and with love, for every minute had suddenly begun to matter. It was ironic, wholly, as her ordinary loathing for iniquity evidenced itself in her assigned management of Mr. LaCoste. What I did know is that she would be the first to fall back into destruction after wearing the tight-fitting garment of borrowed, metaphorical motherhood, requiring, in her mind, a harshness more encompassing than her leniency.

When describing him one night to Mason as I stood nearby and wiped down the face of the soda counter, Sonya said, "He's a stupid old mean motherfucker with money that had no connection with his own kid, man. Didn't know who he is. Who he..."

She trapped herself in impetuous softness and looked away from Mason a moment, just before he would reach his thick, gentle fingers out to the back of her neck, which she stepped away from while reaching again for the wine bottle. To each his own tug-of-war.

"But it doesn't matter, right?" She continued. "What matters is that we're all still here."

She lit a cigarette and looked over Mason's shoulder at me and my occasional glances at her. "Well, most of us," she said, lowering her voice.

But what I didn't know was how expeditious Mr. LaCoste would prove to be. And how stealthy. Brody's car was towed from the Stone, three days out, to a dealership in Mountainbrook in Birmingham, the day after Brody's father came to Mobile for a collection of information from the restaurant. Not to collect anything else—clothes, notebooks, anything—just information on his son's employment for reason of taxes and loans. He had visited the small house off Mohawk in Midtown, fearlessly inviting himself in to the new resident's digs in order to survey the old home of his son's, the last address he'd been sent from Mobile. Apparently the new inhabitant of the tiny apartment was a friend of Blain's and was stoned and confused beyond expression. And I feared, no, expected almost, that the couch at any moment would be removed by some cabin-sized hand that would punch through the front wall of our house as we slept, with me likely on it, and if I hadn't a survivalist's wherewithal when coming up from sleep, the developing fairy tale of Mr. LaCoste's evil would manifest itself in that gnarled-knuckled hand that came from nowhere, unapologetically entering to crush me and then disappear with the furniture. I wanted the maniacal untruth of that fiction to happen, to alter the environment, but I also was relieved when nothing remotely like this occurred, not even a knock on the door.

Where the anger turned, or rather, *when*, was the afternoon the car was towed. Mr. LaCoste had left Sonya with instructions to post a memo for the staff, a memo I later heard she'd typed out in the office with a wild series of screamed curse words, audible at the bar. I had gotten off late in the afternoon, opting to stay until four-thirty, still trying to shake the overbearing energy of Brody's father, glad he was gone. Unsure if I were being insensitive to the sudden work he'd had to take on, I still reacted coldly to how his eyes barely met with anyone at work as he muscled around the store that last day he was in Mobile, as if he owned us. From the injustice, that affected my body differently than Dawn's, and then the nausea following a strong desire to hit something, I can't recall the exact words of what Sonya posted near our schedules on the corkboard in the walkway between the bar and office. But in this case, full detail is irrelevant when the only specific necessary is this, that no one—*not one of you now, you hear?*—was allowed to attend the funeral service upstate. At first, and then soon later, I felt the rule could bend, *would* bend for at least me, at least Knox and me. We would get in the car again, together again, and in the small cabin, with cigarettes and the radio dial clicked off, say what needed saying, find something within ourselves to lay out on the dash between us, stick it there, stare at it around our sporadic glances at the road—we would stare at it until the shapes and colors of what it was became evident, if only to one of us, and then we would talk about it, a work of art, perhaps still in progress, until the other would see what the other saw, or something alternatively new and churning and breaking. We would dampen it with what had to eventually leave our bodies, leave them together, not to return to what was our home, our *dynamic*, our reality of *then*, for at least we knew without vocalizing it that something had broken and was gone and could not be found anywhere, not again, nowhere—we would cry with the revelation and drive and understand that what was ahead could be better discussed past the casual, noncommittal half-thoughts that leapt from us in passing. Suddenly, we *had* to be there.

But between the efforts to convince myself we'd be the exception, there was rage, my brand of it, influenced perhaps by the movies Knox and Brody and I had watched together, had commented on but never exercised:

"Look at the tension there, right there."

"Yeah, in what she wants to say versus what she'll likely say."

"Exactly, babe. No one ever just comes out with it in movies. Always just hints."

"And maneuvers. I hope if it's not what he wants to hear he doesn't go into a screaming fit."

"Yeah, me too."

"That's cliché these days in film."

"I don't think it happens enough."

"I bet it *would* feel good sometimes to just unload at the sky."

"Shhh, I missed what she said."

"Pass me a beer."

"*Shhh.*"

Yet I did enter a screaming fit, hauling off past the corkboard and in to the walk-in cooler, startling Greg who was inside with a notepad, drinking a beer while tallying figures for the next day's produce order. No classical outburst of irrevocable devastation, just a few swollen swears at the ceiling before noticing Greg and, with heart racing, sitting on a large sanitized bucket filled with fresh sauce for the evening crew. I shook my head and then ran fingers through my hair. Greg put down his notepad and let me steam a while.

"No I agree. I agree. I mean, I'm trying to see it his way, too. You want a private family thing? Fine. But don't come around here and treat everybody like we're nobody..."

"Or that we're to blame," I added, standing up. "Sorry I scared you, man."

"No problem. It pissed me off, too. Fucking asshole. Not you."

"Hey I've gotta...I need to see if I can take care of something. See you tomorrow, Greg. Sorry, again."

"Good side is, at least Brad got him to give up the address for where to send flowers. Right? We're all gonna sign something, too. Sonya went to get a better card than the ones they send with..."

"But that's not enough, man. That's dismissive as hell."

"*I* know. I think so, *too*, brother."

"Ok," I nodded. "Good."

I wiped my hands on the legs of my jeans and made it toward the cooler door and pushed against its heaviness.

"Hey, Pete?"

"Yeah," I said, turning toward Greg, who hadn't moved. His head was cocked to the side, eyes curious, a Knox sort of curious.

"You're not walking around here feeling responsible for anything, are you?" He raised one eyebrow, shrugged and then sipped his beer. I paused to look at the floor and answer.

"Are you?"

"Why, are you?" He blinked at me.

"See you tomorrow, man."

Stepping past the office I glanced in and noticed a stack of employee folders were still out, the second in the pile being Brody's. His father's business card sat on top of the first page, with an "H" and a "C" in separate, stacked parentheses before one upstate area code and two different numbers. I took a piece of paper hanging limply from the fax machine and wrote them down, folded the paper into a thin rectangle and slipped it in my back pocket before exiting the back door. I was energized by the validation of my anger from Greg. *Finally*, I'd thought in the cooler, someone *sees* this thing. His Socratic shit he could keep. But beneath the rest, the renewed thirst for action was on the heels of the previous days' inaction, along with whatever promise existed to be discovered, but it was ahead, something *plausible* was ahead, motion and talks, maybe, maybe a surplus of the needed latter. But then it occurred to me I wasn't willing yet to allow this without a catalyst, and also, that the catalyst itself hinged on something, someone, that was out of my control.

I arrived at an empty house and made a line to the telephone before noticing the time and remembering Birmingham was four-plus hours

319

north, depending on speed. I went out on to the side stoop through the kitchen, past the corner desk, and as I lit a cigarette I realized my manuscript was missing from its surface. I dismissed the idea that it was lost, assumed Knox had grown curious, and stood outside in the humid warmth until curiosity of my own won out and I took to searching the house for signs of its life. But I was moving in too frantic a sweeping motion, actually not looking for it, and not in the mood to fold and re-fold, make and re-make anything across the house, not in the mood to lift the towel from over Brody's clothes box and sift through them, remember what was said when what was worn, and then I saw, fully, that in my effort to leave time alone I was being irrational. Mr. LaCoste had left town shortly after we'd opened at eleven in the morning, and it was nearly night. He's a rational man, I thought, on the way to the phone, briskly hurtling the forgivable swamp that had rebuilt itself since Monday. We're going to be able to talk about *everything*, I thought, without a suggestion past my supposing that what everything was, in my mind at the time, was necessarily what needed to be discussed. I dialed the "H" number, sat on the bed and waited.

After the fourth ring I grew nervous and almost hung up, but a woman's soft voice answered in the middle of the fifth. I turned the receiver away to clear my throat.

"Hello?"

"Mrs. LaCoste?"

Silence.

"Is this Mrs. LaCoste?"

"Yes," she finally said.

I stood over the phone. My back hurt. The house was quiet.

"My name is...my name is Pete Rattigan."

Silence, again. The energy I had brought inside had become what it should have been from its birth at the restaurant, fear, but again, that anger, the loud words, Greg's blinking. I realized I'd nothing planned to say, but instead to plead, at my very best, without sounding pathetic.

"I'm a friend...I was...I was a friend of Brody's, and..."

"*Oh*," I heard her say, more softly than when she answered. It sounded like she dropped the phone. I heard mixed voices in the back, all adults, it seemed, far away but echoing, as if they lived in a cave.

320

I found myself arching my back even more into a semi-circle as the silence from the other end pulsated in my ear, lasting just long enough to induce a sense of insecurity, of self-doubt—ten seconds, fifteen at best.

"May I help you, son?" It was a rhetorical question, from a rough man's voice, startling me as though I had been the one counting lettuce heads, momentarily unbothered in a cooler. My chest folded inward. My back throbbed. My face was near the phone's cradle. His voice was so severe. He's a rational man, I thought. How else do I do this without his *yes*?

"Mr. LaCoste, my name's Pete R..."

"My wife's upset. She doesn't need to be answering the telephone." He called this last sentence out of his shoulder away from the phone, because the echo changed, it got stronger. "How can I help you?"

Thinking of Brody's couch, unwilling at this point to surrender it, Brody's scratched-up jeans and spare bandanas, paint-flecked, too—I knew I couldn't tell him about our house.

"I work with...worked with, Brody here in Mobile, and I know..."

"Which one were you?" He asked, loudly into the phone.

"We didn't meet, sir."

"Does my son owe you money?"

What, I thought.

"What?"

"Does he owe you money? Did he steal from your store? From you?"

"No, sir. Not at all. That isn't why I'm...this has nothing to do with..."

"Then how can I help you, son?"

A conflict arose, in that he called me "son." The other half of the conflict was that I suddenly wanted to laugh, thinking of my own mother, either calling me her "son" in third person or talking directly to the Almighty about my ways—I wondered who she would think I'd stolen from when someone called if I were to no longer be around. And then the anger staged its resurgence because I didn't want to laugh. I wanted this man to see my eyes and read the boyishness that had redeveloped in my heavy shoulders that week and I wanted him to say, All right young man, all right, *son*, come on up.

"Brody meant more to me than...I'm calling to ask you with all seriousness if I may attend the services..."

"Ok, listen up, young man, I thought I..."

"Now I was told at work what you said about privacy, which I completely respect, sir, but this would really mean..."

"I thought I'd made it clear that my wife and I don't need any of you..."

"I know, Mr. LaCoste, it would just be very important to attend, to maybe sit in the back and..."

"My *wife* and I..." he continued, unimaginably louder than before, "... don't need any of you new wave hippies with your nose rings and voodoo values in or around my church and my house. Got it?"

"It would just be me, sir. I understand you..."

"You don't understand a *damned* thing, boy. Not one."

"If you would just let me..."

"You've been allowed enough, young man. You call here again and I'll have that pillbox of yours fined 'til it's shut down. You want to keep your job? Leave it be. Right now. End of story. *No.*"

And with a loud clack of what sounded much heavier than the thin plastic of our own phone, he hung up. He may have done it twice. After a moment of silence, and still bent low to the phone, I slipped the receiver into the cradle and slowly stood. My skin was hot, my spine gone. I'd felt it disappearing, mid-conversation, mid-roar, mid-weakness of mine, though I couldn't, and wouldn't ever, not even much later, produce something in my mind that I thought might have turned him toward agreement.

He's a rational man, I thought, and then Fuck. Fuck. *Fuck.*

———

I returned to work over the next week with the same appeal to distraction, volunteering for long extra shifts without breaks, working straight through, eating on the fly a sandwich or slice that consistently grew cold from being ignored on a plastic, multi-colored dinner plate on the back table beside the sink designated for hand-washed wine glasses. But my approach changed. I worked with a militaristic efficiency at everything, far removed from any disdain I once made evident toward unruly guests in search of something free. I allowed myself a steady trampling from people, gave them what they wanted, what they barked for, with a low-pointed nod as if they were right by their mere presence and I was wrong for my full human inadequacy. Nothing like that stung. I'd bent the rules of myself, directing anger not at any one person, any conversational slight at my judgment or ability, saving it instead to mull frenetically after work, during long drives, sometimes back across the bay to Fairhope, just to have a cup of coffee at an all-night breakfast joint off 98 and then turning back around to face Mobile in the gloaming, in the hum of my engine cutting through it. The anger would stick, I was sure, borne of my brief, feeble effort to win at one thing, an isolated invitation to Birmingham, in order to weaken and eventually break apart the spell, the abrasion of what was on and in me, the gravitational sense of loss.

There was no unity. It was nowhere to be found, unearthed, refitted, attached to something stronger. I hadn't given up on its possibility, and wouldn't, *couldn't* for long, but for the week the emotional lines were darting in their own directions like comets, with no discernible center, and the fires from their haste disappeared too quickly against all the blackness for me to determine their temperature, color, their need.

And it's too simplified to say Knox noticed. Too easy to say some at work were aware. I felt it being studied around me, I felt selfish because of the interest it was drawing. Conversations would lower in volume after hours at the store, when we were cleaning and there was laughter, when new music had been brought to discuss and compare to other sounds, other musicians and techniques and legacies. Nothing was getting new and little remained old, and in my distance, child of disappointment, the money piled up. I was spending it on gas, mostly, darting off toward Biloxi some nights, thinking maybe New Orleans, before turning around and crawling on to the couch as Knox slept. She left me a note in the first days after I spoke with Brody's father, a note declaring that the planet had tilted and had somehow shaken loose a year-long internship on campus, beginning late August, which meant more bullshit for Knox to manage working with a department we both thought detested her and her confidence, her mind. But it also meant four composition classes per semester, decent pay, better than what she was currently receiving even after all the extra hours at the studio. I left her a dull response of congratulations, meant deeply, even in the dullness, as she'd accomplished something I had given up on a half-year back, remaining in my field in wait of something more choice, a window to open and later dive through. But I couldn't be thrilled, couldn't feel thrill, because I knew what she would have to endure to find that window, to come across it. And in congratulating her I also wanted to tell her to not sink so deeply into the mire of the job's lack of grandeur that she might miss the window when the sun, in the darkness, at last shined through. But I would have sounded like a hypocrite. I would have been one, so I left it at "congratulations" and continued on with my nights of driving.

Dawn was spending her nights still entangled in the late hours, juggling both jobs as the semester fell to its close, and even picked back up with her thesis as the department had no need for her during summers. She was still helping Mohler, still had research pages and chapter samples of his book scattered in organized fashion on the floor in a semi-circle around the coffee table. On the nights I'd idle past her apartment and catch the light still on, I'd key in softly to find her sipping wine with the radio on low, shrugging upward at me as I stepped inside, set my keys on the end table by the door and sat in the nearby reclining chair. She was in motion, too. She was driving late into night without leaving her house, finding the motion of moving on with what she'd put on pause a "necessary comfort, not a distraction," she'd said. *This needs to be done.*

Her sudden attentiveness somehow shoved me into the thought, through no fault or real influence of Dawn's at all, that I owed Knox something. From moving and moving silently in and out of each place I entered, I was leaving those who, too, had lost, I was leaving them to lose on their own, and I knew it. The lump in my throat knew it when I motioned to speak, to join a conversation Dawn would have with the neighbors when outside on the patio, when Blain and Mason compared new tattoos on their forearms that first weekend, when Knox quietly read a book I'd never heard of as she balled up in the corner of her bed, leaving open the space where my body had ordinarily, warmly stretched out. I knew I was still in the sky, looking down.

I thought to invite Knox to dinner the next night I had off, to the Italian restaurant in Midtown where we'd first caught up together again, with seriousness, with fervor, where we'd celebrated her dual graduation and supported her preparation to later strong-arm her thesis. But it was a place of another beginning that would remind, both of us equally, of an end. It was too difficult to imagine the two of us, of old and able words, coming up with anything to talk about besides the wine, the good food, the bustle of the small place, the kind owners. Why this would have been a bad start, I wouldn't bear to ask myself, let alone answer.

One morning, after a nap on Dawn's couch, I rose with her as she headed out toward campus to turn over her department keys for the summer months, and then go meet Mohler for a drinking brunch off Royal Street downtown. Knox was home and awake when I entered on tiptoe. She was sitting in bed, hair pulled back, bright-eyed for the hour, and she glanced at me briefly, likely expecting nothing, and then she took to scanning the long row of cabinets across the foot of the bed to my right, the picture frames on top of them, the half-burned candles, anything.

"You're up early. You working?"

I stepped out of my sandals and changed into another shirt, the first I could find, and then motioned toward the couch as if to go immediately to sleep, but she was watching my nervous dance. I felt I was, too.

"I can make coffee if you're interested."

"Ok," she said.

I took my time in the kitchen, with a part of me wishing her to lose interest and to go about the work of getting ready to leave the house. Our old coffeemaker took its usual extra minutes to brew, so I washed a few plates and bowls from the top of the mid-sized pile in the sink and placed them to dry in the rack on the counter. I stuffed empty food containers further down into the full trash bag in the pantry. I considered sweeping.

"I read your novel," I heard her say, clearly.

"What?" I grabbed the broom.

"Will you come in here?"

I took a deep breath, swept the space immediately in front of the cabinet doors below the sink and emptied what I'd collected in the dustpan into the trash, the pantry door still open.

"What was that?" I asked, scratching lightly at my hair, stopping at the corner of the end of the bed. "Coffee's ready. There's that chai vanilla stuff to put..."

"I read your novel, Rattigan."

She lifted a few pages from off the bed. I noticed the rest of the stack jutting out from under my pillow.

"Yeah?"

"Yeah." She folded her face at me. "I've been reading it, these last three days."

I studied the sprawl of pages around her.

"It still needs another edit or so," I told her.

I took a step away from the bed toward the kitchen.

"Rattigan, what are you doing?"

I paused and then turned back to her.

"I'm making coffee, man. It's ready. I should..."

"*Pete*," she said, sitting forward. "What are you *doing*?"

"Nothing."

"Can you even look at me?"

"I did, Knox. I am. You're being silly."

She turned her head in a manner I'd seen before, playfully before, just as she was going to light into me about some grave injustice I'd done to her in a facetious banter over drinks somewhere downtown, in the long long nights of the recent, yet far gone past. But instead of following through, which I wanted—I wanted her to be responsible for shaking me out of myself—she shook her head and went into the bathroom and shut the door behind her. I returned to the kitchen and rinsed two used mugs and filled them from the boiling, brown pot, becoming more clear than brown as I poured. I studied it change its identity, its mind.

"Fuck it," I heard her say. "I'm late anyway. As usual."

"What?" I asked, setting down her cup on the makeshift table she'd constructed for the floor beside the bed, where she usually rested her laptop as she slept. It was still in the bed, at the feet of my half, farther away from her than normal.

"I don't even have time to shower. So fuck that, too."

I sat on the bed beside her computer as she resurfaced a few minutes later. Knox had run the air cold overnight, and the hot mug felt good against my palms. I didn't want to drink, just hold. She watched me as she flipped through a few outfits draping over the top of her thin chest-of-drawers. I watched her, too, as I'd been watching everything, from the side of my eyes, and I blew softly at the coffee's steam.

"I'm just trying to tell you I read your novel, Rattigan."

"I hope it was..."

"It's beautiful. Fucking stunning, actually."

"It's raw, still," I said, still blowing.

"I know it might be and I don't care if it is." She wrestled into a thin, collared shirt. "I'm just making the point to...will you look at me?"

I glanced up at her with my lips hovering over my mug.

"This is really hot."

"Fuck the coffee, *Rattigan*. I'm telling you...you know, I'm not just bullshitting you. I read it. I love it, and I want to tell you why, and I thought some fucking part of you would be willing to listen to me."

She began to softly cry, slightly defeated. I wanted to pour the entire cup of coffee in my own lap. I was being such a bastard. I was leaving her by sitting there, invisible. But as soon as she started, she stopped as she buttoned her pants and wiped at her eyes.

"Knox, I'm..."

"I need a smoke, man. I can't do this right now."

She grabbed up her things and put an unlit cigarette in her mouth and stepped into a pair of shoes by the door. I set the mug on the floor by my foot and pressed the bottoms of my palms against the top of my forehead.

"Knox, I know it doesn't seem like I'm trying to..."

"No," she said, stopping at the door, a lighter in her free hand already up toward her cigarette, which she removed from her lips. "You're not try-ing at all."

She motioned to leave, but stepped back into the room. My eyes felt dry and I'm sure, to her, they appeared red, dumb maybe, alert and somehow also confused. I didn't deserve her, suddenly, at all. Or perhaps she didn't deserve who it was that sat at the end of the bed. Until I could release it, or learn from it, I wanted her own anger to be what we could have in common.

"There's a message on the machine you need to listen to. Probably this morning. Who knows when you'll be back around."

She shook her head again, stepped outside on to the top step, lit the cigarette and shut the door. After a short moment I stood to follow her out, to say unplanned things, to say something based on apology and follow it, like her, into the new unmet world in which we both had reluctantly found ourselves. But I got caught by the solid light on the answering machine, a light meaning the message had been listened to and saved. I walked to it and pressed play, thinking in my absence I had surrendered a chance to go upstate, I had surrendered *our* chance, that Mr. LaCoste had not changed his heart but discovered it. The voice was different.

"Ok, this message is for Brody LaCoste. Brody, this is Meena with Penguin. In New York. I hope this is a good number at which to reach you. Short and simple—we didn't discuss a reintroduction of character, I don't think. But these people, these Flanagan, Dixon people brought with them an altogether new storyline that follows well the basis we agreed would work. A young person's novel, mostly about love? That doesn't slip into kitsch or, pardon me, stupidity, let alone cliché? It's modern because it's redefined. The theme, that is. So bravo. It will sell. It's going to sell. The next step is getting you to the city again. Call me at my home, not too late. But soon. More work to come, but it will sell. Quite well, I think. I hope this is a good number. Ciao."

Tears flooded my eyes. Nothing else happened with my face, just the business of eyes. I meant to run out the front door, but turned toward the closet. I spun, I leapt over the bed's old wooden corner. I needed Knox, instantly. I hurled myself through the door and let it bang against the shelf behind it, ran barefoot toward the iron gate, over the thick level of pebbled stone, and once at the gate I reverted the force of my oncoming body into a pull to heave open its heaviness, to continue running. I ran out into the middle of the drive, to the edge of the street, but Knox had already driven away. There was no trace of bumper, taillight, not the scent of engine disappearing. I caught my breath, my chest rising and falling, and then I walked back into the house, anger inside yet again—but finally, at a person, at someone, at *me*.

————

The next few days were a slow exodus back to myself, not because I was put together, far from it. But I was busy, I felt, because even against my will the exodus had to begin. Some rationalities needed to be embraced, faulty or obscurely accurate. The labor, in any capacity, had to start. So it began with the obvious. Knox had won for *us* with her defense, I had claimed some sense of a forged future from *our* victory in Nashville, and the message from New York had temporarily pulled Brody closer. From these assertions alone, I joined some conversations at work once our doors had been locked, had a drink on occasion and went on fewer drives, kept the car and my body closer to Mobile. I drove over to Pensacola once just to get mixed up with unfamiliar streets off incorrect exits, making my way back from the finally-found downtown around four one morning, not having had a drink, but instead having spent the limited time I had on the boulevard before their own doors were locked and the groups dispersed to be around a crowd that did not know me, that had its own sense of measure in a world not ridiculously far from home. And from the tainted rapport between myself and Brody's father, though I didn't think he'd caught my name, but worried maybe he'd remember my voice, I had Sonya agree to mail him a letter I dictated to her which included Meena's phone number. Assuming the man might have loathed what we represented to him and his sense of wealth, from a money standpoint, this way he could control something of his son's that he couldn't before. And we would experience another win.

Knox had retreated from me somewhat, and justifiably, but I recognized a forgiveness in her eyes when I spoke to her once, maybe twice, about the idea of Brody's novel landing on shelf.

"Yeah," she would say, feeling me out as I let my imagination run, speaking more than I had in days. "*Yeah*, man."

But what I had to assess in those developing days was the swing of the return, which was not a casual glide into a former state that protected any of us from what had happened. Judging from a slight indifference toward my shift in mood at work, I saw that my speed had challenged others away from their own form of recovery, that I had been callous in the handling of how others might be responding to themselves. And it was a fresh wound, too, that such a short amount of time could have brought me back so swiftly, regardless of good news. So the pendulum was there, in me—I still wanted to keep the hurt because it was familiar, unimpeachably so—but I was noticing it in others. I still avoided Westminster Way, still wouldn't roam the aisles of the bookstore where Brody and I had once followed Margaret and watched her ready to sacrifice her life to the first weak offer of love, still wouldn't sleep in bed at home. And more painfully, even in the improvement with Knox, I still bore the weight of having left her alone as much as I had ignored myself.

Dawn had become more playful at work, began talking about her thesis less, making more sense in her convincing rationale that it could wait.

Ortega will still be there when I'm ready, right? It can wait. When I did feel I was taking advantage of Knox's generosity, when I felt I'd invaded her silence, I would stay with Dawn, and we would share a meal and listen to music low on the radio while playing cards, distracted a bit more amicably, not talking of the future, not Mohler, not us, just rotating turns dropping thin paper cards on top of thin paper cards. Back home, the conversation had not been had, but the preface had been skimmed and needed time to air out, to breathe, before its having. But at Dawn's, because there was less owed between us, even if the hurt was receding, the confusion dissipating too slowly for comfort, we had a better grip on the avoidance of it and didn't feel as glum when looking out over the back lawn at night, when the cats were out but not the moon.

And the weather had finally sunk in to my skin, the unimaginable heat that teases in at the front of an Alabama Spring, but one that really comes on once it comes. I would get off the couch when Knox woke, and as she conducted herself in the storm of her usual first hour, I would take my novel's draft and sit at a patio table by the pool and tear through it with a more determined, cleaner focus. I'd be in a light sweat, already by eight, just from sitting, when she would thunder from the door, consistently and more frequently offering coffee or tea she'd made before she padded toward the driveway. We watched a comedy one night, her in bed and me on the floor beside her, not talking but laughing some. I made dinner twice and she cleaned the bathroom. The regiments we assigned ourselves were uncommon and required their own time to be understood, our sudden efficiency, one I had removed from work and had set down in the house, one that she had had all along but then put to use without our knowing whose lead was being followed. I slept more often and stayed tired from all the redemptive acts, studying everyone around me with maybe the same acuity as before, but reveling in the fact that it had returned, my sincere interest in the way others carry on.

Beneath it, though, I was sometimes straining to behave like them, like those at work who could plan without guilt to attend a concert or art show. My hesitance at first baffled me, but I was patient with it and saw there were things, in my own interim, that needed their nearness reset, reconstructed before I could enter the world of getting lost again in a good way. So I stayed around home, worked a little less, made acquaintance with the young college children of the main house who were in for the summer, to do nothing but either play golf with the father across the street, or lie around the pool with the stepmother and spill wine on magazines.

Moments still rose from below the surface where I'd replay, albeit briefly, the conversation with Brody the night before, unsuccessfully seeking out hints at what I couldn't have predicted, and then taking it uncomfortably further, into the analysis of my own powers, then, to have prevented what I could foresee. Those days were the hardest. Those days would become nights, but because I wouldn't leave again, I would spend those nights editing under the gas lamps and getting eaten alive by mosquitoes, as if I deserved that in replacement of what I refused to fully blame myself for. One punishment for another was the cycle, one deprivation here, one glass of wine that tasted in the night like melancholy, and was rimmed with gnats each time I'd lift it from the ground.

After a week had passed since Meena called, there was a late morning, early afternoon where it snuck in—the talk, the ensuing insecurity and then missing him, physically feeling an absence, a phantom energy—I went inside and got ready for work, collected the two bags of aluminum cans that had been ferociously crammed into the limited space behind the trashcan in the pantry, and I took them down Government to a recycling center just before Michigan Avenue.

"Finally putting these to bed," I'd told Knox as I carried them toward the door. She was sleeping in but she looked up and squinted.

"I kept putting it off. Sorry, man."

"Get your rest."

But by the time I'd made it to work, the drive had afforded me the appropriate kind of sunlit solitude necessary to not put on the shoulders of night the sole responsibility of helping things gain better clarity. The change of venue, the opposite side of the city, different faces, different workers achieving different ends, the homeless pacing more slowly down the sidewalk toward the Salvation Army, slower than during winter. The bicyclists were out, restaurants were relocating to bigger buildings, elderly women blocking the sun with their extended palms while waiting for the bus. A new condominium was going up, a tall, grey monument to expensive sleep. Interesting in that they were additions to a list of things to remind myself that more was still ongoing—not that I'd forgotten, but when left ignored, the brick facades, the business, the faces and the newness all seem to matter less, and so exposure, not knowing it was what I required, became reminder to search for more rationalities, more suggestions that eventually seconds would stop seeming so infinitely long.

The Stone would provide a slow night, a good night, with everyone's energies healthy, and strong, and my distraction, when it came in waves throughout the shift, would gently lap against me instead of as an overpowering, disintegrating force. I wasn't forgetting him, in any sense of reality, but the new attempt at distancing meant I was keeping something down still, something was being left out, and I only realized it at the end of this particular night, as I stood in the kitchen at closing time, having a beer with Blain, when Jena stepped around the corner from the bar to tell me one of my customers was waiting out front to talk to me.

"I've already done my cash out, man. That's strange."

"Hey, maybe they want your number," Blain said.

"Yeah, maybe."

I headed toward the front.

"*Stud*," he called behind me.

It amazed me how quickly a scenario could paint itself in the mind. In only the six or so steps it would take to place me in the open space between the bar and soda machine, I wondered who it was, who it could be, and the answers came in grotesquely, almost childlike in their lack of realism. It was Brody's father, come to reconcile with me, the one of all of us who deserved it most. It was Meena, she'd found out, had flown to Mobile all afternoon and night to ask questions, to appeal to my stamp on his work, his story. Knox maybe, to say nothing was over and everything had begun. No, it was Brody, alive and there to proclaim his cruel joke, which I would bear, I would laugh at and accept, and the staff, regulars, too, would amass around him and we would stand back on the tops of the shaky bar stools and read and scream and glance at each other, knowing we were on to something, that nothing had stopped, things could still end, but not yet. It wasn't a customer, it was Brody, saying our full resurrection was incomplete. Brody, saying that this was not just a movie, but real life where these things happen all the time. Brody painted with a smile.

Who stood there, instead, with patience, an almost uncomfortable plethora of it, was a short girl with sandy blonde hair, cut short to just below her ears. Pale skin, small symmetrical face. She wore what looked at first like a lab coat, then at second study, an artist's jacket which, in my mind, made sense because I saw the smears of various colors across it, as if she'd wiped her fingers or maybe a brush across it. But I didn't know if an "artist's jacket" existed or was the proper term. She was someone I knew, but I didn't know her name. The girl who'd sat alone at one of my tables for nearly two hours, who'd ordered a salad and slowly drank her beers while reading a thin paperback in the dim blue light from the hanging lamp overhead.

"You're Pete."

"Yeah." I stood a moment. "Was everything all right?"

She smiled a small, gentle smile and nodded at me slowly, as if I did know her, and now she knew me, and I should have known her name.

"Would you like another beer? I don't think Jena would mind if..."

"I'm Heidi," she said. She extended her small hand to me.

My mouth reacted first, it must have, because I saw her wait for me, again so patiently, to remember her, as if she were part of what I was not forgetting, but leaving out. The *details*. Then my eyes followed my eyebrows up toward my hairline and I said, "Oh."

Her smile grew larger, wider, and she shook her head.

"It's ok, man. I'm Heidi."

I finally took her hand in my right and overlapped it with my left.

"Good to...it's nice to meet you. How did you know it's me?"

I propped myself on the counter with my left hand. She smiled again.

"I heard someone call you Rattigan earlier. Since you didn't tell me your name and all."

"Oh, yeah."

"Not too committed to your job," she joked.

I sighed.

"Not too much lately."

She nodded, her face contorted into sympathy and then back to her odd steadfastness.

"No one really gives a shit what their server's name is around here. Most are regulars anyway that..."

"I'd really like to talk to you, Pete."

"Ok. When?"

"I know you guys are closed, so...I mean, I waited to see if we could..."

"Yeah, absolutely. I'm done. Let me see if I can..."

I fidgeted with cash in one pocket, my keys in the other, looking for some answer on my body, attempting the purchase of time to develop a lie out of it.

"I'll be out front," she said. "Ok?" She had a cigarette in her hand.

"All right. One second."

She walked through the front doors and I saw a flame rise up from her hand, an orange comet glow illuminating her pallid cheeks, bronzing them in the dark.

"Hey guys, I'm taking off," I called across the bar.

"I bet you are, baby," Blain said from the kitchen, having slid down the metal table in back to watch. He was smiling, smoke climbing softly from his mouth. He waved his beer at me. It was comedic, but I couldn't laugh. I wanted to sneak out the back door and drive home and drink gnats.

"Who is she? She's cute," Jena said.

I took a deep breath and shrugged.

"I'm not really sure yet."

"Good night lover," Mason said over the bar, where he stood beneath the large television, packing a smoke on the outside of his thumb.

"Will you clock me out?" I asked Jena.

"You got it. Hey, have a good night Rattigan," she said.

I forced a smile and waved a semi-circle in the air at everyone and turned toward the door.

Outside, I stood beside Heidi as she finished her smoke and looked on into the dangerous intersection across the parking lot. The roads and lanes had been re-lined to alleviate the problem, but it had only caused more confusion and led to bi-weekly wrecks we always left our tables to go out and observe from the front patio. But traffic was slim and quiet, and the few restaurants of the area were closing, too, as the several bars were getting started.

"I found out about Brody a couple days ago," she said, turning to drop her cigarette in a large sand-filled bucket beside the door.

"Ok."

"And I wasn't sure how to...well, I didn't want to overanalyze it, which is funny because..."

"Why's it funny?"

She sighed, heavily, the maternal nature from inside gone. Her shoulders sagged.

"Because I'm going to Georgia State in the Fall for a PhD in clinical psych., so I guess analysis is supposed to..."

"Supposed to be your thing."

"Right." She said this one word with a weakness I welcomed. The scenarios building during the walk to the door included a fear of her strength, the control she seemed to exude inside. She flinched, grimaced, did something with her face indicating tears, and she turned her back toward me. From behind her I could see her fingertips outspread to the left, right and upward in front of her face, as if she were wiping her eyes with her palm. She let a heavy breath and turned around.

"So I wanted to tell you something, and I'm completely at a loss as to whether you'd want to hear, or have time to listen, or need it or want it. But I thought it might help."

My hands were in my pockets.

"I've got time."

"Do you?"

"Yeah."

She exhaled again.

"I have a house off Airport. Right across the end of Bit and Spur. Will you come by?"

"I can follow you, sure."

I jogged around the building to my car, drove it around and found her idling in the middle of the parking lot. After blinking my lights, she pulled off on to University, U-turned toward Old Shell and led us to Airport, where we turned right and drove two miles west before hanging left into the section of the Pinehurst neighborhood that hid behind a furniture store. Sonya's neighborhood. We drove south through three streets until she signaled to turn right into a medium-sized house off the road. I pulled in behind her and cut my engine.

"It's a mess," she said as we walked up the few steps to her door. "Isn't that what you say to first-timers? Sorry for the mess?" She keyed us in.

"I can't judge."

She took off her coat and draped it over a chair beside her sofa, revealing corduroy-looking overalls beneath. The living room was small, the kitchen the same, a laundry room past it that led, I guessed, into a back yard.

"This is nice," I said, seating myself on a chair at the other end of the sofa, my back to the door.

"Thanks to my Dad," she said. "Would you like a beer?"

"I guess so."

I wasn't clear on my role there, and was doubly unsure as to whether or not I wanted to be there. A face to the name was a relief, somehow, but it was something I hadn't required or considered. Again, the details, but what could come with the unforeseen needed to be addressed as much as anything else. Heidi handed me a beer and then sat on the side of the couch closest to me. She faced forward, her back taut and stiff, after setting her beer on the heavy glass coffee table in front of us, and then she folded her hands in her lap. A soft music played behind a closed door through the hallway past her shoulder, but I could still hear the secondhand ticking on a clock above the kitchen sink.

With no time wasted, she started to talk.

"Brody was only here because he was changing his book for you."

I wasn't caught off guard by her directness, as I immediately recalled Meena's message, the character names mentioned, their similarity to mine and Knox's. But I hadn't desired enough to get near it. In Heidi's chair I felt warm, like I was holding a hot coffee again, but the warmth was from a sense of displacement—in this house, I thought. This foreign country.

"For you and Knox. I thought you should know."

"Yeah, we, um...we got a message from his editor about..."

"I think it's important I tell you."

No, it isn't. I'm good. I think I'm good.

"Why?" I asked. I studied the condensation on the table, beneath her bottle, and took a sip.

"He was so worried..." she began, and then paused as if to carefully consider her words, as if she were practicing on me, a future case study in her own professional objectivity. "He was concerned you wouldn't understand why he was here. At least he didn't want to tell you during the process."

"Process of what?"

"Changing the story."

336

The story? Who cares now about the story? I'm sure I looked dejected, dumb again. I felt both.

"Why would he think...why would he do that?"

"Why would he do what?" She asked, reaching for her beer, sipping, setting it back in its exact circle on the glass. The bottle moved on its own a few inches toward the table's center.

"I don't know," I said softly.

"Know what?"

I'm not your patient, Heidi. I know you have a heart, I know you're hurt, too, I saw your eyes in the light of the intersection, briefly, it's best if you're scared here, too.

"Why he wouldn't tell me. Tell us. Why he would change his novel for...I don't know why to any of it." I took another drink. The clock ticked.

"It wasn't supposed to be a surprise, Pete."

"Then why was he here?"

She took a deep breath and exhaled, rolling her eyes slightly at the fact she'd have to deviate from what she'd set out to say. That it seemed rehearsed told me that she, absolutely, was gone, had left herself over this, over what she'd discovered so many days after.

"In the Fall I'm studying 3rd wave psych. theory, mainly with a professor who focuses on ACT. Do you know what..."

I shook my head.

"Nevermind. Neither did...neither did Brody."

"He said he was on to something, I don't know, something about out-of-body experiences, and astral-something..."

"That was all Brody. He took what we'd been talking about and made it his own. He always..."

"Yeah, he always did." I finished my beer. "All right if I have another one?"

"Help yourself. No, I'll get it."

Heidi went to the refrigerator and pulled one out, opened it with a winged gadget on the counter and brought it back in to the living room, sitting exactly the same. She thought a moment.

"He was here, Pete, because he was afraid of being too close to you guys, in proximity I mean, thereby risking inaccuracy about you."

"What?"

"He wanted to get you right. You meant more to him than I..."

"Wait," I said, my eyes watering. I put my hand out to stop her. "Please wait."

I understood what she meant. I understood what he meant. It was too much in front of a stranger. I breathed in, studied the clock in the other room, exhaled and looked at her.

"I just wish he could have told..."

"He didn't feel he should, Pete. He said it would make sense once it was out."

"But that was *his* book, man."

"I realize that," she said.

"It shouldn't have had anything to do with us."

"That's what you're not getting." She leaned forward and traced a finger over the lip of her bottle and then sat back, facing me. "I'm sorry. I didn't mean to sound..."

I shrugged it off.

"His feelings for you *was* his book, Pete. He kept saying that's what it *became*. He was afraid he..."

"*What?*" I asked, my face in my hands. My drink was on the floor beside the chair, and I leaned forward, but I couldn't yet look at her.

"He was afraid it would make the writing too personal, that it would seem like a lie, transparent, like..."

"How can you be so *calm* in all of this?" I asked, red-eyed, face to face with her then, wanting to know. Needing to know.

Again, she took a breath, smaller, preparatory. The anger and guilt and distance was collecting at the top of my chest and rising.

"Because he didn't love me the way he loved Knox, the way he loved you. It's that simple."

I felt my face finally press all of its outer parts into the center, at the point of tears that finally, at last, had come. A full-grown, parent-of-the-sob jangling loose of withheld frustrations and silences, unleashed and spent like coins hitting ground. I could hear the clang on the hardwood, the sound of sharp emotions rounded off from their expulsion and then rolling metallically off into dark corners. I slid from the seat, slowly, and sat on the floor, shaking.

"I'm hurting, man. Holy shit I can't explain how bad this hurts."

Heidi quietly sat down on the floor near me as I cried, not touching my arm, either arm for that matter, as I'd buried my face in them. Instead, she lifted her palm to the lower cuff of my jeans and gripped there, pulling almost as if to say, *yes you can explain, yes I can know*. I could feel exhaustion penetrate the sobs, then reenergize as something stronger, more unrecognizable, a wave of calm entered, then confusion. It was horrifying and necessary and reminded me in the gentle flow of its permeation that I was alive and what was leaving me at that moment needed to leave, it was good to let it be gone.

"I've just felt like a fucking animal all this time," I said into my arms. "Walking around mindlessly, on some kind of, I don't know, hunt for a better reason, *any* type of reason to present itself. So fucking ridiculous."

"It's not, Pete. It really is not."

"And *blame?*" I looked up at her. "That's been the worst fucking part. Knowing not to do it, not knowing I could even be this good at assigning it, but just doing it and doing it, this stupid inner snarl just scaring off everything. *Everything*, man."

"I understand that, Pete. I do," she whispered.

"And then, I dumped all this confusion on top of everything else, that..."

"Confusion about what?"

"I don't know, fully. Combating, I *guess*, selfishness, wanting him still here, but not really believing it's selfish to want it..."

"Only assholes say it is."

"...and then *why* I still want him here, you know? I mean, what is it I think I need or *deserve* so much that I should try to change his direction, change that tiny fucking moment that feels so titanic? It's been swallowing me whole and spitting me up and swallowing me again."

I took a long breath and held it, exhaling only after my body stopped shaking. I wiped at my face and shrugged at the kind light in the kitchen. After a minute or more had passed, I shrugged again and ran my forearms against the outside of my jeans.

"Who knows, Heidi? Maybe I wanted to feel consumed by something real."

Her cheeks were moist but she still maintained control over her eyes.

"I think I know what you mean."

"Do you?" I asked.

"I hope so," she said. "It would make me human."

I nodded slowly, still holding her stare. In the kaleidoscopic shadows of the room, versus the electric near-blue that blended with the white in the kitchen to cast a character of its own light halfway across the woven rug closest to the tiles, and then, versus us sitting in a makeshift corner of the furniture and floor, the house in its silence had little left to say. We finished our beers between small nods and whispered one or two-word sentences. *You ok? I'm good. You? I will be. I know.* We stood together and she took my bottle, added it to the thin row of fingers that held hers, and she walked to set them on the kitchen counter before meeting me at the door. I was making small talk—it was nice to meet her, and thanks. Time was telling me to not leave, but go, get in motion, describe her, to myself, this new person, and then continue to breathe. Begin again to *do* something.

"This may seem distasteful, Pete, but I'm going to say it anyway."

I stood before her, my back suddenly rigid again, punch-drunk of mind and tensed, with the enigma of her losing its shapelessness in my head, becoming a whole distinct thing yet to be made out, and without a name, but teetering on a cliff's edge, prelapsarian, to fall perhaps, or just fall apart. *You're ruining how I plan to remember you.*

"Ok."

Heidi put her palm flat against the center of my chest, her fingers together and pointing at the convergence of two walls near the ceiling. She hesitated, or waited, an intensely long time, her eyes again on mine as though we were still sitting, still drying exposed flesh with our clothes. I took another breath.

"Grace comes after the pain of loss," she whispered.

At this, my entire body sighed, I wiped my eyes, nodded to her nod, our faces having spoken more loudly than our throats, and then I stepped out of the door as she smiled, her least confident yet, and shut it behind me.

———

Northbound, I met the boulevard and turned on, windows down, no sound but wind and passing cars, fewer each tick of the clock. The hours were cannibals, devouring themselves, gnashing their teeth to outmuscle, to intimidate and to mark their own ground in the night. Time was an animal, so were people, the air, the road, Dawn and her blackened lawns, Knox a doe on dew, her agile walk amongst the eggshells at my feet—any impassive thing, anything unreal had a sense of its own prowl in the late dark, the wheels beneath my feet, groaning far down on the food chain of machinery, my steering grip high above the molten rubber, my body back down from the midnight sky, or at least descending, finally, in management of its trajectory home.

Home.

Where I went, though, only led there. It was not the quickest route but, I thought, what is? I'd been seeking it out for nearly two weeks, getting nowhere faster, with a wild briskness, pawing the earth and running, how else, headlong into more nothing, perhaps the promise of another invisible bruise. I saw Knox, sitting up in bed, a wine glass behind her on a shelf of the old headboard, shaking her head at a screen or a hard page of words, hers maybe, mine, a stranger's. I saw the light on through the north window of the guesthouse in the woods, and through the pane I saw remorse exonerated by apology. I wanted to run there, solely in that moment, with no urge to arrive in the future, as I was there already, pushing the car with my feet and fingers eastward, down McGregor, then up it toward the mouth of Dauphin and the Country Club, then left through the arching oaks above the road, the street-pressing bushes, over the speed bumps and around the south-western curve of the golf course, its lights asleep in wait of the sun's break.

But I found myself angling through a yield sign, past The Baker's Stone, and shuttling up the mildly upward slant of Old Shell. A bar was still open to my left, then more driving, slowing the car, another bar, The Blackbird, not yet last call, the blues and greens from their window signs still declaring a collective thirst in need of quenching, the lunch dive to my right, the post office and across from it, the coffee shop that had bands on weekends, but it, too, was dark, with only a soda machine's faint light visible from the street. I was driving home, the longest, and yet swiftest route to the house of climbing vines. I was driving to Westminster.

A car was coming fast behind me, so I turned on to a small service road that would soon intersect Brody's last avenue. The car squealed on to it and jetted in several seconds to the other end and disappeared back toward University. I took a few small breaths and studied the partially illumined soccer lawn neighboring the Presbyterian church across from my front bumper. Children played there almost year-round, afternoons, with parents in foldout chairs, and sometimes there would be some sort of fair or festival, with cars lined north to south on either side of Westminster. I slowly turned on and idled down.

There was nothing cruel about it, no dark fangs protruding from trees, no broken metal across the blacktop signing some thievery of tender hearts. Just silence, guaranteeing its presence beneath an unidentifiable stir in the air. Older mailboxes leaned over curbs, a maybe-dog jumped shadows in a front yard, telephone wires sagged, but hung on. Life was still there, carrying on.

And then I saw him, in flashing bursts, in the middle of the pavement, shoulders high, of course, close to his ears, tucked in, and again his hands pocketed, body walking in oblique lines.

My car nudged forward.

And there he was again—white bandana bright below a streetlamp, both palms clamped down atop his hair—maybe singing, maybe talking out a new line. He was slender and healthy and good.

I kept on.

His eyes grew closer, sparkling, still moist and drying and recovering and whole, seeing what I then saw, himself in better darkness, another realm of blue, of strange and ample light. He was laughing, he whistled, he disappeared and came back whistling, jeans too low, sneakers almost done for, laughing, drumming the air, alive, awake, still very much a part of it all.

I was crying again.

He looked at me, two bright beams staring back from the warm and warming dark above the dash. He stopped, he smiled. Brody waved, his middle and index fingers pointing upward to the sky. He displayed the inside of his wrist, the thin blue veins bright and stretching down to above his elbow, his skin tight and light brown and breathing, his chest breathing, strong, claiming air and surrendering it, laughing and smiling. He was smiling.

I blinked and found my heavy foot on the brake. Glancing up, the sign at the other end of Westminster said STOP. It was quiet and half dark and there was nothing I noticed in the rearview, nothing as I wiped my eyes, nothing dancing alone along the avenue.

www.ingramcontent.com/pod-product-compliance
Lightning Source LLC
Chambersburg PA
CBHW030015180626
46810CB00001B/45